DANGEROUS RENEGADE

82ND STREET VANDALS

BOOK SIX

HEATHER LONG

Dangerous Renegade/Heather Long – 1st ed.

ISBN: 978-1-956264-13-5

DANGEROUS RENEGADE

The mute twin.

The strange brother.

The broken one.

I'd been called so many names over the years. None of them mattered. My mirror cared more than I did. But he never treated me as less. None of them did. My brothers were the Vandals. They didn't always understand, but they never judged, and they always had my back.

I would always have theirs.

They were my life until Starling came to us. Quiet. Hurt. Broken. Those words were tossed around along with stubborn, fierce, impossible, and beautiful. I'd studied her from afar for years, but to have her close changed everything.

Trust. Acceptance. Understanding.

She colored in all my missing pieces. My other half needed her too. We all did. She fought her way back to us, continues to fight to stay, and more she fights for us.

She belongs.

My name is Rome Cleary. Starling is ours. She has always

been a part of us, even when she didn't know our names. We will always come for our own.

For Gina.
I miss you.

SERIES SO FAR

82ND STREET
VANDALS

Savage Vandal
Vicious Rebel
Ruthless Traitor
Dirty Devil
Brutal Fighter
Dangerous Renegade
Merciless Spy

FOREWORD

Dear Reader,

Welcome to book six of the 82nd Street Vandals series. If you have not read the first five, stop. Do not pass Go. Grab book one: Savage Vandal, and start there.

Seriously.

This is a series that really must be read in order.

Okay, back to my welcome. Dangerous Renegade picks up where we left off in Brutal Fighter. Need a snapshot? Grab a drink and sit back. Last time in the 82nd Street Vandals:

After bringing Emersyn home from Pinetree, the Vandals are very focused on eliminating enemies, giving her time to recover, and getting everything back on track. When a struggling Freddie calls for help, though, the Vandals along with Em are ambushed. Caught in the crossfire, Jasper takes a bullet but survives. It doesn't take long for them to put the facts together on who was behind the assault, this sends them on a fresh path, one involves taking out the 19Ds, and the other involves Kellan's bio father, a human trafficker who also washes his dirty money through charities.

Whew and if that wasn't enough, on the night they go after the 19Ds, a group attacks the remaining Vandals at the Clubhouse. It tears the whole place up, but Emersyn (after some lessons from Kellan earlier in the book) saves Liam's life by shooting the guy who had the drop on him. Adam and Ezra also sweep in to help repel the attack. With the clubhouse a wreck, but everyone alive and at least two of their enemies scratched off the list, they think they've bought themselves time.

And... end scene.

Well at least for Brutal Fighter. That's a sketch of everything that happened, but there are a lot of pages so re-reads are not only welcomed, they are encouraged.

This, of course, is where Dangerous Renegade finds us and our Vandals. They are fierce in their determination to find both Rome and Emersyn. While they have taken down some of their enemies, there are more out there. They have more questions than answers, but they are also planning.

It won't be long before these guys take their war to those trying to hurt them and their own. The journey, for me, is every bit as important as the destination. Sometimes, even more.

The seismic shifts that have rocked their lives are not over. Not by a long shot. Please remember that this is a dark romance and there are definitely triggering moments with regard to abuse, assault, violence, and addiction. Take care of yourself.

And now, as always, the housekeeping notes:

For those of you who have never read a why choose, or reverse harem before, first let me thank you for picking this up and giving it a shot. Second, the heroine will not make a choice in this book or any other between the guys in her life. It may take her a while to reach that conclusion, but it's the journey that drives it. There are many ways to frame this kind of relationship, currently why choose fits it very well.

Also, this is the sixth book in a series. While there may be no specific happy endings at the end of each of these books, there will be one to the whole series, that I promise you. Some of these books will have cliffhangers, largely due to the size of the story, but the happy ending has to be earned.

xoxo

Heather

PROLOGUE

EMERSYN

The warehouse was busy—busier than I'd seen it in a while. There were trucks parked inside and out. Rats were moving to offload. There were stacked pallets waiting to be loaded. The doors were wide open, letting in the cold air, but the sun was shining and it was kind of a perfect day.

Rats had died that day and it had shifted the atmosphere around all of them. Liam had paid for their funerals. He'd also given money to the only one who also had a family; it turned out he'd had a girl and she was pregnant.

That just made me feel awful. Rome tugged my hand when I drifted, pulling me back to the present. He nodded toward his new vehicle and ushered me into it. They all seemed to have new cars, but I also thought this might be one of Liam's. It was an SUV and in the same dark blue as one of his sports cars.

"Do I get to know where we're going?"

Rome studied me for a beat. "Can it be a surprise?"

"Yes."

He nodded, then we were pulling out and driving. We

didn't stay close; in fact, he pulled out onto the highway like Jasper had when we were going to the resort. Then again, he'd also mentioned Liam, so maybe we were going to meet him.

That could be fun.

The sun filling the car was actually kind of nice, and I closed my eyes, soaking it up. When we slowed down, I lifted my head to see where we were. He'd chosen an exit that was away from the city. Not quite the suburbs, like where Ms. Stephanie lived, and not the coast, where Jasper and I had gone.

We passed a lot of storefronts. A couple were really cute, like something out of an old movie's main street. When we finally pulled off, we went through an entrance into what looked like an old circus or carnival. I suppose they weren't traveling.

"Liam bought it," Rome said and I blinked.

"He what?"

"He bought the fairgrounds." He pointed to a long wall with brought colors painted all along it. "First place that paid me to paint."

Paid him...

"That's yours?" It was gorgeous. The wall had to be several yards long. Every inch of it was painted with people, balloons, families, and more.

"Yes."

Then his smile faded as wheels squealed over the cracked black top. He jerked his gaze upwards, then ahead, as a half dozen cars surrounded us forcing him to slam on the brakes.

"Rome..."

He frowned as he stared out at the people exiting the vehicles. Men mostly, all dressed in black suits and black ties. All wearing sunglasses and armed to the teeth—or at least brandishing guns. It was like something out of a movie, only we were right in the middle of it.

"Get out of the car, O'Connell," one of the men shouted. "Now."

Glancing behind us, I stared at the equal number of people who were now *pointing* those guns at us. The man in front raised his gun, and it was locked on Rome.

"Don't make me repeat myself." His voice carried a vaguely encouraging note, almost ominous in its intensity. Did he want us to run? Or did he just want to shoot us?

Rome cocked his head to the side, his gaze fixed on the guy speaking. Made sense, he was the one in charge. Or at least, I thought he was. Ice water poured into my veins. Did we fight? Did we get out? Did he try to ram their car?

I didn't actually have a gun with me. I'd kept it with me at the clubhouse, but I didn't think to bring it out here. Note to self, bring one next time. Never going anywhere without one again.

"Stay," Rome said, after a prolonged moment where I forgot to breathe. Stay?

What?

He raised his hands, showing both palms before he dipped one to unlock his seatbelt. Then he opened the door. "Stay in the car," he repeated.

Every protest died unspoken on my lips as he slid out and then shut the door. The locks engaged automatically. The engine was still running. Rome stared at the man.

"I'm out of the car."

"Don't be a smartass." The guy transferred his attention to me. "Get out of the car."

"No," Rome answered for me. Was there a gun in the car? It was one of Liam's, right? The guys all had weapons. Then again, I wasn't sure if I'd ever seen Rome with a gun. I had a knife. But I wasn't that good with it—but I would have to reach to get it.

Moving right now didn't seem like the best idea. I definitely didn't want to get Rome shot.

"Mr. O'Connell, this is *not* a negotiation."

"You said for me to get out of the car," Rome told him, his tone almost as bored as it was plain. "I am out of the car. Your instructions did not include her." He motioned toward me.

The guy nearest him swung his gun, but he never actually hit Rome. In a move I barely comprehended, Rome caught the swing and slammed the weapon back into the guy's face. Blood splattered the car and the ground. When it was over, Rome had the gun and the guy was on the ground.

But he didn't point it or shoot it, it just hung from one of his fingers like an accessory as he returned his attention to the "leader."

My pulse hammered in my ears.

"Don't," the man ordered abruptly, but it was the guy approaching my door who stopped. The gun in Rome's hand was pointed over the hood of the car and I would bet he was pointing at the guy approaching us. "Mr. O'Connell, I'm prepared to be reasonable. Communication is the key here. So let me be absolutely clear with you. There are only two ways this is going to end."

At his pause, Rome said, "I'm listening." Though if I hadn't seen his lips move, I would have thought it was piped in because he was so still, and that gun was still pointed at the guy near my door.

"Excellent. This standoff ends in one of two ways. Each results with you accompanying us. How you accompany us is the only matter to be decided. Because unless you possess the skill to shoot all of us at once, you and your girlfriend will cooperate and get in the car. Or we will load your wounded body into it while we leave her corpse here."

He sounded so very reasonable.

"I'm afraid we are on a tight schedule. Negotiation is not an option. So, what is your decision?"

CHAPTER 1

ROME

Silence filled the vehicle on the ride from the park to whatever our destination was. The man in charge, Brixton as he introduced himself, allowed Starling to sit with me and didn't bind our hands. The blindfolds and bags over our heads were non-negotiable.

I didn't care for either, but rather than let them touch her, I put Starling's blindfold on and then tugged the bag over her head. Even delaying for Liam's planned arrival didn't net us much time. Brixton's idea of negotiation was to shoot Starling.

That wasn't acceptable. Once I'd done that and helped her into the car, I let them do the same to me. We would be together, and her hand was in mine.

"Nothing will happen to your girlfriend," Brixton promised without a smirk or an air of sarcasm. If anything, it sounded like a solemn vow. "You cooperate and I will make sure she is safe."

A reasonable offer. They continued to call me Mr. O'Connell. For some reason, they assumed I was Liam. I did not disabuse them of this notion. My mistaken identity provided Starling with protection. That was all that mattered.

The drive from the fairgrounds took significantly longer than our drive there. I tried to map the turns in my head. Clocking the miles. There was a rhythm to the way the highway felt beneath tires versus suburban roads versus the city streets. A cadence and a sensation I understood. Rougher asphalt versus concrete and tarred blacktop.

From the fairgrounds, they went east, away from Braxton Harbor. They stuck to the highway long enough that at the speed limit, we would be easily a hundred miles away from Braxton Harbor.

As we traveled, we angled northeast. There were a handful of likely destinations. None stood out to me. The concern was leaving Vandal territory entirely. They weren't trying to outrun the Vandals though—and the Royals marked their territory differently.

Liam had explained it once. I should have paid closer attention. Focusing only on what involved him directly meant I discounted the other details as irrelevant.

Starling moved her thumb in a slow circle against my palm. The action soothed with its repetitive nature. Then gradually it shifted.

She spelled out a word. I reoriented my attention to the strokes, circles, and slashes.

Are you okay?

A smile touched me at the question. Covering her hand with my free one, so I could hold her hands between mine. I spelled back my answer.

Yes. You?

Yes. Worried.

Don't.

Communicating distracted from tracking our progress, but not responding to her wasn't an option.

Who are they? It was a good question. One, for which I didn't have an answer.

I don't know.

She tightened her hand on mine. I wanted to offer more. But all I had was *Trust me.*

I'm here. Not alone. Her reply had me lifting my head. Our driver and Brixton didn't speak. I didn't even know if they could see or hear us. I refrained from speaking aloud regardless.

The drive seemed interminable. We were on another highway. Were they making unneeded turns to double-back on their route? Or were we truly heading away from Braxton Harbor at an alarming rate?

Starling's pulse raced, and her fingers tightened over mine. I squeezed her hand and began to rub her palm with my thumb until her heart's pounding beat slowed again. Counting her deep breaths, I kept my attention diverted to try and track our route. It wasn't working though. Every single reaction she had preoccupied me and I couldn't focus on the road, the turns, or even the speed.

Discomfort unfurled within me, an irritation itching beneath my skin. Taking care of her was more important. We'd figure it out once we were there. Time seemed to crawl forward. If not for Starling fidgeting next to me, I might have thought I imagined how long it was taking.

Finally, the car slowed. Another series of turns, stops, and starts followed until we came to a complete halt. The doors ahead of us opened and then closed. Starling's nails dug into my palms and then the door next to me opened.

Me.

Not her.

9

I turned to face whatever was coming, Starling's hand moved to rest against my back.

"Mr. O'Connell," Brixton said, his calm intonation not settling me at all. "I thought I would provide you with some clarity for what will happen next.

The air coming from outside was definitely cooler than what had been in the vehicle. Blinded still, I waited for whatever explanation he planned to offer.

"As we are aware of your skills, it would be prudent for you to understand that any action you take will result in immediate retaliation against your girlfriend."

Her nails dug into my back.

"While you stand a solid chance of eliminating two or more of us before we can act," Brixton continued, seemingly uncaring that he detailed his own demise with such cold precision. "We will be placing a shock collar on your girlfriend."

Shock collar?

My fingers curled into my palms as I flexed my hands.

A door behind us opened.

"That will be my man to put the shock collar on her neck. While it is a distasteful business, it is better that we are all in complete understanding before any more unpleasantness occurs, don't you think?"

"It's okay," Starling murmured. The first words she'd spoken since we'd gotten in the car. The barest quaver underscored those words. The tiniest hint of fear.

"Do you want me to do it?" I asked the question over my shoulder. I still "faced" Brixton, even if I couldn't see him. But I didn't want her to have to endure *anyone* touching her if she didn't want that.

"You don't want to," she said, her voice softening. "I'll be okay." Then she cleared her throat. "They're only putting the collar on, right?"

"Correct, Miss. Trust me, there will be no liberties taken."

"Take my hood off," I ordered. "Let me see."

There was silence, but even with the car door open behind us, Starling remained pressed against me.

"Very well," Brixton said, then tugged the hood. It slid free and I pushed my hand up to remove the blindfold. We were in some kind of darkened underground garage. The light had me squinting, but not so much that I couldn't see. I spared the man a look then twisted in the seat.

The hood over her head hid her features from me. There was a man leaning in to meet my gaze from the opposite side of the vehicle. In his hand was the metal collar. I hated it on sight.

"You don't have to do this," I told her. "We will negotiate something else."

"I'm afraid, Mr. O'Connell, that negotiation is not an option. While I would prefer to take you in unwounded, that remains the alternative and your girlfriend doesn't need to go at all."

Starling pressed her palm against my chest. I found myself missing her eyes. "Let them put it on me," she said. "You don't have to do that."

"You don't want anyone else touching you." It wasn't a question.

"I don't want you to hurt either. I have survived the other."

"Not alone," I reminded her.

"I know, I'm not. Neither are you."

"Mr. O'Connell, as precious as this interaction is, we don't have time to indulge you any further. Are you putting on the collar or are we?"

She pushed away to turn herself to the man outside the car.

No. He didn't get to touch her. I pulled her back and held out my hand. "Give it to me."

Her soft sigh wreathed me as the man pressed the cold metal into my fingers. "It connects there and there," he told me, and I looked at the hateful device.

Releasing Starling, I wrapped my grip around the collar tightly. "Test it."

"Excuse me?" The man growled, confusion in his expression as he jerked a look behind me—at Brixton presumably.

"Test it. I want to know what it will feel like."

If they were going to use it on her, I needed to know. The shock zapped me hard enough to send violent tingles up and down my arm. My teeth clicked together so hard my head ached.

"Satisfied?" Brixton asked.

No. I hated it more.

"Continue to waste my time, Mr. O'Connell, and I can tase you until you are drooling on the concrete, and then you won't be able to do anything for her."

I wasn't fast enough to kill him and the man on the other side of the car. Starling was still here and vulnerable. I didn't know how many were outside the vehicle waiting for us.

"I'm sorry," I whispered as I slid the metal up beneath the hood to wrap around her throat. It wasn't quite a choker despite the snug fit, but once it clicked into place—it was locked.

"I know," she answered in the same voice, then covered my hand with hers.

"Let's go," Brixton instructed. "We're leaving the car here, and you're needed inside."

Inside.

Where? And by who?

With Starling's hand in mine, I eased out of the vehicle. I took my time as though I was still dealing with the shock from the collar. My shoulder and jaw still hurt from the muscle spasm the electrical charge had wrenched out of me.

Easily a half-dozen men stood in a loose circle, with another dozen or more beyond them. They were taking no chances with Liam.

My mirror frightened them.

Good.

"Does she still need the hood?"

"For now," Brixton said. "I will let you guide her." He snapped his fingers and two of the men closest to us backed off.

That was a concession. I nodded my acceptance. Starling held my hand where it rested on her shoulder when I wrapped an arm around her. With Brixton in the lead, I followed him toward the only clear exit. The parking garage had to be underground; I couldn't even see a sliver of external light.

In addition to the SUV we'd exited, there were easily another seven or eight vehicles of equal size ranged around where we parked. They really were leaving me no openings.

At the door, Brixton swiped a card then entered a code. The angle didn't let me see the numbers. The men around us were armed, but they kept their distance.

The doors opened to an elevator. Only four men stepped inside with us. I put Starling against the wall and stood in front of her. They kept their distance. The ride took us up, not down. The markers on the wall detailed twenty-four floors.

Definitely a city building.

The silence moved with us until the elevator came to a halt. The doors opened. Brixton and the man who'd been on the other side of the car stepped out, but the others stayed there.

So, just two of us and two of them.

I liked these odds better.

The hallway was muted, with no art or windows. A camera stared at me as soon as we stepped out. More than one. I clocked four total as Brixton led the way down a wide hallway. More an office building than a residence.

Or so it seemed. A pair of doors waited at the end of the hall, along with a pair of guards.

The odds tilted back to their favor.

Brixton gestured to the men ahead of us. One turned, sliding a card, then entering a code before they both opened the doors to let us into an apartment.

They didn't follow us inside.

"You can make yourself comfortable," Brixton said as he checked his watch. "Our meeting will begin in two hours. Promptly. I will come for you then."

With that, he turned but then paused and glanced back to where I stood with Starling behind me.

"The room is monitored. We have eyes and ears. Do try to relax, but understand that we will not allow you to interfere with our plans." With a motion to the others, he strode away and the doors closed.

The sound of the locks tumbling closed echoed through the room. I tugged the hood off of Starling's head and she dragged the blindfold off herself. Her eyes were huge and luminous when she stared up at me.

"We have two hours," I told her, "Hellspawn."

A tiny frown tightened her brows as I held her gaze, waiting. "Not a fan of this." She swallowed. "Liam."

"I know." I trailed my fingers to the collar. I was not a fan of this either. "What do you need?"

"Right now?"

I nodded.

"I need to pee."

A smile tugged at my lips. "Then let's see what they have for a bathroom."

Fingers linked, I scanned the room as we made our way through the open space. As large as it was, the furnishings were sparse. There was a television, it was dark, and a landline phone sat on a table. Windows were all along one wall, but the blinds were more like metallic shutters and they were sealed shut.

They probably wouldn't open. Cameras were set up strategically in the various corners, the red lights following us down the one hallway that opened to a second large room. Like the living room, there were sparse furnishings—a large bed and an overhead light. Not even a table lamp.

"They really don't want you to have weapons," Starling murmured.

So it would seem.

There was a sliding door partially open to a bathroom. This was larger and offered a double shower and a huge tub. I studied it. The camera in the corner had me narrowing my eyes. "Turn it off," I said straight to the camera. "She doesn't need an audience to use the bathroom."

The light didn't flicker, but I kept staring. It took a full minute, and then the red light went out.

"I could have handled it," she said softly.

"I don't care," I replied. Liam wouldn't put up with this either. My mirror and I were alike in this. "They don't need to watch you in here."

Aware of the collar, I withdrew to stand in the partially open door. They could probably still hear us. Better for them to see me. I locked my gaze with Starling's.

"Not alone," she mouthed the words and I nodded.

Though this time, I really wished I was.

CHAPTER 2

LIAM

*L*ike some bad B movie that Rome wanted to watch late at night, the images replayed over and over in my mind.

No body. No *bodies*.

Car doors open.

Blood on the car.

Phones left.

Her purse.

IDs.

Cash.

Weapons.

Even the gun stored under the passenger seat was still in place.

The other gun was missing.

Engine cool.

Not cold. Cool.

Someone had taken them.

A car door slammed, shattering the reverie, and I cut my gaze to where Kellan and Milo strode toward me. The rage in Milo's eyes echoed the ice-slicked fury in my gut.

"Anything?" He fired all three syllables like he needed to empty the chamber on his gun.

"I have a whole team combing the carnival grounds." I'd called them in right after I'd called Kellan. They were faster. Though in fairness, they were paid to be fast. "I doubt they will find anything."

Kellan didn't comment, just circled the vehicle once before coming back. "The blood?"

"It's being tested," I told him. "There's not a lot." Small measure of comfort that it was.

"Why weren't you here?" Milo asked, biting off each word like they left a bad taste in his mouth.

"Accident on the highway. Burnt out SUV. Since I don't believe in coincidences, I'm guessing it was a distraction or delaying tactic. Particularly because there were no injuries. The driver walked away."

And disappeared.

"You've been busy," Kellan commented, but unlike Milo, there was no reading his tone. Kel was calm because we needed him calm. He would remain calm because it was how he processed.

I got that. It was how I processed, too.

"Now that you're here, take the SUV back, and go over it. I didn't find anything on it that was an obvious tracker, but someone followed them here." If the instruction rankled, Kellan didn't react to it. Instead, he frowned.

"When did Rome pick it up from you?"

"Day before yesterday." He'd had a different car, but we'd already been discussing this "date" with Emersyn. I wanted them in the safer vehicle. "It should have been at the club-house since then."

"No one is putting trackers on it there," Kellan said slowly, but his frown disputed the comment. "Unless we have more problems than I want to consider."

Which meant he was already considering them.

"I'll leave that in your hands. I don't spend enough time there to give you a solid opinion on any of the rats." I'd just as likely say shoot them all and start over. But we weren't psychopaths.

Most of the time.

Milo let out an aggrieved sigh. "The rats are supposed to serve a purpose, but if we can't trust them…"

"It's not about can't, it's won't." Kellan stared at the car as if he could drill out the details of what happened with his gaze. If that were possible, I'd know everything. "We'll deal with it. We needed to take a closer look at them anyway. Especially after all the photographs."

"Is this her family? Do we need to worry about her going back to the facility?"

No, if Sharpe got his hands on her again—I doubted he'd take her to the facility. "He would have no reason to take Rome. If anything, eliminating Rome as a lesson to her, and to us, would be far more likely to be his choice."

The nausea-inducing thought doubled the ice shifting in my veins. If Sharpe and the king were one and the same, then yes, killing Rome and taking her would be the play.

If they weren't…?

"You don't think it was about her," Kellan said, his gaze sharpening as he focused on me.

"I can't assume it was about her," I corrected. At the same time… "Taking Rome was a message. That wasn't for you."

"You're assuming that."

After the king's attempts? I shook my head once. "No. Taking Rome was a message for me. Taking her, too? That could be an unfortunate byproduct of her being in the wrong place at the wrong time."

"You can't see the king alone," Milo said, and while we kept our voices low and even, there was no one to overhear us.

"I'm not going alone," I said as I pulled out my keys. "Ezra will meet me there." Because these two couldn't follow me. "We're already playing fast and loose with all of this. But if the king took Rome to keep me in line, I'll be keeping a promise I made him a long time ago."

"Liam…" Kellan blew out a breath then turned from the car to meet my gaze. "If he took them, you're not doing this alone."

"I'll get Hellspawn *and* my brother back," I told him. "And I'll keep you in the loop. You do the same."

He nodded, and a muscle twitched in his jaw. "We haven't told Jasper or Freddie yet."

"Give me five hours. Maybe we won't have to tell them anything bad before we've already fixed it."

"Five hours."

He wasn't happy about it. Hell, neither was I. Jasper was still healing, though, and Freddie had been on edge for weeks. "I'll find them."

If I had to burn the whole damn city down.

Neither tried to stop me as I left. I'd already told my men to send me the report. Once my guys finished here, they'd take the car back. If I knew Kellan, he'd take the whole damn thing apart.

Fine.

Whatever it took.

I didn't burn rubber tearing out of there, but I didn't go light on the accelerator either. I'd stayed long enough to give them the info and to get a team into place.

My phone rang, but the name flashing on the screen gave

me pause. No, I couldn't talk to Mom right now. Keeping them at arm's length from all of this was second nature at this point. But I wasn't sure I could disguise my worry or my mood. I didn't want to.

Rejecting the call, I sent the generic "in a meeting" message back. That wouldn't hold her for long. Five hours. Five hours to find Rome and Hellspawn, then bury the assholes who thought touching them was a good idea.

I flexed my hands on the steering wheel, keeping the speed pegged just nine over the limit. The next call I answered.

"I'm here," Ezra said. "Any changes?"

"No."

The other man sighed. "O'Connell, we're seeing way too much of each other. It's like we're dating."

I snorted. "You're not my type."

"No, your type is about five foot nothing and built out of muscle and tenacity."

"Yes, she is. Your point?"

"Nothing." Ezra chuckled, though very little humor bled through the phone line. "I haven't heard from him at all. So if he's going to take this meeting, we need to be in place."

"I'm almost there. Five minutes."

I didn't wait for his response, just hung up. Ezra didn't have to keep coming back to Braxton Harbor. In fact, it would be better if he kept his distance entirely. He was here to do me a favor.

Just like he had the week before.

Adam.

Fuck, I rubbed a hand against my chest. The bruises from where the bullets had slammed into my vest still ached. They'd turned some lovely colors this week, too. Bruises that probably went down to the bone. Soft tissue was a bitch, though.

Adam and Ezra had come through for me, and I was about to drag them deeper into this shit. Then again, they were hardly innocents. They'd had no problem with eliminating a common enemy, and Adam trusted me enough to continue playing dead while we played out this hand.

The drive back to the city took significantly less time than the drive out. Course, I didn't give a flying fuck if someone followed me this time. I'd welcome the attempt.

Just the promise of violence was enough to get my blood pumping. Ezra straightened from the side of his Audi when I pulled into the slot one over from him.

The bitter cold air was a slap in the face when I climbed out. The parking structure didn't keep all the wind out, not when it cut in from the bay.

"Good timing," Ezra mouthed more than said as I cleared the hood of the car. He had his phone to his ear. "Yes, sir. He just got here."

I flexed my hands to keep from yanking the phone from him.

"We're heading up right now." He paused a beat then eyed me. "How serious is it?"

I held out my hand.

"He would like a word with you, sir." How he managed to say the *sir* without an ounce of heat or edge surprised me. Ezra was the most volatile of us, the least predictable, and frankly, he had about as much reverence for the system as Freddie did.

Maybe less.

Still, he sounded one hundred percent earnest and genuine in his "respectful" approach.

I didn't even sound like that on my best days.

It was even more impressive, considering our suspicions about Sharpe's relationship to the king. I wasn't wholly convinced, but Adam and Ezra loathed Sharpe more than they did the king, and I hadn't thought that possible.

"Of course," Ezra said, then passed his phone to me with only the barest roll of his eyes. "He said you have thirty seconds to convince him."

Asshole. I didn't need that long.

"Did you take my brother and my girlfriend?" It was a calculated gamble. Rome had always been a vulnerability, one I'd taught them to never try and exploit. Hellspawn was a whole new level of danger for us, but I'd waited too damn long for her.

No one was taking her from me.

Not if she didn't want to go.

The soft look in her eyes, the determination glittering in them when she said she wanted me. It had seared those words to my soul.

I was not letting her go.

"Something has happened to your brother?" There was just the barest measure of uncertainty in his voice. Barely there before it was gone again. But I'd never heard so much as a quaver to it before.

Whatever he'd expected me to say, that wasn't it.

"Go up to the office. I'll start the call," the king ordered before the call was cut off.

"He didn't take them," I told Ezra when I handed him his phone back.

Brows raised, Ezra studied me a beat, but I didn't have time for this game. I needed to interrogate the king for what he knew, then get back out there.

Silence bracketed us as we rode the elevator up. The last time I'd been in this building, the king had ordered me to kill Adam. To kill him and take his place as bishop. In the time since, I'd done a handful of tasks but the king had been almost completely silent.

Too silent.

I'd been preoccupied with getting Hellspawn back. It had meant taking my eyes off the target. We couldn't afford to let it go untracked for long. Not when we were finally getting somewhere.

Then again, I'd throw it all away to get her and Rome back. Milo and Kellan had to know. They knew and they didn't care or judge. We'd deal with the royals and the king another way if it came to it on that level.

Still…

Ezra got to the door to the offices a half-step ahead of me, and he examined it before sliding his card. I put a hand on my gun as he glanced back at me. He gripped his own before pulling the door open.

The office space was empty, decorated like it was in full use but silent like a ghost business.

"Clear the rooms," I said and Ezra nodded. He went left, I went right. We went through the whole place, including the bathrooms.

Paranoid was an ugly word.

It also kept us alive.

The screen was already on in the conference room, and the king stood there, his back to us and the shadows masking him for the most part.

"Tell me what happened," he said without preamble.

I gave him the thumbnail sketch about meeting my brother and girlfriend for a day together. The vehicle. The blood. The items left behind. Even the burnt-out SUV on the highway.

I left out no details.

Save for my call to Kellan and the Vandals. That was not his concern.

"You thought I was involved?" The king didn't turn to face the screen.

I didn't apologize for the supposition. "It was a question. It would also not be the first time you made a move on Rome. Though, I do believe I made myself perfectly clear on this subject, Your Majesty."

"Hmm."

That wasn't a denial, but it also wasn't confirmation.

"With Adam's disappearance," Ezra said, "this could be a move by someone else. Maybe they thought they were bagging O'Connell."

That had occurred to me. It was the king's reaction that I tracked though.

"Then again, maybe it was the girlfriend," Ezra continued. "The rumors circling Emersyn Sharpe the last few months suggest she might have fallen in with a bad crowd. Or gone a little wild."

The smirk he wore had me itching to punch it off his face. This was a play. One designed to see what response it would get from the king.

"You're dating Emersyn Sharpe?" Was that disgust in his tone?

"Who I date or don't is none of your concern."

"It does if you getting your dick wet compromises us in any way."

I just stared at him. That didn't even deserve an answer.

"However, your brother is another matter. An attack on him is an attack on you—which in turn is an attack on me." The dead neutrality in his tone shifted. "For a few months now, I've been aware of a new player trying to get into the game…"

New player?

"I think they've finally made a move against me. This is what you're going to do…"

CHAPTER 3

EMERSYN

$\mathcal{T}$he hum of the refrigerator in the kitchen and the faint whir of the air conditioning seemed almost too loud in the silence of the apartment. A barb-edged hush that cut at my flesh. There was a television, but we hadn't turned it on. There was a phone, but it didn't dial out. In the kitchen, there was nothing like silverware or dishes—at least nothing that wasn't plastic.

They didn't even have coffee, though there were cans of iced coffee—Eiskaffee, a brand I didn't know—in the fridge, along with plastic-wrapped food. We didn't touch any of it. I'd drunk some water from the sink in the bathroom using my cupped hands. Rome studied every part of the place with such intensity I was certain he could describe it with his eyes closed.

He kept me away from the windows. His dislike of the cameras and awareness of them was almost uncanny. Once I followed his line of sight, it was difficult to miss them, even the ones disguised as a smoke alarm or tucked away in a vent. The others were more prominent, and they had a habit of tracking us as we moved.

Their mechanical sound added another razor to the quiet of the room. I wanted to ask Rome a hundred questions, but if he wasn't talking then I needed to stay silent, too. I hated that he was in this position because of me. Somehow, I didn't think they would have had as easy a job of snaring him if I hadn't been present.

Warm fingers curled around mine and I turned my head to Rome. A moment later, locks tumbled at the door they'd sealed behind us when they let us into the apartment. Rome tugged me to my feet from where we'd been sitting and parked me behind him. While he let go of my hand, I pressed my fingers to his back.

We'd taken off our jackets, but the heat rolling off of him seemed to radiate into the air around us. The doors pushed inward, held by two men as a third strode inside. In his hand was a brown, drink carrier filled with three white-cupped coffees.

"Mr. O'Connell," he said as he came in. "Forgive the intrusion, but your keepers noted that neither of you have eaten or drunk anything."

He set the coffees on the table, then snapped his fingers. Another pair of men entered with a pair of large trays. The scents of grilled fish, savory onions, and hints of lemon-butter filled the air. My stomach clenched as I forced my breath to come in slow, measured inhales and exhales.

The trays were placed on the table as well. The silver domes on top of them were removed, revealing black plastic dishes with food piled onto them. Yep. Grilled fish from the looks of it. I was having trouble making spit form in my mouth. The man from earlier seemed even more intimidating up close than he had when he stepped out of the car or wielded a gun.

Maybe it was the expensive cut of his suit. It was a Gucci Signoria Wool Mohair Suit in dark green. It made my skin crawl. Uncle Bradley and his friends wore those types of suits. Custom-made and designed for the man. Their wealth was on display like some overstuffed peacocks. A shudder went through me as I cut my gaze away from the man.

I didn't want to look in his eyes and see Uncle Bradley. I didn't want to see anything that reminded me of them. It was bad enough that he seemed so—*polite*. Almost ruthlessly polite.

"If there are any objections to this meal, I can send for anything you'd like." The man's crisp enunciation made me think that English wasn't his first language. The accent wasn't English, but far more continental European. Definitely not French or German. Maybe Austrian?

"Why?" Rome asked. Unlike our "host," Rome didn't make nice. He just fired the single syllable like a bullet.

"Because you do have to eat. As does the young woman. We do not want either of you to become ill or experience anything untoward brought upon you through starvation or dehydration."

Rome said nothing. The thud of his heart remained steady beneath my hand. The soothing cadence was something that had lulled me to sleep on some truly troubled nights. It did much the same now.

With a long sigh, the man said, "What can I do to assure you that the food and drink are not poisoned or in any way drugged?"

"Release us and I'll get it myself."

"Not an option. Name something I can do." Oddly, he sounded almost disappointed. That disturbed me almost as much as his phrasing.

"Leave."

"Mr. O'Connell... Please be reasonable."

"Why?" The curiosity in his voice had me biting my lip. Because it wasn't real curiosity. Real curiosity was the question he'd asked me that dark night when he first told me his name. *Did it help?*

No, what he asked now reminded me of Liam.

Push. Strike. Push. Hit.

"Because it is in all of our best interests to look after you and your girlfriend."

"Letting us go is in your best interests," Rome informed him in a damn near identical tone Liam had used when he wanted to provoke me. It was unnerving to hear it coming from Rome. Yet, he seemed determined to inhabit the role of his brother.

"Mr. O'Connell, I explained this to you earlier. You have cooperated thus far and we do appreciate it—"

"Explain why we're here."

"We will get to that," the man said, seemingly unperturbed. "What we will not do is indulge behavior that leads to self-harm."

That was a really odd statement.

Rather than engage, Rome merely stared at him and waited. Having been the recipient of both his studying looks, and Liam's outright challenging gazes, I didn't give the man long odds on remaining silent. Yes, I was aware that his name was Brixton. But so far, he'd addressed all of his remarks to Mr. O'Connell.

The guards were still there. Even if they only stood patiently at the open doors, they were present. Awareness prickled over my skin, the hairs rising on my arms. Rome had me behind him, which afforded me a limited view of the pair.

He could handle the suit. The other two were thicker

built than our "Brixton." While they were also dressed in suits, they weren't quite as "fine," and they weren't as refined. No, they looked more like a cross between Jasper, Liam, and Vaughn. Big, tough, and mean.

Rome could take them but he could get hurt, and I could help but how much would I get in the way? Even as I turned that idea over in my head, our host let out a sigh. The sound irritated me. Almost as much as calling him our "host." He needed a name. Needed more than just "Brixton."

Names made things better.

When you could name what made you afraid, you took away some of its power. It also gave you a target. I'd given Liam and Rome the name of the guard who'd hurt me. I was pretty sure he was dead now.

Names were definitely power.

"Mr. O'Connell..." The man began and I pressed my hand to Rome's spine a little firmer. Spelling out trust me with my finger before I leaned against him and then around so I could meet the other man's gaze.

"You could start with introducing yourself," I informed him. "It's rude to keep addressing Liam in that pompous tone when we can't return the favor."

Cool eyes shifted toward me. "Who I am isn't important."

"Then we should be talking to the person who is," I suggested, raising my chin. While I might not like the circles I'd grown up in, I was very well acquainted with them. "You've already made a nuisance of yourself and interrupted our day with your uncouth and rude kidnapping. I'm going to have the smell of that cloth bag in my nose for days."

A muscle in Rome's back tensed as I continued. The cool eyes appraising me seemed to grow frostier, but I swore Brixton's lips twitched.

"Am I amusing you?" It was easier than I could imagine falling back into those old habits. Never, ever, let them

31

dictate to you as Lainey would say. Make sure they are aware that your cooperation was a boon they didn't deserve and that they needed to earn it.

"Miss Sharpe, that was your name, right?" Someone had done their research. "Yes," Brixton continued. "Once Mr. O'Connell confirmed your value, we made sure we identified you."

"How special for you."

"Not particularly. Though there is reason to believe if you are not beneficial to these proceedings, we can make use of you elsewhere."

Now Rome stiffened. "Leave her alone."

"I was merely answering her questions, Mr. O'Connell. As I have told you repeatedly—we can do this the easy way, or we can do it the more difficult." When he shifted his hand to his pocket I stepped back from Rome. "Unfortunately, you seem to require an education on these options to understand we are not playing some street game."

"Don't—" But Rome's words had no effect. They made good on their threat and shocked me with the collar. My teeth clacked together at the first wild surge of electricity burning through my veins. I collapsed into the world of white static all over again.

I fell in a swimming pool once when I was little. The memory was a faint one, like a half-forgotten dream. The world was huge, there was music, sunshine, and water. I was running, and then I was falling.

Falling never scared me. Even as I landed in the water and it closed over my head, I'd been laughing. Even with the bright sun shining, the dark figure plunging into the water with me promised there was nothing to fear.

Nothing to be afraid of because—

He was there. Right there. Scooping me up and dragging me up from the water—I'd never been afraid—coughing and laughing as I clapped my hands together. He got me to the side of the pool and I was ready to run and jump in again.

"Dammit Ivy—"

Milo?

"Hellspawn?" Rome's voice dragged me upward and I shuddered as he tightened his arms around me. Why was he calling me—

"I will leave you both to consider your next course of action," Brixton said in those impersonal tones of his. "This does not have to be difficult, Mr. O'Connell. In fact, I would much prefer if it wasn't. However, you need to also understand how serious we are."

I couldn't see him, but that tone was like sandpaper over my nerves. Shivering like I'd fallen into icy water, I fought to unclench my fingers so I could give the guy my middle finger. I hadn't quite sorted out where everything was before the doors closed.

"Open your eyes," Rome murmured, his voice much lower and far less Liam. "Please."

They weren't open? Shit. I dragged my eyelids up and shuddered again. I couldn't stop shaking. Even my jaw hurt from how hard I'd clenched my teeth.

"Sorry," I said the word in a quavery voice that bounced up and down. I was freezing, but I wasn't. "That—thing sucks."

Oh, it got a little easier with every word.

Rome cupped my face, then he was picking me up and stalking out of the living room. In the bedroom, he kicked the door closed and a minute later, he set me on the bed. He vanished and there was a wrenching noise.

I managed to push up on my elbows to see Rome whacking one of the cameras down with a chair. The camera bounced across the floor. He set the chair down, then scooped up the camera before vanishing from the room.

Forcing one breath after another, I struggled to sit all the way up, and I'd made it to the edge of the bed when Rome returned. He shut the door then brought a bottle of water over to the bed.

"Don't." It was more a request than an order, but there was a core of steel to the word.

"I'm sorry," I whispered, and he frowned as he dropped to his knees next to the bed. With a trembling hand, I touched his cheek. The barest hint of stubble on his jaw rasped against my palm. "I pushed him and he pushed back."

"You don't push again," Rome said, his eyes steady. As my own vision calmed, I got a good look at him and the red mark on his forehead. It was the shape of a gun barrel's opening. At the brush of my fingers, he caught my hand. "They didn't let me kill him. I'll fix that later."

He meant every word.

Leaning forward, I pressed my lips to his temple and held there. He wrapped his arms around me. "We need a plan," I whispered.

"We have a plan," he answered. "Hellspawn. Trust me?"

I didn't like this plan. Leaning back, I searched for an argument against it, but there wasn't one.

"If you can get away," I kept my voice as low as I could. I didn't want it to travel at all. "Go without me."

"No," he said. "He'll find us."

I had no doubt who he meant. At all.

"They all will," Rome continued. "We go together." Before I could make a sound of protest, his mouth crashed into mine and I was clinging to him as his kiss seared all the way to my soul. It was a lifeline I needed. "Say yes?"

He all but breathed those words against my lips.

"You don't fight fair," I whispered back and he rubbed his nose to mine. "But we're not fighting, are we?"

The smile in his eyes was all I needed.

I nodded, but... "I won't let them hurt you," I promised. Even if it cost me.

"I won't let them hurt you," he echoed my oath. Then he kissed me again, his hands cradling my face. Protecting him meant one of us needed to eat the food out there. As soon as I could stop trembling, I'd take the first bite.

CHAPTER 4

KELLAN

*a*fter a cryptic message regarding the king, Liam had gone radio silent. It was to be expected. I didn't like it, didn't have to like it, and frankly, fucking hated it, but I accepted it. Liam would stop at nothing to find Rome and Emersyn. No doubt existed in me on that front.

I just didn't want him getting himself killed. Ezra Graham as his backup was a wild card. I didn't know or trust him. However, he and Reed had both come through to protect Emersyn before. If Liam trusted them, then I'd trust him.

That didn't mean sitting passive. Warrick had "disappeared," and his operation was in pieces. Doc hadn't said a word to me, beyond, "You don't have to worry about him again. Should have happened a long time ago."

That was it.

I accepted it and moved on. I never wanted the son of a bitch in my life in the first place. The dissolution of his organization, however, that was a damn headache. One we couldn't afford to ignore.

Milo's level of interest in it was comparable to mine, but he was one of the only people I knew who understood the complexity in the layers to any organization. More, he was one of the few *I* trusted.

Sending him in alone wasn't an option. Not when he was still healing and so on edge. His time with Emersyn highlighted the damage. But Emersyn's friend had done him good. She'd given him no choice but to rise to the occasion. In the meanwhile, her absence only served to illustrate how deep those wounds were.

He needed someone who could help him, someone who understood the dark underbelly of the unsavory business and what it would would take to dismantle it completely. That person also had to have the wherewithal to stomach it and a vested interest in resolving the situation in a way that benefitted all of us. The people who could fulfill those criteria were greatly limited.

Hence, why I was on the road to a house I had only visited on three prior occasions: twice in our teen years, when Liam still lived here with his adopted parents, and once barely a month earlier, when he introduced me and Milo to Adam Reed and Ezra Graham.

The whole undercover operation Liam and Milo cooked up had been ongoing for over a decade. It had netted us contacts, resources, information, and more importantly —enemies.

Now to see if, beyond Liam, the operation had also earned us allies. Real ones.

Trust needed time, a resource we were precious low on. So if Sparrow could bridge this gap, then I would lean into it, as long as nothing compromised her. Her safety was non-negotiable.

As if on auto-pilot, I glanced at my phone. No messages.

No matter how brief the disappearance had been so far, it left a deep groove on my soul. One that was still bleeding. Telling Jasper and Freddie had only split that wound wider.

Thank fuck that Freddie had taken it better than even I could have anticipated. The news struck Jasper like a physical blow, but he'd immediately focused on three things. One, Freddie was right there. He always held it together for him. Two, Rome was with her. Our brother wasn't letting a damn thing happen to her. And three? Of all things, Liam. Jasper trusted Liam to find not only Sparrow but Rome.

Doc and Vaughn were keeping an eye on them—and in turn—on Milo.

Fortunately, Liam would tear the person or persons responsible apart. If there was anything left of those who took his twin and our girl, I'd be shocked. Then I'd shred them.

The gate opened at my approach. I'd taken the long way and kept one eye on my tail the whole way. Between her family stalking us and this mysterious king, paranoid had taken on a whole new level of meaning. Though it did seem to fit that her uncle and this "benefactor" were one and the same.

My gut twisted at the idea of him taking Emersyn again. We needed to know where he was at all times. Another reason I was on my way to see Reed.

The man in question waited in the garage, a shoulder holster in plain view. There was a Glock in the holster and a second one in his hand. While not the reception I expected, it also didn't surprise me. There was some comfort in his gaze going past the vehicle to the drive as I pulled in. Then he hit the button to close the garage door.

"I took my time. We're clear," I informed him as I climbed out of the car. He tucked the second Glock away into a holster on the back of his belt. Interestingly, Adam Reed wore his power and wealth like a cloak despite the fact he wore jeans and a t-shirt.

The clothes might be humble, but the man was not. He pinned his gaze on me. "What happened?"

Direct. One point in his favor.

"Sparrow and Rome are missing."

The minute shift in his expression betrayed his concern. If I hadn't been watching for it, I would have missed it. "Come in and explain. Is this why Ezra and Liam have both gone quiet?"

"Yes." I didn't hedge the answer or try to vague it up as I followed him inside. The smell of coffee hit as soon as I crossed the threshold into the warmer interior. It was also the first time the growing chill outside registered with me.

It *was* getting colder. We'd almost had Sparrow with us a year, and this was the second time she'd vanished on us. At least the first time had been of her own volition, even if she'd felt forced to protect us.

Shuttling all of that concern to the side, I focused on the task at hand. Getting Adam Reed on our side. As much as I loathed to admit it, we needed him.

In the immediate future and possibly beyond that.

Once we were in the enormous kitchen that seemed almost too bright and open a space for such dark business, Reed poured two large cups of coffee. Apparently, he'd literally just made the pot.

Interesting.

"What happened?" He slid the cup over the broad island and I shrugged out of my coat to drape it over the back of the chair.

Like him, I was also armed. Better to put all our cards on the table. The shoulder holster was comfortable, but it didn't make for a fast draw. Then again, I wasn't expecting some Old West gunslinger draw down either.

"The twins planned a birthday surprise for Sparrow," I informed him, keeping it only to the basic facts with no speculation. "Rome left with her early to take her to meet Liam."

The fact Liam would be there when they got there—or was supposed to be—was why no one, particularly Milo, complained about them leaving without backup.

"Liam was delayed by an accident on the highway. When he got to the fairgrounds he was meeting them at—" I pulled out my phone, thumbed to the first image, and slid it across the island.

Reed set his coffee mug down then began to thumb through the images. "The blood?"

"Not hers. Not Rome's." That helped.

Not much. But it helped.

"Swift retrieval?"

"No idea," I answered. "Based on when they left the clubhouse and Liam's arrival—the window is an hour, ninety minutes at most."

"Plenty of time." He pushed the phone back. "What do you need?"

"Liam and Ezra are working on this."

"So you said," Reed retorted before picking up his coffee mug. His fingers were faintly discolored and his knuckles a mass of bruises. Someone wasn't taking to inactivity well. "If the king is Sharpe, he wouldn't have bothered with O'Connell's brother."

"Agreed. Rome disappearing *with* her suggests this isn't her family."

"But it doesn't mean the king isn't involved." Reed scrubbed a hand over his face. "Does Lainey know?"

"As far as I know, not yet." She wasn't back with us. Sparrow said she would be soon. "But they were talking nearly every day, so she's going to notice the lack of communication."

"Fuck." Bracing his hands on the counter, Reed pinned a look on me. "You still haven't told me what you need."

"I need your help. But not with this."

He frowned and straightened. "Explain."

Despite the brusque tone or maybe because of it, I found myself appreciating his directness. "What do you know about human trafficking?"

"It's a filthy business, and the people who engage in it should be herded together and made to do the work they sell people into."

The corner of my mouth kicked up. "I'd rather just shoot them."

"Efficient. My way hurts more."

No argument here. "We have an organization formally headed by Noel Warrick that's currently headless. Headless doesn't mean toothless though…"

"Planning to take it over?"

"No. Dismantle. Destroy. Scorched earth preferably. Backtrack through their contacts, dig them out before they entrench themselves. Kill the whole damn labyrinth if we can."

His snort wasn't encouraging. "Dismantling it is one thing. Even trying to weed out first, maybe second level contacts. You won't get it all."

"A man can dream." The wistful note was not me, but he didn't know that. So I opened the door, would he walk through it or not?

"Disagree. Boys can dream. Men have to plan and deal with what's in front of them. If they don't… it will surround and destroy them."

After taking a long drink of the coffee, I folded my arms and met his gaze. "What would you do?"

"Convert it. Take it over, replace all the key people with ones I can control. Use their network to pull them apart from the inside out. Shut it down, the traffickers go elsewhere. Stay in control—you are in a position to make things happen."

"Pretty much what I thought," I told him. Though Milo had been far more colorful in his response to that statement. "We don't want to be in that business. Even with noble aspirations, the Vandals are stretched far too thin, and we have graver concerns."

Selfish. I was aware. But I'd put Sparrow in front of everyone, even strangers who never asked to be in the position they were in, every damn day of the week. She came first.

Period.

"That's why you're here... you want *me* to do it."

"Close. While I feel that I might learn to trust you to a point, we are not that tight."

"No," he said, folding his arms and mirroring my pose. "We aren't."

"However, you proved we could work with you when you backed Liam at the clubhouse."

He shrugged a shoulder. Only one. Not both. While he wasn't indifferent to our situation, he didn't want to reveal any investment. "Emersyn is important to Lainey."

"Yes, I suppose she is. But she's important to more than just Lainey. You and your friend Graham have been very clear on wanting Sparrow to choose the pair of you. To let you protect her. To take her away from us."

Reed said nothing.

"What I want to know," I continued because while I'd opened the door and he'd walked through, there were some doors that needed to be closed for this to work at all, "is how much of that is because of her friendship with Lainey and how much of that is because you want Emersyn Sharpe for yourself?"

I hoped his answer was something I could stomach. He held my stare for the longest time, then rolled his head from side to side. "I take it they haven't told you what I asked her."

Not in so many words, but it had to be important, and it had to be something only she could give him. Since offering herself up wasn't an option I was onboard with, nor could I imagine Liam accepting it, I waited.

"This is a trust exercise," Reed said, almost bemused. "You are showing me some of your cards in hope that I will reveal some of mine. You want to trust me, but you don't dare. You're hoping my need to continue the current farce of playing dead will encourage me to trust you and tell you what you want."

I kept my feelings firmly in neutral when he cut an appraising gaze at me.

"Cards on the table?"

"I need you to help us with the Warrick enterprise. Whether we transform it from within or gut it and put all our own people in place..." I dropped from folding my arms to spreading my hands. I hadn't forgotten his description of putting people he could "control" not trust into place. "I'm willing to be convinced. You'll also be working with one of us and any decisions the pair of you disagree on will come to me."

"That's acceptable."

I didn't roll my eyes.

"Profit-sharing?"

"Negotiable." I wouldn't bend too far. "This isn't about money."

"It's about power." He nodded, his expression grim. "Then, on the subject of cards on the table, I asked Emersyn to marry me after she turned eighteen to deliver a blow to

Bradley Sharpe's control over her life, put her under the protection of the Reed family, and acquire access to the assets she controls because Sharpe has hidden leases and other fundamental accounts under her name."

Fuck. Me.

"I would never hurt her," he continued. "She doesn't deserve that. But you should be aware that the person who controls Emersyn Sharpe also controls a great deal of wealth. Wealth that even her family can't access or take away without power of attorney or a death certificate."

The whole concept nauseated me. "Pinetree." That fucking "hospital."

"Most likely. Probably why he always used it whenever she exhibited signs of independence. Our families have been competitors for a long time. I know where more than a few of his bodies are buried. But a man like that doesn't go down unless you can strip him of his power."

"She has it." There was no way she knew she had that access.

"Some of it would have vested at her eighteenth birthday, and more will come in at twenty-one and likely twenty-five—"

"Or if she marries." Fuck that was cold.

"Yes, if she marries and conceives, then she would likely come into all of it, and the considerable wealth of the Sharpes would pass to a new generation."

"You were planning on marrying her and knocking her up?" Killing him had suddenly moved up the list of options.

"I would never have touched her," Reed said in a voice so fierce, I believed him. There was a rage in his eyes that promised bodily harm. "I'll kill anyone that tries to force that on her. Lainey *needs* her safe. Marrying her would give her my name and my wealth as a wall around her."

"Except you're dead now," I pointed out.

Reed's expression shifted. Shock replaced anger.

"Yeah, you asked her to marry you. We took her a week later. Then, just as she's been taken back by her family and committed to Pinetree, the king wants you dead."

That was definitely a move. A bold one. It had the benefit of being both an ambush and efficient. Clearing the board of an obstacle to whatever it was she had.

"She escapes Pinetree, there's a fire, a lot of deaths, but all of it has been swept under the rug and there hasn't been a whisper of her being there or being 'presumed dead.'"

"They think I've already married her," Reed said slowly. Which meant they had a vested interest in keeping her "alive," so her widower wouldn't claim her fortune. Sick, but it fit. "No one knew I asked. Even if they did—I'm presumed dead." Except he wasn't. His "death" had been covered up.

Son of a bitch.

"She knew," I said softly. "And that whole damn company watched her. They wanted control over her, too. Including that shrew who was her chaperone." This was another nail in the coffin on who the king was. We needed to figure out this asshole's identity and eliminate him.

Reed's eyes went glacial all over again.

Yes. We were very much on the same page. "We have a lot to talk about, you and I," I told him. "I'm willing to work with you—for her." I believed him when he said he wanted to protect her.

Words and actions matched.

So, I held out my hand.

He glanced at it then at me before he clasped it. "For her."

Then we had an accord.

"Now let's talk business."

CHAPTER 5

FREDDIE

$\mathcal{J}$asper shoved out of the bed and to his feet.

"Dude," I called. "Watch the stitches."

"I'm fine," he snapped, then raked a hand over his face. He might say he was fine, but nothing in how he moved, from the stiffness of his shoulders to the way he put a hand over his side, confirmed his declaration. "Fuck. Sorry, Freddie. Any word?"

"Nope." I was flipping my knife. Snapping it out, then back, before snapping it out and dancing it over my fingers. The coolness of the blade on my skin offered a kind of relief I couldn't put into words.

Clean almost thirty days.

Twenty-four more hours. It would be a record. The last stint I'd been clean this long had been senior year in high school. The only reason I stayed clean was because the guys never left me the fuck alone. Back then, it had pissed me off. They were so fucking annoying about it.

Then... well, then Jasper said, if I didn't go to college it wouldn't be because of grades or attendance. That shut me up good. It was weird to be clean for so long. The world wasn't improved. But I did it. I fought through it and graduated with a 3.2.

Somehow.

Then I skipped the whole college scene, even if the parties looked interesting.

"Freddie."

I cut my gaze from the dancing knife to where Jasper leaned against the door to the bathroom. Some part of my brain had tracked him as he went in, pissed, flushed, then the sink had come on. He was doing better, which was great, cause I loved him, but I wasn't holding his dick to pee.

Pretty sure he didn't even let Boo-Boo do that.

The whole thought made me smile. "What?"

"On second thought, I don't want to ask what you're thinking about." Grim didn't begin to describe his expression, but that was a flash of humor that had been absent since Kellan informed us about Rome and Boo-Boo.

"I was thinking you're good at holding your own dick and that you probably don't let Boo-Boo do that when you gotta piss." The comment made him jerk, and he shook his head.

"Freddie, I'm not discussing Swan and what she gets to do with my dick."

Manufacturing shock was easy enough, I just put a hand to my chest as I snapped my blade closed. "Man, you let her hold your dick for you while you take a leak? In what world is that sexy?"

With a roll of his eyes, he flipped me off. "I need to shower."

Yeah, conversation about his dick over. Fine by me. Then again, it just made me restless to be out there looking for Boo-Boo. It had sucked when she left before. She didn't leave this time. And before, we had a clue on where to go find her thanks to the Ball-Cracker.

Now…

The water came on.

"Five minutes," I called. "And make sure you slap the shower tape on."

"Fuck off."

"Five minutes," I repeated. "Put the shower tape on or I will."

"Yeah, yeah." Dismissive or not, the sound of the tape ripping told me he was doing it. The little patches went over the incisions to protect them from the soap. The shower and the water wasn't the problem. The soap was. Who knew soap could be a problem? Doc asked me if I wanted the full explanation or just to know he had to wear them. I was good with knowing he had to wear them.

It was kind of fun to boss him around. Boo-Boo just climbed right in the shower with him. I sure as shit wasn't going to be doing that either. I'd help if he needed it, but so far, that hadn't been an issue. The only reason I was still in here was because it was Jasper.

The second reason was Kellan asked me. *"I don't care if you have to use emotional blackmail, you keep him focused on his recovery. The time to fight will come soon enough, but he needs to heal. Sparrow is the only other person besides you that I know he won't lash out at to get out of here."*

"That means I have to fucking stay put, too. You realize that, don't you?" Even before the words were out of my mouth, I'd seen the glint in Kellan's eyes. "You're a real asshole, but you're good at this leadership stuff."

"It's why I'm good at it," he'd retorted. Then he sobered and the look of intensity he wore demanded I pay attention. "Look, the minute *I know anything about Sparrow, you will know. No*

secrets. We're getting her back if we have to burn the city to the ground."

That made me feel better. Not a lot. But some. Especially the burning the city down part. Burning down Pinetree had been a stroke of fucking genius on Bodhi's part. I hadn't intended to do the level of damage he had, but the whole facility had become uninhabitable. At least according to the last story I read about it.

Good.

The shower cut off, but Jasper didn't say anything. I waited. The door was open because if he fell or anything, we had to pick him up.

"Freddie…"

"Yo?"

"I can't just sit around here with my thumb up my ass. Kel said I was supervising some of the reconstruction, but that's bullshit…"

"Nothing else we can do right now," I parroted the words Kellan had given me. "You need to heal. Because that wasn't our last fight. We have more coming."

He appeared in the doorway, dressed in sweats and spreading shaving cream on his face. He was shaving? That—was weird.

Jasper had grown a beard right after Milo went to prison.

Then again. Maybe he was ready to lose it now that Milo was home. That was good, right?

I sucked at this psychology shit.

"You don't believe that," he said after studying me for a long minute.

"No, I definitely believe that we have more fights coming. The only thing I don't know, is if it will be a fight that comes at us or a fight we take to them. Kel promised the minute he knew something about Boo-Boo, I would know. When I know, you'll know."

Eyes flat, Jasper stared past me for a moment, though he kept spreading the shaving cream on. "Whoever they are, they got to Rome, too."

Yeah. That bugged me, too. "If they threaten Boo-Boo, they can control him." It would control me. At least until I got close enough to fuck them up and get her out. "He won't let anything happen to her."

"Fuckers need to go away and leave us alone," Jas said finally, then turned back to the bathroom. The movement was too quick. That was obvious in the way he stiffened for a moment, but he kept going.

Yeah, I wasn't keeping him locked down for long. "There's always another fucker." Why did I have to remind him of that? "Happened at the group home. Happened at school. Happened here. We only keep what we can defend."

Silence greeted that statement, then he let out a dry chuckle. "I didn't think you ever listened to me."

"I always listen, Hawk," I told him. "Don't always want to hear. Sometimes, I can't do shit about it. But I listen." When he spoke to me. When Boo-Boo did. "Vaughn. You. Kellan." I ticked off their names. "Rome. Liam. Doc even. Ms. Stephanie. You guys talk a lot. You know?"

That got me a real laugh. "Bullshit. Rome communicates in middle fingers and dry stares most of the time."

"But you know what he's saying when he does, you know?" That was one of my favorite parts of Rome. He didn't waste words. Hell, Liam didn't waste them. Me? I spread them around like they were fucking confetti and it was a New Year's Eve party.

"Yeah, I know." Quiet followed for another few minutes, and I glanced down at my blade. Then at the Kindle on the table. I'd been catching up on the last book Boo-Boo had read to me. There were some spicy parts that she just did not read aloud. I loved reading them to her. Her face was hilarious.

My gut sank and my hand began to shake, so I started playing with the blade again. Where was she? What the hell were they doing to her? The last time I'd found her, they'd been drugging her to high heaven, shocking her, strapping her to her fucking bed, and seemingly trying to *erase* her.

Maybe we should go kill her uncle. The knife stopped moving. We could do that. We knew where he was—at least where he should be. We could kill him. Slow. Maybe skin him.

The weight of her back against mine as she told me what he'd done to her. Had been doing to her—for years—flashed through me. I swore I could feel the soft frailness of her, the scent of tears, hints of sweat and chemicals, and that ineffable scent that seemed to linger in the air around her.

The depth of sadness lingering in her words. The darkness inhabiting them. I'd been in that darkness. I heard every single thing she didn't say. Killing her uncle would be a sheer fucking pleasure.

We could really take our time, make sure he was well and truly trash before handing him over and letting Boo-Boo decide his fate. Death, obviously, but the how could be fun.

How would she like to kill him?

Humor splashed through me and then I caught the handle of the knife and sat all the way forward. How would *he* kill them? "Jas, I have a really bad idea."

Patting his clean-shaven cheeks with a towel, Jasper exited the bathroom. "How bad?"

"Pretty fucking terrible, but also just what we need." What Boo-Boo needed. "I know a guy…"

"Yeah, I've yet to hear a story that ended well when it starts that way." But he wasn't dismissing me and the more I turned the idea over in my head, the more I liked it. Maybe I should get high and shut the noise off for a while. Cause inviting *him* here could go wrong in so many ways, but he *had* helped us.

More, he'd helped Boo-Boo.

"Tell me," Jasper said as he crossed the room to his dresser. He pulled out a clean t-shirt and despite the stiffness from earlier, he was moving a little easier. The stitches on his abdomen were pretty puffy looking and his back was downright angry.

"You sure you're okay?"

"No," he said as he turned to face me and pulled the t-shirt over his head. The grimace as he moved and stretched the stitches worried me. "Talk."

"Take your pain meds? I know what Doc told you. Not to be afraid of them, that they can make you more comfortable, which means you will—"

"I flushed the meds," he told me flatly. "I'll survive. You don't need the temptation here. Now, tell me about the bad idea."

Fuck.

"Don't," he told me in a measured voice as he moved to take a seat in the chair to the left of the sofa. The relief was palpable when he sat down. "I don't want to take that shit because it makes me foggy. If I turn down the pain from the stitches, I'm a lot more likely to tear them. The over-the-counter stuff helps." He lifted a bottle as if to demonstrate, then tapped out four into his palm before he knocked them back and dry swallowed.

I sighed. If not for me, he'd have the good shit and maybe he'd be able to relax.

"Get the fuck out of your head and talk to me." The order was unmistakable, as was the growl. Frankly, it was welcome as hell.

"When we were in Pinetree," I began, and Jasper's

eyebrows shot up. "Boo-Boo and I met a guy. His name is Bodhi. Boo-Boo recognized him. Said he was Cavendish or some shit. That part doesn't matter, the thing about Bodhi was, he was full on cracked. Makes me look like the normal one."

"You are the normal one. What's this Bodhi got that we need?"

"Not sure he's got anything except..." How did I phrase this? "I don't even know why he was in Pinetree. He was really good at killing people. Killed someone for me. Told Boo-Boo that he killed the doc. I mean that guy had to be dead, but he snapped the doc's neck to be sure. Then he got me when Boo-Boo wasn't responsive. Helped us get out and he got me my phone."

"And he was someone who worked there, or a patient?" Jasper frowned. "You mentioned you had help but not who..."

"Didn't think it was important. He had his thing. I had mine. He helped Boo-Boo. That counts for a lot." The doctor had been touching her. Bodhi never told me why he was there that day in the doctor's office. Course, it wasn't like we had time to chat. What he had done was gotten me and helped her.

That was all that mattered.

"He's creative as fuck with killing and really efficient."

"We can handle our own killing," Jasper reminded me.

"We can, but he liked Boo-Boo." That counted for a lot.

"Where is he?" Jasper asked. He wasn't dismissing my idea out of hand. "And have you told Kel?"

"Not yet. Just thought about it. I don't know where he is. But I do have his number." The tremors in my hand increased. "Thinking about calling him. Terrible idea. We already have enough trouble, but what if we can bring in trouble that's on our side, you know?"

He seemed to be turning the idea over in his head, so I went back to flipping the blade. Fuck, the shakes were hitting me harder now than they had the night I killed the dealers that ended with Jasper getting shot.

We were just sitting here. I needed to be doing something. Jas wanted to do something. But Kel wanted us staying put 'cause Jas needed it. Fuck. I clenched the blade again. "Jas?"

"I'm here, Freddie," he told me, his voice a hell of a lot gentler than a few minutes earlier. "What do you need?"

"Talk to me? Just—talk to me about anything. Tell me how you seduced Boo-Boo or something. But—you can keep the graphic parts to yourself, unless you really feel like sharing. I've seen that pretty pussy, I can imagine the rest...just... Tell me something that will keep me from getting a hit of something. There's nothing here and I'd have to go score it and I don't want to score it."

The last few words gave me pause and I lifted my gaze to meet Jasper's.

"I don't want to go and score any. She needs me to be clear, but there's so much noise..."

"I told her I was sorry," he said.

"What?"

"You asked me what I did to seduce her. I started by telling her sorry..."

CHAPTER 6

DOC

Blood splattered the wall as Milo drove his fist into the guy's face and it snapped his head to the side. Already sporting what would be a black eye soon enough, a fat lip from where the blows had cut his mouth on his teeth, and blood pouring from both nostrils, Weavil was not going to be in much shape to answer questions for very much longer.

"Milo," I said in a low voice. It wouldn't carry far, not with traffic on the road, the tall buildings around us with their thick, brick walls that dated back to 1920s art deco invention. The overflowing dumpsters at either end of the alley also provided some shelter from view as well as sound.

But we didn't need to drop a body here.

Making sure everyone got the message required a *messenger,* and we didn't need to try and do a body cleanup in the middle of the fucking day.

He threw me a dark look but pinned the guy to the wall

by his throat. "You know," Milo said, almost conversationally as a muscle ticked in his jaw.

You'd have to be a fool to think he was anything remotely appearing to be calm. Then again, Weavil didn't know him except by reputation. He'd earned the name Raptor because whether through stealth, speed, or strength, he never missed a target when he made his decision to hunt.

"Maybe I had it wrong," Milo continued. "Maybe I'm just assuming you were out here trying to deal on our streets, peddling..." As if an afterthought, he patted the guy down but his hand never left Weavil's throat. Milo easily outweighed him by fifty pounds of solid muscle; the skinny fuck wasn't going anywhere. "Huh?" He pulled out a dozen packets of white powder. "You baking a cake or something, Weav?"

Wild-eyed, the punk cut a look at me. "Doc—you just gonna stand there?" Blood flecked his lips. "You're a doctor. Aren't you supposed to do no harm or something?"

"I don't see any harm," I told him in a firm voice. "I see education. I see information. I see the chance to figure your shit out before you make fatal mistakes." And there wasn't a court on this planet that would get me to testify against Milo.

As far as I was concerned, he wasn't here. I'd go down for the crime before I let him go back to jail.

"Man," Weavil blew out a breath, then cast his frantic glance at Milo. "Raptor, man, I didn't know you was back."

"Shouldn't matter if I'm here or not," Milo kept his tone so even and laid back, it had *trap* written all over it. Hopefully this dumb punk didn't wade in any deeper, especially since Milo was emptying all the packets of pills and powder out of Weavil's pockets. "This is a lot of shit for one guy, you know? Not judging, but there are easier ways to off yourself. Like dealing in Vandals' territory..."

Weavil licked his lips, not that it did much for the scarlet tinge around his mouth or the fresh blood trickling from his nostrils. His pupils were just this side of dilated, though I'd bet the pain was eating away at his high. He wasn't gonna be a happy camper here in a bit. "Man, I wasn't dealing in Vandals' territory. I'm not that stupid."

"But you were dealing," Milo said like he was almost sympathetic. "You were bringing your little packets of— cocaine? Heroin?" He held up a smaller bag with pills in it. "Codeine? These are medical-grade, aren't they, Doc?" The near casual over his shoulder toss only worked 'cause I'd been watching for it. I caught the pack.

The number was stamped right onto the pills. Milo wasn't wrong. These were pharmaceutical grade. "Where did you get these, Weavil?"

"Man, I just pick up the stuff, you know. They give me the stuff. I—I wasn't gonna sell it."

"Uh huh." Milo's manufactured sympathy suckered Weavil right in. "Just planning to share it with a few friends?"

"Nah, I mean…not supposed to give it away, you know. And I can't afford all that stuff." He cut his gaze to the scattered packets on the ground. "I just—run it. You know." He shot me another look. "That's not selling, Doc. You know me. I'm a good kid."

"Weavil, you'd sell your mother if she was still alive."

He hung his head. "I'm trying to be a good kid. It's hard. But—I'm not selling on your streets, Milo. I promise. I wouldn't do that. I know better. Jasper promised to castrate me last time he caught me doing a delivery—"

As if his confession registered with him, Weavil choked on the last word.

"Hawk's got a temper," Milo consoled him. "When was that conversation? Cause you know, we all have bad days."

The guy didn't answer. I closed my hand over the pill packet and shook my head. "Weavil, who you running for?

Cause it sounds like he's the one we need to be having this conversation with."

Clutching the lifeline I tossed him, Weavil cast me a pleading look. "Doc, they'll kill me. This is 19D territory, we pay them—"

"Protection. But the 19Ds aren't going to protect you, Weavil." I kept my tone sympathetic, but my eyes were hard. "There are no more 19Ds. This isn't their territory."

"No," Milo said, patting Weavil's blanching face with his free hand. "It's our territory, which means you're running in our territory. Not as bad as selling—so not gonna castrate you, but if Hawk were here, you'd lose a couple of fingers."

Maybe. Jasper had mellowed some. Then again, with Little Bit having gone missing—again—there was every chance in the world this guy would be leaving headless. All of my humor evaporated. Liam better fucking call soon. I'd already put in a call to Alphabet and the guys, but they hadn't returned it.

If they were on a job, it could be a hot minute or ten. I'd been leaning on them of late. Though not for everything. Some jobs were personal.

Little Bit was really fucking personal.

"I didn't know," Weavil stammered the words, but a hopelessness drifted into his eyes. "I swear I didn't."

"I believe you," Milo said slowly. "But you know it doesn't matter…"

Tears leaked out of his eyes and the distinctive scent of urine filled the air. I glanced down to see the wet stream marking the front of Weavil's jeans. Milo didn't so much as flinch. "If you cut off my fingers, it'll hurt."

"Yep," Milo agreed.

"I need my fingers."

"Do you?" The faint hint of curiosity in his voice made me

shake my head. "What you doing with your fingers that you need them, Weavil?"

"I mean—how am I supposed to feed myself?"

"You lose two, you still have eight."

"Man, that's cold. What about girls? They like fingers."

"You do that right, you only need one." Yeah, that sympathy wasn't going to be there for long.

"Please don't cut off my fingers, Raptor. I didn't know. I'd never break the rules. You know I wouldn't—I mean, even when Freddie—"

Yeah. That was a mistake.

"Even when Freddie, what?" Milo asked with all humor and warmth draining from his voice.

"Even when...when they asked me to get Freddie hooked. I didn't do it. I swear to *God*, I didn't do it."

"Who asked you to get Freddie hooked?" I interjected the question because Milo's knuckles were turning white where he gripped Weavil's throat.

"They'll kill me," Weavil said, shooting me a look of desperation. "You know how it is Doc—I heard rumors about you—Vandal. I heard the rumors when you were..."

Vandal. Yeah, that was a name I hadn't used in a long time. One I had no intention of reclaiming.

Or I hadn't.

"I know we will kill you if you don't tell us who has you dealing on our streets." The threat rolled out of me as easily as any I'd ever made. Only this was different. I had the scars of battle. From war. I'd survived these streets. Then I'd survived in deserts, mountains, and dark hellish places far away.

Every fucking scar on my body was a testament to that. Weavil was a kid. They were all kids in a place we'd never been allowed to be children. I could pity him, but it wouldn't save him.

"Please..."

"Talk to me," Milo ordered, devoid of emotion as he flexed his grip on Weavil's throat. "Tell me who sent you after Freddie and who sent you here. Tell me before I squeeze it out of you."

The scent of the urine stained the air as well as Weavil's jeans. "Chaser—Jason Chaser."

Milo cut a look at me and I shook my head slightly. I didn't know the name.

"Give me more," Milo said. "Don't make me ask again." Cold edged his tone.

"I don't know more, Raptor. I swear. Guy's name is Jason Chaser. He works in some big fucking building downtown. It's—it's like one of those charities, I don't pay attention. They just pay me to show up, pick up the stuff, then get it to where it goes. If I don't show up, I gotta pay for this stuff—they know where I live..."

Milo shut him up with a tight squeeze on his throat. Weavil went from complaining to grunting as he raked his fingers over Milo's grip. His face went red and his eyes bulged.

"Milo." It was a warning. He wasn't killing this guy. Weavil was worse than a rat. He was just a street kid like the rest of us, trying to feed his addiction and his life with the only way he saw out.

Running was easy money. Just hang onto that morally gray center and do it.

"Don't," I added when Weavil's fight began to leave bloody rivulets along the back of Milo's hand.

The silence stretched taut, punctuated only by Weavil's frantic fight and just about the moment his eyes began to roll, Milo dropped him. The skinny bastard hit the ground, and his breathing was rough. If nothing else, he'd damaged his trachea.

Casting pleading looks up at us, Weavil waited. Survival instincts had kicked in, and his fight had fled. So had his flight—

"Leave," Milo said abruptly as he turned away. I said nothing because every sign was there. The damage was coming, but Weavil reached for the first of the packets and then Milo slammed his booted foot down on the extended hand.

A raw scream tore out of Weavil's throat as he flopped around, his hand trapped. He might leave with all his fingers, but those bones were broken. It would take time to set them all—I could map it in my head.

The tug of my conscience couldn't shift the compass of my rage. The drug dealers weren't going to rush in to fill the vacuum left by the 19 Diamonds. The Vandals wouldn't allow it.

No more drugs on our streets. Freddie wanted out of it. We could control only so much...

"I said leave," Milo told him dispassionately. "You aren't taking the drugs with you."

"They'll kill me," the punk complained, but even in his complaint there was loss.

"Then leave town," I said, already pulling out my wallet. I dropped ten one-hundred-dollar bills. "Wrap up that hand, go to the bus station, get on a bus and go. See a doctor a hundred miles away, then keep going."

I ignored Milo's sharp look of reproval as he removed his foot from Weavil's hand. Bending, I grabbed the kid by his shirt and hauled him up while he grabbed at the bills and fisted them in his one good hand.

"Buy some ice and stick your hand in it on the bus. Go. Don't come back."

"They'll hunt me down..."

"Then don't let them find you."

It was the only advice I had.

"Now get out of here."

Trembling, Weavil glanced at Milo as he clutched the money to his chest. "I'm sorry." The two words fell from his lips in a half-whispered declaration before he ran. Flight kicked in and he was gone, vanishing as he turned the corner onto the busy street. If he knew what was good for him, we wouldn't see him again.

With him gone, I faced Milo. "You can't do that."

"Don't tell me what to do, Mickey."

"I will tell you that you can't just kill someone because they annoy you."

"He's a—"

"A runner. A nobody. An unthinking asshole who doesn't give a fuck about people on either side of the equation. He's in it for the easy money, pick it up, drop it off, fuck off to wherever. He's *not* the problem." I should know. I'd been that dumb fucking kid. I'd run the drugs. I hadn't cared who I hurt…

Or even cared that I had hurt someone.

Helped kill them.

"Right," Milo said, then shook his head as he turned away from me to look at the scattered drugs. "Those prescription drugs are probably from one of our shipments."

"Maybe." I scrubbed a hand over my face. "I'll find this Jason Chaser and figure that out."

"Mickey…" Milo began then shook his head as he began to gather up the little packets. I agreed with the silence. It didn't take us long to gather it up, then set a fire in one of the drums and drop the evidence inside. It burned and we watched until the last of it was gone.

The air around us turned bitter as the wind picked up and the sun sank. The days were getting shorter. Milo's phone vibrated, the buzzing almost loud in the quiet. He pulled it out and stared at the screen.

I waited.

"There's a shipment in…"

"Go," I told him. "I'll make sure this is cleaned up."

There was still blood here. Some of it might be his.

"Mickey—"

"Just go, Milo. Keep your head on swivel, watch your back."

"None of us are supposed to run alone," he argued, and I quirked a brow. "Don't give me that shit, *Vandal*."

I snorted. "I can watch myself, *Kid*."

"Right. And if somebody knifes you in the back before you can make up with Ivy, you're gonna be sorry… and so is she."

"It doesn't matter. She has the boys." They would look after her.

Milo just shot me a dirty look. "Lie to someone who believes you." Then he turned his back on me to head over to the blood and clean it. The fire was dying down and most of the packets were gone. The last was disintegrating. We just avoided the smoke.

Jason Chaser. Charity downtown. Had to be the shit with Warrick. That piece of shit was gone though, what remained of the body dissolved into chemical soup and washed down a drain.

Freddie. Always they circled back to Freddie.

The weak link. Or so they thought.

But who were *they*? The 19 Diamonds, but they were gone. So who had they been fronting for? And did any of this have something to do with Little Bit and Rome going missing?

Who knew us like this? Who knew to target Freddie—the weakest link because of his addictions? Who knew to come at the Vandals' businesses? I had a lot of questions, but when I checked my phone Alphabet still hadn't gotten back to me. That was fine. There were things I could do.

I fired off a message to Liam. I wanted a response.

I needed to know where we were with finding Little Bit.

Milo waited it out with me though. No one ran alone. Not even me—apparently.

That was fine. The kids would be busy soon and then I'd do what I had to.

CHAPTER 7

EMERSYN

*N*o light trickled from the blackout curtains. Rome had closed them as soon as he realized what they were. Two days we'd been here. Two days with no contact beyond Brixton and his rotating bodyguards. This would be our third day. After the first, and the little object lesson with the shock collar, Rome and I had taken turns on eating the different dishes.

I'd offered to test them all and he'd just looked at me then said, "I'm bigger." Afterwards, he took a bite and we waited. Only after an hour of nothing happening did we proceed from there. I took my share of test bites, much to his consternation, but eventually, we split the tempting of fate.

So far, nothing had proven dangerous or even particularly inedible—if cold because we would wait between bites before we'd eat. I didn't mind the cold food. I minded the fact that Rome barely slept. I'd caught him: he'd taken to wrapping me up against him then "dozing," only every time I woke, he was already awake.

The night before, I'd played at sleeping, and no, he never went to sleep until I sat up and made him put his head against my lap. Then I stroked his hair while I watched the door until he went to sleep. If we had to take turns sleeping, we would. I hadn't meant to drift off, but I was tucked up against his chest with my ass snug to his groin.

Like I had with him the night before, he palmed my hair in slow, smoothing strokes. It eased away all the tension tightening up my scalp and bunching my shoulders that waking brought with it. The lack of nightmares helped. Rome being there helped. The ever-present awareness of being prisoners, though, that reality struck the moment my brain slid to waking.

Soft pressure from his lips pulled a smile from me as he pressed a kiss to the back of my head. The gesture and the contact communicated, "I'm here," without a word being spoken.

Need unfurled in me at the way his muscles flexed. Rome surrounded me, one leg tucked between mine, his arm tightening across my shoulders, and I ground back against his hard cock where it nestled along the crack of my ass. A soft hum escaped him, but almost at once he began to pull away. I twisted and he stilled when my gaze found his.

"Not safe," he murmured, though he traced his finger over the seam of my lips. No, it wasn't safe. I agreed. Still, I sucked his finger against my lips and then into my mouth. The light in the room was too low to make out his expression fully. His sharp inhale at the contact made me smile, then I ran my tongue around his finger. When he pulled it back with a slow drag against my lip, I let him go, only to suck his digit back again.

Tracing a light hand up his thigh, I only brushed against

the erection straining the fabric of his sweats. Like Rome, I had on some clothes, but only a shirt and sleep shorts. No sleeping naked.

Not when we didn't know when someone could come in. But the door to the bedroom was closed, and it was also barricaded with a chair. The cameras were off in here, and even if they were on—they'd need infrared to see anything.

That made me bold. Rome deserved every ounce of privacy, and I didn't want to share a moment of him with any one of our captors. When he pulled his finger from my mouth only to drag me in for a kiss, I smiled against his lips. I loved how Rome kissed, how he leaned into it. In his own way, he kissed like we were dancing.

He tested each step, growing bolder as I matched him and sank into the contact. When his hands feathered up my hips to the shirt and beneath it, I let out a little sigh. I wanted to touch him everywhere. Just as he would touch then pause, so did I until we were both rubbing against each other. It was almost like we were cats.

A laugh escaped me a moment before he cupped my breast and then pinched my nipple. That laughter turned to a gasp as I arched my back. Rising, I half-pulled away and he went still. The deference wasn't lost on me, but I didn't want any barriers between us. I dragged the shirt off and let it fall away, then found his hands in the dark.

Rome clasped our palms together until I placed his hands on my bare breasts. My nipples were already taut and beading against the cooler temperature. The brush of his lips over one was exactly what I needed. A hard pull of suction, followed by the bite of teeth and the lave of his tongue, sensation layered over sensation.

"Yes," I exhaled the word and he hummed a sound, pulling the nipple against his teeth as it vibrated against his tongue. Oh, that was even better.

When I slid my fingers into the waistband of my shorts, Rome's hands hooked over mine and he flipped me over so I was flat against the bed and then he was dragging the shorts off. I had no idea where they landed, because his hot mouth locked around my previously ignored nipple as he licked and sucked kisses between them and then down.

The moment he pressed his lips to the apex of my thighs, I spread my legs. I loved the feel of his tongue, but I wanted to do more than just soak up the attention.

"Twist," I beckoned, half turning onto my side. Rome hesitated and then he shifted his whole body. The rasp of fabric peeling away just made my smile grow as the first brush of his cock touched my lips. Hot, silken skin beckoned for my caresses, and I loved the way his dick seemed to flex under my touch.

It was already heavy with need, the tip beaded with a drop of pre-cum, and the vein along the underside pulsed. I took shallow strokes, lapping at the pre-cum before I sucked the tip into my mouth. On our sides, I could control the speed and access. His hips trembled, the muscles of his thighs corded beneath my nails as I petted him, swallowing around his cock until he was almost to my throat.

The pressure of his hands on my thighs encouraged me to lift my left leg and I curved it up against my side and fully out of his way. At least that flexibility remained, and I nearly choked at the open mouth, carnal kiss he pressed to my cunt. The flat of his tongue traced me from entrance to clit, then he swirled it around my clit before scraping the bundle of nerves with his teeth.

It added just the right amount of edge to the pleasure blasting through me. I loved the feel of him touching me, trusting me. I swallowed around his cock, and he let out a low sound as he pushed all the way to my throat. The tears in my eyes were a joy as I took him so deep my nose pressed against his balls.

Humming around him caused his hips to flex, and then he returned the favor and I swore he laughed. The low sound in the dark was a tantalizing seduction. I wanted to hear him make that sound again. I wanted to be the *reason* he made that sound again. Then he speared a finger into me followed by another as he licked and sucked around my clit.

Like a ravenous man, he waged a campaign of pure pleasure that left me shaking, but he hid nothing of his own reactions. Each time my throat tightened around him, he would push a little deeper. When I bobbed my head, he braced against my hands so that he didn't thrust and only when I pulled did he push as far as he could.

The edge was right there, but Rome was the perfect dance partner, never pushing too far, or pulling me too fast when I pulled back, he released my cunt and I twisted to chase after him. His breaths came in as short and fast of pants as my own. Wrapping my fist around his cock, I straddled him so I could sink down even as he pushed up.

Our mouths fused in the middle. The taste of me coated his lips and I thrust my hand into his hair as he slid a hand under my ass. For a moment, everything in me fisted and I stiffened. Rome's kiss eased, but he didn't pull away from me and instead, we hung there with me impaled on his cock while he teased his tongue against my own.

It was Rome. Rome's hands. Rome's cock. Rome's chest against my nipples. Everywhere he touched me, I burned for more. The pressure of his hands against my ass was no more or less than when he touched me anywhere else. Lifting my head, I pressed my forehead to his while he palmed my ass slowly as I began to roll my hips.

"Starling?" The single, strangled whisper threatened to undo every part of me. He hadn't slipped once in the days since they'd surrounded the car in the parking lot. I'd been Hellspawn and it would never not be weird to have Rome call me that. It left me aching for Starling and even more for Liam himself.

"I'm here," I promised. Then I kissed him again, trusting Rome as I rolled my hips to grind against him. He thrust upward, pushing me down as though determined to cram every inch of himself into me. Now that the thought crystalized, I wanted more.

The dance analogy reasserted itself as he shifted onto his knees, keeping me braced against him. Then he was slamming into me until I saw stars. Every stroke ground his pelvis to mine and then his cock struck sparks within me. I held onto his shoulders.

Sweat slicked his skin as our breath fused. I didn't know where his exhales ended and my inhales began. I rocked with him, matching the furious rhythm. There was just the barest hint of a squeak. Whether it was from the bed or from the way our flesh slapped together—I honestly didn't care. All I wanted was more of Rome.

We hung there, suspended forever at the precipice as we writhed together. He flexed his hands, squeezing so tight, I swore his fingers would leave indentions on my ass. Claiming it. Marking it. It only took that singular idea for my cunt to spasm. Rome plunged me into a hard, deep orgasm so intense I didn't think it would end.

Rome lasted a bit longer, but he wrapped his arms around me as he came in a series of spurts that left us both sticky. Breathless, we clung together, shuddering and gasping. For the first time since we'd been taken, there was no fear. None, just the two of us clinging together.

I never wanted to move. A distant part of my mind registered Rome rubbing my back. The feel of his skin under my hands as I flexed around his still semi-hard cock. The trickle of release coating my thighs and his just seemed to fuse us tighter together.

The room smelled like sex and Rome. It was the best ever. Too soon though, Rome moved and I let out a little complaint.

"The front door opened," he said as he carried me straight into the bathroom, finding his way even in the dark. "Lights." I squeezed my eyes shut at the warning, then blinked as the light flooded the room around us.

We were a picture in the mirror, my body still wrapped around his and his cock still pressed tightly to my cunt though he was slipping away. "Shower," I suggested. "Together. Then we'll go out there—when *we're* ready —together."

Leaning my head back, I studied Rome's gaze as he considered the suggestion. When he set me down on the cold tile of the bathroom counter, I startled. It was almost too cold against my flushed body. A quick kiss, then Rome murmured, "Stay." A moment later, he was gone and the bathroom door closed.

Irritation at the timing of intrusion simmered in my blood. I touched a finger to my collar and then glanced at it in the mirror. It didn't threaten to choke me and it wasn't so tight I couldn't slide a finger between it and my skin, but there was no way to remove it.

Not easily. Rome had studied it for quite a while. The place where it locked was also where a light was always on. A sensor that would probably stun me if we tried.

I was willing. Rome? Not so much.

A minute later, Rome slipped back into the bathroom, clothes in hand. He moved with such economy, muscles flexing with every step. I loved looking at him. So beautiful in his own way.

"I told them to not bother us."

"And they accepted that?" Why? Why would they—

"I have to have coffee with Brixton after." An apology gleamed in his eyes.

"Alone?"

He nodded.

"I don't like that."

"I know," he said, cupping my face. Then his gaze went to my throat. "I don't like that."

"I know," I echoed him and then pushed up on my toes to hug him. "We're going to get out of here."

"He'll find us," Rome reminded me, then leaned back. "You might have to reward him."

I laughed.

Rome was being one hundred percent serious, but at the same time… "I'll think about it."

"Thank you." Rome opened the shower and turned the water on, then walked right under the cool spray without waiting for it to warm. "He will need you to feel better."

What Liam would need was his brother. "Hopefully, they will tell us *why* they took us." Took Liam.

"They will," Rome said, holding out a wet hand to me. "Come, Hellspawn. I made them promise to let me make coffee for you before I talk to him."

It wasn't funny, and at the same time, it left me with questions. "Made them?"

He pulled me into the shower and I sighed as I rubbed up against him. "Yes," he said. That simple.

"Then they're going to wait until you're happy," I mused aloud. They were very agreeable when it meant "Liam" cooperated. "I want something else before my coffee."

Rome paused to study me, but I was already sliding down to admire the cock I hadn't been able to see in the dark. It was already thickening under my scrutiny.

When I ran my tongue up one side and then down the other. Rome nodded slowly. "You want me?"

"Yes, please."

I didn't have to ask twice.

And we definitely kept them waiting.

CHAPTER 8

ROME

"Be careful," she admonished in a tight voice even as she glanced at the door. My blood still hummed from playing with her in the shower. I'd like to have sex with her every day. Need for her grew every single time.

Touching a finger to her cheek, I traced down to her jaw until her eyes once again sought out mine and let me gaze into their honey brown depths. Her eyes, though like Milo's, held different facets depending on the light.

"I'm here," I promised. "I'll be back. Will you stay in here?" We'd dressed and I'd brought back her coffee after taking the time to make it correctly and then testing a cup for myself. She didn't know the second part. I didn't want to trust Brixton or his words.

So far, however, he had not lied. I needed to accept that part.

"I will," she whispered then cradled my face as she pushed

up on her toes. Dipping my head at her touch was no great hardship, nor was the feeling of her lips beneath mine. Soft, yet supple. Fragile, yet strong. Beautiful, from her movements to her stillness.

Perfection.

Sighing against her lips, I pulled back or I would never leave. As it was, the choice to go was a bargain for keeping her safe. "I'll be back." Repeating the earlier phrase helped to remind me as well as her.

"Liam…" The strangled look in her expression made me smile. I missed the sound of my name coming from her.

"Stay, Hellspawn." Firming my voice, I echoed my mirror. It was easy enough to do. We had done it for fun before. Her expression transformed briefly, worry giving way to a frown. Yes, that was how she glared at my other half sometimes.

Then she winked and I had to turn before I laughed. This game would be a lot more fun if we didn't have to worry about her safety or that shock collar. That was one of the first things I wanted them to remove.

Though, I already knew what their answer would be.

Brixton waited for me at the table Starling and I never used. He had a digital tablet open and his attention was on the screen. "Have a seat, Mr. O'Connell, I'll be with you in a moment."

After pulling the chair out opposite him, I sat. Two mugs sat on the table. One next to him and the other near me. His had steaming coffee. Mine was empty. The message was clear. If I wanted my own coffee, I could make it.

Acceptable.

Since I agreed to sit with him for coffee, I rose, collected the mug and carried it into the kitchen. After washing it, I brewed a single cup of coffee from the single-cup brewer that had made an appearance.

It had made Starling laugh. Though I was sure she would

prefer the coffeemaker at Liam's or the clubhouse. The one we still needed to replace. Brixton said nothing as I fixed my coffee. Awareness rippled over me though between one breath and the next.

He had finished whatever task had occupied him and now watched me. Saying nothing, I cleaned up and threw away the now used single cup before returning to the table with the hot coffee.

My mirror drank it black, so I didn't bother to add anything to it.

Brixton waited for me to take my seat before he leaned back in his chair. The tablet he'd been working on was closed and rested beneath his hand. Eye contact was something Liam would do, so I locked my gaze on his and held it.

The sensation wasn't pleasant, but the role demanded it. Keeping Starling safe required it. I didn't like being my mirror. But I could do it.

"Thank you for joining me," Brixton said finally, breaking the silence between us. I only nodded. Because I had very little to say until he explained how we might leave or offered to remove that collar.

Brixton seemed unlike others who moved in Liam's circle. His hands had no calluses. His suit seemed to disguise any hint of muscles and build. It gave him a long, lean look. The tailoring didn't betray anything beneath.

Nor did his facial features. He possessed a rather unremarkable face, a couple of cut angles for cheeks, but his jaw line was neither sharp nor defined. Average build. Average looks. Average.

Nothing about him would be memorable if he hadn't been the one to put the collar on her. The one to shock her as a lesson.

For that alone, I would never forget his face.

I took one sip of the coffee then put the mug down. I had

agreed to have coffee with him in order to give Starling privacy.

"Every report I have on you, Mr. O'Connell, really does not do your taciturn nature justice."

That didn't require a response, so I didn't make one.

With a sigh, Brixton set aside his cup, then drummed his fingers against the digital tablet. "This will go easier for you if you simply cooperate."

"I have cooperated." The only reason we were here, having this conversation, was because I'd cooperated.

"Yes, you've worked within the parameters we established and only to a point in order to protect your girlfriend. Leveraging her keeps you in line, but it hasn't bought your wholesale cooperation."

I shrugged. "You have given me no reason to cooperate with you more than I have."

"True, we haven't asked for more, but I'd rather hoped our actions spoke louder. You do as you're told, you're given privacy and safety. You disobey or challenge, Miss Sharpe pays the price."

"You haven't told me to do anything else." Understanding threaded through me. "This is why you're here."

"Very good, Mr. O'Connell. We've given you a few days to settle in, and now you will begin working for us."

"Who is 'us'?"

"Not something you need to concern yourself with. You obey, you do as you're told, and Miss Sharpe continues to have a happy, healthy existence."

"What do you want?"

"Well, the identity of the king would be a good start," he suggested.

Since I didn't know who he was, nor did Liam as far as I was aware, I just said nothing. Tired of staring at his eyes, I focused on a point just past his head. They'd trained me to do that when I didn't want to look someone in the eye. It kept my attention on them without me having to look at them.

"I thought that might be pushing it." Brixton seemed almost amused. That pulled my attention back to him, but the physical cues indicating humor didn't seem present. "Keep in mind, that information on him is valuable and can be traded for things like freedom."

Owing no allegiances to the figure pulling the strings in Liam's life meant I would offer him up immediately for Starling's safety. I didn't know.

"That said," Brixton continued clasping his hands together. "I thought we'd work on building the trust between us. After all, life and business are negotiations."

"If that translates to you telling me why I'm here," I said. "Then please, continue."

The man chuckled. "Brusque and taciturn to the point of insultingly rude. Yes, the descriptions do not do you justice, Mr. O'Connell. Fine, let's get to it then. My employer wants you to take on a series of fights over the next few nights."

Fighting?

"You have a fearsome reputation, Mr. O'Connell, and one well-earned. I am aware that most of your fights are for your own pleasure." Brixton spoke as if each word was a revelation, one I should be impressed by. "Or so we assumed, in the beginning. But then I noticed a pattern developing between your opponents and the businesses associated with them. You see, I like patterns. Patterns can be more revealing than even general actions can be."

I drained the coffee down to one last swallow. I had agreed to talk over coffee. When the coffee was finished, I would walk away.

"The king targets other wealthy families, particularly those who own the majority stock in their own companies. You go in, soften up their progeny through a series of fights, escalating the bets each time, until they are—how shall I put this—more easily persuaded that compliance with the King's wishes are far more beneficial than their own independence."

He seemed very pleased with himself.

"So, with that in mind... you're going to deliver a few fights for us."

Liam didn't always fight for the king. Sometimes he fought because it was how he relaxed. Other times... but they wouldn't see that.

"Why?"

"Excuse me?" Brixton frowned.

"Why will I deliver fights for you?"

"Because if you don't, every fight you refuse I'll turn up the voltage on her collar. Pain is a powerful motivator, don't you agree?"

"You misunderstand." Or perhaps I wasn't clear. It could be both. "Why do *you* need these fights?"

"That's not important. All that matters is obedience. You will fight when I tell you to fight. Do you understand?"

"It would be difficult to not understand," I told him. "When?"

"Tonight." He rose, checked his watch. "Transportation will arrive for you at six. Be ready. Miss Sharpe will accompany you. Be sure she is also dressed and ready."

"She doesn't need to see this."

"Perhaps not," he said, collecting his digital pad. "But she will be in attendance. If you are not ready, you will not enjoy the response. She will enjoy it even less. Have a good day."

With that, he let himself out. The guards were right there on the far side of the doors. Watchful and waiting. Two more were beyond them near the elevators. The guards were always in pairs or fours, never singular.

Smart.

I could take four. But could I take them fast enough?

Turning over Brixton's orders, I considered what he required. I'd been to many of Liam's fights. Backed him when he needed it. Sometimes when he didn't. Most of the venues knew *me* as well as him.

After washing out the mugs, I found food to take back to Starling. Sandwiches were easy and we'd tested most of it already. That didn't stop me from taking little bites of each piece and waiting a few extra minutes.

The fact they wanted Liam to fight made me think they couldn't afford for me to get sick. Thus, Starling would also be protected.

Starling sat on the floor, legs extended in the splits when I came back into the room. A smile quickly flared to life on her lips as relief melted over her face. "You're okay."

"Yes," I said. "Food."

Moving over to where she stretched, I sat down on the floor in front of her and set the plate there. I'd made four sandwiches. I'd eat after she did.

"Did it go okay?"

"I don't know," I admitted. She eyed the sandwiches, then me. "I tested them. I don't think we need to anymore though."

Frowning, she picked up a sandwich and swiveled her hips so she could face me as she kept her legs extended to either side of her. She was pure symmetry in even the simplest of her movements.

"Why?"

"They want me to fight." Because Liam fought for the king, but not always. At the same time, Brixton discussed patterns.

"Fight who?" Worry slipped into her voice, and I brushed my fingers down her cheek. I locked my gaze on hers. Meeting her eyes was no hardship for me. So many possibilities reflected back at me, so much emotion. The first glimmers of trust. Pleasure spiking. Also, pain. Then there was fear. The fear I couldn't stand.

But I would never look away.

"I don't know. He hasn't told me. Only that we will be going tonight. He insists that you go." I still didn't like that part. "There are clothes for us."

We'd already found them in the closet. Neither of us much cared.

"You don't want me there." She chewed on her lower lip. "But he wants me there to make sure you do what he wants."

"Yes."

Starling was leverage. They would hurt her to keep me obedient. I studied the device around her neck. Smooth, cool metal betrayed its purpose. But nothing about it resembled jewelry.

"Don't let him hurt you," she said. "I don't care what he threatens me with."

No. "He will not hurt you. No more pain for you... Hellspawn. I can fight. It will be fine."

I wasn't Liam. I didn't have to be. Fighting just meant making sure the other person didn't get back up. I could do that. Losing wasn't an option if it got her hurt.

"I hate this," she said, making a face. "I hate that we don't know what they want or why they want to make you do this."

"They want the king."

Starling frowned.

"Giving him up is not an option." I wished it was. "But he will find us."

If they were listening in, they would think I meant the king and if they weren't—it was still safer.

"Liam..."

I still missed hearing her say *my* name. Ever since she asked me what it was, then told me that if she knew, it might make her feel better.

"What do you need me to do?"

Starling lifted her chin. Even eating a sandwich while doing the splits in the middle of this empty bedroom, she was so beautiful.

"Do as they ask—but only if it doesn't hurt you." If they asked her to do anything she didn't want to do... Then again, to use her, they had to make sure I could see her.

"I will."

"Don't watch the fight."

She frowned.

I shook my head. "It will be messy. Don't watch."

"If it's messy, then I'm not letting you face it alone." When she linked her fingers with mine, I sighed. "I'm here."

For the first time, I wished she wasn't.

CHAPTER 9

EMERSYN

hile there were clothes in the closet, it turned out an outfit had been sent up for me along with "gear" for Rome. Gear. The sweats, shorts, a t-shirt, and shoes. Wraps for his hands would be available at the arena. I hated the idea of him having to go into a fight. It wasn't a lack of faith in his ability; he could fight. But why the hell were they making him? That thought just chased its tail around in my head until I remembered it wasn't *Rome* they were making fight. It was *Liam*.

He would hate this. I hated it.

The dress they'd sent for me though made me grimace more. There wasn't much room for imagination in it. Instead of a gown like my uncle preferred, it was more of a cocktail dress. The cut meant it left my back bare, while a sheer panel in the front offered a similar suggestion with only the cups to cover my breasts being slightly darker than the rest.

I'd worn far more revealing costumes, but this just felt...

"You don't like it?" Rome asked, worry coating the words, and I summoned a smile. He had enough to worry about. That said, I didn't want to lie to him.

"I hate when other people dress me up to show me off," I admitted. *Other people* was my uncle for certain, but I hadn't liked it when Liam arranged for all of those clothes, either, and his intentions had been far kinder.

Regret itched through me, and I curled my fingers. Not for the first time since we'd arrived, I longed for the stapler. It was a stupid need, but it wasn't here and we couldn't go get it. Pulse racing, I dug my nails into my palms and tried to get my breathing to calm, but that only seemed to make it worse.

The air backed up into my lungs. Warm hands closed over mine. He worked his fingers into the grip of mine, pulling my nails away from my skin. Words hummed in the air as he spoke. The vibrations of them translated from his skin to mine. Pressing my head to his chest, I soaked in the pounding of his heart. So much steadier and slower than mine. I tried to breathe when he did.

Some part of my mind scrabbled to get out of the darkness and escape. The stapler wasn't here. The bear wasn't. The others weren't.

"I'm here," Rome repeated, the words surrounded me, a lot like he did, and it took effort, but I got my eyes to open. His were right there. "I'm here."

He was there. "So am I."

The corners of his mouth lifted when I found his eyes. "Yes," he said. "We're here."

A shudder worked its way up my spine even as chill raced over my skin. It hurt, but I sucked in a deeper breath before I let it out. "Broken isn't bad." Maybe if I said it enough.

Rome slid his hand around my nape and then tugged me closer, and I wrapped my arms around him. The hug was everything I needed and didn't even know how to ask for right now.

"I'm sorry," I whispered.

"Why?"

"I'm freaking out." The last thing he needed to deal with was one of my panic attacks.

At first, he only shrugged, his arms tightening. Then he asked, "Do you feel better?"

"Yes and no." Rubbing my cheek against his shoulder, I sighed. "You always make me feel better, but...I'm worried about tonight."

What they wanted him to do.

"Hellspawn," he whispered the name, and I made a face. Then Rome's smile expanded and a laugh escaped him. "It does suit you."

"Okay, to be fair, I only punched him in the face 'cause he startled me."

That pulled a real laugh from him. Gentle fingers framed my face as he tilted my head back to study me. "Don't be afraid."

I let out a shuddering breath. "I don't want to be."

"Then don't. We can do this." Head tilted, his smile dimmed a fraction. "How do I fix this?"

"Win," I whispered. "Don't let them hurt you."

He nodded slowly. "Don't let them hurt you." That sounded more like an order.

"We're a pair," I admitted then sighed before I wrapped around him again. He cradled me closer. "Hugs help too."

"Hugs and kisses?" The last came out almost hopefully.

"Yes, always your kisses." Then because I wanted to cheer him up too, I squeezed his butt. "Everything with you."

"Good. Then we will make it better later."

Later.

I blew out a breath.

Right.

We could do this.

Rome needed me to do this. I *could* do this.

I would do this.

It wasn't two hours later before they came for us. The dress did not hide my collar. If anything, it seemed to emphasize the platinum band. It wasn't impossible that someone would think it was some chunky piece of jewelry. I didn't really follow fashion.

The dress seemed even more revealing once I had it on than I'd imagined. The only thing that kept me from throwing up was the very real appreciation in Rome's eyes. But I'd seen the same appreciation when I was wearing one of Vaughn's hoodies and a pair of yoga pants.

They'd sent up heels with the dress, but I went with flats. I'd rather be able to move if I had to, and I would be even better off barefooted. At least, I'd already stretched fully and my muscles were warmed. Rome looked downright dangerous in the gray t-shirt over sweats, and a black hoodie that he'd zipped partially. It hid all of his beautiful ink but also disguised the fact that he didn't sport the sleeve tattoo his twin did.

We were in the front room when the door locks sounded. Rome pivoted and moved to stand between me and the door. Brixton looked pleased as the guards held the doors open. "Excellent, I do appreciate promptness."

The urge to flip him off slid through me. "Too bad," I replied. "We definitely didn't do it for you."

Rather than show irritation, Brixton laughed. "Of course not, you did it for yourself, Miss Sharpe. As you should. Mr. O'Connell has been well-briefed on the consequences for disobedience. Should I give you a similar briefing?"

"No," Rome answered him. "Hellspawn will behave."

It was equal parts eerie and hilarious how much Rome

sounded like Liam. That tug was there, the longing for it to really be Liam standing there with us. He would *hate* this. Hate that his brother was in the middle of this. I hated it.

And I missed him.

Missed all of them.

Closing my eyes for a moment, I took a breath before standing.

"We will be taking you both down in the elevator. If you can behave, you may ride in the same vehicle." Brixton smoothed down the lapels of his suit. "If not, I will put Miss Sharpe in one car and you in the other, Mr. O'Connell."

"We already agreed," Rome stated.

"You agreed, Mr. O'Connell," Brixton said easily, before shifting his gaze to me. "I need Miss Sharpe's word."

"Why do you need my word? You have an electro shock collar on me. I step out of line and 'bzzt,'" I countered, moving to stand next to Rome, but staying just a bit behind him. The tension in his muscles seemed to practically vibrate under my fingers as I rested them against his back.

"Because you are not to interfere in his fights tonight, Miss Sharpe. That is why I require your agreement. You will be there. You will be sitting where Mr. O'Connell can see you, and you will be accompanied by a pair of guards..." Brixton motioned to the men at the door. They were thickly built, dressed in suits, and wearing utterly unimpressed expressions. If this was out of character for Brixton, you wouldn't know it by them.

"Or?"

Rome frowned, but he didn't take his gaze off of the men.

"I'm gathering there's a threat at the other end of that statement. You want my agreement to behave or... what?"

The corners of Brixton's mouth actually turned up into a hint of a smile. "I have to say, for someone aware of the physical danger you are already in, you have a great deal of spirit."

"I'm a hellspawn," I said with a shrug of indifference I definitely didn't feel. Then again, I'd been performing on a stage my whole life. I could damn well do it here. "Have to live up to the name."

The man chuckled. "I see why you like her, Mr. O'Connell."

"Then stop looking," Rome informed him and it got the attention off me and back on him. "Answer her question."

"If you can't behave, we will separate you. Mr. O'Connell has already demonstrated his willingness to keep you safe and that your continued well-being will assure his cooperation. You can be moved to a different location and locked away—for your own well-being of course."

"That's the stick. If I want to stay with Liam, I cooperate." Never hurt to clarify.

"Precisely. Do we have an understanding?" He seemed genuinely interested in my response. Something to think about later, for sure. But also something to address now.

"Don't touch me."

"Excuse me?"

"You will have my cooperation provided that neither you nor any of your men *touch* me. Agree to that and I will agree to the other."

This lesson didn't come from Lainey but from a lifetime of surviving on the road with troupes that were often as much strangers before they became families. And from an uncle who never hesitated to exert his power.

"Interesting," Brixton said, almost thoughtfully. "Provided you continue to cooperate, I find those terms acceptable. Understand, that cooperation means you go where you're told, you sit where you're told, and you behave as if you are meant to be there."

Rome spared me a look and I gave a little shrug. The corner of his mouth twitched, but he nodded. "Those terms are acceptable. My cooperation will increase as long as her terms are honored."

"Excellent. It's good that we're all on the same page. Miss Sharpe, meet Wulfric and Gerhard. They are your escorts this evening. Where you go, one of them will always be in attendance, they will also ensure you are not at all bothered during the evening's fights." With that, he glanced at the pair of guards in question. "You have your orders, guide, escort— don't touch."

"Wir verstehen." The one on the left spoke. "I am Wulfric," he informed me. "I will be doing the driving. If there is work to be done, I will be stepping away. Gerhard," he continued, motioning to the man with the sandy dark hair, flat eyes, and muted expression. "He will be your escort for all things. Do not leave his sight or his side. If there is trouble, *he* will deal with it."

The phrasing seemed almost odd. Like the trouble they discussed wouldn't just be from me. For now, however, I merely nodded. "This is acceptable."

Some control was better than none.

"Glad to hear it. Let us move along. We have a schedule to keep."

Rome held out his hand to me and I slid my fingers through his. The ride down in the elevator was claustrophobic. As dressed up as I was, the men in their suits seemed almost overdressed while Rome was underdressed.

That was the point.

He would be fighting. They would be working. Me?

I was both the carrot and the stick.

Fun.

The air outside was brisker than I'd expected, and I hadn't brought a jacket. Clamping down on the need to shudder, I didn't complain when they hustled us into the darkened back seat of a car. Our host didn't join us, and there was nothing to see out of the blacked-out windows. A partition separated us from the driver as well.

All told, the drive took us almost ninety minutes to reach the venue. Without a jacket, I wasn't looking forward to getting out of the car. Rome had reached for his hoodie zipper, but I shook my head. If he took it off, then his arms would be out.

Maybe no one else would notice… they were both beautiful, even if Liam's beauty had a harder edge to it. But I would, and I had no idea how much of a risk it would be if they realized that Rome wasn't Liam.

To my surprise, they opened the car up in another parking garage. How… ubiquitous. The air was still definitely colder and goosebumps raced up my arms. To their word, Wulfric and Gerhard didn't touch me, but they were right there.

"Miss Sharpe, if you will accompany the gentlemen inside, I will take Mr. O'Connell back to get ready."

At Brixton's statement, I met Rome's brief frown before I narrowed the distance between us. Brushing my lips to his, I whispered, "Kick their asses."

The flash of his smile softened his eyes, but he nodded. "Where I can see you."

"I'll be where you could spread my legs if you wanted." It was a bold offer and it got me another nod.

"Good. No one else."

I winked. We were on the same page there. Then I did the hardest thing yet. I let him go and took a step back. Facing my captors, I raised my brows. "Well, lead the way. We don't want to be late."

I also wanted out of the cold, but irritation warmed me enough for the moment. They didn't take my haughty words at more than face value. The parking garage we were in led to a set of double doors into whatever venue had been chosen.

Weirdly, I would have put the marble floors and conservative decorating scheme down to something like a bank. Big, wide hallways, and a larger open area with desks, and some teller windows said it probably was a bank.

They were all dark, however, and the only lights inside were low, muted, and left pools of shadows to surround us. No matter how light my steps, my shoes, like the guards', tapped as we crossed the marble floors.

They went to one of the rack of elevators, pulling open the old-fashioned gating to let me step in first. I shifted to a back corner. I'd rather face them both than have one behind me in this confined space. There was a definitive loud squealing noise before the elevator began to descend.

Okay, there was classic and then there was broken down. Hopefully, this leaned far more toward the former than the latter.

We descended two floors, then the doors opened to a loud room. Like above, the floors were marble, but unlike the lobby we'd crossed, this room was packed. Chairs were set around an arena. The guests ranged from those dressed to the nines to others in more casual clothes.

A man who just radiated "bouncer" turned at the elevator opening. He glanced at my escorts then at me before checking his tablet.

"Front row, east side," he informed them and stepped back.

Not that I recognized anyone in this crowd, not really. But I swore I saw more than one familiar face or someone who *should* be familiar. The chills from the parking garage were back, but I kept my arms down, my chin up, and my gaze moving.

Despite the cacophony of noise, skimpily clad women

moved amongst the throng. Some appeared to be serving drinks, one was definitely passing out some kind of pills, and a third—

I almost stumbled as she accepted a payment before going to her knees in front of one of the men and then had a cock down her throat.

That was unexpected.

"Easier to not watch," Gerhard said in a low voice from just at my elbow. "Depravations are readily available at these events."

I believed him but still wasn't prepared for the older woman who sat with one leg on another chair while a man knelt between her legs. She wore a blissfully patient expression, but there was no mistaking what the man was doing as he ground his face against her cunt.

Bodies were bodies but this was...like some Dionysian orgy with every type of hedonistic pleasure available. I let my gaze linger a moment too long as the woman took notice of me. Her smile was that of a Mona Lisa, secretive, amused, and she nodded to me as she stroked her hand over the man's head.

The polite thing to do would be to nod and smile back, but when she gestured to the open chair next to her even as she swept her gaze over me, I was glad I could decline.

Not because she wasn't beautiful and certainly not because I didn't appreciate the admiration. No, I didn't want her to get in trouble with my keepers.

"Go away," Wulfric snapped and that pulled my attention from the elegant beauty to the man who wore a collar a lot like my own and absolutely nothing else. His dick was out, red, pointed, and he licked his lips as he eyed me.

"I'm here to make the lady's evening more comfortable if she wishes." Sex laced his voice, sex and something a little darker. His eyes were glazed and his pupils fat. He was a party favor and my stomach rolled a little for him.

My uncle had only done that to me once. An object lesson.

One I'd never forgotten.

"I'm afraid I'm already a favor," I told him as I ran my fingers over the collar. It took him a moment to focus on it and then he nodded.

"If no one takes us home, I'll find you after." It was almost sweet.

Almost.

"Thank you."

But he didn't linger as Wulfric gave him a killing look, and finally we reached our seats. The little area was roped off with no one behind us or ahead. Gerhard took the seat next to me and Wulfric sat behind us.

I didn't like it, but I accepted it.

Across the ring, I found the older woman studying me again. She really was beautiful, from her pure white hair to her regal expression. Her lips parted as our gazes locked and then she let out an almost silent sigh as her body stiffened.

Her orgasm was a visceral thing and I swore my whole body clenched in tension witnessing it. The man between her legs sat up, his face slick under the lights and the collar he wore visible.

She gave him a sweet kiss, not once looking away from me and when her gaze went to my collar, I got the message.

They bartered in the various party favors and she'd already noted I was one.

This was going to be a long evening.

Panic licked along the sparks in my blood. Even when I kept my gaze off of her, my awareness told me she didn't return the favor.

More than one suited figure came to sit in our "section,"

but the seat on my left side remained empty. The only person nearest me was one of the guards. No one touched me.

The opulence, the sex in the air, and the murky darkness promised that this was so much more than just an underground fight. This was…

The lights came up and a pair of combatants entered the ring. I didn't know either of them. The battle was swift and brutal. Over almost before it began, with blood splatter striking the marble not that far from my feet.

The contestant in the ring let out a roar, and another fighter came in to meet him. The conversation in the room surged. Cheers. Betting. I couldn't follow all of it as a second brutal battle was waged.

The champion in that ring had no pity for any fighter who entered against him. His size, larger, or smaller, it didn't seem to matter. In five fights, he'd been the decisive victor and not one of his opponents had gotten up after.

The last one stared at me from empty eyes before they dragged him out.

Bile crawled up my throat and I fisted my hands together.

Then Rome entered the ring. The roar in the room rose to unintelligible cacophony. Liam O'Connell, the Renegade. That was what they called him. Rome ignored the whole crowd; he didn't even look at his opponent as his gaze sought mine.

Despite the size of the room, the temperatures climbed from the heat. Behind me, a woman screamed in pleasure punctuated with the meaty slaps of flesh on flesh. Across the ring, the dame who had been eyeing me currently smoked a single cigarette, her collared lover at her feet.

More skimpily clad and naked figures moved swiftly through the crowd, serving drinks, drugs, bets, and themselves.

"Stay here," Gerhard ordered, as one of those girls came

to him. He rose and glanced behind me—to Wulfric presumably—before he moved over to the wall not far away. The girl went to her knees for him and I looked back at Rome.

If Gerhard wanted to fuck someone, I did not want to watch.

Wreathed in sex and violence, this whole place was like something out of a Faustian nightmare. But I was here for Rome. For Liam. Only for them.

His hands were wrapped, but it was the only difference from when he left the car. Unlike his opponent, he hadn't stripped out of his hoodie, sweats, or shirt. He turned to face the other fighter.

The vicious other had been pacing back and forth since Rome entered the ring. Restless for the battle to begin. Where I'd barely been processing the other fights, I couldn't tear my eyes away from this one.

Somewhere, a buzzer sounded and the man leapt toward Rome. My beautiful artist flowed like liquid. I'd seen him fight before, but always when I'd been right there in the middle of it. This gave me some distance and where the guy had at least fifty pounds of raw muscle on him, he didn't have Rome's height or precision. As swiftly as that man had defeated his first opponents, the brutalizer went down to slam against the mat, blood trickling from his mouth and nostrils.

He didn't get up again.

The roar from the crowd cheered him on, and I put my fingers to my lips and whistled. Just for Rome. He slanted a look toward me, the corner of his mouth ticking up once.

Then another opponent entered the ring. They didn't last any longer with Rome than the first. A third and a fourth came in quick succession. Teaming up to fight him.

Two on one.

They got in two hits. Both made me wince, but it didn't

slow Rome down. With a kind of poetic efficiency he dispatched them both. One landed outside of the ring with a sickening crunch. The other—the other Rome wrenched their arm until it cracked and they were screaming.

After he finished each time, he drifted back to his corner where he would check me before he faced the next fighter. It was now his fifth fight, this guy moved faster, and it took Rome effort. He blocked more hits than he took, yet, the guy still managed to score a couple of blows that made me flinch.

As the fifth opponent hit the mat, I let out a shuddering sigh. A cut had opened above Rome's eye. The blood trickling from it slid down his face. Still, he checked with me and I summoned a smile for him.

How many more of these did he have to do…?

Rome's eyes narrowed a moment before Brixton took a seat next to me in the previously empty chair on my left. "He has done well," Brixton said. Something in his voice made my blood run cold. "Too well, and he's not obeying his orders."

Something cold pushed right up against the base of my skull even as Wulfric leaned forward against the back of my chair.

"I thought you wanted him to win," I countered.

"I want him to obey," Brixton corrected. "That .22 will not make as loud a noise, but you will be very dead. Consider that as he takes on this next fight, and because he did not listen, you must not look away."

My stomach plummeted.

"If you look away, I will make sure it lasts much longer for him."

Rome stared at me as a new opponent entered. He hadn't even turned to face them. *Don't*, I wanted to tell him. Dread curled through me. They wanted me to watch him get beaten and they wanted him to take the beating.

"Mr. O'Connell is a strong man, and his affection for you

is admirable, if foolish. But you will both learn, I don't make idle threats."

Ice threaded my spine. The barrel of the weapon pressed a little harder against my scalp, but I kept my expression as neutral as possible. Rome had to focus on the fight.

But he didn't turn to look, even as the buzzer sounded and his opponent lunged for him. He blocked two hits.

Two.

The rest? The rest he took.

I wanted to look away. I wanted to look anywhere that wasn't a man raining fists down on Rome as he took body blows and more than one fist to the side of his head.

But instead of going down, Rome kept getting back up. Tears burned in my eyes. Tears and fury. Both I had to hold on. Both meant I had to keep looking.

Only when Rome collapsed—finally—did the buzzer sound.

My heart just stopped.

All the sound in the room retreated.

Rome wasn't moving.

His eyes weren't open. Blood and bruises marred his beautiful face.

The gun against my skull went away and Brixton rose. "You listen very well, Miss Sharpe. Perhaps you are more than the princess you appear to be."

The word scorched in my brain. Wulfric took Brixton's place, Gerhard hadn't come back. The whole place was on their feet and a woman paused in front of me, speaking to Wulfric, I presumed. She blocked my view, but there was a weapon attached to her dress.

A long, cylindrical blade.

A perfect stiletto.

The silver caught the light. Rising, I brushed against her

and apologized. She gave me a warm, almost sultry look before she told Wulfric. "I'd love to serve both of you…"

Wulfric snorted and I didn't listen to what he said before I slammed the stiletto right through his chest. It hit bone and jarred my whole arm, but his body went stiff. Our sexy new friend let out a scream and Wulfric glared down at the silver blade sticking out of him and then at me.

Bastard deserved it.

The roar swept in again from the crowd and I smiled. After all, I was right here. I hadn't looked away or run away.

If I was lucky, I'd get to watch him die.

The one I really wanted to stab, though, watched me from nearer to the ring with a barely moving Rome. Behind him, my classy admirer raised a glass of champagne to me then blew me a kiss.

Crazy fucking people.

CHAPTER 10

JASPER

$\mathcal{M}$y side throbbed, more bruises than real pain, but worse, the stitches just fucking *itched*. For the most part, I ignored them. Everything was healing or it wouldn't be so fucking irritating. The last time Doc checked, he said the stitches could come out *soon*. Whatever the fuck "soon" meant.

For now, I headed down to the kitchen. The hallway between the bedrooms was a series of obstacles, torn down walls marking one end of the hall from the others. Two of the bedrooms had been compromised, so we were just knocking those out entirely and redoing them.

Bare struts, raw wood, and dust seemed to be everywhere. The carpeting from the threadbare to the functional had all been stripped up. Where bloodstains had been, bleached out marks remained. Those would be gone soon with a little judicious application of sander.

The kitchen and her dance studio had taken some of the

worst damage. It still pissed me off to think of all the mirrors shattered, and how they'd torn up the wood floors. Kel said we were ordering more—*after* we reinforced those walls.

Agreed. Nothing would get through them again. Her dance studio should always be safe.

Freddie glanced up from the kitchen table, braced against the wall with a couple of two-by-fours at the moment. "I said I'd bring the food up."

"It's fine," I told him. "I need to be up and moving."

"You're not supposed to tear your stitches."

"He's lucky I haven't cut the fucking things out myself," I grunted, yanking open the fridge. It was on its last legs. The whole thing vibrated, and I don't know what Kellan had done to keep it running, but we'd be getting new appliances in once everything was fixed up.

Plaster cracked off the ceiling and landed on the floor next to me. Shooting a look up, I grimaced. The whole place was going to shit. We definitely needed to get it all fixed up, and that meant I needed to be out of bed.

"You haven't cut them out cause then you'd have to explain it to Boo-Boo," Freddie said, returning his attention to his phone. There were two coffees on the table in front of him and a bag of takeout.

"I'd love to explain it to her," I countered. Love to just fucking see her. Even when she'd been trapped at Liam's, I knew *where* she was. Since her return from Pinetree, I craved seeing her like I needed my next breath.

Shutting the fridge door to hide the barrenness inside, I snagged one of the bags and opened it. Subs.

"You're not supposed to go to Kelly's," I reminded Freddie.

"I didn't," he said, tapping away on his phone. "I sent that twat Doug—Dirk—Dougan..."

"Mark?" I supplied.

"Yeah, him. He wasn't doing shit, so I sent him out to grab us food and coffee. Just hadn't had time to bring it up." Squinting at me, Freddie added, "And I'm not banned from Kelly's anymore. I paid my debt and he dumped that chick anyway."

Shaking my head, I sat in one of the less damaged chairs and ignored how it listed. The meatball subs were fully loaded and perfect. I drained half my coffee before taking my first bite.

"Still not a good idea, Kelly's not a bad guy," I reminded him. "But he does hold a grudge and I'd prefer if he didn't spit in my food. Cause then I'd have to beat his ass. It would be a whole thing."

The comment worked because Freddie snorted. "Kelly would never spit in your food. Mine? Sure. Yours? Never."

"What's got you so tied to the phone?" If it was word from Liam or the others, Freddie would have told me. A door opened from the warehouse, but the heavy steps sounded like Milo as the door slammed.

"I called Bodhi," Freddie said quickly and in undertone, then mimed zipping his lips as Milo walked in. The thunderous expression on his face didn't bode well for anyone.

"Doc is here," Milo said, as if warning me. "We're gonna have to deal with some of the rats this week too."

Yeah. I rolled my head from side to side. Time to cull some of them. "You don't have to deal with them," I said as I leaned back in the chair, careful not to stretch. "Most of them signed on during my watch. You and Kel didn't have much to do with it."

"That's why we'll do it," Milo corrected as he opened the bag of sandwiches and then glanced at Freddie. "You're not supposed to go to Kelly's."

"I'm aware, *Dad*," Freddie said with a smirk. "I didn't. I sent Bingo or Bongo or…"

"Mark," I supplied and Freddie grinned to himself. Yeah, he could pretend all he liked that he didn't know all their names, but he couldn't fool me. Freddie knew them. Knew their weaknesses. Knew where they dipped their dicks and who wanted to suck them.

Freddie didn't like strangers, and while he didn't like most of the rats either, he wouldn't let them be strangers.

"Yeah," he said. "Him. I can help with the rats."

I paused mid-bite at the offer and Milo swung around to look at him. "What?" Milo frowned.

"I can help with the rats," Freddie volunteered. Freddie never volunteered. He just didn't like anyone that close to him and I'd never ask him for it. "Gives me a break from Jas and lets us feel useful, since no one wants to let me go find Boo-Boo, even if I found her before."

"Freddie…" I got it. I wanted to be the fuck out there too, but a door slammed announcing a new arrival. Probably Doc.

"Hello?" A very *not* Doc voice called and Milo whipped around.

"Ball-Cracker!" Freddie rose with a grin, but Milo was out the door first.

Oh, this was going to go really, really well. Or really, really badly.

Wrapping up my sandwich, I followed Freddie out to the torn out living room. We had a chair and a sofa left. One table. It would all be replaced once the work was finished.

With a bag slung over her shoulder and looking like she'd just walked off some New York fashion runway, Emersyn's best friend looked around the destruction slowly before she focused on Milo.

There was no mistaking the longing on his face even if he stuffed it all under a blank expression. "What happened?" she asked before she cut a look at Freddie. "Where's Em?"

"Missing," he told her, not even sugar-coating it. "Someone took her and Rome. We've been trying to find them."

"Freddie," Milo growled, but Lainey let her bag fall to the ground.

"Are you fucking kidding me right now?" She dragged her gaze from Freddie to glare at Milo. "Someone kidnapped her? Why didn't you call me?"

Mutiny crowded his expression, and I'd bet even money if I were standing close to him there would be no mistaking the grinding of his teeth. "You couldn't do anything, Mayhem. We'll find them. Liam has a lead."

Did he? He could. Liam would turn the world inside out to find Rome. I didn't doubt he'd crush a few heads to get to Emersyn.

"You're such a jackass... but that explains Ezra." At the mention of Graham, Milo's expression tensed. "He vanished on me a week ago."

"Look," Freddie said. "We got food. We can tell you what happened and you can yell at Milo after. Or you can finish yelling at Milo and we can eat. Whatever works for you, Ball-Cracker."

I didn't laugh, but Milo's incensed expression was *almost* amusing.

"Tell me," Lainey said, bypassing Milo without a backward glance. "Tell me everything. Just tell me it wasn't her family that got her."

"Far as we know," I told her as she passed me, following Freddie. "It wasn't them. We've been trying to keep an eye on them but they're hard to track down."

"I can help with that," she said and Milo scowled. Before he could plow past me, I put a hand on his chest to slow his progress.

"What?" he snapped at me.

"Easy, Raptor," I said, pitching my voice low. Freddie's mouth moved a mile a minute, so we had maybe three before he'd be finished giving her all the details we know. "She's Emersyn's friend, she's an ally…"

"She's going to get hurt."

"You don't know that," I corrected. "We don't know a lot of things. One of the problems we've all had is assuming anything."

Eyes narrowing, he focused on me. "Since when did *you* become so reasonable?"

"Since I fell in love with your sister." That stopped him cold. It felt good to say it to someone else. Loving Emersyn, embracing that? Yeah, I could live on that. "So back off on her friend."

"Or what?"

"Or I'm going to be ripping stitches. But she means something to Swan. That means we protect her too."

Milo snorted, but it wasn't derogatory or disbelief. It wasn't even skeptical. "You still think any of them should be in our world?"

"Doesn't matter what I think." It hadn't for a long time. "It matters what she wants. Matters what that girl in there wants. Long as Emersyn wants us, she gets us. I will burn this world fucking down to make sure she gets what she wants."

I couldn't make it plainer.

"You might want to think about—what did you call her? Mayhem? What she wants and stop getting in her way, unless you really don't care if you're there on the other side."

Leaving him with that to chew on, I returned to the kitchen. Lainey had her phone in her hand, tapping the top of it against her chin. Her eyes were cool, thoughtful, and her expression was set in stone.

"So you have no other leads other than they were taken with only a small amount of violence?"

"There was blood," I answered for Freddie. "It wasn't hers or his. Their phones and IDs, everything electronic were left behind. Liam was supposed to be meeting them for some surprise for Swan... when he got there, the car was open, empty, and they were nowhere to be seen."

"The reasons you don't think her family is involved?" Rather than wait for an answer, Lainey canted her head. "No, he's too proud of his reputation. There would be photographs. We'd have heard. We did *before* he sent her to Pinetree this last time."

"We don't think they would have taken Rome," Milo said, grudgingly maybe, but he still offered it. "The family doesn't seem to have any compunction about hurting others. If they were taking her back, then one would expect them to have left Rome."

Even if Rome would have fought to keep her safe, they'd have left a body. We knew it.

"Then whoever took them may have nothing to do with the Sharpes."

"That's what Liam thinks," I said as I leaned back against the counter, careful of my stitches. As long as Lainey was on her feet, I'd stay standing as well. Freddie scowled.

"That means someone is after us..."

"No," I said simply. "If they took Rome to get at *us*, they wouldn't have taken Swan or else, like with Rome, we'd have found a body."

That made me sick to think about. I hated pointing it out to Freddie, 'cause he blanched.

"That's not a guarantee," Milo countered. "She has been seen with us." But he didn't like the idea either. Our enemies weren't the type to take prisoners. They took body parts. They took lives. They took cargo.

They didn't kidnap people.

"No," I agreed. "But for now, I think Liam's right. I think

it's tied to this business with the king, the Royals, and whatever fucking game they've been playing."

"Then we really don't know where they are?" Lainey asked, her expression growing more troubled. "No leads?"

I glanced at Milo and quirked a brow.

"We can go over what we know," he offered, his tone and expression gentling for the first time since she blew back into our lives. "Not sure how much it will help."

That got a smile out of her. "Well, Pretty Boy, we'll never know until you tell me."

Freddie grinned before he unwrapped his sandwich. "Almost wish I had popcorn for this part. Ball-Cracker is here. That means we get to find Boo-Boo soon."

Fuck, I hoped so.

CHAPTER 11

KELLAN

The message from Vaughn shifted my plans. Instead of working with Adam at Liam's old place, I brought Reed back to the clubhouse with me.

"Not sure what the point of playing dead is, if I keep heading back to Braxton Harbor and the one place I *really* shouldn't be seen," he'd commented, almost idly.

I merely shrugged. Reed might act "put upon," but he'd agreed to join me with zero hesitation when I said we had some news. What would that news turn out to be? I wasn't sure. "If anyone asks," I told him before pushing the door open. "You're just a new rat."

The derision in his snort actually pulled a smile from me. Vaughn pushed away from the door to the clubhouse. Despite my comment, I had been running ideas to cover Adam's now regular, if infrequent, appearances here. A change in his look would help.

His clothing was too expensive for a rat's, and his attitude would get his ass handed to him. If we could manage to sand some of that off and teach him to blend, it could work. Then again, the cover of his "death" was for his protection and not ours.

Frankly, I was a little over the fucking lies.

"What happened?" I asked as I met Vaughn halfway. He spared a glance behind me and then raised his eyebrows. I nodded. We didn't have to go into specifics, but for now, Adam Reed qualified as an ally.

"Dove's bestie is back," he said without preamble. "Milo's in a mood, but Jasper and Freddie have been plotting. Liam's not answering his goddamn phone, and Doc just got here. He and Jasper have already gone three rounds."

"So, just another day in the neighborhood," I replied and Vaughn shrugged.

"If Dove were here, it would be fine."

Agreed. "Let's just get this over with." I cut a look back at Reed. "Try not to bait every single person in there. I've only got so much patience, and you're far more useful to me alive than dead."

"Noted." The bland expression he shot back made zero promises. Well, it wouldn't be the first time we spilled blood inside. As it was, I had only so many fucks to give on the subject.

Sparrow and Rome were out there, and until they were *home* and *safe,* everyone else needed to get the fuck over themselves. I added Liam to that list. His need to get his brother back wasn't a question, nor was his affection for Emersyn.

But he was too used to working on his own. That needed to stop.

Now.

Reed followed me with Vaughn holding open the door to

let us both in before trailing after us. "This is not going to be fun," he muttered.

No, I didn't suppose it would.

"Hawk, I'm not taking those stitches out until you've finished healing. It *seems* like it's healed because the stitches are there, but you had internal damage, and wounds don't heal from the outside in. They go from the inside out." Doc's patience was on a shoe-string budget.

Interesting.

"They fucking pull, and I need to be free to move." Jasper scowled. "At least take the ones on my back out."

"No."

"You know," Jasper continued with a snarl. "I could just cut the fuckers out myself."

"Is there a point to this argument?" Lainey asked, her tone crystal clear on her opinion of said argument. "Or can we return to gathering useful information?"

"Lainey." Adam swore and that dragged the attention of everyone standing in the remnants of our living room around to us. The renovations were on hold. Right now, we had far greater concerns.

The woman at the center of all of Reed's aggravation barely spared him a look. "Aren't you supposed to be playing dead? I don't talk to ghosts."

Freddie snickered, but he also shifted his stance from leaning against the sofa to standing. "If he's here, does he have something useful for helping us find Boo-Boo?"

"I'm sure he does, and if the dead could speak, he still wouldn't say anything useful while I was in the room." Her disdain was a tangible thing, as was her own rapidly brewing anger. Clearly, the pair had issues.

"Mayhem," Milo rumbled, and she made a face then threw her hands up in the air. That sounded more like a request than a warning, but I would steer well clear of the whole debate. We needed everyone present. Period.

Reed came to a halt next to me, his posture stiff and a muscle ticking away in his jaw. His gaze fixed on Lainey and behind her, Milo focused on him.

Yeah. No.

"For the time being, everyone put your pride and your pissiness in your pockets. I don't give a damn what you like or don't like. Until we have them back, nothing else is more important. Not your personal lives." I stared at Milo. "Not your temper." Jasper glared back, but he spread his hands. "Not your impatience." Of all people, I didn't think I'd have to give Doc that look.

To my surprise, he snorted, but folded his arms and then nodded.

When no one else offered an argument, I said, "Better. Reed is here because he is going to help us with some issues, but also because this involves Emersyn."

Lainey frowned, but she took a step back and actually leaned against Milo. Yeah. There was trouble waiting to happen, but he wrapped an arm around her as she brought her gaze to mine.

"You," I continued now that I had her attention. "You're here because you're her friend and you will always be welcome. I don't know what's between you two—or three—and right now, I don't care. Is working with him going to be an issue?"

Her chin came up, and the haughtiness she could affect reminded me of those first few days when I'd been driving Emersyn and she hadn't relaxed her guard around me at all.

But I'd seen her curled up with Sparrow, the two of them sleeping with tear tracks on their faces. I'd seen her fierce devotion and equally hot temper whenever Milo tried to back her into a corner.

Freddie called her Ball-Cracker and that name suited her too damn well. I wasn't touching the Mayhem comment, however.

"Of course, I can *work* with him," she told me, her tone cultured and calm, though I didn't doubt her temper wasn't still active. "What do you know?" she asked, transferring her attention to Adam, "that would be useful."

The silence dragged out and Freddie made a face, but he had his blade out and it danced over his fingers. Whatever he really thought of the whole situation, his agitation was right there on the edge.

Jasper let out a breath, then leaned against the back of the sofa. It was his concession to taking it easy. I'd take it. "Maybe we start at the top, pool what all of us know…" He focused on me. "Liam was the first on site, but you and Milo were there next."

"That's an idea," Doc said, flicking a look at me. "Read us all in."

Fine.

"Liam called us ten minutes after he got there…" I walked them through the phone call, our subsequent drive over, and arrival. We went over everything that had been in the vehicle and outside it from the blood—not theirs—to their phones and bags. The supplies.

The location made pinning down any footage impossible. Liam didn't have security cameras on the property, something he planned to correct. While he hadn't said anything to me directly—I saw it in his eyes. We'd added cameras here in all the public areas, and we all knew they were here *now*.

"He went to meet with the so-called king," I continued. The arrogance implied by that name rankled, but that wasn't our problem right now. "He reached out to Graham because the undercover game means taking us as backup isn't an option he wanted to exploit—yet."

"That makes sense," Reed offered. "Ezra is still in. Them working together wouldn't be seen as anything more than allies being called in. His brother is off-limits; the king knows this. But… that said, he would be the first person I'd look to in light of the identity of those taken."

He cut a look at Lainey, but he didn't keep his gaze there.

"The king," Reed continued, his tone crisper, "is complicated and cagey. His secrets have secrets. Everything is a puzzle, a game, or a mission. He won't care for any accusations. But…he will care less for someone attacking one of his people. This is an open assault on Liam. At his rank, the king would perceive it as an attack on him personally."

"Is that good or bad?" Jasper asked and Reed didn't answer immediately. If anything, he appeared to be considering it.

"It could be both, I'm afraid."

That was not the admission I wanted to hear.

"How?" Lainey demanded.

"Lainey—"

"How could it be both good and bad? It's not a difficult question." The pair locked eyes for a moment and Reed shook his head.

"Good, because he will use his resources to help." Reed sighed. "Bad because he could take an interest in Emersyn because she was with Liam's brother."

Fuck. Definitely not what I wanted to hear.

"We can deal with that when we have to," I said, though it was Doc who frowned.

"Is he a threat to her?" Doc demanded in a cool tone. Maybe I shouldn't enjoy seeing Mickey J more and more, even with elements of the old Vandal creeping in. But fuck if I didn't enjoy it. Doc was a solid guy, but Mickey J was hell in a fight.

Milo's expression darkened even as Reed spared Lainey another look.

"He's a threat to everyone. When was the last time Liam and Ezra checked in?"

The silence that greeted that question had me checking my phone. "More than twenty-four hours. But he said they might have to go dark." I didn't like it and I didn't want to give him a lot of time to fly this on his own.

If we were getting them back fast, that would have happened day one.

"Give me a minute," Reed said as he pulled out his phone and paced down the hall. Freddie shifted to keep an eye on him, but I lifted a hand.

"Let him go," I said. "He's had plenty of opportunities to be a threat. Right now, we have an agreement. We're trusting him."

"We are?" Milo eyed me and I nodded once.

"We are."

Freddie shrugged, but it was Lainey who looked from where Reed went to study me. "Why would you trust him?"

"For the same reason we trusted you."

"Em."

I inclined my head. Some of the mutiny in her expression eased. "Sparrow trusts you, and to a certain extent, she trusts Reed." His offer to her, his protectiveness of her, might be tied up in his feelings for Lainey. At the same time, he'd been trying to protect Sparrow.

This was fertile ground we could navigate and upon which a foundation could be built.

But in case anyone else needed a reminder, "He and Graham also saved Sparrow, Jasper, and Liam not that long ago."

"I wasn't arguing," Jasper countered. "For once, I have no complaints. Don't know them well enough to trust them, but

Liam does and so does Swan. That's all I need to know for now."

"You keep getting all mature like that, Hawk, and no one is going to recognize you soon." Vaughn's dry remark earned him a middle finger from Jasper.

Lainey's expression turned inscrutable, and I scrubbed a hand over my face.

"Guys…"

"You said Liam's been unreachable?" Reed asked, returning faster than I expected.

"Said he hasn't been sending answers, pretty sure he's getting the messages." But being in a position to answer them were two different things. "Why?"

"Renegade went down in a fight last night—after winning several."

I hadn't heard that name in a long time.

"He's fighting?" Vaughn asked. "Would he be fighting right now?"

If it got him closer to Sparrow and Rome…

Yeah. He would.

My phone chose that minute to buzz, and I turned it over. "Speak of the devil…" I hit answer and put it to my ear. "Tell me that fight got you something on where she is? And are you alright…"

Dead silence greeted my comment, then Liam fired off two words, "What fight?"

I flicked a look toward Reed. "We just got word that Renegade went down in a fight last night."

Liam didn't explode. Jasper was the hot and volatile one. He burned. Ripped into people and got loud as hell. Liam? He was ice. Went cold, deadly quiet, and even his beatings were chilly, almost impersonal.

"Where?"

I repeated the question to Adam and then put the phone

on speaker. "Everyone is here, including Sparrow's friend Lainey and your buddy Reed."

"Fight took place at one of the palaces," Reed told him. "Renegade doesn't go down so it's making the rounds."

More silence.

"You weren't in a fight," I said, filling in the blanks, which meant the only person who could be doubling for him was Rome.

"I'm going to kill every single one of them. Which palace? Get me the info, then find me the next one. If they are fighting on that circuit, I need an invite to get in, and if they are running Rome as me, I'm not getting in that way."

"That could take a minute," Reed admitted.

"It'll go faster if I help," Lainey jumped in, and Milo clamped down his jaw on what looked like an objection. Reed gave her a long look, then nodded.

It was grudging, but they were in.

"Head back here," I told Liam. "Bring your friend."

"Just get me the location—"

"If you want the location, you get back to us. You aren't going in alone."

"Kel..." There was a wealth of unspoken words on the end of that exhale.

"Tell it to my face," I said, then hung up on him.

"Find out where these fights are. If they are running Rome in them, then Sparrow may be there too."

It was the first thing looking like a lead we'd gotten.

CHAPTER 12

VAUGHN

*T*he next time Kellan handed out assignments, I didn't want the one that involved Milo, *Lainey*, and Reed. She was a nice girl. Stubborn, pushy, and more than a little confident in her own power. I liked that about her.

Milo was *almost* human around her. But Reed? Holy shit, the tension between the three of them was going to give me a headache. Going to? Correction, had given me a headache.

"I've got it," Lainey said, a thread of excitement in her voice. Reed reached for her phone, but she pulled it back to herself and Milo glared at him. "I said I have it, I didn't say you could have it."

"Mayhem," Milo said in that same tone he'd used earlier and she gave him a faintly sour look. That scowl promised a lot of things, like maybe Milo should be careful where he slept.

If this was any other time and we weren't trying to find

Dove and Rome, I'd be entertained. As it was... "Location?" I interjected and all three of them swung their heads in my direction. Yeah, they'd forgotten I was here. "After we get them back, you three can settle whatever this is."

But I would object to spending any more time on this *right now*. Milo nodded, the corners of his mouth turned downward, and I got it.

"Or not. Long as Dove is safe, we can pretty much figure anything out." I focused on Lainey. She'd taken a lot of risks to get to us in the first place. Maybe not as many now. Whatever the hell was going on with her and Reed, it also involved Dove.

Milo liked Dove's best friend. We all got that. But right now, Dove came first.

Period.

Lainey flushed then shot me an apologetic look. "You're right. Here," she said, passing the phone to Reed. "Does that look correct?"

"Conrad got you this?"

"Don't start," Lainey said with a sigh. "You hate him. You hate everyone. But he answered. He also offered to get me in..."

Expression set in granite, Reed shook his head. "No. The last place you should go is one of these events," he said, but before Milo's Mayhem could erupt, he added, "They traffic during these events. If he's offering to get you in, he's expecting quid pro quo."

Her nose wrinkled. "I can have him meet me at the location, play dumb—then we ditch him and just go."

Milo frowned.

"And before you start," Lainey continued, "I know damn well what some of these places are like." She glanced at Milo. "We've done this before. We can do it now. The more people we have there, the safer it will be, right?"

Reed pinched the bridge of his nose. "The location is a former casino, one of about a dozen scattered across the country. It's easy to get in and hard to get out. It also has acres of camera coverage. Unless one of you is hiding some especially useful skill at hacking..."

Milo grimaced, but Lainey tapped at her lower lip. "We could call..."

"No."

"He'd say yes," she argued.

"That's why I'm saying no, he wanted out of the family business. I'm not dragging him back in." Reed frowned again. "Maybe we don't have to try and sneak in..."

"Walk through the front door," Milo said slowly. "Wear your wealth like a shield and use the privilege to gain entrance."

For a long moment, Reed studied Milo. The tension crackling between them climbed, but this wasn't violence directed at each other.

It was a *promise* of violence, however.

"We need to get close enough to get Dove and Rome. Liam knows these locations like you do?"

"He'll know them better," Reed admitted. "I didn't go to the fights as often." Distaste marked each word. "But I've been. So has Ezra."

"Good."

I pulled out my phone and then held out my hand to Lainey. She handed over her unlocked phone with the name. I sent the info to Kel, including the invitation Lainey wanted to accept.

Not watching my audience took effort, but there was no mistaking the long, brooding looks or all the unspoken epithets, questions, and accusations burning in the air. In the handful of days since Rome and Dove went missing I'd focused on what needed to be done.

This close to an actual clue had tension coiling in my muscles. The urge to just *go* simmered in my blood. Kicking down doors was usually Jasper's thing, but I would be fine with it right now.

"Accept the invitation," I told Lainey as I passed her the phone back. "Tell him you'll meet him near the location. Someplace out of the way and private."

Milo and Reed both glared at me. I ignored them as she took her phone.

"Tease him?" Lainey said. "Not a problem." She typed into her phone and since the hostility rolling off Milo and Reed seemed pointed at me for a change, the air was a little easier to breathe. I really didn't care what Reed thought, and Milo would get over it.

Especially when he got to deal with the son of a bitch.

"I also need a picture of what the guy looks like."

Reed supplied it so swiftly, I wondered if he was tracking where the guy was right now. I studied the image for a beat.

"When you go into these things, do they check ID or just a visual sweep? I'm assuming if they're by invitation only; you can't just show up without an invitation or you wouldn't know where it is."

The guy wasn't anything extraordinary. Dark hair, dark eyes—Milo could pass, but Milo might be too big a build for him.

"Usually, there's a phrase. It's sent with the invitation. They are very particular about who comes to these events."

Underground fighting and criminal activity? It'd be shocking if they didn't. I'd done my share of fights with Liam, but not these. Rome had gone to some with him, but Rome was there.

Right, so we needed Liam to not dive in without us.

"The fights are tomorrow night," Lainey said. "He wants me to meet him outside Beldini's."

"That gives us twenty-four hours. Try not to kill each other. Milo...we need to talk."

That was leaving Lainey and Adam alone, but she didn't look alarmed. We wouldn't be far, but I needed to pass a message to Milo that those two didn't need to hear yet.

Not taking his gaze off the pair, Milo said, "Kel wants to take out this guy and replace him?"

"Yes," I said. "That's not why I pulled you aside."

He cut me a look. "I'm fine."

"You sure?" I nodded to where Reed now faced Lainey. We could see her face, but not his. "That's potentially messy."

"I can handle it."

"Milo, you don't have to handle shit if you don't want to. He's an ally and he's useful, we will back you and you have to know that."

The corner of his mouth kicked up. "I do know that. I also know her. She's not thrilled with him being here, but she's angrier that he wants to keep her out of it."

"Well, maybe there's a lesson to be learned there."

That earned me a dark look. "What do you need, Vaughn?"

"I need Dove back, and I need you to hold your shit together when we go in. If what Reed is saying is true, this is not our scene—at all." It was even less Milo's. "We need to get them. Afterward, we can burn the whole damn thing down and I'll help."

He chuckled, but the lack of humor actually seemed to pull Lainey's attention toward him. The concern in her eyes was hard to miss. "I can handle it."

Some days, I wish he didn't have to handle shit. One step forward, two steps back. "Right..."

Eighteen hours later—and three hours away from Braxton Harbor, I dumped a stripped-down Conrad Masters the Fifth into a trunk. Hands and feet tied, and we'd gagged him for good measure. Jasper had insisted on coming for the meetup, but he and Freddie were taking our friend for a drive and dumping him somewhere.

"You sure we can't kill him?" Reed asked. "It would be more efficient and save time. Also keep more resources here."

The speed at which Milo had taken Conrad down had left Lainey staring, but I didn't worry about that right now. Milo was never going to fit into the suit, but we had a dark one and a light colored one, so we went with what worked then handed off the guy's wallet and phone, after we unlocked it with his face.

Facial recognition to unlock phones was really fucking useful. Reset the passcode then we were free to get rid of him.

"We don't have time for that and we don't know who he told he was meeting Lainey," Kellan said in a crisp tone. "Better for him to think he was mugged, she can come up with a story to deal with him later."

Reed's expression suggested he'd take care of that part later too. Fine by me.

"Three cars," Kellan continued. "Doc, you're with me. Vaughn, you're Reed's muscle. Milo, you're Conrad Masters for the night."

That left Lainey. "I know what I'm doing," she said, then motioned to her dress. It left a lot of skin on display, a fact neither Reed nor Milo had commented on but they'd both definitely noticed.

"You also stay with one of us at all times. I don't care if you need to pee, you don't go through a door without one of us with you."

Defiance flooded her expression, but she only nodded. "How are you and the doctor getting in if we're going separately?"

"I'll handle it," Kellan told her, and I just kept my expression neutral. Warrick would come in useful, what did you know? That had to be what he'd use, but I still wasn't going to worry about it.

"Don't get dead," Jasper ordered as he headed for the last car with Freddie. "And bring them back."

"That is the plan," I called before I followed Reed to his car. He drove a liquid-black Ferrari. Liam pulled up as we opened the doors. He sported a couple of new bruises from something. He didn't offer and none of us asked.

I waited while Milo helped Lainey into the car they were taking. Reed stared at them broodingly. He wasn't alone. Graham, who was riding shotgun with Liam, looked pretty pissed, too.

"Let's go," Kellan said before he headed to his own car. I climbed in, Reed started the car with a single push, and we were accelerating after Liam. That left Kellan and Milo behind us.

The silence inside the vehicle wasn't unpleasant. I wasn't really here to make friends anyway. Even if the car felt too damn small for me.

"I saw you fight once," he commented. "Five or six years ago."

"Okay?" Did he have a point?

"You still hit as hard now as you did then?"

I grinned. "I hit harder."

"Good to know." He pressed his foot down. Despite the fact we'd already driven several hours, the former casino location was in the middle of fucking nowhere. No city lights to provide coverage, no civilians to worry about, and no cops.

It seemed ideal.

According to Reed, what law enforcement was out there

would be on a payroll somewhere and the local sheriffs made way too much money off these events to worry about what happened during them.

No bodies.

No crimes.

Course, they also had their own security and their own rules. We were the ones flying semi-blind. I kind of wished Jasper was with us on this one. At the same time, there was no way he wouldn't wade into whatever fight waited for us.

Better to give him a little more time to heal. Besides, he and Freddie were also backup if this shit went sideways.

An hour later, I sent them a text with the exact GPS location before I followed Reed toward the doors.

Liam and Graham were already through them, and the others were still pulling into the parking lot. The interior was loud, bright, and filled with people…

People. Sex. Drugs. A hedonistic circle of hell where everything someone could desire seemed to be available. Men and women alike wore collars and served the "guests." The guests in this case ranged in age from ours to senior citizens.

Old money and new. Blood money and…

"Next up in the ring will be the Renegade…"

The name echoed through the room and cut through some of the chatter. The ring—or cage in this case—was hard to miss. It occupied the center stage of the whole room. Rome headed out of a side door toward it. His face was a riot of bruises.

Liam was going to kill a lot of people today. Following Rome's gaze, I stiffened.

"She's here."

Reed shifted next to me. "Where?"

I nodded toward the ringside seats. Dove sat there,

expressionless in a black cocktail dress. Her hair was pulled up, leaving the collar completely on display.

They had her in a *fucking* collar.

Liam wasn't the only one who would be killing someone tonight.

CHAPTER 13

LIAM

$\mathcal{F}$ive days.

Five days of looking. Kicking over rocks. Tearing apart other operations. Doing the king's dirty work to find little or nothing on *who* or *what* had taken my brother and our girl. In fact, the only thing we had found was a name.

Constantine.

The name told us nothing. The king's actual irritation told me more than the name had. He had no idea who this person, or persons, was. It pissed him off.

Normally, I'd be fine with that. As it was, what few strands of patience I had left had begun to snap one at a time.

Then word came down that I'd lost a fight.

Me.

Or rather, my fighter name had lost a bout. The Renegade didn't lose. I'd cultivated that reputation to the cost of broken ribs and internal bleeding.

Kellan wouldn't give me any information on where, save

for a clue I'd gotten out of Adam. It was one of the palaces. Those fight locations rotated on a circuit that changed at the whims of the promoters.

Palaces were safe locales, open for staging huge events. The fights also worked as ideal locations for networking, sales, information gathering, and if necessary —assassination.

Rome *rarely* attended these events. We always made sure we looked different enough during them that they knew I had a brother, but they wouldn't see us for the twins we were.

The only person who could be fighting in a ring as me *would* be him.

The coldness slicking over my blood from the day I found them missing penetrated all the way to my bones. All of us going wasn't the best idea. It wasn't the worst.

"You're not thinking," Ezra pointed out when Kellan hung up on me. When I cut a look at him, he just raised his hands. "I get it. I was there not that long ago."

A pointed reminder.

Fisting my temper into both hands, I locked it down.

"We're going to get your brother back. Moody asshole is the only one who makes you look like a peach."

That didn't make me laugh.

"And we'll get Em back. I'm pretty sure she can pull the stick out of your ass and beat you with it."

"Fuck off," I said, but it still helped. Then I'd glanced down at the guy I'd been beating information out of. He was still unconscious.

Not that he probably knew anything anyway. Or anything useful, that was. Still…

"If they're running Rome as me," I said slowly. "They were after me."

"Yep," Ezra said, folding his arms and leaning back against

the broken concrete wall like we were chatting it up in some parlor.

Rolling my head from side to side, I studied the man bleeding on the floor. "Still think the king isn't in on it?"

"I think he isn't even more now," Ezra admitted. "First, he sounded genuinely pissed and he never even sounds ruffled, even when we disobeyed him directly."

True.

"Secondly, he *knows* you have a twin. He also knows what you'll do. If these people are running your brother as you— they either don't know he's you..."

"Or they want to lure me out. Push my buttons, piss me off, and get me to act rashly."

"Pop, pop, pop." He said dryly as he pulled a gun out of his holster, then the noise suppressor from his pocket. "If you were me, you would have already made so much noise that they wouldn't miss who had been taken."

The dry look I'd given him made him laugh.

"But you're not. Also, are we done with this asshole?"

The asshole in question was a low-level enforcer for some group out of South America. I seriously doubted the cartel would miss this idiot, but at the same time, if one does not have to piss off a whole cartel, then one should not.

At least not today.

Maybe next week, after I got Rome and Hellspawn back.

"Clean up," he told me as he took my place. "Then we'll pull the info we need. Whoever took them runs in the palace circles and games. That actually narrows our list."

It had.

It did.

Now I was standing inside the doors to the old Three Coins Casino, where its public-facing business had been shut down for more than twenty years. Privately, the palaces had probably been using it before the chains were added to the doors. It just meant now they didn't have to worry about civilian clientele.

Access to palace events required knowing someone. You didn't get through the door with only a name, you had to be invited. That invite only came when someone vouched for you.

There wasn't a single Royal who didn't have access. It was why I fought on these circuits regularly. I'd pulled a knit cap on before I headed inside, and I wore a jacket. It was hardly a disguise, but no one was looking for *me* out here.

Not with sex for sale at the tables, money changing hands to cover payment for the workers—most of whom were willing but not all. Not all by a long shot. We shut those down when we found them, but they were getting better about indenturing sex slaves these days.

Collars for debts.

Run up a big enough bill and some of these fuckers would sell their mothers, their sisters, and their daughters. A few would sell their sons.

Jaw clenched, I locked down that thought. Find Rome. Find Hell—

"Next up in the ring will be the Renegade..."

The name rebounded off the walls and the change in the lights offered some cover for the instant anger rolling through me. Rome stalked out of the back with two guys "escorting" him. He wasn't dressed like I did for fights, though his hands were taped.

Bruises decorated the left side of his face. Split lip. Swollen eye. Very discolored cheek bone.

I couldn't see any bruises on his body, but he was still dressed in sweats, a shirt, and hoodie. Smart.

Covering for me.

Taking beatings *for me*.

Rome's gaze wasn't on the cage or the opponent waiting for him. It tracked right to Hellspawn.

Relief swarmed me. They were both there. Both—safe. The collar around her neck registered on me in the same breath as Ezra's hand gripping my arm. I was going to break his arm off and beat him with it, but the yank pulled me up enough to scan the room.

She wasn't alone.

There were guys in suits on either side of her. While palace events didn't have dress codes, suits weren't out of place, but these guys were both armed.

"They aren't alone," Ezra said. "Babysitters have watchers."

Rome was almost to the ring, I was going to have to watch my brother fight or call it right here in the middle of everything.

I disliked both parts of this plan.

Kel moved up next to me. "What's the play?"

"Deferring to me now?" Was I being a prick?

Yes.

Did I care?

No.

"Choose or I will," he said. Milo and Lainey were on the far side, but Milo had already found his sister and he had an arm wrapped around Lainey to keep her from approaching.

I'd wondered why Kel wanted her here. Now I got it.

"Give me a minute," I told Kel. "Don't let Hellspawn out of your sight."

"I don't intend to."

Adam and Vaughn were in. Expressionless, Vaughn's body language told me he wasn't going to last long before he acted.

"I need to replace Rome, then we get Hellspawn and out of here." It was a split-second decision. "Fight card."

"On it."

Ezra moved without me having to even glance at him. Adam's attention moved over the crowd. Between the three of us, we knew the faces of most of the major players. The opponent in the ring wasn't familiar, but he moved like he was already injured.

Rome barely paid him any attention as the announcer ran down the stats.

Warm-up fight.

Made sense. They usually held my bouts for the end of the night and it was still early. But the Renegade had lost—so softening the ground.

Were they trying to lure someone out?

"Got it," Ezra was back, sliding up next to me like he was made of smoke. "This is a demo match only, first blood and it's over."

The buzzer rang and the guy who'd been favoring his side stopped and lunged right for Rome.

It was short. It was brutal. And first blood or not, Rome put the guy on the mat. He didn't bother with playing him. Then, he wouldn't. Pride fisted in my chest at the hard crack of his fist to the guy's face. There was no way he didn't break a bone in that guy's cheek.

Hopefully, he hadn't damaged his hand.

"Four more guys on the card," Ezra said. "Spaced out. Looks like you've got some cartel lunatics on the list."

I scanned down the names he had on his phone. I knew two by reputation. The other two were just ringers. They were more softening the ground. Someone wanted at the last two for something. But no way in hell was I letting Rome take a fight with Carver.

"Fucking great. I'm getting my brother. Keep your eyes on Hellspawn. Then I'm getting her out of here." Following logic right now wasn't enticing, however, I wanted them in one piece. There was enough firepower in this room, we risked one or both if I started the fight. We needed to get one clear, *then* free the other.

Rome would not like this plan. He would not want to leave with her still here.

Bro was going to need to trust me.

I caught Vaughn's eye then nodded to the back where the fighters waited. He was big enough to get through that door as a fighter, and even if they didn't want to open it, if we went through it together, they weren't keeping us out.

Rome had already disappeared through a door to what worked as a locker room. More a holding room for fighters. There was security back there, but it was mostly to keep fights from spilling over into the back. It also gave us a place to get cleaned up between bouts.

There were usually a couple of ways in. I spared Hellspawn another glance. Perfectly composed, gaze laser forward, and her hands were…

I paused and Vaughn bumped against my shoulder before he twisted to follow my gaze.

She wore a pair of handcuffs.

Curling my fingers into a fist, I forced out a breath then continued to the door. "Fighter," I said to the bouncer at it and he just gave me and then Vaughn a look before he slid a card and opened the door.

Not my first rodeo.

The lights outside hadn't come up because more fighters were being announced.

"Get his attention," I told Vaughn before I diverted to the bathroom. It was actually on the far side of a door so I just went into a stall and waited.

Vaughn was good. Five minutes later, Rome walked into the bathroom—alone.

I pulled the stall door open and glared at him.

He glared right back. "You're late."

"I know." And I did know. "How bad?"

He shrugged, then faced me. "They put a shock collar on Starling."

A muscle in my jaw ticked as I clamped my teeth together. But I was already stripped out of my shirt. "Swap with me."

"Starling—"

"Everyone is here. Swap with me. They wanted me. They are going to get me."

He didn't move, and I cut a look at the door. We didn't have time for this.

"I'm sorry."

"Not your fault." He glanced at the door. "They want something on the king."

"Okay. Anything specific?"

He shook his head, but he started stripping.

We exchanged clothes. I needed his sweatpants, and he took my jeans. The bruises on his chest stopped me dead.

"Looks bad. Starling kissed them."

Of course she did. "They're keeping you together."

He nodded.

"What happened with the losing?"

Cause Rome didn't need me in a fight, even if I'd never let him wade into one willingly without me. He tugged on my knit cap then eyed my face.

"You need another bruise."

"You can hit me in a minute," I told him as I wrapped my hands. "What happened at the fight?"

"They were going to kill her if I didn't throw it." The admission carried a lot of unspoken emotion and weight. He was angry. In a way, Rome did not get angry. "You can't kill the guy who did it."

"Why the fuck not?" Because that guy was definitely at the top of my list.

"Starling already did."

That… An image of her shooting the guy who had the drop on me flashed through my mind. "That's beautiful."

Rome grinned. "I thought so."

"Come here," I said, and he let me hug him. It wasn't something he allowed often, but he didn't even stiffen at the contact. If anything, he returned it.

"Don't be mad at her."

"I'm not," I promised.

"You will be."

I chuckled. "That's probably true, but I'm not mad at her now." Backing up a step, I met his gaze. "Hit me."

The best thing about Rome: He didn't hesitate or make me wait for it. The blow staggered me and I blinked against the tearing in my eye. Fuck that hurt.

He studied me for a minute.

"Another?"

I checked the mirror on the wall, then my mirror.

"Yeah. One—"

The blow rocked my head back.

"—more."

He shook out his hand and I rotated my jaw. There was definitely blood in the back of my mouth.

"Get in the stall. Give me five to get back to your keepers, then get out of here with Vaughn."

Resistance flashed in his eyes.

"I know. I won't leave her behind. I'm late, not stupid."

"Sometimes," he said, a hint of a smile touching the corners of his mouth.

Jokes.

Now he had jokes.

I spit out some blood, left the jacket unzipped, and headed out of the bathroom. I didn't even spare Vaughn a look as I went for Rome's expressionless mask. Not quite me, but it would do.

Right now, I didn't really give a fuck if it impressed these guys or not.

The pair that had followed him were waiting.

"You're up in five," one of them said, tossing me a bottle of water. "Hydrate." But they were both keeping their distance.

Smart.

Hopefully, Rome expressed to them the error of their ways at every opportunity.

"The boss wants more of a show this time," the second guy said.

I really didn't give a fuck. I unscrewed the water and took a swig, rinsed out my mouth then spat it on the floor at their feet. They actually jumped and I didn't laugh.

But it was tempting.

Fighters came and went. There was a guy in the corner eyeing me, but I didn't let on that I'd noticed. The keepers were a pair of heavy set men, both armed. Neither seemed particularly balanced on their feet and one had on a pair of orthopedic shoes. They weren't here to keep me in line.

No, that was why they'd kept Hellspawn when they took Rome. They used her as leverage.

That was their second mistake.

"Let's go," the first guy said and I just walked away from him. I didn't even care if they were behind me. They were smoke, but they had no idea I was the mirror.

Outside, the sound had cranked up. Music blared through the speakers as a fight cleared out of the cage. Both of the fighters were still standing but bleeding heavily. The salty stink of sweat mingled with the copper-tinged blood lingered in the air.

If I had to fight first, that was fine, they weren't getting a show. I tracked to where Hellspawn sat as I stripped off the hoodie. I wanted nothing hampering my movement.

The minute her gaze locked with mine, and recognition flared in her eyes. Good girl, focus on me... She cut her gaze away just as Adam stepped up to where she was sitting.

What the fuck was he doing?

CHAPTER 14

EMERSYN

*L*iam was here.

Between the first fight and the second, Liam had arrived. I hadn't even seen when that happened. But it wasn't Rome walking out to head back to the cage. The gaze zeroing in on mine held so much leashed violence. My heart slammed brute force as sweat dotted my skin.

The air inside was far too cold, to the point my flesh had prickled with goosebumps. I tried to suppress the shiver and every other reaction though, because in addition to my dress and collar, I also had to endure handcuffs.

Brixton had been less than impressed by my impalement of Wulfric. Not as much as Wulfric himself. My aim proved impressive. He'd gaped at me, then staggered before he collapsed.

More shocking than his downfall had been the utter lack of response by any of the people around us, including the girl who'd been flirting with him. She gave me an impressed look then fluttered a little hand wave before she'd wandered away.

In fact, no one had been particularly moved by the action. Except for perhaps Gerhard. His reaction had been apoplectic, his eyes incensed and his face red as he stalked toward me. But he never laid a finger on me.

I'd expected punishment from Brixton or the shock collar. None of it was forthcoming. Instead, we were ushered out and back to our confinement. Rome had been conscious by the time we got there, but he'd also been a mess. They brought me medical supplies to take care of him.

On our next trip out the following night, I'd been in handcuffs. They hadn't made Rome fight. Tonight, that changed.

Liam was *here*. The bruises on his face weren't as pronounced, but he distracted from a lot of that by stripping off his hoodie and his shirt.

When Adam entered my line of sight, my attempt at no reaction failed. Wasn't he supposed to be lying low? Now he was here *too?* I started to stand, but the guy to my left—they didn't offer names today and I hadn't asked—gripped my arm.

"Let go of my fiancée," Adam told him in a cold voice. "Or I'll break that hand off." He didn't appear armed with anything more than attitude and disdain. Both added a depthless layer of threat. Not once in my life had I ever been afraid of Adam. Not even at his most caustic with Lainey.

Right now? I didn't envy the men standing on either side of me. Death stood in front of me and Hell was right behind him.

Brixton approached, his gaze traveling from me to Adam then to Liam. "Mr. O'Connell, you have a fight. I suggest you get to it."

The look Liam sent to Brixton seemed to unsettle him

more than anything else had since he'd taken us. The guard gripping my arm had loosened his hand, but it was still there.

Adam apparently had no patience for the conversation either. He struck like an adder, his fist snapping forward. At first, I expected the blow to land on the guy's face and for bones to crunch. Instead, Adam struck the man's throat, leaving him gagging as he released me and doubled-over, trying to catch his breath.

"Better," Adam stated coolly as he held that same hand out to me. He dipped his gaze like he gave me a once over. The gagging guard dropped back, but Brixton and the second guard both stood their ground.

I really hoped Adam knew what he was doing. Grasping his hand, I let him pull me to my feet as the buzzer sounded on the fight.

Shifting his posture, Adam wrapped an arm around me, but didn't move us away. I glanced from our audience to the ring. Liam moved like a lethal predator, not even slowing as he struck the guy. A fist to his face, a kick to the guy's knee, then around him and down, he rolled into him and slammed him against the far side of the cage.

There was definitely an audible crunching sound before the audience roared and the music blared. The bout was over.

"I hope he's not that fast in bed," Adam commented and I swung my head to look at him. "Cheating on me with a three second wonder can't be that much fun."

"Maybe it's what he does in those three seconds that would blow your mind."

The corners of his mouth twitched. "I'll take your word for it."

Brixton cleared his throat. "Mr. Reed, I don't recall inviting you to this negotiation."

"When you took my fiancée, you absolutely invited me. You're going to release her now…"

"I'm afraid that's not open for discussion. Mr. O'Connell—"

"—can't do a fucking thing for you." Adam gave him a thin smile, sharper than a knife's blade. "He's always been kept at arm's length from the king because of his ties to the 82nd Street Vandals. You can pull a rat out of the gutter, but you certainly can't dress it up or take it out into polite society."

What the hell was he doing…?

"My *fiancée* might enjoy slumming it up with the vermin, but I assure you, they will never give her what she really craves or needs." His gaze seemed fixed on Brixton. Raw anger ripped through me. I wanted to trust him, but this was…

Then I saw Lainey. *With* Milo.

Her lips were flattened into a thin line and her eyes blazed. All the sounds around us seemed to fade. The roar of the crowd, the music, the slapping of skin—both the couples fucking away in some of the corners and the fresh fight in the arena.

"O'Connell is a pretender. You want access, you need an actual Bishop."

Brixton quirked an eyebrow. "That would be you?"

"For more than five years. I know far more than the king would probably like to admit."

"And you're just going to help us? Just like that?" The scoff in Brixton's voice didn't have to be imagined. I wanted to move away from Adam, but he kept his arm firm around me.

"No, not just like that." Adam paused for a beat then glanced down at me. "For her. The one decent light in all of this. She doesn't come from a family of whores, thieves, or murderers. She certainly doesn't belong here…not getting this filth on her."

"Subtle, Mr. Reed," Brixton said in a clipped tone. "But bargaining for your fiancée—" He managed to make the word sound like *slut*, impressive. "That doesn't lend a lot of weight to your offer."

"No?" Adam traced his fingers against my bare arm. "I owe the king very little and O'Connell a small amount, and like I said… my fiancée here."

If he said *my fiancée* one more time…

"Reed," Liam said in a harsh voice.

"Hush, O'Connell, the grownups are talking." He didn't even look at Liam. "Be grateful I'm not castrating you for putting your dick in her. She seems happy enough with it… *for now.*"

I was so utterly fucking lost.

Brixton's frown deepened.

"As I was saying," Adam continued, every word enunciated with a kind of flawless execution of those who were trained from birth to monitor every syllable that passed through their lips. It was both arrogant, unyielding, and a raw challenge. "You need a bishop. You need someone with access and a personal stake. The king wanted me dead. So I owe him no loyalties."

What was happening right now?

"This involves O'Connell?"

Adam gave a shrug. "He could have killed me. He didn't. That buys him forgiveness for a lot."

"And apparently her bed." Distrust and dismissiveness combined in Brixton's tone.

"Not your concern." Adam gave me a squeeze. "Here is what I'm prepared to offer you. Release her and O'Connell— I'll stay in her place."

I snapped my head to look at him. "Adam—"

He dropped a kiss on my lips that startled me enough to shut me up. "Behave," he instructed. "You can take your lover and go. That's all you need to do right now. Be glad I'm letting you have *him*."

The automatic urge to slap him warred with the need to shake him, and I could barely do either with my wrists in cuffs.

Without taking his gaze off me or relaxing his grip, Adam said, "Do we have an agreement?"

Brixton hummed a sound. "This is very convenient."

"Not really," Adam stated as he lifted his head. "At this point, there are a half-dozen weapons fixed on you. It will be messy, cost quite a bit to clean it up, but you can agree—and perhaps even get something out of the deal."

"Or?" our captor asked in an inquiring tone that suggested he didn't quite believe him.

"*Or* you can die…like your man there." He nodded and I turned to look almost as swiftly as Brixton did.

The guard who'd been choking was lying on the ground, not moving. Blood trickled from the corner of his mouth and more… was spreading on the floor beneath him.

How…?

"Decision? I'd really like to get my fiancée home." The possessiveness every single time he said that seemed to be delivered home on the point of a blade. I swore he was inflicting it on Lainey.

It made me hate him a little even if the *reason* for it seemed unrelated.

Maybe.

Brixton's phone rang and it solidified what Rome and I had thought. He wasn't the one in charge. Answering it, he spared me a look then looked past us to Liam. Noise from around us rushed in, shouts from the gaming tables, more sounds of fights in the ring.

The conversation wasn't a long one. "Very well. Uncuff her. You will take her place, that means you get the shock collar as well. If anyone tries to interfere with us leaving, she will be the first target to go down. You are not the only one with resources here."

That was it?

"So we understand, all of you will die if so much as a hair on her head is disturbed." They sounded like they were discussing the weather and it was insane. Adam couldn't be—

"Ow," I snapped as the guy trying to take off the handcuffs gripped my arm to turn me to him. A second later, he was on the ground screaming following a sickening crunch of his arm bending at an unnatural angle.

Keys in hand, Liam faced us and unlocked the handcuffs. "The collar now," he ordered with a glare at Brixton.

"Mr. O'Connell," Brixton said. "I haven't agreed to let you go."

"I haven't agreed to not kill you either," Liam countered. He ran his fingers over my wrists, then up my arms as he gave me a once over. The faint burn marks on my neck had faded, but they were there.

"O'Connell, you know, I don't have to let you go with her," Reed said, almost conversationally. "You could at least show some gratitude."

"Have I broken your face?" Nope, Liam wasn't playing and to be honest, the whole thing seemed so surreal. Brixton moved behind me, and the only reason I didn't flinch away was because Liam stayed right there, his gaze tracking him.

Behind Liam—Kellan drifted closer. Doc was there. My heart slammed against my ribs. I didn't see Rome, but if Liam was here, Rome was out, right?

The touch of icy fingers to my neck had me stiffening. A moment later the collar was off and Liam dragged me to him and we were a couple of steps away.

"Adam," I said, as I faced them.

"Go," he said, not even fighting that collar going on. "Get her out of here, O'Connell." He wasn't even looking at me anymore.

Was he seriously doing this?

An explosive sound cut through the noise. That was definitely a gun.

Bedlam erupted. Someone crashed into us and Liam struck with a raw brutality that sent whoever they were to the ground.

"Stay with me, Hellspawn," he ordered one arm around me and we were moving.

I searched around for the others. But there were fights. Lights exploding. A guy rushed in front of us lifting a gun like he was going to point it at us, but Doc was just there. He wrapped his arms around the guy's head and snapped his neck like it was nothing.

"Go," he said, echoing Adam's earlier order. "Get her out. They've set up a crossfire. We've marked most of their guys."

His gaze lingered on me a moment, then he was gone. Liam didn't slow. Anytime someone got in our way, he took them down with efficiency. I lost track of where we even were because the painful lights were gone—it was just darkness, smoke, and the flashes of muzzle fire and I swore—actual fire licked away at something.

Then we were outside and Liam hauled me up off my feet and sprinted across the open ground. It wasn't until we were next to his car that he put me down and I whirled to look up at him. "Liam—"

"Hellspawn." Then his mouth slammed down on mine.

CHAPTER 15

EMERSYN

The move of his mouth over mine burned. I fisted his shirt. I didn't even know when he'd dragged it back on. He blanketed my body with his, pressing me against the cool, unyielding surface of his car while the hot wall of muscle caged me in. Nothing bad would happen in this cage. All that leashed violence around him seemed to crackle in the air, superheating it. When his tongue thrust toward mine, I tilted my head back, just letting the car hold me up while my lips parted to welcome him.

I had *missed* him so damn much the last few days. No one said *Hellspawn* like he did. No one growled it with so much possession. No one made me feel safe. Even when Rome—

Flattening my hands against his chest, I gave a little push and Liam lifted his head. The smell of sweat and blood on him tickled my nostrils, as the warmth of his breath touched my cheek. He cupped my face in one hand, the wrap was still there, rougher against my skin but another reminder of where we were.

"Rome?" I licked my lips. Liam already got him out, I knew it and still…

"He's with Vaughn," Liam promised, and I swore I wilted a little. Then I cut a glance back toward the building where fresh sounds of violence spilled outside. "In the car, Hellspawn, now."

He tugged me forward as he opened the driver's side door. I didn't care how not ladylike it was to crawl in and climb into the passenger seat.

"Down on the floor." He was right behind me. Terror threaded through the heat his kiss had ignited. But anger swiftly followed the terror as I crouched into the well of the seat, ducking down below the window. "Not for long."

The engine already rumbled to life.

"Everyone else?"

"We have a plan, trust me. They need to blow off some steam on the way out. We're all angry."

Yeah. I felt that. "Rome is fine." Not a question from me.

He shot me a glance, the dashboard lights playing with shadows over his bruised face. Yes, he and Rome were twins, but they were wholly different individuals. Both beautiful in their own ways. Rome's violence was swift, surgical and gone in an instant. Liam's lived there, housed like some exotic beast whose beauty dazzled you before he struck.

Deadly. Gorgeous.

"He's fine," he repeated and even as the vehicle jolted into motion, Liam slid his hand toward me and I grasped his fingers. "Hold on, Hellspawn."

He didn't have to tell me twice. The bouncing over the road—or whatever we were on—calmed and then we were on a smoother straightaway. His phone rang and he answered it without taking his hand off the wheel or his hand away from me.

"I've got her," he said by way of greeting.

"Sparrow?"

I blew out a shaky breath. "I'm here," I promised. "Safe and in one piece."

"Good." Kellan's relief was palpable. "Vaughn and Rome are out. Doc and I are finishing up. Milo's got Lainey and Ezra."

I swallowed. "What about Adam?"

Silence greeted the question, then a sigh. "Sorry, Sparrow. They were gone before we could close the net. We got a couple of their guys, but Adam was out with them."

He traded himself for me.

"He'll be fine," Liam said, his expression didn't match his tone. "He planned that. Not that he discussed it. But I get it… he was chafing being stuck down."

"You watch your back," Kellan said. "Bring her home. We'll see you soon, Sparrow."

"We'll be there," Liam replied, but ended the call before I could say anything. I frowned. "He'll be fine," Liam repeated. "Adam knew what he was doing."

"But he traded himself…"

"To get you out," Liam agreed with me. "He did. We had Rome, next was you. It saved on the bloodshed. Maybe." He didn't sound thrilled about that.

"I stabbed someone." It was the weirdest thing I'd ever offered to someone as comfort, but a grin flashed over his face.

"Rome told me. Said the guy put a gun to your head and you put a blade right into him." He squeezed my hand. "Good girl."

"They used me to hurt Rome," I told him.

"I know, Hellspawn. You did the right thing." He glanced

down at me. The motion was brief, then he was up scanning the road again. "Climb up. We're clear." He kept his hand there if I needed it, but I was fine.

The car was warm. The collar was gone. Rome was safe. Worry for Adam made me sick to my stomach. As soon as I had the seat belt snapped in, Liam put his hand on my thigh and I covered it with my own. He pulled away only to knock up the heat in the car, then put his hand into the back and dragged up a jacket.

"Put this over your legs."

"What?" It was a leather jacket and huge, but the interior was lined and as soon as I had it over my legs, some of the shivering seemed to penetrate my awareness. I was shaking. I grasped onto his hand again after I got it tucked around my thighs. "I'm fine."

"You are fine," he murmured. "But you're also shaking. Cold? Or fear?" Neither sounded okay with him and I tried to shrug even as I ran my thumb over the wrap on his hand.

"Can I take this off?"

He glanced at me, then down. "It's fine…"

"I want to feel your hand." I didn't even know where that admission came from, but I did. I wanted to feel more than just his fingers.

"Go ahead," he urged in a gentler tone and I went to work loosening the wrap. It didn't take long to unwind it. Beneath, there were discolorations on his knuckles. A fight outside of the ring? His face had been bruised too. When I cradled his hand in between mine, he closed his grip on me. "Does it help?"

The soft question threw me back to the night I met Rome, when I asked for his name. "Yes," I admitted. "I missed you."

"Then stop disappearing," he said with a rueful chuckle.

"We didn't mean to…"

"I know," he said. "This time it was my fault."

"No," I countered with a shake of my head. "Not your fault. Brixton's fault. Whoever this king person is. The people Brixton works for. Not you...they wanted you. Told Rome they could do it the easy way or the hard way. One way was to shoot me. As long as they had me, they controlled him. But they never realized he wasn't you."

Liam's smile at that was fierce and my heart clenched at it. "Rome can act despite what some people think. I hate that they thought he was me though. My world shouldn't touch him."

"I think we're kind of past that." I leaned my head against the seat, turning so I could study his profile. "Your world and my world are a lot closer than we thought. We're both in their world."

He sighed, the sound long and almost resigned. "The fact you know Adam Reed kills me."

"I know him because of Lainey. It's weird to me that you knew them, too."

"I don't know Lainey," he told me. "Not the way Adam seems to know you. Also—I don't give a fuck what he said back there. He's not your fiancé."

"He did that to get me free," I defended him. Maybe I shouldn't. Not everything he'd said had been about me. Some of it—some had been directed at Lainey and Milo. How could he be so kind and so cruel in equal measures? But he had gotten me out...he did want to protect me. So damn complicated.

"He fucking kissed you, Hellspawn."

I'd half-forgotten that. "He was playing a part."

"I don't care," Liam muttered. "He kissed you. Not okay."

"Gonna beat him up for me?"

He pursed his lips, then slid me a look I couldn't read in the shadows cast by the dashboard lights. The road we were on had grown steadily busier, but it was too dark to see in the other cars. I didn't even know if the guys were with us on the road or somewhere else.

"I might," he admitted. "After we figure out what is going on and he's free. I'll wait that long."

A real smile slipped out of me. "He's a good friend."

"He's an asshole."

"Those things aren't mutually exclusive," I reminded him. "You're kind of an asshole, too."

His laughter filled the interior of the vehicle and my grin grew. "I guess it's a good thing you like assholes."

"Apparently," I murmured. "So maybe Adam isn't so bad…"

It was a teasing comment only, but his hand tightened on mine. "Hellspawn, I will spank your ass one of these days. Don't think I'm not keeping a list."

"It's good to have goals." The little thrill I got was completely at odds with his "threat," but this was Liam. He let go of my hands to reach up and caress my cheek, but before he could say anything, the phone rang. He answered it from the steering wheel, before reclaiming my hand again.

"Report," ordered an older male voice voice I didn't recognize.

Liam's hand tightened on mine and he shot me a single look that I didn't need to translate. Say nothing.

"I have my brother and my girlfriend," Liam informed him. "I'll get you a full report after I have them secure."

"Bring your girlfriend to the tower…"

His girlfriend? Surprise followed by pleasure filtered through me.

"No, sir," Liam countered, his tone inflexible and polite, though his expression was pure fury. "I'll get them home, then I'll meet with you. She has nothing to do with this."

"That's not your call to make, Bishop," the king said in a tone as dismissive as Adam's had been earlier. As though nothing Liam had to say was worth being uttered. "It wasn't a request."

"Sir..."

"O'Connell. If your girlfriend was important enough for someone to take, then she's important enough for me to speak with. I want the details of her contact with these individuals. Bring her to see me within a week, or there will be consequences."

The call ended abruptly, and Liam let go of my hand entirely to slam his fist against the steering wheel. He let out a snarl of sound that echoed in the close confines.

"Liam—"

"No," he snapped at me. "You are *not* involved. I don't care what he said. You shouldn't have been taken in the first damn place. You are not going anywhere near this guy."

Dislike rolled off him in waves.

"This is the same son of a bitch who wanted Adam shot, no warning, no crime, no explanation. Just shoot him and take his place."

"But you didn't do that," I reminded him. Even if he hadn't partially explained some of this before, the fact Adam was *very* much alive more than served to illustrate his choices.

"I'm not giving him the opportunity to involve you," he reiterated. "Period."

"But—"

"Hellspawn. Leave it alone."

A sigh escaped me when he slammed his fist against the steering wheel again. The quiet of the vehicle echoed with all his frustration.

"If you don't bring me," I asked softly, "what happens?"

"Whatever it is, it won't happen to you," he said with a sharp shake of his head.

Yeah, I got that but...

"Please," he said, and it was that single word that made me swallow my next objections. "Just leave it alone. We just got you back, I'm not dangling you out there again like chum for the sharks."

"I don't want you to be chum for sharks either."

"I can take care of myself."

"So can I," I responded. "But I still appreciate the fact you guys didn't abandon me even when I made bad choices."

"Goddammit, Hellspawn," he grumbled, before he switched lanes, and then we were off the highway and racing through the dark toward—nothing that I could see. Finally, he turned, and then the whole vehicle stopped. He killed the lights, but the engine was still running.

I waited long enough for him to put it in park before I reached for his face. Maybe I was reading his mind or his physical cues, but he was already tugging me to him, and then his mouth fused with mine. Cradling my face in his hands, he devoured my lips, tongue teasing mine until I groaned under the fierceness of it.

Anger infused his kiss. I tasted something coppery, and with care, I put my own palm against his bruised cheek. He leaned into the contact, chasing my tongue and then nibbling little bites against my lower lip. I don't know how long we were there, suspended in time as he kissed me and let me kiss him.

Some of his raw fury abated, then he pressed his forehead to mine as he trailed the fingers of his left hand to my throat. The wrap was still on his hand, so I caught the edge and began to work it free. He let me, his shadowed gaze fixed on mine. Even if I could barely make out the blue of his eyes, I could see them clearly.

I'd know their color anywhere.

"Let me handle this," he whispered, the command was

there but so was the whispered plea. "I just got you and Rome back."

"I don't want to lose you either," I answered him. "Please don't ask me to not want to protect you, too."

He sighed then kissed me again. This one was far sweeter and held less demand. But it didn't take the edge off of anything. He didn't offer me any promises as he buckled my seatbelt once more, and all too soon we were back on the road again.

"It's going to be fine," he said instead, but he was still holding my hand. "You'll see. It's going to be fine."

)

CHAPTER 16

FREDDIE

Body disposal was not my favorite job, but at least the dude we dumped wasn't dead. So we literally just dumped him—unconscious—in a field about a half hour's walk from the asshole of nowhere. Left him in his underwear because I wasn't touching that. I also carried him a solid thirty feet from the road before I dropped him.

Thankfully, it was dark and not hot, but I was still sweating when I finished. The guy stank like expensive cologne, a little weed, and expensive booze. He grunted when he hit the ground, but he didn't rouse. Slipping out my blade, I cut the ties on him then the gag and took the evidence with me.

"So long, sucker," I said with a hum and headed back up the road to the car. Jasper stood outside of it, his gaze behind me. Even the intermittent light provided by the flashers casting their red glow over him before draping him in shadows once more said he was ready for anything.

Well that and the gun in his hand. He'd already done more today than he had since he got shot, but I kind of liked having him watch my back, so no bitching here.

"Ready?" he asked when I made it up the sharp incline back to the road and I spread my hands before flipping my knife closed and sliding it back into my pocket.

"I was born ready."

"Get in the car, smart-ass." His grin was brief though, and with a shake of his head he glanced back down the hill. Jasper could be overprotective sometimes. It wasn't always comfortable, but it reminded me that he cared. It had to be killing him to not be in with the rest to go get her.

"They're gonna bring Boo-Boo home," I said as I slid in and he eased into the driver's seat.

"Yes," he said with a nod. "They are. I just—"

"Hate being left out of the ass kicking and the violence?" I leaned back in the seat, phone out to check for messages.

We'd had a drive to get to the meeting spot in the first place. By the time the others had traveled to the casino where the fights were being held, we'd only just gotten the text of the location and reached this dump spot. It was off the main highways and about three miles to the nearest location before he could get a phone. Too bad it was cold. Not so cold that he'd get hypothermia or anything, but still cold. The mosquitos and other bugs would feast. It would suck for him, but the prick would survive.

"Hate that she's missing again," Jasper admitted. "Definitely hate that I'm not up to being out there swinging."

"You will be," I promised him and Jasper shot me a look. "What?"

"When did you become Mr. Optimistic?"

I snorted. "Definitely not me. But you're too stubborn to not get better. Besides, Boo-Boo will be back soon, and then you'll have her kissing your wounds and looking after you. Makes staying in bed easier, you know?"

He laughed at me. "You're a closet romantic."

I snorted. Still, we were back at the clubhouse before we got the second set of texts.

Got them. Coming home.

They were safe, and for one bleak moment, anxiety flared through me, setting my skin on fire. Then ice. The itching came hot on its heels. All I wanted to do was rip my flesh off and shout out the noise.

Safe.

Coming home.

Boo-Boo was coming home.

"Tell you what," Jasper said, and his voice cut through the cacophony. "Play me a game to see who gets to kiss her first when she gets here."

I lifted my head from my hands. I wasn't even sure when I'd put them there. "You wanna play for kisses? Shouldn't she have something to say about that?" It came out strained and uneven. My heart slammed so loudly it echoed in my ears.

"Okay, winner gets to ask for a kiss first, how about that?"

"That sounds better," I admitted. "And yeah…we find all the balls for the table?"

"I'll spot you one," Jasper said. "Besides, I'm gonna have trouble bending, and I think the table's a little uneven, so we'll have fun."

The pool table had been broken in the raid. We'd put it back together and braced the legs, but it was gonna have to go. The felt had scorch marks. One of the balls—the solid green six—had vanished. So far it hadn't been found anywhere.

I bet it was in one of the holes in the wall, but we hadn't gotten that far toward looking. The game took forever, but it helped. Focusing on the balls helped. Jasper grimaced a couple of times, but he was still moving.

I should've probably made him rest. This nursing shit was hard when all I wanted to do was go stand outside—

The door opened and I pivoted to check who was coming in. Vaughn entered with a bruised-up Rome. He lifted his chin to me and Jasper exhaled.

"Where's everyone else?"

"They're coming," Vaughn said. "Kel was right behind me. Milo's about five minutes behind."

"Liam's not here?" Rome asked as he glanced around.

"Not yet. Is that a problem?" Cold prickled along my neck. We really didn't need any more problems.

"No," he said.

"You want some ice for your face?" Jasper asked, but Rome shook his head.

"It doesn't really hurt." He dropped to sit in one of the remaining chairs.

"I'm getting food," Vaughn told us.

It wasn't long before Kellan and Doc filtered in, along with Milo, Ball-Cracker, and the Ezra dude. Jasper and I gave up the game while the guys got food together. Tension crackled in the air. Everyone looked okay. Doc had a couple of bruises. There was blood on their clothing. The worst of them was Rome, and he wasn't really talking.

Made sense to me.

It was an agonizing thirty minutes… and then the door to the warehouse opened and I bounced to my feet before I even realized I was moving. Boo-Boo was the first through the door. She wore a gorgeous dress and was barefoot, though she did have a pair of heels dangling from one hand.

"Hey," she said and I snapped my gaze up from her feet to her face. Exhaustion reflected in her expression, but the

164

darkness that lived in her eyes sometimes wasn't present. "Miss me?"

"Hell yes, I missed you." I wanted to hug her, but I didn't want to charge her. Spreading my arms, I hoped the invitation was implied, and she rewarded me by folding right into me. Boo-Boo gave the most amazing hugs. I closed my eyes and held her tight.

Not too tight. She was so tiny sometimes. She made me feel like a huge guy and I wasn't. Closing my eyes, I took a deep breath of her.

"Don't disappear again," I told her. "Might have to LoJack you or something. People keep trying to steal you from us."

I was joking.

A little.

Leaning away from me, Boo-Boo grinned. "Something to think about?"

I held up a pinkie to her and she hooked her pinkie around mine. When she leaned in to press a kiss to my cheek, I sighed then brushed my lips against hers. It was a brief touch. Some part of my mind tracked the fact Liam had followed her inside and that the whole room had gone quiet.

"Shit..." I started to apologize, but Boo-Boo squeezed my finger then pressed another kiss to my lips. Though firmer than the brush I'd given her, it was definitely as swift. I wanted to apologize, but she just grinned then kissed my cheek.

"Sorry we disappeared. I promise, not going unarmed again. And I'll think about the LoJacking." She tilted her head. "Though I don't know if I can do a piercing..."

"I'll take care of any you need, Dove," Vaughn promised from somewhere behind me, and the air around us seemed to lighten all at once as laughter flooded in. I let her go after one more squeeze of our pinkies, and then Ball-Cracker was there to hug her and the others spilled around me like I was the rock in the stream.

I didn't even mind them crowding around as everyone got a good look at her. Liam looked past all of us, and it had to be at Rome. When Boo-Boo eased around to him though, I pivoted to track her progress. She collapsed against Rome in a hug and her laughter eased some of the fear that had been digging into me. Even Jasper looked better.

Ball-Cracker was right behind her, and the Ezra dude didn't hug her so much as brush her hair back from her face. She caught his hand and murmured something to him. Neither looked happy about it. I kind of wanted to know what she said, but then food was delivered, so we were all finding spots to eat. Jasper got the most untorn piece of sofa with Boo-Boo perched next to him.

Rome got the spot on the other side of her. For some reason, Liam was keeping his distance. It was kind of weird. Now that she was back, the tension holding me hostage drifted away. Doc and Kellan were in an intense conversation, but they kept glancing at Boo-Boo whenever she moved. Vaughn refilled her plate a second time and got another for Rome. When Rome wasn't eating, Boo-Boo teased him and fed him until he started eating on his own.

They were both bruised and weary, but they were okay. Milo seemed riveted by all of it, or maybe I was projecting. Could be. Though his attention was definitely split between Boo-Boo and Ball-Cracker, who perched on the uneven coffee table in front of her.

We really needed to get back to fixing this place up. It was a wreck. I could get up early and start hauling all the other broken pieces out. Talk to Kel about when we wanted to pick up new furniture. There were still walls to repair—

"We should go soon," Ezra said abruptly, interrupting the

hum of conversation. He'd disposed of his plate and stood not far from where Lainey perched.

She spared him a look. "I'm not going…"

"The hell you aren't," Ezra said in a tone that didn't hide an ounce of his hostility. "I'm not leaving you here with him."

"I don't need your permission," Lainey said, ticking off one finger. "And I'll go where I damn well please." She ticked off a second. "Also, your manners are appalling; these are our hosts."

"They're…"

"Be really careful," Liam warned in a cool tone. "You're pissed about Adam. I'm not a fan of it at the moment, and we're not leaving him. But what happened was *his* call. Not ours. Definitely not mine."

Boo-Boo caught Lainey's fingers in hers as she sat forward. Jasper shifted his weight. He'd gone from relaxed to tense as he eased to the edge of the sofa. Yeah, if Ezra started toward them—I slid my blade out.

"Lainey, don't be a little bit—" Yeah. Big mistake, Ezra buddy. Huge.

From utter stillness to full motion, Milo surged up from where he'd been sitting, his fist caught Ezra right across the jaw. It staggered the other guy, and for someone who didn't look like much, he proved a scrapper. He just charged right at Milo and they went down.

Thankfully, Lainey had already abandoned the table as Milo and Ezra collapsed what was left of it. Rome plucked Boo-Boo up and put her on the far side of him, even as Liam herded Lainey right to her. The twins got between them and the brawl.

Vaughn just moved to the side and took another bite of his sandwich, while Jasper watched. None of us were interfering in this fight. Ezra grunted when Milo shoved him back with a foot, then they collided again.

When they hit the wall where the television used to hang, Milo's fist actually went through the drywall as Ezra dodged the strike, and I winced. There was blood dripping from both of them and now smearing the wall.

"Liam…" Boo-Boo's voice carried and he swore.

"Fine." As soon as he moved, so did Doc and they were wading in to separate the two. I circled the mess and stowed my blade. Frankly, I could just stab Ezra and be done with it, but Boo-Boo seemed to like the guy for some reason. The look on Ball-Cracker's face said she might not be as opposed.

"Come on," I said to Boo-Boo. "Let them figure this out. You probably want to shower and change. Then I can watch, and it will be a much nicer show." The last line slipped out and she shot me a grin.

I liked that she always got me.

"Lainey?"

"No," her friend said. "Freddie is right, you should go grab a shower and change. Your doctor friend probably wants to go over all your injuries."

"I'm fine," Boo-Boo assured her and she ran a hand down Rome's arm. "You okay?"

"Go," he said, then gave me a look. It said stay with her. Right, not a problem. When I held out my hand she took it, but she shared looks with all the guys. Jasper and Vaughn shooed her off, but not before I noticed Jasper sliding Vaughn a five-dollar bill.

Fuck, did I miss a bet?

I'd check that later.

Thankfully, they'd gotten the guys apart by the time I got Boo-Boo to the stairs. She was quiet all the way to her room. Once we were inside Kellan's room and near the door to hers, I said, "Okay, I can wait out here."

"Freddie?"

"Yes, Boo-Boo?"

She turned to look at me. "Thank you."

"For what?"

"For wanting to LoJack me. I think it's really sweet."

My face heated. "I just don't want to lose you."

"You won't."

"Pinky swear?" I dared her, raising my pinky. She hooked hers to mine and then drifted closer. I swore my gaze dipped to her lips then back up again. I wasn't supposed to be thinking about kissing her. I'd already stepped over the line.

"Kiss and makeup?" At the invitation, something in my brain seemed to short-fire. Did she mean…?

"We didn't fight," I said slowly, but she was so close I swore I couldn't see anything that wasn't her.

"Then pinky swear and kiss to seal the deal."

That seemed completely reasonable. I dipped my head, and where I hadn't worried about my breath earlier, it occurred to me there had been a lot of onions on my burger. But she didn't retreat. When I touched my lips to hers, just a whisper of a kiss to the corner and then to the other, I told myself I would be fine with that.

But Boo-Boo leaned into me, our pinkies still locked in their embrace and when she parted her lips against mine, I took a taste. Just one. Then she kissed me like I was everything she'd been looking for and I clung to her like a drowning man.

The tingling warmth that a single touch of her lips had ignited rolled through me like a thunderstorm, but I didn't want to let go. Then her tongue slid against mine and I stopped fighting it and just sank into the kiss, aware that I'd pulled her hand to cover my heart where it beat fiercely, wanting to leap into the palm of her hand.

A groan escaped as my dick gave a wicked throb. Thoughts about her pretty pussy filtered through my brain and I suddenly wanted a much closer and very personal view of just how pretty it was. Like a dousing of icy water, the thought pulled me out of the haze and I lifted my head.

I wanted to curse about breaking the kiss, but at the same time… this was Boo-Boo. She deserved so much better than me. Her smile stopped that thought dead in its track.

"Welcome home," I whispered. That wasn't what I meant to say. A dozen apologies formed and died without ever finding my voice.

"I'm really glad to be here."

Me too. "LoJack," I said firmly.

Then she laughed and everything just seemed *better*. "LoJack. We'll find you the best."

With a careful touch, she brushed her knuckles against my cheek. "Wait for me while I shower?"

"Forever," I said, and I meant it. I was good. I could wait right here for however long she needed.

"I'll try not to take that long."

She didn't close her bedroom door, but she did blow me a kiss before she grabbed some clothes out of the dresser and disappeared into the bathroom.

Yep. Forever sounded pretty good.

I touched two fingers to my lips. They were still tingling.

That was new… and very cool.

CHAPTER 17

JASPER

*a*fter paying Vaughn the five for Milo being the first one to throw a punch, I put my wallet away. Freddie was already ushering Emersyn toward the stairs. Good plan. The fact he'd kissed her earlier had filled me with a kind of inexplicable pride. Letting her in was a hard thing for him, and letting her care seemed almost impossible. As much as I'd wanted my own kiss and moment with her, I didn't want to intrude on their moment.

Despite the intervening days, she looked fine. There were a couple of red marks on her throat, and one bruise on her bare arm. Her spirits were good, her eyes bright, and her smile soft. This hadn't been Pinetree.

Liam threw Ezra back a few feet as Doc pushed Milo to a wall.

"You could help," Liam muttered toward me and I grinned.

"Sorry, injured. Supposed to take it easy."

Vaughn fucking laughed. He leaned over to give me a high five and then we both grinned as Kellan rolled his eyes.

"Mr. Graham," Kellan said, locking his gaze on the other man. "Lainey is our guest, specifically Sparrow's guest. That means if she wants to stay here, then here she stays. If she wants to go, she is free to do so. You, however, do not get to make that decision for her."

"Get off me," Ezra snapped at Liam, then gave him a shove. Not that he managed to move him far. The guy wasn't a lightweight, but Liam had definitely added muscle mass the last few years. Vaughn might have trouble with him.

Maybe.

"I can't believe you just fucking left him there and now you think I'm going to leave her here with you..."

"She has a name," Lainey corrected him. "No one held a gun to Adam's head. You saw and heard him just like I did. Clearly, he's where he wants to be."

Doc had backed off a pace on Milo, who stood there just staring at Ezra like he was daring him to say another word. Seriously, if he called Lainey a bitch again, twenty bucks said Ezra was gonna be sucking steak through a straw for a while.

"And he trusts me to look after you," Ezra argued. "Why did you come back here?"

"That's a stupid question," Rome declared as he rubbed his jaw. "Starling is here. She's welcome. You don't have to be."

"I got him," Liam said.

"No, Rome is right," Kellan interrupted. "Your friend is a guest. Sparrow likes him. Reed acted in good faith, none of us knew he was going to do it. But you're not gonna create havoc here because you don't like something or someone."

"Let him," Milo said. "I'll happily escort him out."

"You want to do this—" Ezra started forward but Lainey stood up, silencing both.

I kind of wished Freddie was here to offer to make popcorn, and at the same time I was glad they were upstairs and away from this drama. It was giving me a headache. We liked Lainey. We didn't like Ezra. Easy decision in my book, but I wasn't the one in charge right now, so it was Kel's headache unless he tagged one of us in.

"I'm staying," she said firmly. "I want to be here to help Emersyn. Don't—" She pointed a finger at him. "Whatever else I do while I'm here is none of your business. You've made it clear that I'm a nuisance. Now you can go and chase after your king or whatever other nefarious plans you and Adam are hatching, without having to worry about me."

"Lainey, it's not like that." All at once, the other guy sounded tired. "Just—you're not going to budge because she's here."

"No, I'm not. Because in the few weeks I was gone, she got taken again and by someone else. You think these guys aren't safe, but my understanding is what happened had nothing to do with them and everything to do with what you, Adam, and Mr. O'Connell here are up to."

At that, Liam grimaced and Ezra's expression went to stone. Yeah, he didn't like that explanation, it landed like someone had tossed dog shit at him. Without another word, he shook off Liam and bypassed Kellan as he stalked out.

"See ya," Vaughn called with a wave. "Don't let the door kick you in the ass on the way out."

"Damn," Kellan said softly as he glanced at Vaughn. "You good?"

"Tired," Vaughn admitted. "Not really in the mood for more chest thumping bullshit over where Dove's friend does and doesn't get to go."

"She stays," Rome said with a shrug before he dropped back onto the sofa. He looked tired. Really tired. "It's where she wants to be."

"Exactly," Vaughn said. "Besides—we have enough issues, I don't feel like babysitting that hothead."

"He's not that bad," Lainey said with a sigh before she glanced at Milo. "You didn't have to hit him."

"I wanted to," Milo told her bluntly and I let out a chuckle that had me gripping my side. Fuck, it still kind of hurt to laugh. Doc just shot me a look like *"really?"* but damn, it was kind of funny. "Have for a while. He doesn't get to talk to you like that. No one does. You don't have to need the protection to get it."

Lainey just stared at him, and Kellan let out another sigh before he pinched the bridge of his nose. "He's not wrong. Words don't have to actually inflict damage to be disrespect-ful. But in the future, let's try to minimize the bloodshed in here."

"On the upside," Vaughn said, "we still need to paint."

I kept a hand firm over my side as another laugh worked it out of me, and then I glanced at Rome who had his eyes half-closed. That dried up all the humor. Liam was back, so Ezra must have fucked off to wherever he was going. Goodbye and good riddance.

"You sure you're good, Rome?" I asked and Liam frowned at him.

"Maybe Doc should take a look, you took some hits—"

"Tired," Rome said as he stood up. "Bruised. Nothing broken."

"You sure about that?" Doc asked, his gaze assessing.

"He hasn't slept well the last few days," Emersyn's voice rushed in to fill all the cracked places left by the earlier erup-tion. "Fight over?"

"Looks like it," Freddie said as he jumped down the last couple of steps. "And, Milo is still standing and Ball-Cracker is still here."

Emersyn smiled at him and then she glanced at all of us. I

wasn't the only one staring at her. Damp hair hung around her face and she'd gotten rid of the dress, changing it for an oversized sweatshirt and yoga pants. It all looked so large on her. "Are you okay?" She'd paused at Lainey.

"I'm fine," she answered then tugged on her shirt a little. "Bag lady chic?"

With a laugh, Emersyn said, "I like wearing their shirts. They're big and warm."

Milo made a face.

"Besides," our girl continued as she moved back to where Rome was sitting. With care, she stroked her fingers through his hair and he tilted his face up to look up at her. "It's been a long few days…" She wasn't talking to us anymore. "You can sleep here. They'll make sure no one comes after me."

"Damn right we will," I agreed with her. Murmurs of assent came from everyone.

"Think you can sleep?" Her focus was still on him and Liam had shifted his whole weight. Yeah, this was his brother and Rome didn't usually need this kind of care. He really did look like hell.

"Where are you sleeping tonight…?"

"Dibs," I said right as Vaughn voiced his dibs and Kellan cleared his throat.

The corner of Rome's lips turned up, that smile looked kind of painful when it tugged at his bruises. "Rock, paper, scissors." Then he stuck out his fist.

Freddie chortled, but Milo gaped. "Are you for real?"

"You can't play," Rome told him, like Milo would want to decide where our girl slept… then again…he might.

I stuck out my fist. So did Vaughn. Lainey's fist came out and I had to laugh. Emersyn glanced at all of us and then Liam thrust his fist out and I shot him a look. Freddie grinned and walked over to put his fist in, too. That just left Doc, and I wasn't the only one who glanced at him.

"I just want to make sure you two are all right—"

"Doc, you can get all medical with them in a minute. In or out?"

Emersyn pressed her hands to her face, but she couldn't hide the way she smiled or the laughter in her eyes.

Kellan put his fist in. "Let's do this."

"On three," I said, and Doc shook his head but put his fist in. Emersyn stared at him, all round-eyed. Okay, maybe not a good idea.

Right. Beat Doc.

"One," I said. "Two." And on "Three," I dropped a rock. The way we played it, we had to go in a circle, starting with Rome, since he called the game. He had a rock. Lainey had Scissors, so he broke her "scissors." Then to Doc, who also had a rock, so nothing. Next was Kellan, who had paper. Amusingly enough, that took out Doc, not Rome, and I was fine with that.

Liam smirked and cut through Kellan's paper since he had scissors and turned to Vaughn who also had scissors.

"Fuck," Vaughn muttered, because I was after him and my rock broke his scissors and that took me to Freddie who leaned over the back of the sofa. He also had a rock.

"Again," Rome said.

We went three more rounds and then Rome and Freddie were out. It was down to me and Liam.

Three more rounds. I did rock, so did he. He pulled scissors, that was my move. Neither of us went for paper. It was like we were flipping it back and forth. Then another three rounds of rock each.

"Eventually one of them will win," Freddie said, loudly. "Then again...we might need popcorn at this rate."

Lainey laughed and Milo just shook his head, but Swan watched us as she stroked her fingers through Rome's hair. He was half-asleep, like a cat under the attention, and I couldn't really blame him. In fact, I was still staring at them on three and flattened my hand without thinking about it.

"Son of a bitch."

I glanced over to see Liam's hand flat too.

"Okay," I said. "New plan." Cause this was fun, and when was the last time we had fun.

"You give up, and I take Hellspawn and my brother home with me?" Liam challenged.

"Woah," Vaughn said even as Freddie straightened. "No one said anything about taking Dove out of here."

"Right," Liam said. "It was for where she slept or who got to sleep with her. I have a place."

"Ease up, Tiger," I said as I stood up slowly. "I was just gonna say, let's make this interesting. How about we play pool for it?"

That got me some stink eye from Milo, but he could take his girl and go get laid if he wanted. Hell, it might do him some good. But there was a spark of humor in Swan's eyes and it had been Rome's idea, so—we were going with it.

"Works for me," Liam said, moving to the table. "Not spotting you a damn thing because you're wounded."

"Not spotting you a damn thing cause you're a stubborn ass either," I informed him and he grinned. "But to be fair, the six green is nowhere to be found."

He plucked out a striped ball and tossed it. "Even now."

The laughter that erupted from Swan was a beautiful thing. "Five on Jas," Freddie said. "Who wants popcorn?"

"I'll take that bet," Kellan answered.

"I'm feeling the love," I tossed back. Kellan merely shrugged, but I caught his glance at Emersyn. Her smile was back and she looked almost as sleepy as Rome, who was damn near out from where she stroked his scalp.

"Five for Liam," Rome murmured.

"Oh, I'll take it," Vaughn said and there was a round of bets.

"I'm betting on Em," Lainey said. "Cause she's the one who is winning right now." Milo groaned, but Emersyn's smile grew.

"I kind of already won."

I caught Liam's eye and raised my brows. "You can surrender any time you want." We could certainly afford to play tonight. We won the gambit. We got them back. Tomorrow we could deal with the rest of it.

"So can you, Hawk," he rumbled. "Rack them."

Game on.

CHAPTER 18

EMERSYN

"*H*e's fine?" The question slipped out as soon as Doc turned away from where Rome sat on the edge of his bed. Shirtless now, there was no hiding the bruises he sported. Liam had come up with us so Doc could go over his ribs.

"Yes," Rome answered before Doc could and I made a face at him.

"Hush. I was asking Doc. It will make me feel better if he agrees." That was all I had to say, and I didn't want to play that card. It made them feel better when Doc looked at me after Pinetree, and the less I thought about that visit the better. Right now, Rome was exhausted, and I understood *why*, but I needed to know.

"He's got some cracked ribs and should probably take it easy," Doc said. "Bruises. But I'm not seeing anything that worries me. His breathing is clear, and despite the bruising, so are his eyes. You don't need to be so concerned, Little Bit."

Relief swarmed me, and I wasn't the only one letting out a breath. Liam had been stoic through the whole process, despite the fact he lost the game with Jasper downstairs. Their sniping at each other had carried a lot of humor, with only a hint of their earlier disputes to salt the old wounds. Though, they seemed to enjoy that.

Jasper had won. I was pretty sure it hadn't been Liam *letting* him win either. It was all kind of silly in a way, but the kind of silly we needed. Not that anyone asked me where I wanted to sleep. I had a feeling if I said I wanted to stay with Rome to keep an eye on him, no one would complain. As it was, Rome flung himself back on the bed with just the barest wince to indicate that probably hadn't felt good.

"Okay," I said slowly, not at all as sure as Doc was. Moving over to the edge of the bed, I scooted on to give Rome a kiss. "Come get me if you need me?"

"Go see Hawk, Starling. I'll find you in the morning."

"Or later if you can't sleep." The last wasn't a question, but his smile answered that for me. After another kiss to his forehead, I stood. He caught my fingers and squeezed them gently. It was harder to let go than I thought it would be. The last few days we'd been inseparable except for when he had to fight.

But this was *home*. I caught Liam's eye as I forced myself to loosen my grip. He gave me a once over then jerked his head to the door. He wanted to talk.

"Little Bit…" Doc stopped me with a hand raised but without touching me. "You haven't let me look at your injuries."

"I'm fine," I said, echoing Rome's earlier statement, and that earned me a snort from both Doc and Liam. "I really am. They only used the shock collar a couple of times, and it hurt, not going to lie, but I was fine. Rome wouldn't let them do anything to me." I spared a glance back at him and he grinned. The pull at the bruises on his face had to hurt.

When I glanced back at Doc, his expression gave me pause. A very real anger brewed in his light brown eyes. There was a tick in the muscle of his cheek and it looked very much like he'd clamped his jaw shut.

"I really am okay," I told him. "It hurt, but I can handle pain." My pain, yes. Not Rome's.

"Come on, Hellspawn," Liam said abruptly. He brushed his hand along the side of mine, then our fingers tangled together when I took the offer. "She'll let you know if that changes, Doc." But he didn't wait for me to agree or not, just opened the door. "I'll be back, Rome."

Then we were in the hall. When I would have opened my mouth to say something, Liam shook his head once and ushered me toward Jasper's room, but diverted into Kel's—he wasn't in there but that could just be because he was still downstairs with the guys. Not slowing, Liam pulled me into my own room, closed the door and boxed me right up against it.

"How many times?" He pinned me with a look, even as he cradled the sides of my face. Instead of kissing me, his attention went to my throat. "How many…"

"It's not—" I swallowed the word *important* when he locked those deep blue-green eyes on me. The twins might be identical, but they were so different and varied in their responses. This look though?

They both did this.

"Twice," I said as gently as I could. "The first time was because I was being bossy and trying to get answers and the second time was to teach Rome a lesson." The second part I hated far more than the first.

With a careful thumb, he nudged my chin up so he could study my neck. "Twice. How badly did it hurt…?"

181

"I don't know," I said when he brushed his lips over one of the marks. At least I assumed it was over one of them. It was a gentle caress, there and gone again. But it sent shivers eddying over my flesh. "The burn marks were there after… but they didn't really hurt so much as sting."

Another kiss and that one sent a pulse to my cunt as he traced a path from one mark to another. "I meant the shock itself, Hellspawn. How bad?"

I groaned and closed my eyes. He lifted his head, the warmth of his breath feathering along my cheek. When he rested his palm there, I opened my eyes to find him staring at me. "You're just going to get angry."

"So?" He raised his brows. "Let me be angry. They took both of you because they thought Rome was me. This is my fault—"

I pressed my fingers to his lips when he would have kept talking. "It's not your fault. The fault lies with the people who sent Brixton after you. The fault lies with whomever the so-called king is making enemies."

"And mine," he said, after catching my fingers in his hand. He smoothed his thumb over the older scar on my palm. "I was late. If I'd been on time…"

"Then you wouldn't have been able to help find us." That was the one thing Rome had known for certain. The same thing that I had held onto. "Rome said you'd find us, until then—he would be you, and it was weird for him to call me Hellspawn."

A faint, if fleeting smile, turned up his lips. "Good weird or bad weird?"

"Just weird," I admitted. "Made me miss you—though Rome can do a fairly convincing you. Just gets all moody and bossy."

"Moody," Liam repeated, the smile flirting with his lips again.

"And bossy," I said with a sigh. He towered over me but there was no claustrophobia, even if the room was dark, save for the single light next to the bed. "But you found us. All of you did. We're home and we're safe." Except for Adam…

"Don't worry about him, Hellspawn. I have to believe he knew what he was doing. If nothing else, he does have a real issue with the king. We all do, but this one is a bit personal for him right now. So his motivations are going to be a little more granular for our enemies to hold onto."

"Are they our enemies?" I'd wondered about that. The king was no friend to Milo or the Vandals. That much had seemed implied in the work Liam did. But…at the same time… just being an enemy of the king didn't make them an ally. Not after what they did to Rome.

"They aren't our friends," Liam said, dipping his head to press a kiss to another mark on my throat. Or maybe it was just my throat he wanted to kiss. The stubble on his cheeks rasped against my skin, and I slid a hand up into his hair. "But we'll deal with it."

"Be careful," I whispered and he raised his head. "You were the one they wanted, so you have to be careful."

"Worried about me, Hellspawn?" The corners of his mouth twitched, the arrogant grin sliding back into place. But it was too late for him. I'd already seen past all of that.

"No," I teased. "You're far too much of an asshole to worry about. You'd be a bitter pill to swallow."

His eyebrows rose slowly. "You can always spit."

I swore my mouth fell open, because that wasn't what I meant at all, but his grin was pure devilish glee. A knock hit the door before I could respond.

"Who's there?" Liam asked with a smirk.

"You lost the game, let my girl go," Jasper called, though he sounded more entertained than upset.

"Possession is nine-tenths of the law," Liam countered. "And I have her right now…"

I gave him a little shove and he laughed, but he did back up. When I opened the door, Jasper grinned at me before giving Liam a look over my head. "I see she took custody of herself."

"I did," I said, then flicked his nose. "I also have a name and my own plans."

He pressed a hand to his chest and then paused, I swore it was so Freddie it made me giggle. "Wait, am I part of these plans?"

"Are you asking me this time? I thought you guys were all gambling for where I slept."

"True," Jasper said, cocking his head to the side. "I could say I won fair and square."

"You did say you won," I reminded him as I folded my arms. This was—fun. Just picking on him. Teasing them.

"Also true." He tapped a finger to his lips.

"Looking for the way out of that hole?" Liam asked as he leaned against the door jamb next to me. He walked his fingers up my arm and it gave me a little shiver.

"Got myself into it," Jasper mused aloud. While the light from my room was too low to illuminate the storm gray of his eyes, I could practically feel them dancing. When was the last time I'd seen Jasper in such a good mood?

Our date.

Some of my cheer fled because not long after that moment, Freddie had called us for help and then Jasper had been shot.

A long sigh escaped me.

Jasper frowned. "I'm teasing, Swan. You can sleep wher-ever you want. Really—"

"No, I know," I said, taking a step forward and resting my

hand over his heart. "I was just thinking about the last time you were this playful and then Freddie called and there was the ambush."

His expression darkened. "But we all made it out that night and we're all going to be fine."

I didn't want any of them to get hurt like that again. But Freddie had been, then Jasper, and now Rome. When I slid my arms around Jasper cautiously, he hugged me far tighter.

"I'm healing, Swan," he whispered against my hair. "I promise. Freddie is here and he's in good shape. We're all doing well—"

"Rome and Liam…"

"We've got bruises, Hellspawn," Liam said gruffly, then his hand came to rest against my back. "Bruises heal. Rome's just smug cause he got you all to himself for a few days."

"He is not smug," I argued.

Liam snorted, then Jasper said, "Why do you think he brought up the game? He could have played the wounded card, but he was smug enough to know he'd had all your attention."

"You guys are mean," I protested, but Jasper chuckled.

"Swan, where you're concerned, we'll beg, borrow, steal, or cheat."

"Fuck," Liam exhaled. "We'll do all of the above. Come on, let's get the boyfriend to bed then you can get tucked in too."

Another laugh shook through me. "Well, I can't really argue with that. I totally stabbed someone for Rome." And shot someone for Liam. When I turned around, I caught his gaze. Something moved through his eyes, but it was there and gone. He just winked.

"You know how sexy it is when you get fierce and protective?" Jasper asked and my face heated. Sliding his hand into mine, he guided me toward the door.

"She's something," Liam murmured and that "something" sounded like he meant something amazing or good. I stole a look back at him. But he just waved me on. "Go, both of you. Rest and don't worry about Rome, Hellspawn. I'll look after him."

That definitely helped. Some of the tension in my gut eased.

"Go away, Liam," Jasper said. "You can see Swan tomorrow. I promise to not even bitch about it."

"Right," Liam said as we continued down the hall. "Why don't I believe you?"

"Cause I'm an ass," Jasper cracked back. "And you're a dick. But you're not stupid."

They were so mean to each other, only Liam laughed. "Don't forget it." All of a sudden his voice was right behind us. "Hey, Hellspawn?"

I turned and Liam cupped my face before he dipped his head. A moment later, his lips were on mine and the soft gentle kisses of earlier gave way to something far hungrier and demanding. The heat scorching my face scalded the rest of me as he delved his tongue against mine. I balanced between them, like I was standing on the most precarious of ropes.

When he dragged out my lower lip, he lifted his head and gave me a slow grin.

"Good night, Hellspawn."

Oh. It was definitely a good night. I was still panting when he gave me another of those little winks, then turned on his heel and stalked away. All that violence, just right there, and it was so damn… attractive.

Butterflies exploded in my stomach as I turned to meet Jasper's knowing look. Possessiveness definitely gleamed in his eyes and he raised a hand to cup my chin before he stroked his thumb over my lower lip.

"Will you spend the night with me?" The soft question just added fuel to the fire already burning inside of me. Because there was really only one answer to that.

"I'd love to."

CHAPTER 19

EMERSYN

$\mathcal{J}$asper's room was just like I'd seen it the last time I'd left it. There was a little more in the dirty laundry stack, but there were also clean towels on the dresser. The fairy lights were on and so was the light in the bathroom. The bed was disheveled, but everywhere there were signs of his recovery.

A couple of dog-eared books on the bedside. Another stack on a second table. There were more books stacked on the floor next to the bed too. "You've gotten a lot of reading in?"

The signs of bandage changes were absent. Though if Doc did it, he probably cleaned up after. It seemed so strange to be here like it had been ages and only seconds. Twisting, I found Jasper watching me from the door. I curled my toes against the rug and then let out a little breath.

"It feels weird." Volunteering that up didn't seem so hard, but when he tilted his head to study me, I rethought the words I'd chosen. "I mean... it feels like we were gone on some weird trip and not kidnapped or something. But we were..."

"We know you were."

I clasped my hands together then moved to just sit on the foot of his bed. "I'm sorry I disappeared again."

"Swan," Jasper said, turning the lock on the door before he crossed over to sit on the bed next to me. "You didn't do anything wrong. Rome told us what happened, we figured out a lot—"

"I know, but after I left the last time..."

"You left because you thought it would be safer for us. I hate that you had to think that and I hate that you did it, but I don't hate why you did it or you being protective. Pretty sure I just said it was hot as fuck."

I was still staring at my hands when he reached over to cover my clasped hands with one of his own. "Want to tell me what's pinging around inside of you that's tying you up in knots?"

"I kissed Freddie," I said.

"Okay."

That—that was not the reaction, I expected. Turning my head, I studied him. The shadows in here were too deep to make out all of his facial expression. Still, he rubbed his thumb over my knuckles.

"I just kissed Liam, too."

"Yeah, saw that. You've kissed Vaughn and Kellan that I know of..." The corner of Jasper's mouth kicked a little higher. "Pretty sure Rome's gotten his kisses in."

"I've kissed you," I pointed out and his smile grew.

"Oh, that I definitely remember." Still stroking my hands, he added, "What's worrying you right now?"

"Everyone is fine with me kissing everyone and you guys are playing games for where I'll sleep and everyone is..."

Were they really okay with this? "You pulled a gun on Doc for helping me take a bath."

He sighed.

"And you were really mad at me and Vaughn."

"Swan," he said, squeezing my hands before he reached up to trace a finger down my cheek. "Do you want the attention from the guys? Do you want to kiss them?"

"I—yes." I winced. Maybe I should have thought about this before I brought it up, but it was all bubbling up inside of me. Liam's kiss still tingled on my lips, and Freddie's had been so damn sweet. His nerves echoed my own. They didn't all know what happened yet, but Freddie knew it all and so did Rome. Vaughn and Kellan suspected.

Freddie had his own horror stories.

"I never want you guys to think I'm using you or…"

"No one," he said firmly, "absolutely *no one* thinks that. If they do, you send them to me. My bat and I will put them right."

A laugh escaped me but none of this was funny. "Jasper…"

"I love how you say my name, you always add just a little impatience to it. It's my second favorite way you say it."

"What's the first favorite way?" And why was he distracting me again? I was trying to be serious, especially since my stomach was doing all these weird knots.

"When you moan it." A smile pulled at his lips again, and this time I did laugh. The heat in my face was still present as was the heat in my belly. "There she is, better. I like that smile. I don't like it when you look scared of us, Swan."

"I'm not scared of you," I said with a frown, though it was hard not to grin. "Even when you were Mr. Grumpy Gus snarling at me, I wasn't *scared* of you."

"Grumpy. Gus." He opened his mouth then closed it again. "That's not remotely sexy."

"You do Grumpy Gus well," I teased, then twisted to sit

sideways so I could face him. When he went to do the same, he grimaced. "Oh crap...you're still healing and I'm..."

"Talking to me, which I want," he said, catching my hand before I could slide off the bed.

"Okay, but maybe we should get you in bed and talk there."

"Swan, you want me in bed and naked or just naked... all you have to do is ask."

I groaned and then just flopped back on the bed. "I'm trying to be serious, Jasper."

"So am I..." He rubbed my leg. "Come on, let's get me naked and in bed. You need to tuck yourself in there with me. I'll even let you look at my wound if you promise to kiss me and make it better."

Cracking an eye open, I stared up at him. The grin was back. "You're happy." It was kind of revelatory. Jasper yelled a lot. He snapped a lot. He growled a lot. That seemed to be Liam's thing now, except when Jasper was around the others, but not tonight.

Lips pursed, he appeared to consider it. Then he rubbed his jaw.

"And you shaved..."

"Now she notices," Jasper said with a slow grin. "I thought it was men who were supposed to not notice an appearance change."

"Why did you shave?" He still had stubble, but the beard he'd had before was gone. I slid off the bed to follow him around to the side where he began to unbutton his shirt. Knocking his fingers aside gently, I took over. I did actually want to check the wound. The days spent in here with him after he'd first been shot had left me viscerally aware of everything about it.

"I do sometimes," he admitted. "Kind of a clean slate.

Then I let it grow back in. Sometimes it just itches. Do you like it?"

I paused with his shirt half open and rose up on my toes to rub my cheek against his as carefully as I could. The prickle of his stubble was abrasive, but also tangible and real. "I miss your beard," I whispered. "Now I want to see you all clean-shaven."

"You know what," he murmured, "that's a wish I can easily grant." I had his shirt unbuttoned, so he shrugged out of it and then tossed it over to the side, before catching my hand. "Come on."

Did I take a moment to check both the bandage in the front and the one on his back as I followed him into the bathroom? I glanced up to find him grinning at me in the mirror.

"Enjoying the view?"

"Yes," I retorted, then traced my fingers down his back. "There's no blood on the bandage."

"Nope, stitches come out real soon, too. Thank fuck, they itch."

I pressed a kiss between his shoulder blades, and he tugged me around to lean against the counter. A minute later he was running water in the sink then lathering up his cheeks. I just soaked up the view as he made quick work of shaving. I'd showered with Rome and with Vaughn. Showered while talking to Kel, too. I'd helped Jasper with his showers, yet this held a whole new kind of intimacy.

He glanced at me, watching me more than the mirror, but his hand was steady and it wasn't long before he rinsed his face off then patted it dry with a towel.

"Better?"

I wouldn't go that far, but it seemed to have blunted all of his hard edges. He looked… younger maybe? I wasn't sure that was the right word.

"I missed you," I told him instead as I reached up to caress his smooth cheek. It was cool and soft, yet the line of his jaw being visible made his expressions easier to read. "I missed all of you. But...it feels like forever and it was only a few days."

"Anytime you're forced to do something you don't want to do, it feels like forever," he said, capturing my hand and pressing a kiss to my palm. The ghost of his lips over the scar on my hand to my wrist sent another shiver through me. "But we missed you, too. I know I fucking did. Hated that I wasn't out there swinging...if the guys hadn't been right on it..."

"I know you would have been." No doubt existed there. "Even when I don't always get how I deserve all this... "

"Love?" That word was like a silken invitation that pulled every knot inside of me taut. "You are loved," he said, closing the distance between us and then he picked me up and settled me on the counter.

"Jasper..."

"Shh," he murmured, stroking a finger down the center of my face to my nose then to my lips. "Barely felt that, you weigh next to nothing, Swan."

When he nudged my legs, I spread them so he could step right up to me. These guys were all so huge. Only Freddie didn't seem so large, but he was still taller than me. This close, I traced my fingers over Jasper's chest, exploring the tangled vines that formed a circle over his left pec. The ivy made so much sense now.

On all of them.

There were scars too. A circular one below his breast bone. A longer one that went down his side was jagged and rough. The new scar would be on his abdomen and another on his back. Would they be puckered spots? Or smooth?

"Hey," he whispered, tucking a finger under my chin until

I lifted my eyes and met his gaze. "You are loved. I didn't imagine telling you that, did I?"

A soft feeling that I barely understood burst inside of me. "No, you didn't imagine it. I heard every word—memorized it." Then I tapped my head. "Kept in here where it will be safe."

"Good, because the only other person I've ever said that to was my mother." The confession held me riveted. "She died when I was a kid..." So much emotion darkened those words.

"I'm sorry."

He silenced me with a brush of his fingers over my lips. "Nothing for you to be sorry for, Swan. Best fucking decision I made was to bring you back here. I know you didn't get it. I know that you were hurt and confused. I know there's a lot that's happened that you keep locked away." With a light, sweet touch, he slid his hand to my throat and carefully traced around the same spots Liam had been kissing. "I love *you*. For you. I want *you* to be happy and safe. Everything else —it's just a matter of picking my battles."

Head tilted, I studied the sober note in his stormy eyes. The first time he'd stared at me, I swore he could see right through me. Right now, I almost wished he could, and at the same time, I never wanted my past to hurt him. I didn't want my past to hurt anyone.

"You sound almost happy about picking battles," I teased. They made that easier for me easier to just shut out that part of my life and focus on this one. This life I could have here with all of them.

"I might like fighting," he admitted, one corner of his mouth ticking up a little higher. "Sometimes, it just takes a good brawl to sort things out."

"No brawling until you're healed," I told him, and he chuckled.

"Yes, ma'am. Gonna make me stay in bed?"

"If I have to," I said then walked my fingers up his chest to the ivy tattoo. "Are you—" I bit my lip.

"Am I?" he prompted, bumping my chin lightly to get me to look up again. I kept doing that, dropping my gaze to him, and I blew out a breath before meeting his gaze once more.

"Are you up for—more? Or just sleep?"

Licking his lips, Jasper grinned slowly. "Swan, are you asking me if I'm up for fucking you?"

"Is it safe? Doc said no recreati—"

I didn't even get to finish that thought before Jasper picked me up, and I had to loop my arms around his shoulders and hitch my legs to his hips carefully. I was trying to bear my own weight as he walked us out of the bathroom and toward his bed.

The light in the bathroom went out, leaving us only with the fairy lights, and he didn't slow down once on the way to the bed. At first, I worried he was going to fall on it with me, but he paused, brushing kisses up my cheek. "You know what I need?"

He paused to rub his cheek against mine with every kiss, like a cat asking for attention and I threaded my fingers through his hair. "Me?"

"Oh yeah," he said. "Just what I need. Naked. Below me. On top of me. In front of me. Wherever you want to be. I just need you."

A shudder rioted through my whole system and this time when he brushed a kiss down my cheek, I turned to meet his lips. I wanted to say something more, but I didn't want to stop kissing him, so I balanced my hands and dropped my legs from his waist. We were right at the bed so I could rest on my knees.

When I bit his lip, he groaned and then chased my tongue. I worked his jeans open, freeing the button and then the zipper. He tugged at my sweatshirt and dragged it upward. I pulled back only long enough to suck in a breath and let him yank it over my head. Then his mouth was on mine as my shirt went flying.

"On the bed," I ordered him. "And on your back...carefully."

His laughter was a caress all its own. "With pleasure."

CHAPTER 20

JASPER

*T*he stitches pulled and they sucked, but I wasn't complaining when she urged me over on my back. I started to reach for my jeans and shove them the rest of the way off, but she actually slapped my hands. Intrigued, I raised my brows. "You got bossy."

Hesitation flickered through her posture. It was a "blink and you'd miss it" moment, but I focused on her even in the low illumination from the string lights throughout the bedroom. I wanted to soak in every drop of her nearness and the hint of control in her tone.

"Bossy good?" She asked as she followed me onto the bed, still on her knees. I wasn't commenting on her lack of bra— not yet. No, I was enjoying seeing the excitement in the way her nipples beaded. The movement of her muscles tugged at the tattoo on her abdomen and I needed to remember to thank Vaughn for that beautiful piece of ink.

I hadn't really had a chance to do that.

"Or bossy bad?"

I tracked my gaze up to her eyes as she gripped my jeans and began to tug them downward. Right. Maybe if she got my pants off, she'd lose hers next. This was an excellent plan. Bracing my hands on the bed, I pushed up and ignored the twinge of the stitches as she rolled the denim free of my hips.

Having not bothered with boxer briefs or underwear of any kind, I got to enjoy the way she smiled when my dick rocked free to bounce upward. Yeah, we were both laser focused on her.

"Bossy, may I have some more please," I answered, and to my delight she cracked up when she got my jeans to my calves and had to pause to haul my shoes off. For a moment, she hesitated and glanced around. "Throw it, Swan."

She tossed the shoe over her shoulder and something fell, but there was no sound of breaking glass or anything I needed to worry about. The second shoe followed the first, and then she had my socks off. The light scrape of her nails along my instep had me jerking with laughter.

"I will tickle you back," I warned her.

"Threaten me with a good time," she murmured, but her grin grew more playful.

"Oh, I'll threaten you with anything you want." The air in here was cool, but my clothes were on the floor now and it was just nice to sprawl back and stare at her. I'd ridden a lot of different roads where she was concerned. The need to keep her was the one that burned the strongest.

Possessing her was like cupping my hands around a flame, protecting it from anything that might blow out her fire and at the same time, refusing to smother her in the same movement. I wasn't great at it. I'd fucked up in the beginning, but I didn't care how I fumbled it as long as she looked at me the way she was right now.

"Jasper…" she whispered my name and the hairs along my body stood up. "What are you thinking about?"

"I'm thinking you have way too many clothes on and your breasts are too far away for me to play with." At my blunt response, she burst out laughing. The rich throaty sound did wonderful things for my dick, especially when she stroked her hands up my thighs right toward it.

"You need to take it easy…"

"I'll take it easy when I've lined up my cock and sunk it into that sweet cunt of yours, or you do me a solid and come up here and sit on my face."

She paused at the description and straightened. Yes, her breasts were still too far away, but she slid her hands to her chest and cupped them.

"That's a good girl, give those nipples a little squeeze for me then slide those hands down to your pants…oh, Swan, have I mentioned how fucking beautiful you are when you do what I ask?"

The glide of her hands down her chest to her hips had all of my attention. The movement flashed the scars on her arms at me. I hated every inch of those marks. Liam and Rome said they'd killed the guy who gave them to her.

My dick flexed. Okay, so maybe my girl wasn't the only one who got off on torturing and maiming the people who hurt her.

I could have wished for a few blows, but I was fine with the fact they'd dealt out retribution. A little hip swivel and she pushed the pants down and yep, there went the panties with them. The smoothness of her pussy, the way her hips dipped down to that sweet little v sent impatience spiking through me.

Even if I were up for pouncing on her, I wouldn't. Not when she watched me with those enigmatic eyes as she tossed her pants and panties off the bed. I zeroed in on the hawk Vaughn had inked there. A hawk and a falcon. Not subtle, but I approved.

"Head up," I murmured, reading it, and her smile grew.

"Wings out," she answered.

"That's perfect." I'd seen it, but even when she'd come to sleep with me before I got shot, it hadn't been about the sex, and then after, I hadn't really had time to appreciate it. "Vaughn does beautiful work."

She knelt again and then dipped her head as she pushed her hair out of the way. Fuck... she wrapped her lips around the tip of my cock and I fisted the sheets to keep from just pushing right up into her mouth. The wet heat sensation was six times fucking better because it was *her*.

Not only that, she locked her gaze on me as she pushed down on my dick. If I thought I was hard before, it had nothing on how fucking rigid and swollen it was getting now.

"Goddammit..." I threw my head back as I flexed my fingers on the sheets. This was going to be a real test for my fucking restraint. Once. Twice. Three times, she pushed down against my dick, until I was almost to my balls at her lips as I nudged into her throat.

Sweat beaded along my brow and my heart fucking pounded. Heaven and hell. This was it. Right here. Then she let me go with a pop and I shuddered. Because instead of continuing upward to let me fucking kiss her, no, she started nuzzling along my dick. First it was little licks and kisses to my balls.

That might be a whole damn new kink for me. Then she lapped her tongue up along the underside of my cock, and I swore my hips gave an involuntary jerk.

"You're killing me, Swan." If I had to keep lyng here while she played and teased and I didn't get to touch her, I might actually die.

"You don't like it?" The throaty question delivered on the edge of a laugh was like a flex of pure feminine power on her part.

"You know how much I like that."

As if to illustrate my point, she wrapped her slender hand around my dick and began to stroke it before she sucked against the tip. I managed to not thrust, and then she stroked her nails down my thigh. Forcing my eyes open, I looked down at her as she began to take me deeper into her throat.

Every stroke kept me closing in on the edge. Not enough to make me come, but more than enough to keep me straining for it. Yep. My perfect swan with her gorgeous eyes, succulent lips, and fuck me—that mouth.

With a swallow, I unfisted the covers and reached down to stroke her hair. Torn between urging her up so I could fuck up into her, and just riding this sensual wave, I threaded my fingers through her hair.

The moment she increased the pace and rolled my balls though, I tightened my grip. Not enough to pull. Never enough to do true harm, fuck no, I'd never hurt her. "Not in your throat, Swan. I want to feel *you* wrapping around me. I want to make you come, too."

Not being selfish meant sharing pleasure, but it also meant that my restraint was stretched to the fullest extent. I blew out a breath when she released me with a pop.

"Don't let me hurt you."

"Trust me," I whispered, beckoning her closer and to my absolute delight, she began the slow ascent to crawl up to me. Everywhere her skin brushed mine, her softness seemed to assault my senses. The glide of her cunt along my cock registered just as her lips reached mine.

Capturing her face, I pulled her in for a kiss. Her tongue dueled with mine as she began to roll her hips. Back and forth, the friction wasn't even close to what I needed. The bump of her clit though caused a little sound to escape her throat. Flattening my feet to the bed, I tested a push of my hips to grind up against her.

That earned me more than a moan. The stitches pulled, but I seriously did not give three fucks. One hand on her jaw to keep her mouth on mine, I teased one breast, then the other.

Oh, I needed to spend at least an hour just playing with those. I wanted to suck them until I made her cry out. Yes, I put that on the to do list. We had all night, and it had still been early when we came in here to go to bed.

No one would need us before tomorrow.

Maybe I could bribe someone to bring us food and I could keep her for another twenty-four hours. I didn't think the others could go that long and not see her. I sure the fuck couldn't. My fingers met hers on my dick and I wrapped my hand around hers.

Squeezing, pulling, stroking. She bit my lip and I chuckled, but between us, we lined me up and then she was sinking down on me. Slick with need and so fucking soft, she soaked my cock with one downward thrust. Then she lifted her head and I let her, but I kept my hand on her face, I didn't want her to go far.

"Let me ride you," she said. "Just let me do all the work."

"Maybe not all of it," I warned. I needed to drink in her pleasure too. Not just mine. She put a hand on my shoulder, then shifted her weight as she lifted her hips. The next thrust took me to the hilt and we both groaned. Fuck, that was amazing. Two more strokes and she was moving at the speed that had me pumping into her.

Fuck, I gripped her hair and her chin and then glanced down to where her feet were on the bed on either side of my hips. She rolled and swiveled her hips, twisting with each downward thrust and my brain began to short circuit.

"Not coming until you do, Swan," I warned and it was a threat I planned to make good on. She was so damn gorgeous riding me like this and I pushed up to meet her, stitches be damned. The slap of skin, the heat as she clamped down around me, it was all so fucking intoxicating. I snaked a hand down to her cunt and then found her clit.

Circling it, I increased the pressure, pursuing her pleasure with single-minded determination. I wanted to burst. I wanted to fuck up into her until she was soaked in my cum, and then I wanted to do it again.

"That's it," I coaxed, dragging her mouth down to mine to swallow her cries. I found the right rhythm because she stiffened, her hips slamming down, and I let go as she shuddered and spasmed around me. Fuck yeah.

We clung together, the kiss going from urgent to slower, then to panting breaths punctuating our kisses. She wasn't letting her weight settle on me.

"Not going to break," I whispered. "Trust me. Too much to fucking live for right here. Lay down, Swan. Let me feel all of you."

There was another hesitation and then she settled against my chest. The weight was perfect. Everything I wanted, and she flexed around me. So perfect.

Head up, she stared down at me as she caressed my cheek then kissed me soft and slow.

"What did you decide?" I asked as my heart began to ease from its frantic pace.

"Smooth is nice," she whispered, "but I miss the beard."

"Yeah?" I'd fix that.

"I loved how it felt against my thighs."

Really? I pressed my head back against the pillows for a moment, then tumbled her over. She let out a squealing laugh, and I stared down at her. "I've been a very good boy. Laid there and everything. Now it's your turn."

I didn't wait for her argument, just worked my way down until I was lying on my stomach and found myself face to face with her cunt. Full of my cum and swollen a beautiful pink. Yes, I'd definitely missed this.

"You need to let me know if you really miss the beard," I teased, rubbing a cheek against the inside of her thigh, and she let out the most delighted laugh. "I have a few ideas. Want to make sure we check everything."

When I sucked a kiss right where her thigh joined her hip, she let out a low laugh that shivered through her. Yeah, that was the sweet spot.

"Let's begin…"

CHAPTER 21

VAUGHN

As soon as Dove vanished upstairs with Doc and the twins to get Rome checked out, Kellan said, "We're back to renovations tomorrow. Keep it normal."

Milo frowned.

"And before you say it, no, we're not letting this go. But I want it normal for Sparrow." He spared a look at Lainey, but for her part, she just shrugged.

"No argument from me."

"That's refreshing," Milo said and earned a look from her that had me biting back a laugh. Freddie didn't pretend to even show restraint; he flat out snickered.

Sleep should have been easy now that Dove and Rome were both safe, but I didn't manage more than three or four hours before I was awake again. Restlessness invaded my dreams, and I rolled out of bed. The clubhouse was quiet. Unsurprising at two in the morning, but I glanced down the hall toward Kellan's door.

Dove's room was tucked away beyond his, at least for now. Though she wasn't in it. No, she was with Jasper, and while we did need to check on them in the morning, I didn't want to wake them if they were sleeping. Knowing Jas, they probably didn't get to sleep anywhere near as early as they went to bed.

I grinned at the idea. After Pinetree, I was worried she'd come back to us with fresh damage. If there was any, it wasn't visible on the surface. Rome looked a lot worse, but we'd seen the burns on her neck. Getting Rome out of there had been important. Still, I wish I'd been able to get my pound of flesh.

On the way to the stairs, I paused at Rome's room. A half-knock before I nudged the door open. Liam glanced up from where he dozed in a chair and squinted at me. "Just checking on him," I said in a quiet voice. If I hadn't woken Rome up, I didn't want to. We both glanced at the bed. Rome seemed sound asleep with an ice pack on his face.

"Getting the swelling down," Liam said. He had his own ice pack in hand.

"Cool, need anything?"

"Ten hours horizontal and a blow job." The faint smirk made me chuckle. "Maybe not in that order."

"You can crash in my room if you want," I offered. "You're on your own for the other."

He flipped me off and I pulled the door closed. Downstairs, I surveyed the damage. Right… time to get to work.

I spent the next three hours working. First, I hauled all of the damaged furniture out and into the warehouse to be discarded. We had new stuff on the way. Or it might have come and just been stored out here in its crates. I'd check later.

After the furniture was out, including the broken pool table, two of the broken cue sticks—mine and Kellan's. We'd get those replaced too—I dragged up the rugs and took them out as well. Once I'd swept up the debris, I headed into the kitchen. A new coffeemaker sat unopened on the counter.

When the fuck had anyone had time to go and get that?

Right, I wasn't looking that in the face. Everything in the kitchen that was broken or damaged went into a bin, and I hauled it out. The main warehouse was quiet; the doors were all sealed. I did a circuit each time I went out before resuming my cleaning.

The kitchen was pretty bare; the table and chairs hadn't survived. The fridge was on its last legs. The microwave was toast. The stove, so far, appeared intact. Needed to make sure all the lines were solid. We'd already blown a couple of lamps.

Electrical work was not my favorite, so I'd leave that for last. After draining two bottles of water and compacting more trash, I surveyed the walls. We'd need to finish filling in the holes. At least two of them just needed to be ripped down and put up again.

Though, I had a feeling if I took a sledgehammer to the walls, I'd kick open an angry nest of Vandals. Just because I was restless didn't mean I needed to wake anyone else up. Right, wall repair required some tear down, then we could paint. We'd need to sand some of the flooring or put down new entirely.

I suspected that bullet hole chic was not the way to go. Upstairs needed work, but definitely not touching that. Wiping the sweat off my face with my shirt, I went for another water, then headed to Dove's studio. I hadn't glanced inside there in a few days. It was a wreck. From the blood-stained boxes in the closet to the shattered mirrors and broken barre.

Not every board of the flooring had been damaged though. This was as good a place to start as any. I'd worked most of the damaged boards up and pulled them free. It was a half-dozen total. We'd need to measure them, cut and place them, then sand everything before we polished it.

No splinters for Dove.

The sweat on my skin had me checking my shirt for smell as I straightened. Because the sweeter scent wasn't…

"Hi," she said from where she leaned in the doorway. Dressed only in a shirt and little else, she watched me with a sleepy focus. Her hair was disheveled, and there was an imprint on her cheek from sleeping.

"Hey," I said, setting the damaged board aside before I hung the hammer I'd been using to claw off the boards back on my belt. "Did I wake you?" 'Cause fuck, as much as I hated the idea of disturbing sleep she needed, she really was a sight for sore eyes.

"No," she told me, rubbing her arms as she padded forward, neatly sidestepping one of the missed board spots.

"Watch your feet." I slid an arm around her and picked her up. Granted, I stank of sweat and work, and she smelled like sex and sin. No complaints on my part, but I really didn't want her hurting her feet.

Toes curled, she wrapped her arms around my neck. "I just wanted to say good morning."

"Floor isn't safe in here for bare feet yet. No splinters for you, Dove." Then her lips brushed mine. Whether she intended to quiet my objection or just kiss me, I had no idea. My cock swelled at the first touch, and I slid an arm under her ass to brace her.

Her very bare, warm, and sweet ass.

A groan escaped me. Devouring her mouth, I sucked against her tongue. Then whispered. "I'm sweaty."

"Okay," she told me before she cupped my face and rubbed against me. Then she nibbled kisses around my mouth. A touch of her tongue to one corner and then I turned to chase her lips. God, she tasted amazing. There was a fresh hint of peppermint, like she'd brushed her teeth before she wandered down here.

The belt around my hips loosened and then crashed to the floor. I carried her toward the nearest wall...oh fuck it was a mirror. There was a crack in that one so I moved to the next pane. It was smooth, and let me enjoy the sweet view that was the clench of her ass.

Another groan escaped me as Dove got my jeans open and then her hand wrapped around my cock. I pumped against her palm as I thrust my tongue in time with it. She was so fucking soft everywhere.

Lifting my head, I dragged her lower lip out a bit before I released it. She gave my dick a squeeze before she teased the piercing. "You up for this, Dove?"

Need for her detonated in my system like a match in a fuel tank. Pure liquid fire spread out from my balls and all I could picture was turning her around and planting her hands on that mirror...

"Yes," she said in a moan and I chased that sound, kissing it out of her as she ground her cunt against me. That denim couldn't be comfortable. "I just want—you."

"Then you're getting me."

I checked the floor at our feet before I balanced her against the mirror.

"Don't let go."

"Never," she promised.

I hauled my shirt up and off then tossed it down at her feet. Sliding my hands down to her hips, I pushed them under her shirt.

"Off."

She squirmed, releasing my dick to wiggle out of her own shirt. As much as I missed the feel of her hand, the sight of her sweet body bared to my perusal had me harder than a stone. Before her shirt even hit the floor, I lifted her up so I could suck on one breast. Then I turned my attention to the other. Hot laves of my tongue in between scrapes of my teeth and her moans turned to softer cries.

With sharp tugs, she pulled at my hair, dragging me closer so I tormented those nipples until they were flushed red and stiff. The whole time I ground against her cunt, not letting myself slip inside, but her panting breaths said she was enjoying it. She flexed her legs around me.

So flexible. Dove could bend in half and let me fuck her with her legs at my shoulders and our mouths fused together. That image sent another pulse to my cock. Right, I needed inside of her. Right now.

Dragging my mouth from her breast with a pop, I looked up at her blown pupils that turned her eyes so dark they might as well be black. "Can I fuck you from behind?"

Panic skittered through her expression. "My ass?"

"No," I whispered. Though I cataloged that response, I filed it away for later. This wasn't about pushing her. She'd already expressed reticence about her ass, and that wasn't what I craved anyway. Fuck knew I wasn't sure I had it in me to be gentle. "I want your cunt. But I want you to watch me in the mirror while I do it."

A flush spread over her face and then down to her breasts. Desire softened her eyes once more and she nodded. "Yes, please."

Fuck. Fighting my own need to just slam into her right here, I set her down and spun her to face the mirror. The heated look she sent me was a caress and I smoothed my hands over her breasts. Her feet were on our shirts. The wood here was solid. This was perfect. When she arched her ass out in invitation, I ran my hands down her hips, just grazing the curve of her ass as I nudged her legs apart.

Cum smeared against her pussy, and I grinned at the trickle of it trying to escape. Wetting two fingers, I pushed it back into her and she let out a little mewling sound that was almost a purr. "Did you just roll out of Jasper's bed and come down here?"

"He woke up," she murmured, pushing back on my fingers. "He was so sweet, but after that I couldn't go back to sleep."

"So you came down here and found me."

She licked her lips and nodded. I held her gaze in the mirror as I thrust those fingers a little deeper. Slick and tight, she was already so warm and inviting.

"You sure you're up for this?" Jasper definitely had needed her and there were hints of bruises at her hips. Bruises from where a man would put his hands and hold on. Right where I wanted to put my hands and fuck into her until the only thing she could feel was me.

"Yes," she insisted, thrusting back against my fingers and arching her head.

"Don't worry, Dove," I crooned her name, just a little, to soothe as I worked my fingers free. "I have you." And I did. She'd always been a woman of her word and I told her to tell me what she needed.

If she needed and wanted me? Then that was exactly who she was getting. Even at this angle, she was still a little short so I pulled her hips out a little, arching her back farther and she curved to give me a sensuous little wiggle.

Bit by bit, my restraint frayed, and I lined myself up and thrust into her in one move. It pushed a low scream right out of her, and I wanted to curse. Her inner muscles just spasmed around me like I'd already ignited a damn orgasm. I picked her up, guiding her a little higher so the angle was better and she flattened her hands on the mirror as she shuddered.

When those pleasure drunk eyes opened and fixed on me, I nodded. "That's my sweet Dove. Now get ready to fly."

She flexed around me as I began to thrust, but she was thrusting back with equal force to meet my forward momentum until my balls were slapping against her. Bracing an arm around her middle, I clasped one of her breasts and pinched the nipple. She curved back toward me, and there, I found the spot she liked so much.

The intensity of her cries rose, pushed out in perfect time with our rhythm. I savored her every expression as she gripped my arm with one hand and pressed the other against the mirror. She felt so fucking good, especially when she twisted her hips and I seemed to go even deeper.

Sliding my free hand down to her cunt, I spread it wider as I arched her up. Oh, there it was, soft and glistening and full of my cock. Rubbing her clit, I braced her as she began to thrash. My own need had me melting down and the minute she twisted her head to kiss me, she came.

The strength of her second orgasm yanked me right over and I swore I came in hot spurts. Now it wouldn't just be Jasper's cum dribbling out of her. A wave of sweet possession rolled through me as I lifted my head. She rested hers back against my shoulder as we stood there, locked together.

She was on display and absolutely fucking gorgeous. The need to have her again vied with the need to keep her right there.

"Welcome home, Dove," I whispered before kissing her damp shoulder and she let out a low laugh.

"It's so good to be here," she answered and I grinned. It was definitely good to be here.

A little under an hour later, I had her sprawled on my bed, sated and smiling. I'd gone down to get her coffee and found Kellan. He eyed the signs of my work.

"Did you get any sleep?"

"Some." Not that I minded. Nor did I object to him following me up with a coffee of his own. Dove rolled over as we came in and her smile hit like the sledgehammer I wanted to take to the walls.

"Good morning," Kellan said with a chuckle as I handed her coffee over. She sat up, almost fluid with ease.

"Morning... we didn't wake you up did we?" She sent me a playful grin and I laughed.

Kellan shook his head. "No, someone was a bad girl and didn't. Maybe next time."

Her eyes widened a little and then she took a sip of her coffee. "If you'd like...and Vaughn doesn't mind."

"Nope, don't mind a bit," I promised her, giving her another kiss before I dropped back to sit on the chair while Kellan took a seat on my bed. He held out an arm to her and she scooted forward carefully to curl against him.

"Good girl," he told her, then kissed her shoulder, before he shot me a look. "I was going to suggest taking it easy today and do some administrative tasks, but Vaughn's already begun renovating the downstairs."

"I didn't miss anything while I was gone?" The sudden hint of worry in her voice gave me pause. It never occurred to me she might object to us making changes while she wasn't here.

"No, Sparrow. We still had some cleaning to do. Next is knocking down walls."

"We're knocking down walls?" Jasper asked from the door, we hadn't closed it all the way. "Sounds like fun."

I chuckled because Rome was right behind him. He gave Jasper a pointed look and Jasper stepped aside. Despite his bruises, he definitely looked better and he made a beeline for Dove. Not leaving Kel's side, she just shifted up to her knees to give Rome a kiss. He caught her coffee, then nuzzled the kiss deeper until she let out a happy little sound.

215

"Want a sip?" she asked, in a breathless voice and he settled next to her.

"I can get him his own," Liam said from the doorway, his expression thoughtful where it rested on her. Yeah. She was back and naked, definitely looking thoroughly fucked, and none of us could keep our gazes off of her.

"I don't mind sharing," she told Liam with a wrinkle of her nose.

"Clearly," he said, for a moment, there was the barest edge in his voice and I frowned but then he chuckled. "You also look too damn delectable for this early in the morning."

"Come have coffee and don't be grumpy."

Rome took a sip of her coffee. "After you make Starling another cup."

Kellan laughed. "Or we could put her in clothes and go down for food, coffee, and planning."

"Oh man," I said even as Jasper said, "Does she have to?"

That ignited another round of laughter. Not that Kellan was wrong. If she didn't get dressed, we were definitely not going to be doing anything other than her, and I wasn't altogether certain Dove was ready for that level.

Yet.

"Renovations, Sparrow," Kellan told her in a firm voice. "That means shirt and panties, probably pants…"

"I need to shower," Rome said abruptly, then scooped her right up.

"Hey," I protested when he walked her right out of the room and she was still laughing. Liam put a hand over his mouth, but not before he smirked. Jasper actually chuckled, and Kellan let out an exasperated sound.

"Rome is going to Rome."

"Nope," Liam said. "Pretty sure Rome is going to Hellspawn right now."

Pretty damn sure he was right.

CHAPTER 22

EMERSYN

*a*fter showering with Rome, I was more than a little loose-limbed and limber. I had to mention stretching to him again, particularly after the ideas that he had. The fact everyone had been wandering into Vaughn's room while I was lounging naked filled me with an inescapable warmth. I was still seriously aching from how fucking glorious it had been with him both in the dance studio then again in his room. He was always so careful and at the same time, he gave me what I needed.

All of them did. Rome pulled one of his shirts over my head and he'd gone to my room to get me fresh panties and yoga pants. My cunt was definitely feeling a little on the bruised side, but a good kind of bruised. The kind that said I'd well and truly worked out. Even my thighs burned.

I twisted my damp hair up into a knot before shoving my feet into shoes that had made their way from my room to here. Then again, construction and renovation. No bare feet.

Rome waited for me at the door. I paused when I got close to study his face.

"Starling…"

"Shh," I pressed a finger to his lips. "I tried to get a good look at this in the shower, but you kept distracting me."

He grinned.

"But you do feel better." He shouldn't have been carrying me with cracked ribs. Not that he seemed to care. Or struggle. Jasper was being bad about his stitches and Rome about his ribs. Then again…

"I am here," he said. "That's always better."

With me. He was here with me and honestly… "I like being home." The swelling had improved. The discoloration still looked bad, but bruises tended to look worse while they were getting better. He could open his eye all the way.

"Good."

Catching his hands, I looked at the bruises over his knuckles. There were paint stains around his nails, a visceral reminder of what he normally did. My stomach chose that moment to gurgle loudly.

"Eat," Rome said, nudging me toward the door.

"Fine," I huffed but kissed his knuckles. I didn't miss his hint of a smile as I headed for the door, claiming my coffee cup on the way. Unlike his room at Liam's, his bedroom here was cluttered with a lot of different items from paint supplies to books to magazines. I'd spied canvases in the corner, but as much as I wanted to explore, I didn't want to intrude.

Downstairs, I stared at the stripped empty front room. I already missed the pool table and the sofa. I missed the wooden coffee table with its worn patterns. I even missed the rug that had been there.

Darkened stains from where some of our attackers had lain after they'd been shot didn't help. They'd bleached away the signs of some, but the rug's absence revealed another. It had been weird when I came down earlier, before I'd followed the sounds of Vaughn working to my studio.

Eliminating the damage or at least removing it was the first step toward fixing things. The guys were in the kitchen, though it wasn't as crowded as having all of them in here would usually be—there was no table or chairs.

"Right," Liam was saying. "We need more furniture for here. Rome, you want to go with me to get some?"

Though he asked Rome, his gaze was on me. I grinned at Liam but Jasper wrapped an arm around me from where he leaned against the wall and pulled me to him for a morning hug. It seemed more like days than hours since we went to bed the day before. So much had happened. All good things.

"No," Rome said. "Walls need patching first."

"Depends on which walls," Vaughn countered. "We actually need to knock some of the walls down."

"Hell yes," Jasper said. "We've been talking plans. Have we worked out how we want to do the layout?"

"I have thoughts on that," Kellan replied, then beckoned to me with a curl of his fingers. After I nuzzled a kiss to Jasper's chin and then his lips, he let me go with a grin.

"Food incoming," Milo called from down the hall, and Kellan pushed away from the counter. He caught me in a loose embrace, then picked me up and settled me on the counter next to where he had been standing with Liam.

"Take Jasper," Kellan said to Liam.

"Oh, c'mon, I don't wanna go furniture shopping," Jasper complained. "Swinging sledge hammers is my thing."

"No, it isn't. You can supervise or shop or go back to bed. Right now, healing is your thing," Doc said as he came through the door ahead of Milo and Lainey. I grinned as she avoided the guys to head over to me. Kellan rubbed my leg and then brushed a kiss to my lips before he made way for her. She hopped right up onto the counter next to me and held up a brown bag.

"If I go back to bed, I'm taking Swan with me."

"Standing *right* here," Milo groused.

"Then close your ears," Jasper replied and everyone laughed.

"Breakfast burritos," Lainey leaned over to tell me as the guys started parceling out their food.

"I can smell them." They smelled great.

They were also hot; I was careful taking the foil-wrapped deliciousness. The breakfast burritos came from a cart a couple of blocks away. We'd had them before and they were amazing.

"We got juice, too," Milo offered as he carried two large bottles of OJ over.

"Thank you." We hadn't really had a chance to say much, but he gave me a searching look and I gave him another smile. "I'm okay."

"Just making sure." He turned and caught one of the burritos that Kellan tossed to him. The guys were shelling out ribbing and jobs to each other. It was—nice. Listening to them just chatter.

"Where's Freddie?" I asked abruptly and Liam glanced at me. I hadn't seen him since Jasper and I went to bed the night before. He should be down here with us, unless he didn't sleep. Concern slipped through me. I'd been playing all night and had the sore cunt to show for it, but...

"He's on a mission," Doc told me and I cut my gaze to him.

"A mission?" At my question, the others went quiet, and I glanced at them. No one seemed worried so that was good, right?

Into the quiet, the sound of the door slamming carried louder than normal. Wow. It was easy to tell there was no real furniture or art out there. We definitely needed to fix that.

"I found them!" Freddie crowed as he came up the hall. Then he was there with two giant white boxes in his hands. "Took a lot of charm, Boo-Boo. I do not just turn it on for everyone, you know?"

His grin was pure mischief.

"No?" I tilted my head. "So, I'm special cause I always get it?"

Jasper hid a smile as Freddie puffed up his chest. "You *are* special, Boo-Boo. So, in light of yours and Rome's return from the unplanned vacation—I would like to reiterate my request for a LoJack, but we'll discuss that later—I went all the way to Gambino's at the Marina to get you these beauties…"

With great fanfare, he flipped open the top box to reveal dancer donuts. Every single one was decorated with shoes, dancers, music, or something else, along with the donuts in the middle that said, "Welcome home."

Tears burned in my eyes. Lainey rescued my burrito because I had nowhere to put it down, and Liam reached out to balance the donuts so Freddie could open the second box. It was little paint cans, splashes of color like paint splatters all over the donuts, and in the middle, it read, "You're late."

Rome looked at the donuts then nodded. "Liam was," he said before he took out one and then a second to pass to me. I laughed and then hopped down to give Freddie a hug. He caught me in one arm and squeezed gently.

"I love them," I told him and he grinned.

"Worth all the charm I had to expend."

Everyone laughed, and there was some rearranging to put the donuts where everyone could get them. I made sure to give Freddie the home donut and he actually flushed. Kellan caught my eye after and gave me an approving nod. It was—

nice. The camaraderie of the night before seemed to extend into the day, and I was excited to help with the renovations. I also needed to stretch, but we needed to work on the studio for that and…

"I hate to be the one to bring it up," Doc said quietly as the guys began heading out to the former sitting room to argue about colors, wall repair, and furniture type. I didn't even care what they picked so much as I wanted it to feel like their home again and not a war zone.

"Bring up what?" Lainey asked for me since I had a mouthful of burrito. I shot her a grateful look and she grinned.

"Physical therapy." Doc really did sound apologetic but I groaned anyway. I hadn't been a fan of it before. It had only been a week, but still…

I glanced down at my arms and then at him. "I wanted to help with the renovations."

"We can still do that," he offered and I didn't miss the emphasis on *we*. It seemed like he was around more, and there was less—hostility with the guys. Then again, he'd been there with the guys, with Liam, when they came to get us. He took that guy down so fast. "We don't have to rush it, but I also know how much you rely on your flexibility and your strength."

"We can," I said, glancing at Lainey. "You're right, I do need my flexibility and my strength." I didn't miss the surprise flickering over Doc's face at my quick acceptance. Then again, Doc hadn't been my favorite person for a while. Then he saved Jasper. He kept looking after him. Then he came to get Rome, and me.

Jasper and Liam headed out for furniture, with Freddie volunteering to help. Their expressions had been kind of comical, but they actually looked like they were having fun. Vaughn went for the sledge hammers with Milo. I really wanted to do that part, but they said they'd save some walls for me to knock down. Lainey promised she'd supervise, and Kellan had some work to do, but he said he wasn't leaving the warehouse. Doc and I went upstairs for the PT because there was literally nowhere downstairs to sit that we wouldn't be in the way.

"Thank you," I said once we got settled and he started rolling my arms. It didn't hurt anywhere near as much as it had before.

"I promised I would help you," he reminded me. His light brown eyes held just a hint of reproach. "I know you're mad at me, Little Bit, but I'm not doing this just to make you miserable."

I shifted a little under his scrutiny. "I know you're not. Some of this is…some of this has just been strange and maybe a little strained."

He studied me for a long moment. "If I asked how you were doing, would you tell me?"

Turning the question over, I considered it as he applied more pressure to the roller. The scars didn't shock me anymore. They were still angry and pink, but they weren't so fresh. Or maybe after the ambush, Jasper being shot, the shooting here at the clubhouse, and then Rome and me being taken… I survived these cuts. The scars might be a fact of life, but the wounds were the past.

"I think I would," I said slowly. "I mean, yes, I would."

Mickey chuckled, some of the humor softening the concern in his expression. "You sure?"

"I don't sound sure, but I also don't mind the question. So, you can ask. I'll answer—and ow." The last came out as calmly as the rest, but the stretching sensation over the inside of my forearm just burned in the most uncomfortable way.

"Few more seconds," he cautioned. While he didn't ease

up on the pressure completely, he did soften it a little, and then he was done. I blew out a breath. "You're doing great."

"Okay, well when I'm in the corner crying later, just remind me I asked you to do this."

"I'll keep that in mind," he said, reaching for my other hand. Okay, yay, fresh torture. "Now, tell me, how are you?"

It wasn't quite the way I thought he'd ask, but I had said I'd answer. "Physically? My arms hurt—not as much as they did. Okay, correction, my left definitely hurts more than my right, right now." I tried to smile, but I was pretty sure it was more a gritting of teeth.

He flashed a grin. "You still have a sense of humor; that helps."

"Better to laugh than cry—fucking ow." At my complaint, he traded the roller for his thumbs and began to massage the tissue around the scar. "I really hadn't been paying that much attention to them."

"No, I can imagine. You've had a lot on your plate. Especially with the kidnapping."

I made a face. "They didn't hurt me. Much." I added the qualifier as an afterthought. "It wasn't about me. It was about trying to control Rome. Technically, Liam but it was Rome."

"Well, I'm not a fan of you hurting in any way." He nodded to me. "Pain isn't something to be shrugged off."

"Sometimes it is," I corrected him. "Mickey, I've had a lot of pain over the years. If I couldn't push past it, then I couldn't perform."

"You love dancing."

I did. *I do.* "It was my life. I know it doesn't *have* to be anymore." Not like it was before. "But there's a freedom that comes from flying, when I'm up there…"

I had no idea how to explain it. He slowed the massage to hold my hand for a moment. "I get it. We'll get you back up there."

"Mickey, if I ask you a question, will you answer it?"

"I think so," he said slowly. "Maybe."

When I wrinkled my nose, he squeezed my hand then went back to working on my arm.

"What do you want to ask me, Little Bit?"

"You…" I frowned, trying to figure out how to word the question.

"I?"

"You—you came with them to get us." I studied him. "You grabbed that guy and you…"

"Removed the problem," he said carefully. "Does that bother you?"

I shook my head slowly. "I just—you told me once why you wanted to be a doctor."

"Hasn't changed, Little Bit. Taking care of people, helping them? Absolutely. But I won't let anyone hurt one of you and get away with it. Not you. Not the boys. No one. Just because I would prefer peace doesn't mean I can't make war."

A shiver slid up my spine at the description. "Thank you, for this… for helping me and for coming to get us."

"Always," he promised, and when he raised his hand to brush his knuckles down my cheek, I didn't move but I also didn't lean into it. I wanted to forgive him and to trust him again. Part of me did. He saved Jasper, but… "It's okay," he murmured as if addressing my unspoken thoughts. "One day at a time. Right?"

I nodded. "One day at a time…and maybe some swinging of a sledge hammer."

He raised his brows.

"What? I've never done it, and it sounds like a lot of fun." I didn't even have to manufacture the tone, but the lighter note helped, and he chuckled.

"Right, well, let's get you to some real exercises with your arms then. Warm you up."

I flexed my hands as he let me go and let out a shaky breath. "I'm ready."

For the first time since we started this whole PT nightmare, it didn't seem so awful. Just mostly full of suck.

Mostly.

CHAPTER 23

EMERSYN

$\mathcal{H}$aving Lainey back with us was amazing. Especially when it came to swinging a sledge hammer. She actually wielded one like an expert, earning an impressed look from Vaughn and a speculative one from Milo. I wasn't quite as talented, but Vaughn helped me brace the hammer so I could swing it without having to worry about throwing it.

Rome found a hard hat to stick on my head, and a second one for Lainey. The guys weren't wearing them,, but I didn't argue. He wasn't going to listen anyway. We all had on face masks, and Milo had hauled in a couple of huge fans and cracked open the door wide to the warehouse itself when we were working.

It wasn't long before I realized why.

Dust.

Lots of dust.

I was pretty gray with it. So was Lainey. Funnily enough,

with all the dust we kicked up from knocking out the walls, we kept trying to outdo the other.

"And you're done," Milo called as he caught Lainey's sledge hammer.

"Killjoy," she said with a smirk, but he just shook his head. The indulgent look in his eyes seemed pretty damn revealing, and I stole a look at Lainey, who watched him as he walked away.

"Get cleaned up. We're going to get pizza and air this place out," he called. To be honest, we'd done a lot of work. It didn't seem like it took long, but watching Vaughn go to town to take down a wall had been entertaining.

Even more when he and Milo had been swinging in tandem. Lainey and I got our share of demolition. It was way more fun than it had any right to be.

But between the demolition and the physical therapy, I was tired. It also took some serious work to scrub all the dust off. Even with the hat and mask, it seemed to be everywhere.

By the time I came back downstairs, there was a new table and chairs in the kitchen. Freddie was sprawled in one chair, with his feet up in the other.

"If I ever volunteer to go shopping with those two again, please thump me." He didn't even open his eyes as he issued the statement.

"That bad?" I asked.

"Worse," he said with a grin. "They can literally argue about *everything*."

Despite his words, he seemed pretty damn entertained. I glanced around. "Where is everyone?"

"Jas went to crash."

I frowned and Freddie cracked his eyes open.

"Don't worry, Boo-Boo. He's just tired."

"But he's admitting it." That did worry me.

When Freddie slid his feet off the chair and pushed it out

for me, I settled on it.

"Doc busted him when we got back," Freddie admitted in a low voice and cut a glance toward the doorway. "Now, I'm telling you this not to get him in trouble, but to make sure you don't worry."

"If you say he's all right, I'll believe you," I promised. "You don't have to tell me any secrets." Huh. That little self-revelation made me smile. A few months earlier, I didn't believe anything they said—not just because they'd "kidnapped" me but because I didn't trust anyone.

No one except Lainey.

Freddie studied me a beat, then said, "He's okay, Boo-Boo."

"Good." Propping my chin on my hand, I studied him. "How are you?"

He darted a look toward the door then back at me. When I raised my brows, he leaned toward me and beckoned me closer with a crook of his finger.

Angling on my chair, I eased closer, and then he pressed a kiss to my cheek. "I'm good, Boo-Boo."

Smiling, I turned my face to him and he brushed his lips against mine. A there-and-gone-again kiss.

"This is still okay?"

"Yes," I promised and held out my pinky. He locked his pinky to mine with a sigh. "It's more than okay."

"Good."

"Freddie," Vaughn called. "Trucks are here."

Oh, I hadn't even realized we had trucks coming in. Well, hell, I hadn't really paid attention to much since getting back. Had it really been less than twenty-four hours?

Freddie groaned, but I stood up and tugged his finger. "Come on, I'll help."

"You're not off-loading a truck," he informed me, but he stood and moved with me to the door.

"Okay," I told him, not arguing. "I can stand there and look encouraging though, right?"

He appeared to consider that a minute. "How bad would it be if we pretended we didn't hear and went upstairs to hide and watch television?"

"Do you need to hide?"

Instead of dismissing the question, he rubbed the back of his neck and seemed to consider it. "I don't think so...but you need a jacket before you go out there. It's cold."

"I'll go get one." Then I bounced up to my toes to kiss him again. I hesitated though, giving him a few seconds to close the distance in case he didn't want the contact. He met my kiss with one of his own. The brush was light but electric.

"I'll wait for you," he said, after making a shooing motion, and I grinned wider.

First demolition, and now, off-loading trucks? I'd never gotten to help with the breakdown and set-up of a show before, and that was the closest I could come to associating this.

I hurried back to my room to find a jacket and a pair of boots. The shoes I had on weren't thick, and I wanted warmer ones. I definitely didn't want to keep any of them waiting.

～

THE NEXT COUPLE OF DAYS FELL INTO A PATTERN. A comfortable one. The guys moved fast once the walls had been torn down. Kel and I had to move everything out of our rooms, and so did Rome. For now, the three of us were taking turns on where we bunked. Sometimes with Vaughn and sometimes with Jasper. Though, we'd moved most of the furniture down to an empty room at the other end.

They weren't really set up for what the guys wanted to

do, and they needed to rework the hallways. The fact they had it all mapped out was kind of fascinating. New walls were going up, along with new doors. They didn't bring in any construction workers for it.

The guys literally did everything. Lainey and I had front row seats to the erection of the first set of walls. There were some arguments about space, then plumbing. The fact that one of the pipes broke led to a lot of laughter and water.

As chaotic as it all was, they always seemed to know what they were doing. Liam disappeared after the first day. They'd picked up furniture, but a lot of it was wrapped and sealed on pallets in the warehouse.

"Hey," Milo said, when he came into the kitchen. I'd just made coffee and stolen a breakfast burrito from the box Kellan had left. He'd gone out for food and brought it back, delivering it with a scorching kiss before he had to head to the shop.

Vaughn was going to work with him today, because they had to pick up more materials on the way back. Then again, there was something in how they said Vaughn was gonna work with him that had me worried.

A part of me wished I'd volunteered to go with them, but I had physical therapy later, and Jasper had an appointment with Mickey after. Fingers crossed, he'd be getting his stitches out. Though, I had concerns about keeping him from overdoing it *when* the stitches were out.

"Hi," I said as Milo moved over to the fridge. He was hot and sweaty looking. Kind of like he'd been… "Were you working out?"

He chuckled. "Yes and no." After he drained a bottle of water, he used his t-shirt to wipe at his face. "Had to finish swapping a load around on some trucks and the lifter broke."

I made a face. "Kel already went to work."

"It's fine; he'll look at it when he gets back." Milo took

another long drink of his water. "You busy today?"

"No," I said slowly, after I finished a bite of my burrito. "I haven't seen Lainey yet..."

Milo grimaced. "She left last night. Fuck, she left a note for you. I'll get it."

She left? My heart sank.

"She's coming back," he raced on to assure me. "Said something about needing to see her grandfather. Hang on... give me five?"

"Sure."

He vanished out of the kitchen and was back in a little more than the five minutes he'd asked for in fresh clothes and carrying his phone. But it was an envelope he handed me, not the phone.

I recognized Lainey's crisp writing on the front.

Don't freak. The dates snuck up on me and I needed to be back in New York for a dinner with my grandfather. I'll be back as soon as I can. I told tall, dark, and growly to make sure he gives you this note as soon as you're awake rather than rousting you from whomever's bed you were in. He wasn't thrilled, but he better have done it.

Be back soon.

L.

I glanced up to find Milo watching me again. "Thank you."

"No problem, I still think you would have probably wanted to say goodbye in person, but she told me I didn't get a vote." Disgruntled *and* amused. Lainey was making progress.

"Yes, I would have liked to say goodbye myself," I began but held up a finger when he got cheerful about it. "But she's right to have not interrupted, too. I wouldn't intrude on you two."

For a moment, I thought he would argue the point, but

then his mouth snapped shut. With a nod, he sat down across from me. "If you're going to put it that way…"

"Hey, let's make a deal?" I offered. "You and me?"

"What's the deal?" Suspicious wasn't quite the right word for his look, but he didn't look altogether trusting either.

"I will make a concentrated effort to not walk in on you naked and you do the same."

"Oh," he let it out like a shout, his expression drawing into a grimace and I couldn't help but laugh at him. "You did *not* have to put it like that."

"Well, I could have said something about your—"

"No," he said firmly. "Deal accepted. We shall confine all of our interactions to the common rooms. Just make sure you're always dressed in them."

Another snicker escaped me. He truly did look appalled, and after a minute, he started to laugh too, even as he shook his head.

"You know… just when I think I have you figured out, you just rip all my expectations to shreds."

I sobered at that description. "I'm sorry?" I mean, but was I really? I suppose I should be sorry but…

"Not at all," he said with a wry, if genuine chuckle. "I know I keep trying to paint you into a box and locking it up, and I don't mean to. Of all people, I know better than to just judge someone based on where they are from or what I think they do." His laughter dried up and he shook his head. "But I'm just as fucking guilty as the people who look at me and see scum."

"You know," I said, studying him from the thick network of tattoos on his arms to his troubled expression. "I never saw scum."

"I wasn't saying you did, Ivy."

"No, I know. I saw an asshole. But not scum."

His jaw snapped shut with a little click and then a laugh

escaped him as I grinned. "You're such a brat."

"And that's what *you're* allowed to see when you look at me." I really didn't mind it anymore. "We're not so bad at this sibling thing."

"I'm amazing," Milo informed me. "You suck. You're supposed to be sweet, gracious, and always do what you're told."

I stared at him for a minute and canted my head to the side.

"What?"

"The only other siblings I know you know well are Rome and Liam."

"And?"

"Do either of them do that?"

Lips pursed, Milo narrowed his eyes at me, but rather than fierce, he looked amused. "No. But that's different…"

"Because they have penises?"

He spat out water as he choked. Thankfully, he didn't spray me with it. I took a bite of my breakfast to keep from laughing, and when he finally caught his breath, he said, "I would like to add, 'we won't discuss anyone's penises' to our list of not trying to see each other naked."

"I can live with it. So, no genitalia at all." I extended my hand to him and he shook it, still chuckling.

"Agreed." Then he reached for his water as I took another bite.

"How are you doing?" It was a lot more serious a question than the earlier ones, so I considered it.

"I'm—okay. I mean, I'm home so that part is great and it feels like home here, which I love." I studied the burrito for a moment, then looked at him. "I know you didn't want me here, but—I love it here. I love it here with you and with them. This…this is everything I never realized I didn't have and always wanted."

"I hate that you didn't have that kind of family." His frown deepened. "I hate....I hate that look in your eyes when you talk about them."

"Then don't look at it." Having brought it up though, I could hardly fault him. "No, I don't mean it that way. I just— we're still getting to know each other. You're getting past this image of me, and I'm getting used to you being overprotective."

"Good." But his smile was fleeting. "Will you ever trust me enough to tell me what happened with your family?"

"It's not about trust, Milo. I promise." But the idea of telling him? Telling anyone was hard enough. Telling Freddie had broken something loose inside of me. The same with Rome. Confessing to Lainey had played its part, too. I didn't run from it, but I also wasn't in a hurry to embrace it.

"Then what is it?" He studied me like he could peer into my soul and find the answers. "Wait, don't answer because you're not ready to. I can respect that." Maybe he could find his own answers. "But when you're ready...will you tell me?"

"I won't promise to tell you," I said after a lot of thought. "But if I can tell you, then I will."

"Okay."

The silence that followed that was so heavy, it made me want to just lay my head down. "Tell me something..."

"What?"

"Anything. Something about you. About our mother. Something I don't know."

He raised his brows. "There's a lot."

"Tell me? Help me get to know you?" Maybe that was where we could build some bridges.

Together.

"Mom...was really pretty," he said slowly. "You look just like her in so many ways, but your smile—that's hers. When I was little..."

CHAPTER 24

KELLAN

"Take the next left," I said, splitting my attention between what was behind and ahead of us, while Emersyn navigated a lane change. Morning traffic had made for a lot of stop and go. Vaughn was pacing us a couple of car lengths behind.

As much as I craved the uninterrupted time with her, I also wasn't taking any chances. She and Rome should have been fine, but they'd gone to an isolated location and then been surrounded. We still didn't know if that had been a "planned" assault or one that asshole Brixton and his crew simply launched to take advantage of the situation.

We also didn't know the identity of the people behind the kidnapping. The name Brixton seemed to be a dead end. We'd all seen him, and Doc had even managed to get a picture of the guy. Nothing.

Also, they appeared to have vanished and taken Adam Reed with them. That left another loose end that needed to be tied off, and there was still the issue of Warrick's business. I'd actually been looking forward to handing it off, but I should have known better.

"Doing good," I said after she made the turn and cast me a quick grin. For all her confidence on the dance floor and in the silks, she actively seemed to need and responded to praise for her newly acquired skill. I would have done it anyway, but the way the smile lit her up? "You're ready for the highway."

"It's only my third lesson!" Her smile gave way to laughter and more than a little disbelief.

"Technically," I reminded her, "it's your fourth. Driving on the highway is no different from a parking lot or the street. You need to accelerate to keep your speed up when you're getting on, and you'll need to merge with traffic. Highway driving can also be easier because there are no traffic lights and no cross traffic."

"Just the other assholes in the other lanes."

"Yes, Jasper, I'm aware we're not fans of other drivers."

The swell of her laughter at the comment pulled a smile from my lips. I'd warned Vaughn we were gonna hit the highway if she was comfortable. Where she'd been reluctant to leave the clubhouse before, this time she'd leapt at the chance.

At least this particular escapade hadn't left any lasting damage. We could only hope that would continue. Especially since I needed to keep her away for at least a couple of hours and I wanted the time anyway.

"We're going up one more block, and you need to get into the right-hand lane. Then we'll take a right onto the access road. You'll have about two minutes to get up to speed before we get to the on-ramp." I checked the time on the dashboard. Traffic shouldn't be heavy right now. So that would be excellent practice.

Her head moved like she was on a swivel, her gaze darting from the side mirrors to the rearview then back as she flicked on the indicator. She moved over like an expert, and I kept my arm relaxed on the door.

For all that she was driving my baby, she was infinitely more important to me. The girls were doing a very good job together. Whatever reckless soul Sparrow possessed that let her throw her body out into the air to dance without anything to catch her if she fell was missing when she drove.

A handful of lessons and she'd never needed me to repeat one. She applied every single nuance to what she was doing. She should have been driving a long time before, but I got why she hadn't *needed* it. What I hated was the fact no one made the effort because if she could drive herself, that would have been one more chain she broke.

Without any prompting, she took the next right and then we were cruising up the access road. "Punch it," I told her. I'd already gotten a look at the highway, lots of wide open spots. "Let my baby show you what she's got."

The sweet purr of the engine revving as she put her foot down was enough to make me smile. My girl could handle this road, and Sparrow was not afraid to grasp that power.

"Good girl," I murmured as she let out a triumphant little laugh. Not only had she hit the speed she needed to merge into traffic, she'd also outpaced a couple of cars and changed lanes without any instruction. "You're a natural."

Especially when you relax, but I kept the last few words to myself. Emersyn wore confidence so beautifully. Then again, she was pretty much gorgeous in everything.

Except shock collars and cuffs. That mental image killed some of my humor.

"This is a lot of fun," she admitted. "Is something wrong?"

"No, Sparrow," I assured her and reached over to rest two

fingers against her nape. I didn't want to distract her, but I also liked feeling her pulse. I liked *knowing* she was back.

I wasn't the only one checking in on her a few times a day either. I caught everyone doing it. Except Liam, but he probably had another angle at play right now and wanted to trust us—or more likely Rome—to know where she was. Then again, I'd seen him ghost in and out in the middle of the night.

So, maybe not. Maybe he wasn't immune to the need to check on her like the rest of us. The sooner we wrapped up this bullshit with the king, the better. The Royals themselves, so far, did not seem to be our problem. But I was ready for Liam to just come home.

"Kellan?"

"Hmm?" I dragged my mind back to the present because she was casting me quick looks, though most of her attention was on the road. That was good, but I needed to make sure *I* didn't distract her.

"Do you mind if I ask some questions?"

"Ask me anything you want, Sparrow," I said. "I don't know that I can answer everything, but I will do what I can." No more lies or half-truths either. If it was something I couldn't tell her, then I'd tell her that.

While I had no idea what she wanted to ask, I figured it would be something along the lines of how legal was the business we ran? The trucking? She knew we'd killed people. Fuck, *she* had killed people, a fact that still amazed me and left me worried.

Killing wasn't easy and never should be. I made my peace with every death I'd ever dealt, but I didn't want those deaths to come back and haunt her. If I had a single regret about her choice to stay with us? That would be it.

"I want to feel useful," she said slowly, taking a direction I hadn't even noticed. "Not just feel useful, but be useful. I mean—you fix things, Vaughn had a job and he is really good at the construction stuff, Jasper has the trucks and Milo's been helping him. Rome paints, but he's also doing the construction, then Doc has the clinic and Liam…"

I didn't laugh, but I got the hesitation.

"Liam is playing a lot of angles that could get him killed."

Yeah. She really paid attention.

"Basically," she continued, "everyone has a job. Even Freddie, whether it's helping or running errands or just bringing in spare cash. I want to be useful, too."

"Sparrow, you are useful. Alive. Smiling. Happy. That's—"

"Really sweet," she told me with more than a little side-eye. "I appreciate that you want me to look after me. But I want to do more."

"I get that. I respect that. But one of the things you're doing is healing. Just like Jasper isn't just going back out on the road until Doc gives him the all clear, I don't want you doing anything that interferes with your recovery."

"Oh."

"However," I continued because that single syllable held such a wealth of disappointment, I couldn't *not* address it. "You have been helping in a lot of ways. You looked after Jasper, and he *listens* to you which is a huge achievement in and of itself."

"He's not that bad."

"Oh, yes he is," I informed her. "I love the guy like a brother, but I'm not blind to his flaws. He's a pushover for you, and you keep him calm, which has let him rest. That's good. You also help with Freddie."

"Freddie has helped me," she countered.

"I believe it," I said. "But you are a grounding influence for him. You accept him as he is and he *trusts* you. Trust is not something any of us do easily and Freddie least of all. There are times when I worry he doesn't trust us."

Not all the time but it was there.

"My point, Sparrow, you are doing a lot more than you realize, but I hear you wanting to do more. Let me think about it for a while? Not all the jobs we do are going to be a good fit for you. Unless you want to do some road trips with Jasper, or come back to the garage with me."

She grinned. "I'd like to go back to the shop. We were having fun that day before… you know."

Yes. I did know. "Okay then, let me think about it ,and take the next exit and loop us back around to head back to the city. You've been handling her like a dream."

"How many businesses do you guys actually have?"

"Legitimately? Two. But we all have or had jobs to supplement income. Trucking brings in a lot of money for us. Transport is expensive though, and we have to maintain the fleet. Short-term cargo storage is another business we have, but that's not quite as lucrative, nor as interesting."

I rubbed my chin, giving it a beat as she took the exit. The sweet purr of my baby's engine promised that Sparrow's touch was as light with the car as she was with me.

"We have our jobs, too. Occasionally we take on a rehab project, especially in the neighborhood. Most of those we do for free. We also keep an eye on the streets, the kids on it, and the drugs being run on it. But those aren't as legitimate."

"The mechanic's shop?"

"Not mine yet. Someday," I told her. "For now, I enjoy the work and there's something really satisfying about taking cars apart, putting them back together. Even more satisfying to listen to what the engine is really telling me about what's wrong with her."

"And then someday?"

"Someday, when the owner is ready to sell, I'll buy the shop. Or if that doesn't work out, I can always open my own." Frankly,

I hadn't really thought about that in a while. "If we keep growing the trucking the way we have, Jasper's got it set to really become a cash cow. Until then, we pool resources to keep costs down."

After everything that happened with the Diamonds, the stolen shipments and trucks? We didn't trust anyone else to service the trucks.

I checked the time again. We'd been out for a couple of hours, but she was handling her like a pro.

"Is there something you want to do?"

"I've only ever really been good at dancing. Technically, I haven't graduated high school. I mean, I finished all the work, but I never took the test."

"Well, we'll figure out what you're good at. I mean, you can always do college if you want." I wasn't totally sure how we would make that work, but we'd find a way.

"Only if I can go to school with Lainey," she declared then made a face. "That probably sounds spoiled but…"

"It doesn't sound anything. You like your friend, you're allowed." I also liked that she would *tell* us what she needed and what she wanted.

"Truthfully, I don't even know what I'd go to college for, so maybe I should practice with all of you and spend more time together so I can see if there's something I'd like."

"I don't have a problem with that. You can also work on your dancing, building your strength up—I bet Doc knows some kids who could use lessons if you were up for that."

"Teach?" She sounded so startled I frowned. Had that never occurred to her? "I don't know…maybe." Only she didn't sound so certain. My phone vibrated with a message.

Everyone was back and we were clear. "Something to think about," I said. "We don't have to decide anything today. You ready to head back?"

"Yes." Relief marked her response, something else to keep

in mind. She was worried about more than just helping out. We'd need to dig into that.

"Do you remember how to get back to the warehouse?" I kept it teasing, and she laughed.

"Let's find out! Don't correct me!"

She did circle one block, but she got back there, and I gave her a thumbs up when she cheered at the sight of the warehouse. I'd already sent the message that we were here.

As soon as she hit the button to open the warehouse, the music and lights spilled out of it. A huge banner had been strung up that said happy birthday across it, and Freddie had a pair of sparklers in hand.

Right. Fire hazards. But Vaughn also had a fire extinguisher—either planning ahead or there had already been a mishap.

"Happy birthday," I said as she stared, wide-eyed. Her shock gave way to an entertaining kind of joy. Thankfully, she put the car into park before she climbed over to give me a kiss and a hug.

I was still laughing when Lainey came to get her. Happiness rolled off Emersyn in waves as they hurried inside. The guys all welcomed her back with kisses and drinks. There would be cake. We'd enjoy tonight. I moved the car inside and parked it, closing the warehouse door after I scanned the area.

Tonight, we'd have her birthday.

Tomorrow, we'd get back to work.

CHAPTER 25

ROME

*T*he birthday party was fun. Lainey had been adamant that no one had ever given her a surprise party. The minute she told Milo, a surprise party was what we all had to do. I liked it. It made Starling happy. Liam and I still needed to make sure we gave her the surprise we'd planned. Though he seemed reluctant about a lot of things, particularly Starling.

Some days, I just wanted to hit him.

I supposed I would have to.

Again.

A door closed further up the hall. The lack of any weight to the steps said it was Freddie or Starling. It could be Lainey, but if she were leaving Milo's room, his heavier steps often followed right behind. If she were with Starling, their laughter served as musical accompaniment.

I waited, my gaze trained on the new door we'd just hung. We'd changed this entire side, essentially building a new wing in the clubhouse. It made more sense to tear out the rooms we rarely used or only used for storage. Then we reworked my room, Starling's, and Kel's into a safe room. We needed to finish the welding in there, but the layout and the designs came from someone Liam hired.

This section would be different. It would be bigger, comfortable. Hopefully more like a home. Privacy had been Kellan's word on it, and that privacy meant that there was a space for Starling and us to be secure in. The door pushed in a little more and then she was there. Dressed in a pair of her dance pants, and a tank top with a cut up sweatshirt over it.

"You working in here by yourself?" she asked as she made her way across the floor. We had plastic down everywhere to protect the floors, not that the final flooring was done yet. The argument over carpet versus wooden floors had escalated to Jasper and Vaughn making a bet. Kellan didn't care and neither did I. No one asked Liam.

Maybe we should let Starling decide. So far that seemed to be the best way to settle ties.

"No," I said as I set aside the paint I'd been mixing to take the hug she offered. Hugging Starling was better than almost anything else. Except when she hugged me back. And sex. I liked sex. "You're here."

"This is true," she said with a laugh. Her hair was damp and piled up on her head. She was warm from a shower. She smelled like oranges and cookies. My stomach grumbled. "Did you have breakfast?"

"No. Want to get started." The majority of the main room here was done. The bedrooms would be arrayed out in a semi-circle, with hers the farthest from the door. We had more work to do, but Starling wanted to make the place "brighter." That was my plan.

"How about I get us coffee and food and bring it back up, and then I can help?"

"I'll finish mixing the paint."

She leaned back to stare at the cans I had set out.

"I've never seen you paint with anything other than spray bottles."

"I can." She didn't need to worry about that.

"I'm sure you can. You didn't do that one on my wall with spray cans." That had been the one area she had hesitated. I promised to do another one. I could even do the same one if she wanted. I would make her anything she wanted. "Will you show me? I've never painted anything—like for real—when I get back?"

"Yes."

Her smile warmed me, then she brushed another kiss to my jaw before she headed for the door. It wasn't long before she was back, the scent of coffee stronger than the paint and there was...

"You made bacon?"

"Nope," she said with a laugh. "Kellan was fixing food before he left for work. He made us bacon and egg sandwiches with cheese. I'm still trying to figure out how to cook."

"Someone else can do it for you." I didn't mind. I didn't cook much. Not because I didn't know how, but I didn't like it. If Starling needed food, I could cook for her. I put aside another can of paint that I'd mixed. There were a few different colors we'd need. After wiping my hand on my shirt, I took one of the sandwiches from her hand and then the coffee.

We didn't have much to sit on in here yet, so I moved a couple of the older buckets and a painter's bench over. We used the bench for a table and the buckets to sit. There was a fresh little red mark on her neck that hadn't been there before and her lips seemed redder. What I liked even more was the softness in her eyes and the ease of her smile.

"So, what's our plan?" She asked after she finished her sandwich. She was as hungry as I was apparently. I was washing mine down with coffee and then looked around the room.

"You want brighter?" That was what she'd said, so I wanted to make sure.

"This is going to be the sitting room? Or the living room?" Her expression took on a thoughtful appearance. Like me, she studied the blank walls. Well, not blank. They were finished and sanded. The drywall had set. Now we just needed to paint them. Then we'd move on to the flooring and the bedrooms.

There were no windows. No natural light. So the lighting would also need to be taken into consideration. We would have a runner around the edge of the ceiling for low light and one on the floor too.

"The ocean..." At her suggestion, I could see it. A rocky shore. Water crashing against the jagged landscape as the tide rolled in. Beautiful, but deadly. "Maybe the sky—definitely blue, not sunrise or sunset." Azure skies, seagulls maybe in the distance. "And everything stretching out as far as the eye can see."

Peaceful and chaotic.

"I like it." Did we want it on all the walls... no. Just one. One that could be the focus and the rest would be a softer shade of blue, stretch out the sky and add wisps of white. I tilted my head to check the ceiling. We were going to need a longer roller. Might have to do three layers.

"Do you think the guys will like it?" The inexorable tug of her presence pulled me back to the present.

"I don't care." I really didn't, but she laughed.

"Rome..." But she did.

I shrugged. "They will like it because you picked it." Kel wanted this to be her home. She said she wanted it to be her home, too. We'd never really decorated. If I wanted to paint, I painted. I left their rooms alone unless they asked. "The ocean and the rocks—that's Braxton Harbor."

It was home.

For us.

Lots of our beaches were like that.

Her smile grew. "Okay… so where do we start?"

"With the blue." I glanced at the buckets I'd been mixing. We had a couple of different kinds of blue. We'd need more. By the time Starling finished her coffee, we were ready to go.

Rolling the base coat on was just basic work, but we needed a canvas. Starling was also having a lot of fun with it. I just followed her to clean up the drip marks and smooth them out. Blue paint flecks decorated her face and there was some in her hair. Her hands also had splatters of paint from the roller too.

We had to close the door so I could tape it, and then I painted the edges of the frame with the white, followed by a swift coat of blue. I wanted it to blend, not be a stark border. Starling leaned in close as I used a smaller brush, and I paused on adding streaks with the wood grain to paint her nose.

Laughter burst out of her and I grinned. Normally, I'd just lose myself to the art, but I liked being here with Starling, too. I didn't want to turn on the fans from the other rooms to help pull the excess of the paint scent out. I kind of liked it.

"Rome…"

I turned at her voice and she painted three fingers across my face. The cool stickiness of the paint was a familiar sensation. At the same time, it was different because she did it to me.

With the brush, I added another streak to her face, this one down her cheek like she'd done mine. Only she needed more than just the pale blue. Her eyes rounded as she stared at me and then we both looked at the paint. She stuck her finger in the blue and I abandoned the brush to do the same.

When she painted a wave on my cheek, I went still and then she tilted her head so I could add a starling to her neck. There wasn't a lot of skin on her face to paint. I glanced down at myself, then stripped off my shirt so she could paint my chest. When she created wings with her palm prints and fingers, I nodded. I liked that.

A minute later she was shrugging out of her clothes. Paint got all over them. Not that I cared. Neither did she. "What is your bird?"

The question made me pause. "Hummingbird."

That earned me a blink.

"Milo decided I was the hummingbird. Too fast to see. Always on the move." I liked the description.

"Always seeking beauty and sweetness." Her addition was also welcome. "I have no idea how to paint a hummingbird."

I switched to a different brush and curled my finger at her. I wanted her to turn away so I could work on her side. The birds on her abdomen were beautiful, but this one would take more space. Arms above her head, she posed as I painted the lines of the bird and then added a twist so that the hummingbird was seeking her nipple like it was one of those feeders.

It took me longer than I thought it would but she only sighed as I worked. She was so smooth everywhere, so the canvas was perfect.

"I want to paint you," I said.

"You already painted me," she pointed out. "On you."

I had. "I mean you…" I smoothed my hand over her ass and then up her back. "I want to paint you."

"Can I paint you?"

Putting aside the brush, I shrugged out of the rest of my clothes. We took turns; she finger painted and sometimes used the brush. Wings, she painted me with lots of wings, and I liked that. I added a mockingbird to her other side, mirroring the hummingbird. Liam should be on her, too. I added a kestrel to her back with a sparrow—in this case a sparrow hawk just below. Her nipples stood out, pebbled and puckered. The air in the room had grown cool.

When I knelt to paint her thighs, I studied her pussy. I liked the way the skin glistened and the soft pink color when it flushed.

"Are you still going to paint me?" The question escaped her on a breathless exhale. No, I wanted to taste her now. No more painting.

Abandoning the brush, I wrapped my hands against her thighs and lifted one to go over my shoulder. I kissed her cunt with a fierce thrust of my tongue and she let out a little shout. Then her hands came to my hair. Balancing herself. I wouldn't let her fall.

Alternating between licking, biting, sucking, and scrapes of my teeth, I reveled in the way she began to rock against my face. The more she grew slick with need, the more I lapped at her.

"Fuck," she swore and then she ground against me and it was amazing.

"More," I said as I lifted my head. She gazed down at me all flushed and panting. "Yes?"

"Yes," she whispered and I helped her down and then she was sinking onto my thighs. The hot fist of her cunt wrapped around my dick and I found an unpainted spot on her neck to bite before she fused her lips to mine.

We didn't need words. Her muscles rippled as she moved against my lap and when I twisted to lay her down, one of the paint trays tipped over. It spilled against her arm and mine, but I didn't care.

Instead, I rocked into her and when she bit down on my

lip, I rolled to let her be on top. I liked looking up at her. Paint streaked her chest and mine. It smeared the birds but also seemed to give them life. Handprints—hers and mine—decorated our chests and when I grasped her hips to increase our pace, she threw her head back.

It reminded me of when she flew. This was what I wanted to paint. Starling in full flight, breasts bared, and pleasure in her expression. The rush of heat spilled out of me as she let out another shout and then she collapsed, slowly, folding down until our lips brushed and we were touching everywhere.

"We made a mess," she murmured.

"Art," I answered, tracing a paint streaked finger down her back. She let out a little shudder and her body fisted me tighter, keeping me deep. This was where I should always be.

"We're definitely covered in it," she said with a smile as she lifted her head. Starling was always beautiful. "Though I don't know if sex-painted walls was what they had in mind."

I considered that for a moment. "Want to try?"

"Try?" She blinked slowly. I reached out to my right and tipped over the big pan of blue into the spill of white, then rolled us both through it. Her shrieks of laughter filled the room and then we were up. I pushed her back to the wall and then kissed as I ground my hips into hers.

It might take us a while.

It did.

A whole hour for one wall.

Lying on the floor together, we stared at the streaks of white and blue and how they marbled the effect on the wall.

"I kind of like it," she admitted and I grinned.

So did I.

"This is how we will paint my room." Paint her. Use her to paint. I wanted her everywhere.

"Maybe mine too?"

I turned my head to look at her. "Yes."

"Eventually, we have to clean this up."

"After we do the next wall."

"The next one?" I rolled over to scoop her up and she let out another laugh.

Even if we didn't finish another wall, I wanted to try.

CHAPTER 26

LIAM

The day at the store had run long. Too damn long. I hadn't meant to let so many of my own responsibilities go or just flat out ignore them. However, between Hellspawn disappearing first to her home and then to Pinetree, to Rome and Hellspawn being kidnapped, I'd just fucked off of the rest. My managers were all talented people, they sure as shit didn't need me telling them what to do.

For the day-to-day stuff, the exclusivity of the boutiques coupled with the special touch each manager had to provide helped. But they couldn't make the bigger decisions, the far-reaching ones—like setting the budget and choosing the designers. That had to come from the top. My parents counted on me.

I'd loosened my tie before I even got in the SUV to drive home. If I hadn't been carrying, I would probably have lost the jacket. In the car, I checked messages. There were more than a dozen. Two from Rome though.

Both had question marks. Nothing else.

At the first traffic light, I sent him a thumbs up. He just wanted to know I was all right. Kel had questions. So did Milo. There was even a message from Freddie. He wanted to know why I'd skipped Hellspawn's surprise party.

A lot of reasons, but none I wanted to discuss with him yet. There were more messages on my other phone. One of them was an order to call the king. Right. I'd get on that.

Later.

Between the shit at the store and the endless parade of meetings interfering with my hunt for who the fuck Brixton was and, better still, who the fuck he worked for, it had been a day overflowing with frustration, aggravation, and in some cases, pure boredom. There were more important things in the world than some up and coming designers or the new thing.

The managers had a better sense for what sold in their stores than I did. The problem, however, lay in giving even one of them more than the others. Competitive as hell, it would just lead to more problems. So I sucked it up, and sat through the five hours of presentations, slideshows, outfits, and designer stories.

Not how I would have spent my day if given a choice. The parking garage was quiet. So was my apartment. I'd added motion detectors as a secondary line of defense and locked my floor even from deliveries if I wasn't home. The doorman now had a partner, one I paid well to make sure any deliveries and delivery people were vetted upon arrival.

Another check of the apartment cameras before I backed the SUV into one of the sealed spots. I'd added three more to the garage in the last couple of weeks. We'd also gone over the cars for trackers. Found two on my cars.

Not anymore.

Every measure required a countermeasure. No one was getting past me to my brother or Hellspawn again.

Period.

In the elevator, I entered my code to take me to my floor. Sliding my gun out, I waited for the doors to open. A mirror let me see both sides of the hall as I stepped out. No movement. I hadn't seen any on the cameras, but I refused to be complacent. Unlocking the apartment, I went inside and did a full sweep before I reset the alarm and then put the gun up in the case.

I had five others secured around the apartment if I needed one. Jacket and tie off, I unbuttoned the sleeves and rolled them up on my way back to the kitchen. I needed a beer, then some food, and I should probably hit the treadmill and run but I was not in the fucking mood for it right now.

At some point, I needed to make time to look at the Warrick Foundation finances and infrastructure. Kellan planned to have Adam do it, but he wasn't available and if I asked Ezra for a favor, he might stab me at the moment.

Lid off the cold beer, I tilted the bottle up and took a long drink. It went down smooth and I drained the whole damn thing. After dropping the empty into the recycle bin, I grabbed out another. Two beers and no run.

I was living life dangerously.

Fuck it, I'd run in the morning.

Nothing in the freezer looked good. Nothing in the fridge either. If I was going to live life on the edge, I might order a pizza. Or I'd suck it up and eat what I had. Pizza meant letting someone come up.

Right.

Grabbing one of the frozen dishes out, I turned the oven on and just slid it inside. It would take a little longer, but fuck the pre-heating and fuck worrying about what it was. I'd had worse meals.

Impatience stung like nettles under my skin. The food would take time to cook. Shower, finish my beer, find something to watch… I could check the cameras at the clubhouse. Just see how she was doing.

Or I could jack off while I was in the shower. Something to get my fucking mind back here and off of Hellspawn. She was better off there and away from me. The guys kept it on solid rotation at least one, preferably two of them around at all times. We'd increased security on the perimeter and we'd be adding more.

I could add more too.

Doc had spent more nights at the clubhouse than his own apartment. Had to wonder if she'd even realized yet. I'd seen him a few times when I slipped in to check on Rome and make sure everything was secure. The nights I couldn't get there directly, I checked on the cameras. Every time, there he was. Even after they'd stripped so much out and started repairing the walls, I caught sight of him.

The new furniture was still packed out in the warehouse. Flooring needed to go down and then they'd unpack it. But between building a safe room, repairing the external and internal security flaws, and taking their sweet time on the walls, the floors just hadn't been picked out.

That reminded me. I needed to check on the lumber they needed to fix her studio. Reinforcing those walls was on the list, but from the outside in, rather than the inside out. Yeah, I'd check the cameras when dinner was ready. Rome had already checked in. I needed to call Ezra, then check in with Kel…

An alarm pinged on my phone just as I got to the bedroom. The elevator was coming up to my floor. Pivoting, beer in hand, I flipped to the cameras in the hall. The doors parted and I sighed at Rome's expression as he stepped through the doors.

My other half was on a mission. Abandoning the shower idea for now, I headed back to the living room. If nothing else, it would be good to see him. Even if he'd come because he hadn't seen *me*. The alarm disengaged and the door opened.

It was Rome. But he wasn't alone. At five foot three if she was an inch, Emersyn stepped in ahead of him. Her soft brown eyes seemed to lock on me the moment she was inside. Backlit from the hall, their shadows stretched across the room. I swore they extended until they touched me.

But it wasn't her shadow I focused on. It was the flushed color of her cheeks. They were pink from the chill outside. Someone needed to turn up the heat in their car. It was the oversized jacket she wore, clearly borrowed, maybe from Rome. Not that I recognized it so maybe one of the other guys.

Her dark hair fell in a cascade around her face and seemed to emphasize the fragility of her bone structure. It also hid the red marks left by the shock collar from view. If they were still there, I amended. A few days had passed since then.

"Hi," she greeted me, bringing my mental assessment to a screeching halt.

"Hellspawn," I said slowly, still drinking in the sight of her before focusing on my brother. "Rome. You aren't supposed to be running solo. Either of you."

"We're not," Hellspawn began but Rome just flipped me off.

"Vaughn's downstairs."

Oh.

"Starling missed you." Then without slowing, he dropped a kiss on top of her head. "I'll be back."

"Wait a sec…" But he'd already closed the door behind

him and my phone buzzed at the elevator being summoned. Fuck.

"Vaughn really is down there," Hellspawn assured me and I switched my gaze back to her. "I promise. I wouldn't risk him."

All at once, my reticence crashed to a halt as I locked eyes on her. "I know you wouldn't." She'd protected him. Rome made that clear. She'd killed for both of us now. Not that I had a single problem killing every single thing that came at her. "Neither of you need to take risks."

"I didn't think coming to see you *was* taking a risk," she retorted with a flash of a smile and then she set a bag down at the table. She brought a bag? Was she planning on staying?

"The last time someone mistook you and Rome for being you with me, the two of you got kidnapped. Tell me again how I'm not a risk?" A muscle ticked in my cheek and I had to concentrate on *not* grinding my teeth.

Stripping off her jacket, she revealed the oversized sweatshirt and dance pants she'd worn so often to our training sessions. She toed off her shoes too, leaving her in fuzzy socks, oversized clothes and looking far too damn delicate and delectable.

Then she smacked a hand to my chest, reminding me that my little hellspawn definitely had some bite in her sweetness. "Do you mind if I have a beer too? And you're not a risk because you were one of the people who came and got us. You got me from Pinetree. You got us from Brixton. Pretty sure you guys would come find me anywhere."

A smile softened her lips and she let out a little whoosh of breath as she brushed past me on her way into the kitchen.

"Most likely," I agreed with her even as my brain shouted of course we would. "But let's not test that theory any time soon, shall we?"

She glanced at me from the other side of the refrigerator door, beer bottle in hand. "Do you want another one?"

At some point, I'd drained this one, too. Fuck, I needed to get my head out of my ass. I knocked back the last swallow before dropping it in the recycle bin. She pulled out a beer and handed it to me. I knocked the lid off of it then traded it for the one she got herself and opened the second one for me.

"As for not testing the theory," she continued as she closed the door and faced me. This close, it was impossible to miss the sweet warmth of the vanilla and honey—was that honey? Whatever it was, she smelled good. Softer. The hint of citrus underscored just how fierce she could be, but it was hard to focus on that. "I'm seriously thinking about Freddie's LoJack idea. Just not sure how that would work."

"Possible, but nothing like being able to track your latitude and longitude." I rubbed the bottle mouth against my lower lip. "At least not safely. An RFID chip can help you get in and out of things without a keycard. A locator would have to be something you wore, not something we put into you— at least not until they've safely developed one that wouldn't cause long-term harm or infection."

"Oh."

She looked so disappointed, I frowned. "There are things we can do, Hellspawn."

"I just—don't want to disappear."

I don't want you to disappear either. But I didn't say those words aloud. Instead, I brushed my fingers down her cheek. They were damp from holding the bottle and left a little trail of moisture on her skin. Instead of pulling away, she leaned into the contact, and I sighed. "You won't disappear," I promised her. "I'll find something. Make sure we can always find you."

Fuck, I'd promise her anything just to chase away the

disappointment in her eyes. She gave me a little smile. "Thank you. And I'm sorry."

"For what?"

"For being all melancholy. I didn't come here to get you to fix my problems or my worries. I mean, Kel's teaching me to shoot and you're teaching me to fight. I'm learning how to drive a car. I even got on the highway." She sounded so fucking proud, I grinned.

"So why did you come?" I could have kicked myself for asking the question, but I really wanted to know. "And do you want to sit?" We were just standing in the fucking kitchen.

"In the living room? Or do you want to change?" Then she paused as she looked me over. "Were you getting ready to go out?"

"Fuck no," I said with a little more of a growl than I intended. "I just got home and yes, I want to change. Go sit down and I'll be right back."

Pivoting on my heel, I stalked out of the kitchen and down the hall to my room. I needed to get my shit together. Having her this close was not in my game plan. It was easier when she was at the clubhouse and I was here. I could check on her. Ghost through at night, make sure she and Rome were safe, then get out again.

But with her in the apartment? Opened a lot of fucking doors that I should leave closed, and fuck if I didn't want to storm through all of them. I set the bottle of beer on the dresser and stripped off the shirt, dumping it in the laundry stack on my way to the closet.

I'd planned on a shower, but that could wait. Wallet and keys went on the nightstand on my way past, and then I was losing the pants and looking for some sweats. My dick throbbed as soon as it was free and I gave it a dirty look.

Damn thing adored her. Steel hard-ons around her were

a fact of life. I gave myself a vicious squeeze to remind my dick that he wasn't in charge, then dragged on the sweats. Leaving the closet, I jerked to a halt.

She was sitting on the edge of my bed, beer in hand and looking far too young, far too sweet, and more than a little annoyed.

"Problems with the living room, Hellspawn?" I kept my voice even, but the last place I needed to picture her was on my bed especially when my dick was already all in. She had enough issues in her life, she did not need my problems.

Or any more of my problems. Especially with the king wanting to meet her.

Just… no.

"No," she answered, lifting her beer bottle. "But I want to know why you don't seem to want to see me… you told me we were okay and then… you just walked away."

Fuck.

"I get that I'm with the other guys too and maybe that's a problem for you."

I curled my fingers into the palms of my hands, flexing my fists before I forced them to relax. *None* of this was her fault.

"But I'm also worried about you…and Rome was right."

"About?" I forced the question out.

"I missed you." My chest cracked at that admission. "I *miss* you. Will you tell me what I can do to fix this?"

Kicking my own ass wouldn't make up for the hurt glimmering in her eyes. "Hellspawn… it's not you." *Liar.*

"Then what is it?"

I tilted my head back to stare at the ceiling. I needed to stop picturing how beautiful she was naked and sated. How slick her cunt would be or how fierce her grip.

"Liam…"

"I'm trying here, Hellspawn." I swore when she moved

and came to stand toe to toe with me. How the fuck was I supposed to not touch her when she was right there and so goddamn…

"Then try harder," she said, throwing down a challenge. "Yell at me if it helps. I can take it. I can take *you*."

Goddamnit.

"Don't bait me," I warned.

"Or *what?*"

I grabbed the beer to keep it from falling before I dragged her to me. "I don't want to scare you." It was the only thing stopping me *right* now.

She pressed her hands against my bare chest and I swore the cool fingers scorched all the way to my soul. "You don't scare me. I know how to drop you if I have to. You showed me."

Yes. I had. I was still turning that over in my head when she slid a hand around my nape and tugged my head down.

Fuck it.

Her lips had already parted when my mouth slammed against hers. My whole body shuddered.

She wasn't alone. I'd missed the hell out of her, too.

CHAPTER 27

EMERSYN

*W*hen Rome said he was taking me to Liam's, it had caught me off-guard. We'd spent most of the day before covered in paint and making an even bigger mess, yet somehow, the walls of the new sitting room for what would be our "apartment" I supposed was the right word was done. It was marbled on the whole front half of what was proving to be more a semicircle wall that featured the door to the rest of the clubhouse. Then the second semicircle wall boasted doors to the bedrooms.

Currently there were seven, including mine. The wall with the doors included the ocean crashing against the waves. It wasn't close to being done, but Rome had mapped it all out so I could "see" it. The spacing would be awkward if we didn't take up the full half of that floor now, especially with all the bathrooms.

They were giving me the biggest bathroom too, which I

found funny, but Vaughn kept coming by with pictures of bathtubs and other interior looks.

The craziest thing was knowing the stairs were going to be moved. I didn't even know *how* you moved stairs. The guys assured me it would be fine. They wanted to reinforce struts under the safe room anyway, so this gave them an excuse to do a lot of tearing out.

They wanted me to have everything I wanted. It was difficult to explain to them that I did have everything I wanted right now.

I had all of them. I had a home. I had a brother. I had my best friend. They were all safe... the only thing missing really was knowing *Adam* was safe. Well, not the only one missing. I missed Liam. Despite his declarations, he'd disappeared again. I hadn't been kidding when I told Kel I was worried about Liam's reckless disregard for his own life.

Apparently, I wasn't the only one. Rome had me put together the bag because he suggested we could spend the night at Liam's apartment. They were going to be tearing out a lot of walls and more, it would likely be really noisy. At least that was what Vaughn said. I wasn't sure how Vaughn was going to get back to the clubhouse on his own since everyone was taking the no traveling alone seriously until Rome dropped me off—and then left himself.

That was when his actual choice of phrases occurred to me. "You can spend the night at the apartment..." coupled with Vaughn's "while we tear out these other walls and reinforce the struts."

Rome was giving me time with Liam, something Liam had been avoiding. At the same time, Liam looked like I was the very last person he wanted to see. If that was the case, then why kiss me like he had been? Why make demands? Then just—walk away?

He blamed himself for me and for Rome. He blamed

himself for us being taken. Blamed himself for Rome being hurt. He blamed himself for a lot...

If he wanted to play the blame game, then I would just have to point out all the times he'd come for me. Hell, he'd taken a bullet for me just a scant few minutes after our first kiss. Maybe he'd forgotten. I hadn't.

All of that gave me the courage to keep pushing him, even when—no *especially* when he said, "Don't bait me."

For a moment, an all too precious moment, his own fear reflected back at me from within his blue-green eyes. The low light in his bedroom cast a lot of shadows, but that shadow shifted and moved. Self-loathing and terror, a potent combination. It was what drove me to go back to my uncle even when it was the last place I wanted to be.

The combination ended with me in Pinetree and with Freddie coming in to get me with Liam and Rome waiting for us just outside those walls.

He didn't scare me. How could he possibly scare me when he taught me to fight, taught me to protect myself, and *still* came to save us?

Heat ignited the moment his mouth fused to mine. There was no mistaking the waves of warmth that seemed to radiate off his bare skin. The tattoos that set him apart from Rome, the shadows in his eyes, and the fierceness in his expressions all told me exactly who he was. Liam had taken control of the beer bottle, so I let it go and wrapped my arms around his neck as he angled his head down to keep our lips together.

The hot invasion of his tongue sent another ripple of tension spiraling tighter through me. He tasted like the beer we'd both been drinking, but there was more to his kiss than just the alcohol. It staked a claim, demanded I let him, and in the same breath pulled at me to never let him go.

That fear in him echoed one so deep inside of me I

couldn't even put it into words. Our brothers gave us up for *better* lives and we would sacrifice ourselves to protect them and keep them safe. Scraping my nails across his nape, I stroked my hand up to his hair. The softness of it feathered over my fingers. He kept it shorter than Rome did, closer to his scalp.

Less for people to grab and yank in the ring. Some distant part of my mind cataloged those differences not to compare but because I wanted to map everything that was unique about them so I could keep it safe. I would never mistake them for each other. The simple truth was, I adored them for being who *they* were and loved everything that tied them together and set them apart.

"Fuck," he murmured against my mouth, in between invasions of his tongue that left me longing to surrender to this intoxication. I didn't need alcohol. At all. Not when I had him. "Hellspawn."

I pushed up with a little jump, holding him tighter as he took one step to the left then there was a clunk as the bottle settled on his dresser. Hitching my thighs to his hips, I got our heads level.

"Hellspawn," he repeated, running his hands over my back. Twice he dipped his hands toward my ass and both times he retreated until he'd threaded his hand into my hair, the other arm locked around me. Not even a breath of air existed between us. If anything, the temperature in the room skyrocketed.

With a gentle tug that lit up my scalp, he pulled back. Not far, just enough to let our eyes lock on each other. His lips glistened from the kiss and the faint roughness to his cheeks just added to his rugged appearance. Like Rome, he still sported some bruises, though the worst of it had healed.

"Liam?" *Please don't reject me now.* But that plea didn't leave my lips, I just raised my eyebrows as he searched my gaze, and in turn, I studied his.

"I'm not a gentle man." The husky admission sent a pulse straight to my cunt, and I flexed my thighs against him. The sweatpants didn't hide any of his erection. The heavy weight of his cock was right there.

"Okay."

A smile flashed briefly across his face. "I tell you I'm rough, I don't know if I can be gentle, and you just say, *okay?*"

"What do you want me to do? Scream and cry?" Was he for fucking real right now? "I've punched you in the nose before, remember?"

"Goddammit, Hellspawn," he swore. His hand flexed in my hair and there was just the faintest shift of his weight, the way his arm loosened. He was going to put me down.

No.

Just. No.

Locking my ankles together behind him, I dropped my hands to his shoulders, then twisted. Hoping like hell I hadn't miscalculated, I used shifting balance against him and we toppled right onto his bed, with him on the bottom and me over him. I managed to squirm my ankles out because that hurt a little, and then I stared down at him.

"If you don't want me," I told him slowly. "Then say that. If you don't want something to happen between us, then say that too. But don't try to scare me off or make me think that you don't even trust yourself with me. Because I *know* you won't hurt me."

"You do, do you?" His mouth set into a firm line. "You *know* I *won't* hurt you?"

"I do," I said, reaching for the sweatshirt and tugging it up and off. "The question is, do you know that?"

The icy finger of unease that tried to wiggle through the coils of tension sent a wave of goosebumps over my skin.

With care, he moved his hands to my hips. I swore he telegraphed every motion before he gripped me there. The guys were all bigger than me, Liam—like Vaughn—was thicker than the others. His fighting gave him a well-muscled, but trim, figure.

But you would have to be a fool to mistake any part of the corded muscles along his body for something soft. No, he was gentle because he was so strong and so aware of that strength. When I slid my fingers to the hem of my shirt, he shook his head.

Okay, I'd pushed us this far, so I paused and rested my fingers on his chest as he pushed my weight down against his dick. There was no mistaking the hardness resting right against my ass.

"Three questions, Hellspawn," he said after a prolonged moment that began to feel like he was going to tell me no, period. Pushing him was one thing, forcing him was something else.

"Okay."

He licked his lips as he thrust up once. The move didn't unseat me. If anything, his grip kept me firmly in place, but it definitely rubbed all along my clit and sent a little pulse of lust to riot through my system. Another bump and then I realized he was moving us, rather deliberately to the center of the bed, but every inch we moved involved him grinding against me.

Thighs tensing, I tried to help him with the adjustments, but that just ended up with him rolling my hips for me until my breath caught in my throat. The tension in my belly stretched out and all I wanted was more, but he kept it just out of reach until we were in the middle of his bed.

"Better."

I swallowed. My heart hammered in my ears. I was glad he thought it was better, because right now, I was definitely aching for more definitive action. Like getting naked and repeating those thrusts with no barriers.

"You had questions?" I was very proud of how steady my voice was. Very proud. He tracked my tongue when I wet my own lips, and he gripped my hips a little tighter.

I really hoped he left bruises there. I'd begun to crave those little signs from the guys. The bite marks from their hickeys. The faint imprints of their fingers. The bruises never *hurt*. Far from it they…

"Why can't I play with your ass?" The record-scratching sound of that question ripped right through the haze of desire. He didn't move his hands, but his whole attention seemed completely focused on me.

"Do you really need to know?" I swallowed around the sudden lump in my throat and the hammer of my heart.

"I need to know how to make sure I don't hurt you. If it's off limits, it's off limits. But it scared the hell out of you, Hellspawn." He paused there for a moment, before he released my hip with his right hand and brought it up to cup my face. Leaning into the contact, I let him pull me closer. "Let me fight that fear for you."

Shock danced along my nerves. "I don't know how to let you fight it…" I wasn't done but I also wasn't sure how to answer him fully. "I don't—I mean, I know why. I know what I feel and see when it happens, and it doesn't happen all the time just…just when I'm vulnerable."

I'd intended to say naked but it had happened when I'd been dressed too. No, it was when I was open or vulnerable or emotional… I frowned, but I didn't avoid his gaze.

"If I let you help me, will you let me help you?"

He raised his eyebrows. "Do you think I need help, Hellspawn?"

"I know you do."

The corner of his mouth kicked up as he stroked his

thumb along my jaw. "Then yes. You let me help you and I'll let you help me."

I almost wanted to make him pinky swear, but Liam had always been pretty straightforward with me.

"Someone hurt me once...they wanted to punish me. To teach me a lesson. And...it was very painful and I had to get stitches afterwards. Now...whenever I think about it or it feels like that's where we're going...I freak out."

His expression didn't shift, but the darkness in his eyes promised so much violence. That violence didn't scare me in the slightest. If anything, it made me feel better.

Covering his hand with mine, I moved his touch down my body until we reached my ass. Yes, I was still in clothes, but I rested his fingers there and pressed my hand over it. My heart raced, but I refused to be afraid of *Liam*. Holding his gaze, I concentrated on breathing.

"Will you tell me the name of the person who did that?" His voice was so soft, a silken promise of bloody retribution.

"Is that your second question?"

Lips pursed, he glared at me.

"Hey, it's fair, you said three questions and while the first was an icy plunge of water, I haven't forgotten what got us into this position in the first place. If being with you means answering these, then I will... I just want to know if that's the second question."

He tilted his head from one side to the other, the vertebrae cracking and I swore I could almost see him fisting his temper and wrestling it to the ground.

"I want to know." Simple and direct. "But," he continued, "I will not demand it of you. When you are ready to trust me with that name, all you have to do is tell me. No explanations required."

"Okay."

He gave my ass a very gentle squeeze. The flexion of his

fingers beneath my hand helped but my pulse leapt no matter how much I told myself he wouldn't hurt me, there was no need to be afraid.

"Second question."

I braced for it.

"Beyond your ass, is there anything else you can't stand? Anything that causes you fear or pain?"

The echo back to when Kellan asked me the same question couldn't be ignored. "I can promise you what I promised Kel."

That got his attention. "That was?"

"No pain for me. My body is mine. You have to let me give it to you if I want to give it to you. If anything hurts or scares me or I just need you to stop—all I have to say is stop." I hadn't even realized how much those words meant to me until they spilled out. None of them wanted to take anything from me I wasn't willing to give.

"Do you want to give me your body?" Nothing coy in the question. If anything, he'd asked in a low voice like he was almost afraid to voice it. Like he didn't deserve something. We really were a matched set in some ways.

"Yes," I told him, keeping it as simple and direct as his question had been. "I don't always know what will set me off, but I do know I want you. I know I care. I know—I've *missed* you so much the last few days. I don't want you to pull away, but I also meant it when I said I wasn't going to force you to do anything either."

He chuckled. "You know, Hellspawn. I was right about you."

"Were you?" I tilted my head as he slid his hand up to my shirt. When he hooked his fingers under the hem of it and lifted his brows, I nodded. He sat up so fast, I didn't even get to enjoy the ripple of his muscle as he tugged my shirt up and off, then he had my arms trapped behind me in the shirt.

I could wiggle out, but there was something so intense in the way he stared at me. "Yes, I was," he murmured. "You're not a sparrow or a dove, you might be able to be those, but you're a fighter. You're tougher than old boots, and you're willful and full of fire. You challenge me every fucking time you look at me."

My stomach went taut at that declaration. He dipped his gaze to my chest then back up to my eyes.

"And I crave you like a drug I will never get enough of. I want you in my bed all the goddamn time. I want you naked and sated. Or fierce and fighting. I just *want* you. You're the first girl my brother has *ever* wanted. The only girl who lights him up. I would rather slit my own throat than fight him, and I want you so fucking much, I actually thought about it." His whole expression tightened. "And I know the others want you. I know Vaughn and Jasper and Kell—even Freddie —they all have a claim on you."

He leaned in and ran his nose along my throat, the faint rasp of his stubble a stinging reminder that he wasn't all soft. His words. Not mine.

"I know even Mickey wants you. He's lying to himself. But I've seen the way he watches you. I recognize that hunger...I feel it myself. My life? It's not safe, Hellspawn. None of our lives are. We have enemies and our enemies have enemies. The only people we've ever been able to rely on are ourselves..."

"And for too damn long, you've been out there on your own," I said, picking up the thread. "You're not alone anymore, Liam."

"Hellspawn, the last thing I want to do is take you down with me, but I don't know if I have you if I'll *ever* be able to let you go. *That's* why I don't know if I can be gentle."

"You can't take me anywhere I don't want to go." My arms were still trapped behind me, bound by the shirt, and it thrust my chest out at him. But all he did was tease kisses along my throat, nuzzle at my chin, and then leaned back to stare at me. He brooded.

Fuck, could he brood.

"Liam...don't be gentle. I don't need gentle."

"What do you need?" The dare was there and so was the challenge.

"Right now?" I flexed my abdominals and then rolled my hips, rubbing against his erection. His pupils flared at the contact and a breath hissed out of him. "I need you."

"Tomorrow?" Oh, he wanted to up the ante.

"Think we'll be done by then?" If he wanted to play, I could play.

"Oh, Hellspawn, you should know better than to challenge me."

"Why?" I tossed out, brows raised. "I'm right here. What are you going to do about it?"

A half-growl left his throat and he pulled me forward, his hand firm on the shirt and my breasts were against his chest. "All you ever have to tell me is stop," he said. "And more. I want to know what you want. Every. Single. Thing."

Not that he gave me a chance to answer before his mouth and mine locked together again. Relief and desire collided as the very real trepidation that he'd reject me evaporated.

He was right there and it was everything.

CHAPTER 28

EMERSYN

The hunger in his kiss just left me starving for more. If I was a craving in his blood, then he was the thirst in mine. From the first moment we met, he'd managed to piss me off. No one could quite get under my skin like he could. I was delighted in the way he kept me still as he all but devoured my mouth.

The wild need to collapse into laughter or sobs or screams was just right there. Every kiss just made me want another and then another. Something in my bra snapped, and I couldn't drag my mouth off of his to check, but the fabric fell away and the heat of his palm on my breast destroyed any chill before it could register.

A groan slipped free when I twisted to the left and then the right. My hands and wrists were tangled up in the shirt. The way he fisted the fabric kept me from just pulling them away. Even if I couldn't use my hands, I had other ways to touch him.

Clenching my ass, I focused on his kiss as I began to flex and relax, gripping his cock at times as I rolled against his lap. He swore, a word I barely heard, and then I bit my lower lip. "Hellspawn, if you make me come in my pants…"

The threat dangled there and laughter, ragged and free, burst out of me. "You'll come all over the inside of them and make me clean you up?"

A sound that wasn't altogether human rumbled through him. He bit my lip hard enough to make it sting before he let it go and studied me. "Keep it up, Hellspawn."

"Keep trying to make you come?" I grinned as I rocked back and forth over his erection. Each time I rolled forward, it pulled at my shoulders because Liam kept my arms trapped, but I didn't care. Holding himself aloof or not, he couldn't hide the way he wanted me.

No, now he wanted control. He wanted to fight for it. He wanted me to take it if I could. A shiver worked its way up my spine, and my nipples went taut. I needed to know if he fucked like he fought, like he taught me to fight. Push. Pull.

Liam let his gaze drift down as I continued to rock. The pace I set wasn't fast, but it was firm. I had to clench and release all my muscles along my ass and through the inside of my thighs to keep up the pressure no matter what part of his dick I rested on.

When his eyes fixed on my breasts, I had a chance to just enjoy the way the muscles in his cheeks moved. A clench around the base of his cock made the muscles in his throat stand out. Teasing at the tip had him licking his lips.

At the first sign that his breathing shifted, I began to rotate my hips. Figure eights added a distinct amount of pressure, and I could engage my whole core into the action, keeping myself firmly in place even as I moved.

After wetting his fingers, he began to trace a circle

around one nipple. Then across the puckered surface until he'd left it damp. Then he blew, the cool breeze tightened my nipple even more and sending goosebumps racing over my skin. Abruptly, he went to his knees, and I had to clamp his hips to stay in place.

Bracing my arms firmly at my back, he lifted me with just a little tug. "Bend for me, Hellspawn, show me that gorgeous curve of your body." My cunt spasmed and clenched at that dark invitation. The shift in angle let the full weight of his cock grind against me. I needed to keep working him. "Ride me like you did the pole that day, when you showed everyone in that fucking club just how wild and on fire you are."

The change also ground my clit against the hard cord of muscle that made up his cock. It wasn't all muscle, I got that, but fuck it felt like that. At this angle, I couldn't see him but I could feel him. He nibbled, licked, and sucked along the underside of my breast. Then he bit down in one place, just hard enough for me to feel his teeth.

"Who left this hickey?" The question was a hum in my ears as I focused on teasing him and myself. I could do this, it felt so good to trust my balance and his grip. Liam wouldn't let me fall, and I pushed myself up, locking a leg around his lower back so I could change the angle. "Fuck!"

The expletive and explosion of air against my breast made me laugh. Some of it was triumph, because really getting to Liam took effort. The rest of it was just pure delight at how *good* it felt. How good *he* felt.

"Who?" The question accompanied a thrust of his hips and it didn't matter that we were both still clothed from the waist down, I felt him. Fuck, I wanted more.

"Probably Vaughn," I answered. Honestly, I wasn't sure where he was indicating at the moment.

"This one?" He bit down against the edge of my nipple, the pain and pleasure mingling into the most profoundly provocative way. It just sent another pulse from my breast to my cunt and back. The burn in my shoulders enhanced the pleasure of his breath teasing over the nipple.

"Kel," I said on a harsh exhale. "At breakfast yesterday…" Right. Making out in the kitchen while he cooked.

He kissed the spot like he wanted to soothe it then nuzzled his way to my other breast.

"This is Rome." He locked his lips around the same nipple that Rome had tormented that morning before we even got out of bed, and I bucked against the competing sensations. With my legs flexing around him, I mimed thrusting us together as I ground against him and rode him like that pole.

"How…" I panted a little trying to get the words out. "How do you know it's Rome?"

"Jasper's is on your neck, he has a thing for it." Liam pushed me upwards until we were face to face again. A vein throbbed in his forehead; his face was flushed and his eyes dark. "Doc's still in the shit house. Freddie's not marking your body in any way if he can help it. So, that left Rome… and my brother does like to tag his work."

Laughter swelled up through me. "We couldn't get all the paint off."

"I don't care," he whispered, staring at me. He loosened his grip on my arms and the shirt fell away, but he was already lowering me to the chill of his blankets. A second later, he peeled off my pants, panties, and socks all at once. One moment they were there and the next they were gone.

Honestly, I didn't care how easily he slid them away, all I cared about was the way he stared down at me. It was like he wanted to memorize everything. Then he traced his hands down my sides and settled them right over the bruises that were there.

"You don't need gentle," he whispered in a voice that bordered on wonder. A part of me wanted to respond verbally, but Liam needed something more than verbal. He needed to *know*.

Curling my right leg up to my chest, I stretched it up and then hooked it over his shoulder. He followed the line of my leg, stroking the soft skin where it joined to my hip then up my thigh to my calf.

"Showing me how flexible you are?" he teased.

"Yes," I said. "Also showing you that you can tag me anywhere you want."

"Anywhere?" He rubbed his thumb against his lower lip.

"Anywhere."

"Grip your ankles, Hellspawn. Both of them."

Push. Pull.

Challenge. Respond.

I pulled my other leg up, then gripped my ankles. It left me open and vulnerable to him. But I was safe here.

Tongue touching his lip, he whispered, "Pull those ankles to your head."

Nice. I almost grinned, but I just kept my gaze locked on him as I pulled my legs up. The burn in my arms was already gone, but the fresh burn in my legs told me I hadn't warmed up for this. But I would be shortly.

He kissed the back of one calf, then paused to brush my lips with another kiss before he went to the other leg. Then he moved to the back of my knees, the sensuous brush of his lips light as a feather but the rasp of his stubble leaving a mark that confirmed he was there.

When he got to my thighs, I swore my cunt clenched again. He paused there, just above my pussy, and blew a little breath. Hips thrusting upward, I arched my back again.

"Beautiful," he whispered, then he laved a kiss right against my cunt, his tongue thrusting in to dominate and possess me every bit as much as he had tried with his kiss to my lips. I rocked against his face as he took his time delving against me over and over until I was shaking. Then, and only then, did he move his kiss to my clit.

One vibrating thrum of his tongue and I came. My orgasm rolled over me like a storm-tossed wave and I submerged. Slickness seemed to soak out of me and he nuzzled, lapped, nipped, and sucked as I tried to not cry out. Then his hand slapped against the back of my thigh, the sting profound and it pushed a shout out of me that was half-howl, half-scream.

He rubbed my thigh slowly, massaging the heat out and he lifted his head to stare up at me. Face wet from his carnal kisses, he said, "Don't hold anything back from me, Hellspawn. You give me every fucking thing."

Then he hooked his fingers into me, plunging them in like they were his cock, and he rested his thumb against my clit. There was no patience, no gradual build up, he pushed, thrusting those fingers as he rubbed my clit. The friction took my already sensitive nub up another notch.

"Scream for me, Hellspawn. Give me every one of them."

Rebellion crashed through me. The need to make him push harder vied with the desire to give in, and somewhere in the middle, I came apart, sobbing as the first cry of release ripped out of my throat.

It was almost too much, too sensitive, but I couldn't escape his fingers as he ruthlessly pushed me to come again. Then again.

Tears on my face and my throat sore, I stared up at him as he finally eased his hand away. He stroked the back of my thighs. The intensity in his gaze raised the temperature in the room another notch.

"This okay?" One question, he asked as he stroked the back of my thigh where he'd slapped me. Was it...

"Yes," I told him, almost dazedly. "It hurt…but good."

"Good?" he repeated like he needed confirmation.

At my nod, he slapped the back of my other thigh, so close to my ass, I swore the ripples of heat spread across the cheek. He kept his gaze on me as he rubbed that thigh too, spreading out the heat. Then he did something I didn't expect.

Couldn't have.

He tilted his head and went almost flush against the comforter and he kissed the spot just below the curve of my ass. Kissed it almost reverently, then he sucked against it and left what felt like the most intimate hickey.

The shudders rocking through me were some vicious combination of pleasure and want. I was drowning in it and I wanted so much more. He straightened, and when he tugged his sweatpants down, I swallowed. The angle was perfect for me to see the angry nature of his cock as it slapped against his belly. Long, thick, and blunted at the crown. A vein pulsed along the underside of it.

His dick was so flushed with color, I swore it was almost purple. He slapped his cock against my pussy twice, just teased me as he ran his hand up and down the length.

No, not just rubbing himself. I let go of my ankles and rolled up to cover his hand on his cock with my own. It burned against my finger; the silken skin was corded tighter and harder than the muscles on his chest or arm.

The erection had to be painful and he was *squeezing* himself brutally. "Don't," I said.

"If I don't…"

"No, you don't get to hurt yourself, Liam. I can take you, in all your glory. I want you—just like this. Hot. Demanding. Pushing me. I told you I wanted to give myself to you." I slapped a hand against the center of his chest. Like every other challenge I'd ever issued to him, I had to glare up at him. Even if I was trembling from multiple orgasms and my voice shook. "Now take me, damnit."

Controlling his cock with pain? Not on my watch. Not unless it was something he truly enjoyed, but the taut expression on his face said it wasn't. In an explosion of movement, he dragged me forward and I was lining him up, and then we collided, with his cock filling me to the brink.

The stretch was right there, right at painful, and he pushed in deeper. I said I could take him and fuck yes, I did. The heat was like hot iron filling me up and lighting me from the inside.

He kissed me like he wasn't sure whether we were fighting or fucking, and we went down together on the bed. He rolled onto his back and let me take the top. His hands were everywhere. My back. My breasts. My face. Not once did he even let me up from the kiss to breathe.

Spots danced in front of my eyes, but if this was drowning then I didn't want to breathe. I rocked my hips, riding him for real, and with every twist of my hips, I wrenched another curse out of him. He clamped a hand down on my hip and slammed me downward as he pushed up.

There, right there, he nailed that spot that sent sparks through my eyes, and we were fighting to get closer. I dug my nails into his shoulder and his hair as he kept me there, and then his hand landed on my ass, palming a full cheek as he squeezed and urged me in tighter and faster.

Apprehension shivered through me and died in an explosion of heat as another orgasm wracked me.

"Look at me," he ordered as my eyes blinked closed. "Focus on me, Hellspawn. Me. You're here with me."

"Yes," I whispered before his lips fused to mine once more. Wet and aching, I sucked on his tongue as he dragged me down to slam against him. The bruising force was just fucking everything, and when he flipped us over so I was on my back and he could shift the angle, I came again, sobbing as he shuddered and then drove home once, twice more. I flexed around him, needing him to stay there, and he came in a hot rush.

Harsh panting filled the air as sound gradually returned that wasn't the hammer of my heart or the growl of his voice. He draped me, a hot masculine blanket that covered me everywhere. Gradually, the pressure of his hand on my ass was there, floating along the surface of my consciousness and I just didn't care.

It was Liam. Liam left his mark somewhere that fear had kept me captive and I liked that. I loved the feel of him filling me. Even half-soft, his cock was a heavy weight inside. Or maybe it was just Liam who was a heavy weight.

A whisper of kisses ghosted over my forehead and then down my face, and I fluttered my eyes open to find him gazing at me then kissing me gently. My eyebrows. My lashes. My cheeks. He swiped away the tears and then left the sweetest of kisses against my lips.

"I win," I murmured, happiness bubbling up inside of me.

"Do you now?" he asked in a chuckle, dragging his hands up to frame my face as he pushed up on his elbows. But he didn't leave me, he just stared down at me like he couldn't get enough.

"Yes, I do." I managed to lift a leg, though I swore every limb was loose and almost impossible to move. I stroked my foot down the back of his thigh and he chuckled. "I said I could handle you and I did."

"Oh, yes, you did," he agreed then pressed his face against my throat. Silent, he took in a deep breath like he needed to memorize my scent. "My hellspawn, full of fight and fire and fury. You consume me."

"Not yet," I said with a huff of laughter. "Give me a few

and then I will happily consume every inch of you. You know —if you're up for it."

His cock gave a definitive twitch and he lifted his head. "Oh, trust me, Hellspawn, my dick has wanted you for a long time. He's going to become your trick pony. Just lick those lips and see what happens."

Curious, I ran my tongue over my lower lip and he gave a low groaning thrust and his semi-soft dick definitely began to stiffen. I repeated the gesture as I stared into the fatness of his pupils blown wide.

"I guess we need to find out if you can handle me." I tossed in the gauntlet and his laughter rumbled out of him as did a groan, because the sound made him give another convulsive thrust.

"Hellspawn, do your worst."

Oh, I just might. His lips collided with mine and it didn't take long for me to get a second or maybe it was a third wind. Our time was only interrupted when his oven alarm went off and he carried me out to the kitchen to rescue the meal he wasn't interested in and I sucked him off in the kitchen. We barely made it to the table.

Later, the sofa.

Eventually, we made it back to the bedroom. I really had no idea of when. Only that Rome slid into bed behind me and Liam let out a grunt. I floated on a cloud of hazy pleasure, safe and secure. My whole body ached and I was already thinking about how to recover faster for the morning.

"Your cunning plan worked," Liam grumbled, he sounded almost annoyed. Almost. "Don't think I didn't see through you bringing her here and leaving."

"Good," Rome said. "She missed you."

I smiled and then Liam kissed the top of my head. "Go back to sleep, Hellspawn."

"You missed her too," Rome added.

"Yeah," was the last thing I heard Liam admit on a long sigh. "I did."

Not anymore.

No more running away.

CHAPTER 29

DOC

*T*hree things had definitely changed over the last few weeks. I wasn't keeping my nose out of the kids' business anymore. The choice to leave them to their tasks and not involve myself had been *mine*, not theirs. At least at first. Beginning with Emersyn's first appearance at the clubhouse to Milo coming home, I'd been forcing myself to face them and the choices they'd made in my absence.

Jasper's aggravation with me had escalated to dangerous levels. The kid was pissed cause I'd left. I got that. I always had. What angered him more was when I refused to come home. Returning to the Vandals, to the life course *I* had set them on, seemed hypocritical at best and downright criminal at worst.

Not that staying the fuck away had helped. They still came to me for patching up before they walked away. Freddie came looking for drugs or for help—if he came at all.

Like me, he tended to avoid those conflicts, and I wanted to help them. I wanted to help *all* of them.

Then Emersyn's presence muddied the waters even further. No eighteen-year-old, well nineteen now, should look as world weary as she did. They sure as shit shouldn't be carrying a rucksack at nearly twice her own weight because she was in the middle of a battle and she had no idea when her next supply run would be.

Honestly, her injuries from a series of assaults had been bad enough. The more I got to know her, the more I realized we'd barely scratched the surface. Even more, I wanted to dig below the surface. I wanted to climb into that hole, however deep it was, and help her get the fuck out of it.

For the first time in what seemed like a lifetime, I had made an active choice against the boys. I'd helped her to leave. That… turned into another series of problems.

A headache pulsed behind my eye as I hit the button that would roll open one of the external garage doors on the warehouse. This was the first of the changes. Not only did I have internal access again, I had my own remote, and the rats had been informed if I gave them an order—they should follow it like I was one of the Vandals.

One of.

Milo raised a hand as I backed the truck into a spot between Vaughn's and Kellan's cars. I lifted my chin in greeting. Once parked, I pulled out my bag and let myself out. I had the clinic closed this morning so I could take care of Emersyn's physical therapy. I might have to start looking for some staff to fill in for me, because I'd been closing the clinic more and more.

That, however, was a problem for later. Anyone I brought into the clinic needed to be trustworthy, not just with the patients but also with the Vandals. No two ways about it. Rats were out in force in the warehouse. They'd been making structural changes out here as well as to the club-house itself.

Starting with increased security. After seeing the war zone the whole place had become, I couldn't agree more. JD and Shaun greeted me with waves, but Shaun kept his attention on the loader as he removed pallets from one of the trucks. Shipments had been on a sharp increase over the past two weeks. If we'd needed a clearer sign that eliminating the 19Ds would remove a thorn from our sides, this was it.

"Hey, Doc," JD said as I approached. "Need anything?"

"No," I told him. "I'm good. Don't let me interrupt."

Couple more of the rats I was familiar with from the neighborhood called out greetings. There had to be a dozen or more here working. That were a lot of recruits who'd been cleared. Then again, Milo was out here supervising—so maybe they weren't cleared yet.

"Kid," I greeted Milo with an extended hand. He snorted and clasped my hand briefly in his.

"Old Man," he retorted, before returning his attention to the manifests on his clipboard. "Ivy's in the studio if you're here for her."

"You guys finished it?"

"Yep, while she was at Liam's. First thing we did as soon as the wood was in. We're still waiting on two mirrors, but we got the other two hung. The external wall is still in progress." He nodded to where the new framework stood. The whole place was going into a shell with a new steel reinforcements. Bullet proofing wasn't always one hundred percent, but after the way some of the bullets had just ripped through the walls? I was down with anything that kept the kids safer.

All of them.

"Good," I said, shifting my attention to the shipments. "Your girl with her?"

I didn't miss the quirk of his lips as a faint smile touched his face. "Yes, she is. Though I have a feeling she needs to leave again soon."

Well, that was an improvement. "Don't close your hand too tight. I get the impression she's leaving not because she wants to but because she has to."

"Yeah," he said with a sigh. "I know."

That was another change. Milo's temper had cooled. More, he seemed interested in listening and leading again, rather than just lashing out. Letting Kel take lead had done him a world of good. Now, to get him reinvested in his own life. Emersyn and Lainey might do more for him in that area than anyone else could.

"Good." I clapped him on the shoulder. "I'm going to check in with her. She's had some serious improvement, and I don't want to lose any of the ground we've gained."

"Sounds good," he said, then glanced at me. "You still pretending you're not interested in her?"

"You still pretending that her dating everyone isn't making you crazy?"

The corners of his mouth flattened. "You're still a dick."

"Sometimes." I gave his shoulder another pat then headed inside. That was another change, but it was his—not mine. He was trying to accept that Emersyn wasn't only not leaving this life, she wanted to be here. I got it. I got why he struggled. He wasn't alone in that struggle. I'd walked away from this life, and it had been both a blessing and a curse.

I'd also pushed her away, thinking it was better for her and for Milo both. Fuck knew I was too damn old for her. Most days, the age difference didn't faze me. Not with the boys. But then I wasn't almost twice their age.

Not so with Emersyn.

The interior of the clubhouse was different every single time I walked inside lately. All the renovations they'd had on hold were going full throttle. Made me wonder how much sleep any of them were getting these days. The stairs that were once in the center, and directly across from the door, had been moved. To get to them, you had to go through the ante room, to the hall, and then around.

They'd created a choke point. One that would keep any invaders from just having a direct access to the hall and the stairs. Smart. There was a secondary door inside; the security wasn't fully hooked up yet, but it would require a code and not a key to open it. The engineering and programming for it was interesting. The cost though...they were investing a lot and it was going to cut into their capital sooner or later.

Alphabet could probably do the job cheaper, but I had a feeling that the funds weren't just coming from the Vandals' financial resources, but Liam's as well. He would spare no expense where his brothers were concerned, and Emersyn's presence just meant more to all of them.

The camera in the corner was a nice touch. It tracked my passage from the first door to the second. The interior walls had been sanded and cured. Half of them were painted. Rome had begun work on a wall painting in the new living room. I didn't even have to guess at the subject matter. I recognized her silhouette as she twisted in the silks. It was far from complete, but she would be right there for them to look at every day.

Vaughn glanced up from where he was working on wiring for the new television. "Hey Doc, Dove's still dancing."

"That's what Milo said." The scent of fresh coffee underscored the paint. "How long has she been at it?"

With a quick check of his watch, Vaughn said, "A little under an hour. She promised to not overdo it because she had physical therapy today."

"Good." Getting her to commit to *not* hurting herself as

she trained was not a simple matter. In fact, I'd barely gotten her to agree to *try* and not overdo it. *No promises, Mickey. I have to be able to do this.*

Leaving Vaughn to his work, I headed down the hall toward her studio. Another set of doors was going in here. Lockdown doors. If necessary, they had an escape hatch that would let them get out through the top. One, I knew for a fact, she'd already availed herself of.

Every ingress and egress was being taken into account. The last few weeks had contained far too many close calls. I'd give the boys credit, they rarely ever took a black eye without learning where and how the hit came from. Then they didn't take another one, not easily.

At the door to her studio, I knocked and then waited. It took two knocks before the door opened and Milo's girl stood there with a grin. "I win! Your physical therapist is here," she said with a droll look at me. "She's been dancing for an hour. She literally just took a break."

Did I look that fierce that she needed to defend my little bit? I nodded. "Good. You staying for PT, or is she up for doing it on her own?"

"I'm good," Little Bit called from inside. The smell of sweat in the studio mingled with the fresh scent of sawdust and paint. "Lainey's got to shower anyway."

"I can wait," her friend argued, shooting a look over her shoulder before she opened the door wider for me. "I know this sucks for you."

Inside, I found Little Bit sitting on the floor, legs spread as she stretched. Sweat soaked her hair, which was pulled up into a messy bun, and her flushed face was still pink from exertion. All of that said, there was a real smile on her face, and it didn't darken or vanish at the sight of me.

That was the third change and probably the one I was most grateful for. I'd gone out of my way to hurt her, and I'd succeeded. It had pushed her even further away than she'd been when we first met and left a chasm that gaped wide open with nowhere to cross safely.

"I'm fine," Little Bit told her, glancing at me. There were fresh hickeys on her neck, and the dip of her shirt showed off one near the curve of her breast. Signs of her shared passion with the boys. Marks they left on her. It aggravated me on one level and enticed me on another.

For now, I throttled all of that back. I was here to *help* her and to earn her trust back. Throwing down demands would not help either of us. Milo's comment about her being at Liam's registered. How long had she stayed with Liam? I hadn't seen her in three days, but she'd promised she had been stretching and doing her exercises.

"Uh huh," Lainey said before she gave me a hard look. "Be nice. She's tired. They haven't been letting her get a lot of sleep."

"Lainey!" Emersyn chided her and I had to bite back a laugh. Controlling the reaction was simple enough. For now, I just focused on her best friend and the faint shadows under her eyes.

"Well, I'll make sure to mention to Milo you're worried about how much sleep the two of you are getting."

Her nostrils flared and her eyes narrowed, but it was Little Bit's reaction I enjoyed more. Real laughter escaped her, and then Lainey just shook her head and muttered, "Ass," before she stalked out of the room and closed the door behind her.

Point to me.

I crossed the floor to where Little Bit rested on the mat and slid my bag to rest on the ground, then studied her. "Should I apologize?"

"To me or to Lainey?" Her eyes were brighter than they had been in a while, and the tension in her expression was absent. Even the shadows that so often plagued her seemed to be gone.

"Either?" I peeled off my coat and set it off to the side before I slid down to sit on the mat with her. I didn't have her flexibility, my left leg definitely didn't bend with as much ease, but I could make it work.

"I don't need an apology and she'll be fine. She's just protective."

"And you are still working out your feelings about me." That last wasn't a question. When she came back from Pinetree she really didn't want anything to do with me, much less letting me treat her. I understood and I deserved the sting.

"I'm feeling better about you," she admitted, and that surprised me more than her admission that she didn't need an apology.

"Really?"

"Mickey…" Yes, she said my name with a huff of impatience, but it was my name and the impatience was much better than the upset or the stress. "You apologized and more…you've been patient and haven't pushed. Maybe we don't have the friendship we had in the beginning."

No, and that was my fault. Yet, when I held out a hand, she set her right hand in mine, wrist facing up so I could get a good look at the scar.

"But maybe we can build something better?" The question caught me off guard.

"Maybe," I said slowly.

"We don't have to," she inserted quickly. "I mean if that's not—"

I gripped her wrist lightly, then pressed a finger from my free hand against her lips. "We don't have to do anything, Little Bit," I assured her, "but I would like the chance to build something better."

With a gentleness that seemed as much a part of her as

her temper, she pressed a kiss to my finger. "Then we do this one day at a time."

"I can work with that. For example, maybe you can tell me how you're doing." I searched her eyes. "For real."

"Because I've been so dishonest before." Just a hint of reproach before she smiled and then caught my finger and pulled it from her face. She lifted her chin toward her arm. "They don't hurt as much. I did two handstands this morning, and before you yell at me... watch?"

I squeezed her wrist once and let her go. "All right."

With a flash of a smile, she rolled up to her feet. The speed and balance seemed almost effortless, yet the flexion of muscle and the fact she was building muscle again decried that. I leaned back to observe and keep a leash on any reactions. Three steps back away from me, she bent backwards.

Her whole body went into an arc as she planted her hands against the floor. She didn't fall at all; if anything, she utterly controlled the angle, arch, and descent so that instead of just landing, she pressed her hands against the floor like a body was supposed to bend that way.

She held that position for a long moment, and then she began to push up with her arms. If I hadn't been watching for it, I might have missed the trembling, but she was slowly lifting her legs up and shifting her entire center of gravity until she was in a perfect handstand, and she held it.

Sweat slid down her arm. It was effort, a lot more effort than it appeared, but she was doing it. I clenched my hand into a fist, resisting the urge to tell her to stop or to let it go. It couldn't have been more than sixty seconds, but she held there in a perfect handstand, her lithe body in total alignment, and there was no mistaking how much of her musculature she'd already reclaimed.

Then she completed the full arc by swinging her legs down to the floor and standing up. Flushed, a little breathless, and beaming, she met my gaze. The absolute delight radiating off of her silenced any objection I wanted to make. She was so damn proud of herself.

Proud and full of life.

"That was beautiful," I told her the unvarnished truth. "You take my breath away, Little Bit."

Her eyes grew brighter and she bounced back over to where I sat and dropped into the easiest criss-cross. So much elasticity she'd reclaimed, but I could hear her now...

"It's not perfect," she declared, almost on cue, "but so much better than I've been, and I know you don't want me overdoing it."

"I just don't want you to hurt anymore."

"Sometimes I need the pain."

That part I hated more than anything else. "But within reason," I cautioned and she held out her arm to me again. I clasped it, studying the angry flush to the scars. The muscles beneath my fingers twitched, and I stroked my thumbs along the scar on either side. She'd definitely warmed up and her skin was almost as hot as it was soft.

"Mickey?"

I glanced up to find her watching me.

"Sometimes, I really do need the pain." The repetition of her earlier statement wasn't lost on me. "Not because I want it—though sometimes I do."

I turned those statements over in my head. "Okay. Can you explain that for me? I want to understand."

She tilted her head back, her gaze locking on the ceiling. I kept my attention on her. There were times when her youth struck me almost speechless. Other times, her maturity and grasp on the darker aspects of life snuck in and ambushed me. This was a time when both left me on uneven footing.

The need to protect her was almost visceral, just like the

298

need to take care of her. But sometimes, doing nothing was the right choice. It was also the hardest choice of all.

"Training is demanding, and it can be painful when learning a new routine or recovering from an injury. But it's the fatigue, the real, bone-deep fatigue of pushing yourself to the limits and not only surpassing the limit but achieving the movement you weren't sure you could do."

That, I understood. "Endurance."

"Yes," she said, then she smiled as I began to increase the pressure to massage the tissue around the scar. It had grown looser and looser with every workout. Long term, the scar tissue would be there, but we could keep it from becoming so dense and incapacitating. "That's part of it. Part of it is the freedom in the movement. Knowing I *can* do it."

"Like climbing up a wall in the middle of a firefight?" I hadn't missed that story.

Her grin practically glowed as it grew wider. "Exactly. I didn't even think about it, I just did it. They needed a place to fall back and we couldn't get inside, but there were windows open above."

"You know, some people would call that risky behavior."

"Yes," she agreed with me, "but I would argue that I've been at risk for as long as I've been alive, and there's freedom in climbing and flying. I'm safer up there than I am just about anywhere else…except maybe here."

Maybe here.

"Little Bit…"

"Don't ask," she whispered. "I know you want to. All of you do. You all know bad things happen. I can't keep that part a secret anymore. But I'm not ready to tell you yet."

Which meant she wanted to tell me. That had to be enough for now. Because that was what she needed. "I can be whatever you need me to be."

She scooted forward abruptly and I stopped the massage.

"What if I don't know what that is? What if I don't know what I need yet?"

"Then we can handle that, too," I promised. It was an oath. One I wouldn't break. "When you're ready… tell me. I'll be here."

"Do you want to watch me dance next time? See if I'm doing anything that might hamper my recovery?"

I had no idea what it cost her to make that offer, but there was a hope in her eyes I could not ignore. "I would love to see you dance. But let's focus on physical therapy for now."

Maybe I could talk her into a massage. I was already working her arms, but if she kept pushing herself, we'd need to work on her shoulders and back.

"Deal," she said and I grinned as she parked herself right in front of me; her knee touched mine and I had to stretch my legs a little wider to make sure she could sit comfortably. "I have a weird question though."

I chuckled. "Hit me."

"Do you think there are kids who come to the clinic that would want to learn how to dance?"

CHAPTER 30

EMERSYN

*T*he only place besides my studio I would escape to stretch in was the new sitting room. We'd made so much progress and the downstairs living room was almost habitable again.

The guys had played pool on the new table and Freddie declared the sofa needed some breaking in, so he crashed on it for a nap. Milo and Lainey played one team at pool against Vaughn and Kel.

It entertained me so much, especially when Mickey showed up and put five on Milo and Lainey. I had to take the bet 'cause Kellan and Vaughn. Jasper and Rome wandered in at one point with food. I had no idea where they'd found the burgers, but the meal was probably the most amazing thing ever.

It was also messy.

I was in a full split and lying on my right leg, perfectly flush to it. The two days at Liam's reminded me that I really needed to keep up on my flexibility. He was a very capable partner.

A little shiver went through me. The food and Rome had both been distractions for the fact Jasper had not only been up and out of bed, but he'd been out of the clubhouse and warehouse altogether.

That was a good sign, right?

I'd meant to ask but sometimes when we were all together, I just wanted to soak in all of them just being there. That nearness. The teasing. The comments. It was— refreshing and safe. Even the disputes…

Straightening, I shifted and leaned over to lie flush against my left leg. Okay, not all of the disputes. Jasper and Milo weren't trying to kill each other anymore. That was the best.

Kellan kept a watch over all their discussions. Each time it began to get heated, he would slide in and manage it. I don't think they'd noticed. To be fair, I hadn't, not at first. Then again, maybe they were like me and appreciated the way he could defuse their tempers.

It was so sweet. I was *very* aware that there were still issues. Issues with who had taken Rome and me. Issues with their business. Issues with the head of the Royals. All of those were still out there, but the guys never brought it up around me. Kellan answered my questions when I asked. They all did.

Now anyway.

But these discussions were rarely had around me. They had to be having them. Were they protecting me or protecting themselves?

Maybe both?

I couldn't fault them any more than I could fault Freddie when he greeted me each morning with how many days sober he'd been. That was not an easy journey.

None of us had easy journeys, so I could hardly refuse them the quiet time. Not when I craved it, craved the safety of all of them together. I desired the warmth of their friendship and the very real sense of family they'd built together.

A family they were wrapping around me. Not just my brother. Sometimes it overwhelmed and I didn't know what to do with it, and other times, I resisted the urge to pinch myself lest all this prove to just be a dream.

I sighed, exhaling a long breath.

A slight cough had me lifting my gaze to the door.

"Is it that bad?" Jasper leaned against the doorframe, still clean-shaven and looking sharp. He had on a new shirt from the looks of it, or at least freshly pressed. It was dark gray, just like his eyes, and tucked into jeans with his boots on, and he looked—amazing.

Honestly, he looked pretty good when he was in filthy clothes, too, but I did like his look.

"No," I said as I straightened up and then leaned forward to bring my torso flush with the floor. With my legs extended out to either side, this added a burn to my quads, my hamstrings, and my back.

It also felt fucking amazing because the burn didn't hurt. The heat in my muscles was exactly the sensation I'd been reaching for since I started putting myself back through my paces.

I was preparing for a show that might never happen, but I enjoyed the act far too much to take a break from training. Honestly, I enjoyed the idea that I *could* train at my pace without interruption or worry that I would be called back "home."

"It's not bad at all, just… thinking about a lot of things."

"Yeah?" he said, pushing away from the doorframe and making his way into the room. He moved much easier, the stiffness in his posture had definitely decreased. "What are you thinking about that makes you sigh like that?"

The new flooring had been put down here, but we still hadn't moved in any furniture. Jasper came closer to where I sprawled stretching and dropped to a crouch. I pushed up on my hands and met him halfway. The kiss was gentle, a caress more than a lingering touch.

His breath had a bit of tobacco in it, but mostly just tooth-paste. He'd barely smoked throughout his recovery. Actually, I don't think he smoked at all save for one day. When he tugged my lower lip, I tried to grin, and then he lifted his head.

"Just—thinking about all of you and the clubhouse and the changes and what we all need to do."

"That's a lot."

"I'm crazy about a lot of guys." The admission slipped out and Jasper's grin grew a little wider.

"Yeah?"

"Yeah."

"I'm one of them, right?" The growl of possession in his voice sent a shiver right through me. Even if I wanted to tease him, I wouldn't.

"You're definitely one of them. You kidnapped me first, after all." Okay, so I could tease him a little.

His mouth opened then snapped shut with a little click of his teeth before he chuckled. "I love you."

That would never get old. "I adore you," I responded. "I don't know if I even have the words for how much I adore you."

"You only need to tell me one word."

"Which word is that?"

"Since our last date was cut short and I've been laid up for a while…"

"And I disappeared?"

"Again," he reminded me with a stern look, but it barely touched the softness in his eyes. "I'd prefer to know where you are, even if it's just 'gone to Liam's, back in a couple of days,' you know?"

"Okay, to be fair," I said as I sat up, and when he rose and held out a hand, I let him help me up. He pulled me right to him and then cupped my face in his hands. "That was Rome's plan, not mine and I didn't mean for it to be two whole days. Not that I'm apologizing for it. I did text."

"Yes, you did," he said, a grin slowly curving his lips, "but I think I want to steal you away for a couple of days at some point. Fair is fair."

Okay, a little thrill went through me. "When it's safe," I said. "When you guys aren't so worried about security. Then we can do anything you want."

"Oh, that's an open-ended promise, Swan. I like that." He kissed me. "Speaking of promises...I want a second chance at our first date."

"Second date," I reminded him. "I know you don't think of our night at the resort..."

"Oh, I think of it all the time," he said with a chuckle. "Fine, a second chance at our second date. You and me?"

Before I could respond, Freddie stuck his head in from the hall. "Hey, I didn't mean to eavesdrop, though I was listening to make sure I wasn't walking in at some inappropriate sexy times."

"Are there appropriate sexy times?" I had to ask, leaning to the side to grin at Freddie around Jasper. I didn't have to lean that way for long. Jasper slid an arm around me to tuck me to his side as he pivoted to face Freddie.

"Well, anytime with you Boo-Boo, that's totally appropriate. But I don't know all the kinky shit the guys are into, so maybe it would scar me for life, you know?"

He was and wasn't teasing in the same breath. "I promise," I said, holding up my left hand. "All the freak is with me."

"Oh, well that's totally cool then." He grinned and I laughed. Jasper just shook his head, a look of exasperated affection on his face.

"You were saying?" Jasper prodded him. "You didn't mean to eavesdrop, but you did?"

"Absolutely. You mentioned a date. Since I was a part of the last date, inadvertently or not, I thought we could plan ahead and just let me go with you guys. Kind of a double-date." He gave Jasper a sly look. "Cause you know Kel said we don't go out alone, and if Boo-Boo goes, at least two of us are with her at all times."

Oh, now I hadn't heard that last part.

"Sneaky," Jasper said with a hint of admiration.

"I try," Freddie said with a grin. "Besides, I do amazing dates. There's that new carnival that just came to town. It's over at 50th and Madison. You know that would be a riot. Jasper and I can compete for who gets you the best stuffed animal."

I had to bite my lip because while that sounded fun, I wasn't so sure of a huge crowd at a carnival. That could have hidden danger. Easier for people to sneak up on us 'cause they could hide in the throngs.

"Or," Jasper said conversationally, "we can go to one of the nicer restaurants like that five-star place at the Peabody."

"Five stars?" I asked. "Some big chef name?"

"Yes," Jasper replied, glancing at me. "Not a fan?"

"Their portions are terrible. But the food is usually amazing. They also require suits most of the time." I shot a look at Freddie.

"I have a suit," he declared. "It's even a respectable color." The edge on his retorts was a little sharper than usual. I held out my pinky finger and he moved over to hook his pinky with mine. I swore I could feel the tension leaking out of him.

"I'd rather go somewhere fun, where we can just be us, and if Jasper doesn't mind, I'd love it if you went. If he does..."

"He doesn't," Jasper said before I finished. "Freddie is always welcome. Provided he doesn't start any fights."

"Boring," Freddie said with a flash of a genuine grin, but I didn't miss the gratitude he cast toward me, or the relief. "I won't *start* any fights, good enough?"

"Can I start a fight?" I mean, if we were setting rules and boundaries.

Jasper groaned. "How about we take a pass on starting any fights, but we absolutely wreck anyone who starts it with us?"

"That's like, almost reasonable, Hawk," Freddie said, hand to his chest. "Like, way too reasonable for you. Have you been replaced by a pod person?"

All at once Jasper let out a laugh and instead of responding to Freddie, he glanced down at me. "That gives me an idea."

"It does?" Freddie and I asked in the same breath.

"Absolutely. Jeans, t-shirts, and jackets, kids. Or just pajama bottoms and sweats, make sure you're comfortable." He checked his watch. "I'm going to call Kel, but I think we're moving our date to tonight."

He gave me a kiss and then headed for the door.

"Jasper?"

He glanced back at me.

"Where are we going?"

"You'll see. Go get ready, both of you. Also, grab some blankets."

After he was gone, I glanced at Freddie and he blinked almost owlishly back at me. "Any ideas?"

"Not a single one," Freddie said. "Pod people gave him the idea."

"Aren't pod people from some alien body snatching movie?"

"Yep," he said with a slow nod. "Pretty sure he's already snatched your body a few times, so that's not it."

I elbowed him and he chuckled. Just as swiftly, the humor evaporated from his expression and he stared at me.

"Are you sure you don't mind? I mean, I kind of invited myself and yes, we aren't supposed to let you go out without at least a couple of us with you. At the same time, we could make it work where it was just you and Jas if you wanted."

"Freddie," I said, facing him. "I would love for you to go with us. We've all been so busy and I haven't gotten to spend as much time with you. I also know you're worried about Jasper, he's starting to do more."

And he wasn't one hundred percent healed.

"Yeah," he admitted. "You're also not LoJacked yet."

I didn't roll my eyes because I absolutely agreed with him. "No, and I have no intentions of going away willingly without some or all of you with me."

That reminded me.

"We should make sure we take a gun. And I need to remember to take my knife, though I don't think I'll ever be as good as you." That was such a weird thing to say.

"Armed is good. I got the knife, you get the gun."

"What does Jasper get?" I asked.

"A bat," Jasper answered from the door. "Will you two move your asses? We need to hit the road."

Oh, he meant *right* now.

I brushed a kiss to Freddie's cheek, and he squeezed my hand and then I hurried toward the door where Jasper caught me up and gave me a very real, toe-curling kiss before he let me head down the hall toward Vaughn's room. I thought that was where most of my clothes had ended up. Kel's were in Jasper's, and I wasn't sure where we'd put Rome's.

"How fast do I need to be?" I called over my shoulder as Vaughn stepped out of the room ahead of me and grinned.

"You do not have time to fuck Vaughn," Jasper said firmly. "Shower by yourself."

I laughed.

Really laughed. Then Vaughn flipped Jasper off and I laughed harder.

Okay, this was already fun.

CHAPTER 31

EMERSYN

$\mathcal{I}$nstead of taking Jasper's car, we took a bigger SUV. The Vandals had been adding the bigger vehicles to their collection the last few weeks. The cars were still in the warehouse, but more SUVs were coming in, and I didn't think all of them were Liam's.

My body still hummed from Vaughn joining my shower, despite Jasper's declaration in the hall. Or maybe because of it. We made it *quick*, but the things Vaughn could do left me buzzing. Besides, I still had to wash my hair, and like I'd told him, that always took a little extra time.

Lucky me.

Sitting cross-legged in the backseat, I caught Jasper's glance in the rearview mirror. It was brief, because he had to pay attention to the drive. Freddie had offered to sit in the back, but I told him to sit up front after I lost rock, paper, scissors to him, with his rock breaking my scissors.

Jasper had just laughed at both of us. Kellan showed up as

we were getting in the car and I got a lovely, warm, and utterly toe-curling kiss goodbye. Then he murmured, "I want a date night, Sparrow. Let's carve some time out together."

Sold.

With so much going on, I wanted to take advantage of any opportunities. The look Kel and Jasper shared before we left, though, worried me more than comforted. They were still deeply worried about everything, but they were working to *not* be. Perhaps that was my wishful thinking.

Still, I'd sent texts to Rome and to Liam, neither of whom were at the clubhouse when we left so they'd know I was going out and that I had my phone. I debated sending one to Mickey, but he didn't seem to follow the same rules as the rest of the guys.

Lainey, at least, had been in the living room with Milo when we came down. They were in the middle of some silent argument, so I gave them both quick hugs and a kiss then escaped. Staying out of their relationship was so much harder than it should be.

"Boo-Boo," Freddie said, half-twisting in the seat to look at me. "You need to turn that frown upside down. You look like you're on the way to an execution rather than a date."

"You warm enough back there?" Jasper asked, and that did make me chuckle. Because I also had blankets back here.

"I'm fine," I said. "I was literally just wondering if I should text Mickey or not. I told Rome and Liam we were going out. Vaughn and Kellan know. I saw Milo and Lainey before we left. I'm trying to not worry anyone."

"Hey, Freddie," Jasper said. "Want to send Doc a text and let him know we're out for the evening?"

"Not really," Freddie said with a playful smirk. "But I will."

I giggled. "Thank you, Freddie."

"You're welcome, Boo-Boo. Now, Jas, should we discuss

how you behave on a date or do you think you have that covered?"

Jasper didn't even slow down to lift his middle finger and flip Freddie off. They both grinned and I laughed for real before I shook my head.

"See, Boo-Boo likes it. We learned a lot about being open about our needs."

"I thought that was being open about how we would kill someone," I pointed out and Freddie's grin grew wider.

"Yes," he agreed with an enthusiastic nod, "But dating? Killing someone? It's kind of all the same. You know?"

I tried to imagine how the two would parallel. "I guess you need a plan for both."

The fact Jasper groaned amidst his laughter definitely didn't discourage me.

"Though killing someone doesn't require all participants to be willing." The fact I could even joke about this and at the same time be perfectly serious didn't seem remotely odd to me.

Not anymore.

"Okay, that's true." Freddie scratched his jaw. "But we're going on this date blind."

"No we're not," I countered. "Jasper asked me out and I said yes; you asked to come along and we both said yes."

"We don't know where we're going…" He slid a look at Jasper, but nope, I wasn't going to help them pick on each other.

"But we're going *with* Jasper," I argued and Freddie laughed. "So I'm *already* having a good time."

"Oh man, Boo-Boo." Freddie mock pouted. "You gotta make him work for it."

"Are you two quite finished?" Despite his own growl, Jasper's expression was far from angry. It seemed way more like exasperated amusement.

Freddie and I shared a look before we chorused, "Nope."

We made it another half mile, if that, before Freddie glanced back at me. "Wanna make a bet on where we're going?"

You know... I kind of did.

"Nope," Jasper said, putting his foot down. It was kind of hot. He pinned me with a look in the mirror. "There will be no betting of any kind. This is a date. We're going. We're gonna have fun. You two will like it."

"Well," I mused aloud. "When you put it that way..."

Freddie cracked up and Jasper wasn't far behind him. As it was, we didn't have to wait that long to find out where we were going. While I was still learning to navigate the city, I knew we were a considerable distance outside of it because the streetlights were larger and farther apart.

They were more muted, too. We passed a lot of sleepy subdivisions, lit up but off the highway. More than a few huge chain box stores too. I kind of wanted to go shopping in one. I couldn't really remember the last time I even went to one.

Maybe in the early days of touring before the show started performing for sold-out crowds. Back when we still traveled in a huge caravan. Even when I had my own car because my uncle insisted, we still stopped with the group.

Jasper's destination, however, was *not* a big box store but rather a drive-in movie theater.

"For real?" Freddie gawked as we pulled up and Jasper paid for the car. Apparently, you didn't pay for passengers, just the vehicle.

"Yes," he said with a wry look. "Swan enjoyed the film, and this also gives us a certain amount of privacy and anonymity. So keep the smart-ass comments to yourself."

I leaned forward and stage-whispered, "Or whisper them to me so you don't explode trying to not say them."

Freddie's grin was so wide, I couldn't help but smile back.

"You're not helping," Jasper accused me with a laugh.

"She's helping *me*," Freddie argued even around his own chuckles. It was silly and freeing in the same breath. Also, just, *normal*. What had Jasper said that night we went out the first time? This was what dating was supposed to be? Spending time together?

Why couldn't I remember it exactly? Granted, it had been more of a feeling that lingered with me than the actual words. The rest of the night *after* the movie had been drenched in blood and violence.

Shivering, I dragged the blanket a little tighter around me. Tonight was not going to end that way. I had a bag at my feet that included a gun *and* my stapler. I hadn't taken it out in a while and tonight just seemed a good time for it.

That reminder also helped soothe some of my nerves. Once we'd paid, Jasper pulled into the drive-in. I don't think I'd seen one outside of the movies, so I tried to focus on the location. There were huge projector screens, at least three by my count. We were at the third one. While I could see the lights flickering from the other two, I couldn't make out what was playing. Jasper took us around to a spot then checked the area before he parked us.

Twisting in the seat, I looked for what he was checking. Behind us were trees, and the building with concessions was off to our right. We weren't centered on the big screen but more off to the left of it, but I didn't think it would hurt our angle.

We were also farther back, which meant we could see the cars between us and the screen. There weren't more than a dozen. None of the cars were near us.

"You need to hit the restroom, Swan?" Jasper asked and I blinked slowly as I refocused on him. "We're going as a group and coming back as a group."

I wrinkled my nose, but that also seemed to make sense. "I think I'm fine."

"You are fine, but he wants to know if you need to pee," Freddie teased and Jasper gave him a smack against the back of the head. It definitely didn't look like it hurt and Freddie just laughed.

"I don't need to pee either, but if you guys do, we can go make our single trek."

Because I got it. Everything with caution, then we could have fun.

"Actually..." Freddie said. "That's a good plan."

So, leaving my blanket behind but dragging on Jasper's heavier coat which he told me to put on, I climbed out to follow them to the bathroom. Jasper had a jacket on, a lighter one, and he was definitely armed.

I didn't doubt Freddie had his knife. When we got to where the bathrooms were, I ducked my head inside the girls' and said no one was in there. Then Jasper made a sweep of it before he came back and out and waved me in.

Overkill?

Maybe. But I was with Freddie on this one. I was really tired of vanishing, and I meant it when I told Liam I didn't want to disappear. My phone buzzed while I was washing my hands and I didn't check it until I was back out where Freddie and Jasper awaited me. I didn't ask if they'd peed and they didn't offer.

The message was from Liam with instructions on how to turn on my location on the phone. I switched to that screen, then turned it on and shared it with all my contacts, which was all the guys and Lainey.

I got a thumbs up from Liam and a quick series of thank-yous from the guys.

Jasper checked his phone and then grinned at me. "Can't hurt," he agreed without me even asking. Once we were back in the car, they turned the radio to whatever we had to listen to for the movie, then Jasper pushed their seats back so they could sit in the back with me, but if he had to, he could slide right into the driver's seat.

It meant shifting the gun and the stapler, but I'd rather curl up between them anyway. Jasper surprised me with a huge cooler in the back that included snacks, drinks, and popcorn.

"It's not hot," Freddie said as he opened the bag. "But it's caramelized and it's even better." He popped a couple of pieces up to my lips and then hesitated.

I didn't. I just opened my mouth and let him feed me. They were sweet and crunchy. "I love popcorn," I confessed after I washed down those bites and Jasper chuckled.

"Now she tells us."

"You never asked before." I was tempted to elbow him playfully, but I was far too aware of his injury to even attempt it yet. He was doing *so* much better. I wanted to keep it that way.

We were halfway through testing the different candies and sorting out the best way to be comfortable—it ended with Jasper and Freddie sprawling a little to the side and me stretching out in the middle, with my legs up on the console, ankles crossed.

We had the blanket over all three of us and snacks where we could all reach—that meant I got all the popcorn. Not that I needed to do more than let Freddie feed me a piece in between each time he took a bite.

It worked for us.

"What are we watching?"

"Hang on…" Jasper pulled out his phone, then flipped to a screen as first a couple of commercials followed by previews began to play on the screen.

"It's an eighties double-feature," he said. "Thought you'd like them."

He held up his phone so I could see it.

Dirty Dancing and Flashdance.

Dance movies.

I laughed. Freddie squinted around me at Jasper and then said, "You know, I kind of want to tease you for chick flicking it, but I don't think *I* have seen those."

"Good," Jasper said. "They're not bad and it's not about us. It's about Swan."

"Bullshit," I retorted, then flicked popcorn at Jasper who caught it with his mouth, then raised his brows at me. "It's about *us.* I want to be here with you guys and having fun. If you aren't going to enjoy the movies…"

"Easy, Swan—though now I'm starting to think I should call you Tiger." The teasing worked, but I still showed him my teeth and clicked them at him like I was taking a bite. "I am going to have a good time because I am *with* you. Okay?"

I considered it, then leaned over to press a kiss to his lips in apology. "Very okay."

Next to me, Freddie let out a low whistle, "And he slides in with the save folks, but can Hawk keep it up or will Boo-Boo take him down in the final round?"

We both threw popcorn at Freddie, but his grin was absolutely unrepentant. It was also the best. The rest of our date, and our night, was perfect. Freddie talked all the way through the movies, his snarky commentary making them even funnier in places. Especially when he and Jasper started adding dialogue. I was still grinning when we got back and went to bed.

So much fun.

CHAPTER 32

KELLAN

"*W*here's Dove?" Vaughn asked as he and Milo carried in another load of flooring. We'd been wheeling it all in, in stages, but we were ready to start getting it down in the bedrooms upstairs and the safe room now that the plumbing was done.

Not my favorite task to do, but we had a neighborhood plumber who was like family and he'd brought in the guys he trusted, with us working with them, and we'd gotten everything sorted with the last set of pipes running and new water heaters.

We'd added a secondary set of emergency water for the safe room specifically that was not accessible from anywhere *outside* the clubhouse itself. The plans were complicated, but the more we added, the more it reinforced our position.

Right now, I wanted a citadel.

"Dancing," I told him. "She and Lainey are probably also having some girl time." Milo grunted at that and I hid a smirk. I liked that she made him happy. As long as none of it made Sparrow unhappy. "Liam will be here in fifteen with electronics, so we're having a meeting while we're all in the same place for longer than fifteen minutes."

"All of us?" Milo asked as he waited for Vaughn to get his haul up the stairs before he turned the hand truck and began to haul his up there.

"Yep. Doc will be here—" A door opened and I jerked my thumb toward it. "Now."

The scent of garlic bread and Italian came with him. "I stopped at Lucretia's," Doc called. "She sent you guys three baskets of your favorite breadsticks."

"Nice," Milo said as he cleared the top and I turned to give Doc a hand, but he had the giant paper bags in hand and carried them into the kitchen.

"Did we do something right?" I had to ask as I rolled up my sleeves.

After sitting the large bags on the table, he stripped off his jacket. His hair was damp. Had it started raining? I didn't think I'd been out of the warehouse today. I had to go over our accounts and that took a while. It also gave me a headache, but I made Freddie help and for all his bullshitting at times, the kid was damn good with numbers.

"They're butt prints," Freddie said as he walked into the kitchen backwards, gesturing at Vaughn. "Tell me they aren't."

"I'm not telling you that," Vaughn retorted with a shake of his head as he went to the fridge. "The food smells good, Doc, thanks for grabbing it."

"What looks like a butt print?" Doc asked.

"I come with beer and flowers," Liam called as he came in. "Where's Hellspawn?"

"She's dancing," Jasper answered from a bit further away.

"But she definitely likes expensive beer, if you got that for her?"

"Fuck off," Liam retorted, but there was a laugh in his voice.

"Fuck my life," Milo muttered on his way into the kitchen.

"You had to ask him that," Vaughn commented to Doc, but I was more than a little curious.

"What did he ask?" Milo peered into the bags. "Lasagna. Nice, Mickey."

"Thought you'd go for that. There's salad in there too, so maybe put that in the fridge and I got the chicken parmigiana Little Bit likes."

Liam scowled. "We need to add more carbs to her diet. She doesn't have to be on a hunger strike, especially if she keeps training."

"She's not on a hunger strike," I told him. "And we're not ordering her around." There was one thing that Sparrow needed above all else, and that was determination and control over her own life. "We can ask her, or check with Doc if it's necessary."

Pausing at the fridge to shove the beers in, he stared at me. "Okay, Kel. You don't have to tell her what to do. I'll take care of that battle on my own."

Rolling my eyes, I just took the beer he offered and popped it open. "Well, I guess that's what the flowers are for."

Instead of commenting, Liam flipped me off and then moved over to another counter and set the flowers up in a pitcher. "I forgot you assholes don't have any vases here."

"Why would we?" Jasper commented as he grabbed his own beer out.

"For Boo-Boo," Freddie answered, opening one of the bags in search of the breadsticks, and I was about to join him.

Lucretia's made the best damn breadsticks on our side of the city. "And the walls in the new sitting room, Doc."

Rome wandered in and took the first basket of breadsticks Freddie was handing out and then slid into a chair at the end of the table. Jasper slid him a beer and we were all moving to sit down.

"What about the walls in the new sitting room?" Milo asked, turning his chair around to straddle it before taking a seat.

"There's a butt print on it."

Freddie's statement landed in a moment of near-perfect silence in the room. Liam pivoted from the flowers to look at him. Milo stalled and so did Doc. I had a feeling that Jasper and I had the exact same *what the fuck* expression on our faces.

As it was, I managed to not inhale my beer. "What?"

"The walls in the new sitting room," Freddie said. "There's a very clear butt print on one of the marble walls. Before you ask, I'm very sober."

I glanced at Rome, mostly cause he'd painted them, but I wasn't alone as everyone else looked at him.

"I took a picture," Freddie volunteered, licking off his fingers before he pulled out his phone and set it on the table. "What is that, Rome?"

Rome didn't even look up from his food. "Starling's butt."

Milo dropped his chin, Liam began to laugh, and Jasper scrubbed a hand over his face, but not before a smile hit it. Even Vaughn started to chuckle.

"Seriously?" Freddie said, his eyebrows up. "You painted her butt *on the wall?*"

The fact that Freddie seemed incensed by it actually had Rome lifting his head to glance at him. "I didn't paint her butt on the wall."

"But you just said it was her butt."

"Yes." Rome nodded once.

"So, you didn't paint it on the wall," Doc said, studying Rome. "But it is her butt."

"Yes," Rome took a drink of his beer and went back to his food.

"I got this," Liam said, grinning at the back of Milo's head. "Rome? Did you use her butt to paint the wall?"

Jasper didn't quite sputter his beer, but it was close. Everyone looked at Rome again.

"No," Rome said without a flicker of an eyelid. "Her whole body."

"Damn," Liam said before he let out a low whistle and Vaughn did sputter his beer. Doc looked up at the ceiling for a long moment, but Milo just groaned.

"It was fun," Rome said. "Looks good." Then he glanced at Freddie. "She had fun."

That clicked everything into place for me from Freddie's reaction to Rome's explanation. "Okay then," Freddie said as he relaxed a fraction then sat down at the table.

It was times like now that reminded me of shit in Freddie's past that made all of us homicidal. The first person we ever killed had hurt him. It was not a death I would ever regret dealing out.

The only regret from then I had ever had was that we didn't get there sooner.

"We need to make sure we don't cover it up with anything," Vaughn finally managed around his laughter and coughing.

"Hell no," Liam said with a slow smile. "How high up is it, brother? We can frame it."

Rome just flipped him off, but Milo groaned. "Guys, can we not talk about my sister's ass?"

"You don't have to talk about anything," Jasper assured him. "But I'm with Liam, I want to frame it. Also, if we're painting rooms with her whole body—dibs for when we get to my room."

Instead of laughing, I just took a drink of the beer then said, "We'll discuss the using of various bodies for painting later, guys."

"Thank fuck," Milo muttered.

"But I do want to see that print in person when we're done," I told Freddie and he gave me a thumbs up. "For now, everyone get food and let's discuss business."

I ignored Milo's grumbling as I pulled out a chair. "Liam, have you found anything on this Brixton and his people?"

Rome looked at his brother just as Liam shook his head. "Nothing. Not even the people I know who run the palace are talking. There's been no word from Adam either. I checked with Ezra this morning. He's—well—he's less than thrilled, but the king has him on another job. He'll fill me on that when he's more secure."

Great. The king was another thorn to deal with. One at a time.

"With the 19Ds gone, we need to keep a presence on the streets. I don't want anyone deciding to fill that vacuum. For the most part, we've got solid relationships with a lot of the local businesses, but I don't want any of those to slip."

"Make regular rounds then," Doc suggested. "Make sure they know who we are, know our faces, and know who they can reach out to."

"That would be the plan," I said as I cut into the lasagna I'd dished out for myself. "That means we need to do circuits. I want the local kids to know who to go to—most of them are probably going to you first anyway."

"I can handle that," Doc said. "I've been looking at bringing in a full time nurse, maybe a nurse practitioner rather than just the volunteers. It will let the clinic have someone else in place and I can be freer to help out."

That gave me food for thought. "Anyone you bring in…"

"We'll do a background check, do a thorough vetting." Doc glanced at Liam. "From all sides."

For his part, Liam just gave him a thumbs up. "I can send you some names for people who would pass the first scratch test, but you'd have to decide if you liked them or not."

Doc nodded once. "As for the locals, I've been building bridges since I got back. I can keep that up."

It was Milo, though, who focused on Doc with a hard stare. "You know you don't have to do that, Mickey. You chose to get out. No one here—" At that phrase, he gave Jasper a look. "No one is going to blame you if you want to stay out. Legit may always be the goal, but we're going to have to stay at a certain level of dirty to deal with potential threats."

Instead of just dismissing the concern, Doc took a long drink of his beer before he set it down and then looked at each of us in turn, before he focused on me and Milo. "I made my peace with what I'm willing to do. I'll protect you boys. I'll protect Little Bit. That also means protecting this neighborhood. You just let me know where you need me."

"Well, Mickey J is back," Jasper said slowly. "Or should we welcome Vandal back?"

"Mickey is fine," Doc told him. "Doc is fine. If Vandal is needed, I'll be here too."

"Welcome back," Liam said as he thrust out his bottle. One by one, we all did the same until the bottles knocked together in a cheap toast. Though Freddie had a can, he definitely didn't get left out. Soda, not beer. He could have one, but he chose not to, and not a single one of us was going to judge it or him.

I gave them all a beat then glanced at Rome. "Check that Sparrow is still dancing?"

He nodded and slid out of the room without a word. No

one said anything while we waited. I didn't want to keep things from her but I also didn't want to make her uncomfortable with some of the discussions that needed to be had.

Rome returned swiftly. "Not dancing, but they are talking and she asked for another half hour."

Fine by me. "Then we'll make this quick."

Milo looked like he wanted to ask what they were talking about, but we didn't need to discuss that right now.

"Warrick still needs to be dealt with. Reed was going to give Milo a hand with that restructuring, but with his current absence, that won't be possible."

"I can help," Liam said before I'd even finished.

"And I may take you up on that," I told him. "But you already have a lot on your plate. Our first priority is Sparrow, period, end of story. But this king and Royals can't be ignored. Nor can Reed's ties to us and to her…"

"He's not tied to her," Milo argued, but clamped his jaw together when I raised a hand. Liam's gaze had gone hard and heated and there was no mistaking the temper in Jasper's expression.

Doc's fierce look surprised me, but only a little. His interest in Sparrow had been there from the beginning, but he was still trying to win his way back into her heart. I didn't think he'd have to work at it as hard as he did but then, she deserved every effort.

So, he could deal with it.

"I discussed Reed's offer to marry her…"

Jasper's fist hit the table and all the relaxation he'd gained around her seem gone in a diamond hard instant.

"Before you start," I warned him. "*Listen.*"

I meant that for all of them and one by one, their lock-jawed expressions gave way to ones of irritation and mutiny, but they focused on me. Freddie's knife was in his hand and as long as he was playing with it, I'd let him handle his own temper.

It was Rome's intense scrutiny that actually might have thrown me if Liam wasn't glaring like *I* had just endorsed Adam or some shit.

"Look," I said, pinching the bridge of my nose before I reached for a beer. "I don't know Reed. I have only what Sparrow has told me and what we've been able to glean from Liam's history with him and Graham, as well as the man's own words and actions. His actions have included protecting Sparrow and putting her first in some cases—to his most recent action which was sacrificing himself to get her back for us."

"We would have gotten her regardless. He made that choice for himself," Liam said through gritted teeth. "We weren't leaving either of them."

"Agreed," I said, meeting the hostility in his stare. "This isn't about who has the bigger dick. This is about Sparrow. This is about the fact he did do something that benefited us and at a cost to himself—much like he was helping you at a cost to himself."

"It saved his life," Liam pointed out.

"This isn't a dick measuring contest," I repeated. "You want to be pissed that he asked her to marry him, be pissed. But do it on someone else's time."

"Excuse the fuck out of me?" Milo said as he twisted to face me.

"Don't start. I'm not repeating myself again. Mouths shut until I'm finished. Save your bitching for after."

Dead silence blanketed the table, then Freddie picked up a breadstick and held it to his mouth, "That's right folks, we're sitting here at the Vandals' dinner table where the dick measuring has taken on a whole new proportion, but Kestrel is laying down the law. Could it be if a dick hits this table that he'll cut it off? Stay tuned for this and much more—news at eleven."

"Combat journalism your new thing?" I asked and Freddie just grinned.

"I don't know, am I going to survive if I answer?"

The tension in the room burst and the laughter started at Milo before it rolled around the room. Dicks.

All of them.

Assholes, too.

"He asked her to marry him to get her away from her family, to provide her a legal out." I just pointed at Liam when he opened his mouth then he shut it with a disgruntled look. "He was doing it to protect her and to get access to funds, accounts, and stocks that have been put in her name."

That had everyone's attention.

"He hates her family. The kind of violent hatred I assume we're all nursing at the moment."

The laughter evaporated.

"But his primary goal was to give her an out. One that got her away from the Sharpes, put the Reed family name and their resources around her—and kept her safe. If he got to use those resources she would come into—including a trust fund…"

"Because she got married, son of a bitch," Liam said as he leaned back in the chair. All at once, the filthy rage in the room turned thoughtful. That was better.

"You believe him?" Doc said, studying me intently.

"Yeah," I said with a nod. "I do. I think where she is concerned, we can trust him. I don't know that we can ever take it further than that, but in this—he has proven himself."

"Fuck," Freddie said with a sigh.

"Yeah," Jasper added, but it was Milo who looked the most disgruntled.

"We have to save that son of a bitch, don't we?"

Yeah. We did.

Vandals didn't leave anyone behind, and we always paid our debts.

"Now that I have your attention," I continued. "This is what we need to do…"

CHAPTER 33

EMERSYN

Freddie knocked on the open door and I glanced up from where I sprawled on Vaughn's bed. I'd been working on floors with Kellan and Vaughn for a while, but I just wasn't as good at laying the wood as they were. So rather than get in the way, I'd gone to stretch and do my physical therapy exercises before showering.

"Hey," I said, rolling to sit up. Soreness was a fact of life on the road, so the bruised feeling in my muscles was a good sign. In fact, it was the best sign. Fatigued enough to have endured a solid workout, but not in enough pain to say I overdid it. "Good morning. I thought you had work today."

"Technically," Freddie said, as he leaned against the door frame and folded his arms. "I don't actually have a *job* job at the moment. So, the work I had was to help babysit the rats while the latest shipments were processed and redistributed then sent out for delivery."

"So, a translation is that you were out in the warehouse

freezing your ass off while they moved a bunch of boxes and crates?" The trucking side of things moved a *lot* of different items. Everything from electronics to furniture to pharmaceuticals. The only things they didn't move were livestock or people.

The fact they made such a distinction, particularly about *people,* said that other people did move people in trucks. That was just a nauseating concept. I didn't live in some ivory tower with blinders on. Human trafficking happened, but it was disconcerting to realize that they had to have encountered it head on.

Of course, that just pitched me back to the fights I'd attended and the sex workers also in attendance. How many of them were trafficked and how many were willing? Did they even know the difference anymore?

"It's not so bad inside. At least I wasn't one of the schmucks going in and out of the rain." Still, he didn't come into the room any further. Twice he glanced away and I had to wonder if he was looking for other people in the hall.

"Freddie?"

"Yes, Boo-Boo?"

"Are you okay?"

Our conversations of late had been mostly light, almost effervescent in nature. We'd had so much fun on the date, but that didn't mean that we were pretending the darker stuff didn't happen. There was no escaping the darkness that was our past.

"Still sober," he said. "Sixty-four days."

I smiled. "That's awesome."

He rubbed his face, then motioned toward me. "You mind coming with me to my room?"

"Not at all..." I scooted off the bed and glanced around the floor for my boots. "We're staying inside?" I had on thick socks, they were mostly to keep my feet warm, but also to hide the bruises from the morning workout.

I'd done pointe work and it had been a while. My toes were not thrilled with me. But they'd toughen back up. I used to joke that dancers had the ugliest feet. That said, it wasn't really a joke.

"Yep. Just going to my room. I wanted to show you some of the furniture catalogs." He shifted on his feet, then rubbed the back of his neck. "The guys are all suggesting new stuff, you know. Better pieces for the sitting room and then for the bedrooms and some of it is expensive."

"Okay." I snagged my phone and padded across the room to him. I was wearing dance pants under one of Vaughn's sweatshirts. I had my own tops, but I loved wearing theirs.

They were warmer and almost made me think of the guys. "Is the stuff not to your taste?"

He shot me a sidelong look. "Boo-Boo, what do you think my taste is?"

I hooked my pinky finger with his as he took lead down the hall toward his room. The sound of steady hammering came from the new shared suite, and I tossed a glanced behind us. While the main door was open, there was no sign of the guys.

"Quirky," I decided for my answer when Freddie opened his room door.

He snickered and flipped on a light switch. The room was far less of a wreck than it normally was. And I said normally because I'd only really been in Freddie's room, what? Three times prior to this, and his clutter had clutter. Between the art on the walls, the stacks of books and clothes, and other random collectible items—that was a generous description of some of the detritus he had stacked in the corners—there wasn't a ton of space in his room.

"I suppose I've had worse descriptions," he said. Like with

Vaughn's room, he left the door open and the light from the hallway filled his room with illumination. He headed over to —oh there was a desk under the stacks of stuff. I wasn't sure where to perch, so I just moved to the bed and settled on the bookcase that made up the footboard.

"Well, it's definitely not an insult," I assured him. "I like your quirky."

He flashed me a grin. "Okay, Boo-Boo. You don't have to compliment me. I'm already wrapped around your finger."

I snorted but just shook my head as he came back with a couple of catalogs. Sliding up onto the bookcase next to me, he tucked a pen behind his ear before he shook open one of the catalogs and spread it over one of his legs and mine.

"Okay, so…as you can tell, I have a lot to match up if I'm getting new furniture…"

Right. I listened while he talked himself into and out of several different types of furniture suites. He liked wood, but natural color, not stained. He definitely didn't want it painted white or black, but maybe black because it wouldn't show as much dirt.

Then again, he preferred darker sheets and would that look weird to have black on black? Essentially, he talked us into a full circle before he groaned. "Maybe I can just skip the new furniture part," he suggested. "What do you think?"

Bumping his shoulder with mine, I said, "I think you can do anything you want."

He made a face before sighing.

"What's wrong?" I asked. "You don't have to tell me, but you can, you know. I'll listen, and what you tell me… it goes nowhere else."

"Nothing is wrong," he admitted. "I mean, nothing that I'm sure of and that's what has me kind of…worried."

"No news is not always good news." Weirdly enough, I totally got that.

Slinging an arm around my shoulders, he hesitated a moment but when I scooted a little closer, he rested his arm there. "Boo-Boo, things don't go right all the time."

No, they really didn't.

"Things are going really right, right now."

"Like the new coffeemaker downstairs?" The replacement they'd gotten me had been upgraded. I had no idea when they'd done it, just that one day it hadn't been there and the next it was. The machine was—well, it pretty much did everything from pulling the perfect shot to making the perfect blend.

I'd been almost scared to touch it.

"Like that, huh?" Freddie asked and I nodded. "Makes you wonder if we stole it or bought it, doesn't it?"

Actually, stealing had never even come to mind. "I didn't really think of it that way."

"What would impress you more then? If I stole it? Or if I bought it?"

"That you think I'm worth either is pretty impressive," I pointed out. "But you being happy would be the best of all."

After releasing a low whistle, Freddie said, "You're killing my mojo, Boo-Boo. I had this whole story about relying on my Cleary credit. Cause Liam's loaded, you know that right? Dude is literally rolling in it and apparently now that I'm official, I get an *allowance*. Not cash cash, because trusting me with cash cash? Bad idea." He danced from topic to topic so swiftly. "But I have my very own credit card now, and carte blanche to get whatever I want. I thought about getting you more of those flowers—you liked the ones he got you right?"

The rush of words had me holding up my pinky. "Freddie? Are you really okay?"

"Promise, Boo-Boo." He hooked his finger around mine and squeezed. "I really am okay. It's just…it's a lot."

"I'll tell you a secret," I said, pitching my voice low

because I didn't want it to carry. "I'm not always sure what to do with how much they care about me, too."

"Boo-Boo—"

I pressed a finger to his lips to quiet him. "Shh. Just listen. You take my breath away because you're brave. Jasper works so hard to keep himself gentle for me. So does Vaughn. Kel— I think Kel sees and hears what I need before I do. Rome and Liam… you'd think they'd be the most overwhelming of all, but the way you guys care about me?"

I didn't have words for it.

"So, I understand that it feels like almost too much. Like what could you have ever done to deserve that kind of loyalty or to feel that safe?"

Surprise appeared in his eyes. Yes, I did know exactly what I was talking about. On impulse, I reached for the catalog he'd been paging through and tossed that one aside and lifted out the one he'd been hiding.

"Can we go through this one? I haven't decided what to get for my room yet either. I've never picked out my own furniture before."

"Never?" He scowled.

"No, my parents and my—family—they chose how the homes were decorated. At boarding school, it was just the basics, and on the road, I pretty much lived out of hotels. When did I ever need to pick out furniture?"

The room they'd first put me in had been the most basic, but I'd loved all the little touches from the painting on the wall to Rome sharing his bear with me, to the chairs they added. The furniture had been mismatched in color and style, but the hodgepodge worked to make it safe and warm.

From the old living room with its ancient furniture, well-used and well-loved to the old pool table, that stuff had also had personality too.

"Whatever we pick," I said slowly. "It needs to be less generic and more...you or me or the guys."

"If we steal it," Freddie mused. "That would definitely be us. In the group home, that was how we got things. We'd beg, borrow, or steal."

I chewed on my lower lip. "How hard would it be to steal a sofa or a bed though? It's not like you can shove them under your shirt and sneak out with them."

Freddie gaped at me for a long moment, then real laughter escaped him in a whoosh of breath and he leaned into me as he laughed.

"Oh my god, Boo-Boo. Have you never stolen anything?"

"Um...I know I've taken pens before. Pretty sure I snitched a candy bar once, but that was because I was in trouble and grounded from all the sugar." And because fuck Marta. She'd always had a bit of a nasty streak. "You wanna show me how to do it?"

"Hell yes, I will show you how to do it." Then he pursed his lips. "Just don't tell the guys cause they'll kill me."

I snorted. "We'll say it's about making me lighter fingered for working with knives." Apparently, I thought way too hard when it came to knife work. Freddie's knife was like an extension of himself. I couldn't quite get there.

"I like how you think, Boo-Boo."

Grinning, I half-twisted so I could face him. His arm was still half-around my shoulders. "Can I give you a hug?"

"Definitely down for that. Bring it in." As soon as I wrapped my arms around him, he closed his around me and squeezed. Eyes closed, I held on. Freddie's heart began to race at first, then calmed again. "Boo-Boo," he said against my hair. "You give great hugs."

"I've been practicing," I teased. After another minute, I said, "Need me to let go now?"

"Nope," he answered in a hurry, his arms flexing. "Need more practice."

I smiled against him as he kept me close. "Sounds good. I like to train for everything."

"Hug training," Freddie said on a laugh. "Sign me up."

"I thought I already had."

That earned me another chuckle. A few more minutes, then we'd pick out some new furniture together. Maybe we weren't used to picking out what we wanted. But together, we could figure it out.

How hard could it be?

CHAPTER 34

VAUGHN

For the last week, we'd been working in shifts to get the renovations done, deal with our own jobs, keep our ears to the ground, and basically maintain vigilance. Through it all, Dove had been an absolute trooper. She didn't chafe at the restrictive protections in place.

When she wanted to go with one of us, we made it happen. When she wanted to stay at the clubhouse, we made that happen too. Everything we did, coordinated, or required, we did to make sure she was safe and felt safe.

Even going to Liam's. I'd gone with her and Rome to drop her off, then made sure Kel was with me when we took Rome back by. On the one hand, doubling and tripling back on our movements to make sure we had everyone covered could be a pain in the ass.

On the other hand, none of us were willing to take risks with Dove, period. Nor were we taking risks with each other. Freddie had been making noises about heading out for more part-time work 'cause his funds were running low, and Kel told him his primary jobs needed to be at the clubhouse for now.

It wasn't just because we wanted him out of the line of fire; we really did need the coverage here for Dove. Jasper's healing had hit the restless as fuck stage. It wouldn't be long before he wanted back on his truck, and that meant we needed someone free to travel with him.

Inside the clubhouse, it was quiet. After endless days of hammering, sawing, and sanding—not to mention polishing, painting, and installing—it seemed almost *too* quiet. I grabbed a beer from the kitchen then headed up to my room.

Shower, beer, maybe catch a nap. It depended on where Dove was. I doubled back and checked the hall to her studio, but the studio door stood wide open. Right, not in there. I pulled out my phone on my way up.

She'd never turned off the tracking on her phone. It shared her location regularly. I hated that she had to do that, but no lie, I loved having access to her location. As long as she had her phone, we'd know where she was.

If it made me a selfish bastard that I always wanted to know, well, I could live with that. I could share her with my brothers, enjoyed it even. All I needed from her was a smile, the occasional cuddle, and if I were really lucky, her hot, lush, and naked in my shower.

Everything else was gravy.

To my delight, I found a Dove sleeping in my bed. Standing in the doorway with the light stretching out to touch her like a long finger, I smiled slowly. I *liked* coming home to Dove in my bed. Having her in the clubhouse at all was amazing, but in my bed?

Hell. Yes.

Closing the door quietly, I made my way over to the bathroom. The softness of her breathing served as the soundtrack. At least the walls were sturdy enough to mute the heavier sounds of construction—not that there were any.

Flipping on the light in the bathroom, I took a moment to just soak in her presence. Rome's bear was on the bed with her and the stapler was there, too. One of her legs was out from under the covers and she wore a t-shirt and, from the bare skin I could see, not much else.

The idea she was relaxed enough to settle like that here was intoxicating. Torn between waking her and sliding between those legs to devour her until she was screaming or leaving her be to sleep, I hesitated in the doorway to the bathroom.

One sniff check told me that I would be better off showering first. I'd done a seven hour ink job today. Good client, but I'd spent half the day hunched to work on it. That kind of detail took concentration, and I'd been sweating bullets thanks to the fact the thermostat was broken.

We either had satan's asshole or a fucking deep freeze. The clients wanted to be warm, so sweltering in hell it was. I grabbed a pair of sweats then headed into the bathroom, closing the door quietly.

She could have gone to sleep five hours or five minutes ago, it didn't matter. I didn't want to disturb her. I turned on the shower, going for cold first to cool off and downed about half of the cold beer before I slid under the water.

It was chilly and bracing, but sluicing off the sweat already improved my mood—and my scent. By the time I'd washed up, the water was warm. When it hit hot, I just braced a hand against the wall and let the spray hammer against my back.

I felt about fifty percent better by the time I finished. I used a towel to wipe off the condensation on the mirror. After that, I brushed my teeth and took time to rinse out my mouth, 'cause toothpaste and beer were a crappy combo.

Sweatpants on, I opened the door to the bedroom and checked on her.

She'd rolled over and her eyes were open but she was still curled up in my bed. "Hey," she said, before stretching as a yawn took hold of her.

Chuckling, I flipped off the light and eased onto the bed before I hit the switch for the low-light lamp next to it. It cast a warm, yellowy glow in a comforting puddle around us.

She slid over as I sat down and then once I was settled, scooted over to curl up under my arm. Okay, this was really just like a sex dream come true. Sleepy, cuddly Dove, still warm from my bed and waiting to climb on me as soon as I was in it?

Hell. Yes.

I slid an arm under her legs and tugged her up further until I had her cradled in my lap. Yes, her ass was as deliciously naked as I suspected. My dick definitely stirred as she settled against him, but getting him wet wasn't the first thing on my mind.

"Afternoon," I murmured to her, before I pressed a kiss to her forehead. "Sleep well?"

"Hmm," she said, stretching. "Really well. I didn't mean to sleep so long. I did a tougher routine after PT this morning though and I was just tired."

Sorting through all of that, I ran a hand up and down her arm. "Did you eat?"

"Yes," she answered with another yawn. "Mickey brought lunch with him."

"That was nice of him." And smart. One thing I had noticed, when she got focused on something—she forgot to do things like eat. Healing took a lot of energy and protein. So did her workouts. If she was gonna keep pushing herself, she needed to increase her calorie intake. "Question."

"Hmm?"

"Do you weight train at all? Or is it always dancing and cardio?"

She tucked her head against my shoulder, then flattened her palm to mine. My hands dwarfed hers, but that never seemed to bother her.

"I have done weight training, sometimes I need to do focused arm and leg strength if I'm coming back from a vacation or an injury."

The weight loss following Pinetree hadn't been a fluke. They'd been starving her. Since she'd been back, and I was assuming even when she and Rome were taken, she had been eating fairly regularly. Her gentler curves were filling back out, and her arms were definitely toned.

"We've got some free weights," I told her. "We'll pull those out if you think they will help. I don't lift like I used to—" Didn't really need it right now. I did enough natural hauling and lifting to keep myself fit."

"Wanna be my lifting partner?" She gave me the most indulgent smile.

"I want to be whatever you need, Dove."

She sighed, rubbing her cheek to my shoulder. "You guys are the best."

"Well, some of us are just a little bit better than the others." The teasing did exactly what I'd wanted it to do. She laughed. "That said… you mind if I ask you some harder questions? I know you're sleepy, so saying no is perfectly reasonable and acceptable."

The sigh that earned was a lot deeper and a lot more melancholy, but she wiggled that sweet ass a little to sit up and then she lifted her head to look at me. "You want to talk about bad stuff."

"Yes, and no. Discussing your triggers and your boundaries are not all bad. It's about defining what you want, when you want it, and how I can help you avoid more negative experiences." It was a conversation we needed to have. One I'd told her a few weeks earlier we would be having.

Then everything else happened. But she was home, and steady, despite everything that happened. The strength Dove had never failed to impress me. Strong or not, I still wanted to tackle her nightmares and pull them apart one at a time until they were nothing but dissipating shadows left to the past.

Nose wrinkling, she looked thoughtful as she began to trace one of the tattoos on my chest. "I know we need to talk about them…"

"But you don't want to."

"Probably never going to want to discuss those things." Which didn't seem at all unreasonable. Who wanted to talk about what brought them pain? "But I probably *need* to face those things even more because I don't want to look at them at all."

I had a feeling that she was actually sorting that part out with herself, so I just rubbed her arm and let her figure out what she wanted to do. For all her remarkable talents, and strength, she was also used to being alone, something it had taken me a while to piece together.

It was in the shadow of that isolation that her friendship with Lainey had grown so fierce and intense. Protecting her meant keeping their whole relationship in a bubble. The rest of the time, she'd been alone, except for the people in her dance company and the dick who'd been hurting her.

Dove was *used* to the pain and the loneliness. It was her normal. Trust took time, but she was trusting us, and now I needed her to trust us a bit more.

"I think that would be a good plan," I told her. "No one wants to hurt you. I think you might have figured out, we'll cut off our own limbs rather than see you suffer…"

That had her lifting her head to study me. "I don't want you to hurt yourselves, either."

"That's why I want to discuss these boundaries. Tear them out from the darkness and drag them into the light. Nothing you tell me will change a single feeling I have about you."

"That's easy to say," she muttered, but I didn't take it personally. "And maybe it is that easy…I just…I hate talking about any of it. I want to forget it happened. Any of it."

"I understand." I really did. "But just forgetting it hasn't worked so far, has it? You're still afraid of whatever it is, on some level, that fear lives in you and each time you duck away from it—you make it stronger."

Dove groaned, but she didn't retreat. No, she twisted so she could straddle my lap and face me. Since I couldn't cradle her anymore, I put my hands on her hips.

"Thank you for not telling me I liked being afraid."

"Okay, whatever dick told you that, just point them out. I'll rearrange their head so it will fit up their ass."

That earned me a chuckle. Pressing her hands to my chest, she met my gaze. "No one has ever put it quite like that, though… sometimes it feels like if I can just keep that door shut and the lights on… if I never ever look…"

"Dove," I stroked a hand up her arm to her face and she leaned her cheek into my hand. "If I thought for an instant that would work, I'd be the one barring the doors."

Another sigh, this one more resigned than anything else. "But it won't."

"No."

It hadn't worked for Freddie and the nightmares he suffered. It definitely didn't help his addiction. It wouldn't help Milo who was still trying to remember who and what he was before his three years in prison. It hadn't done a damn thing for any of us as kids as we tried to repair the damage life had left on us.

"Talking doesn't fix everything. Acknowledging a pain doesn't make it go away." No, the only thing that could heal the pain was to get all the infection out, clean it, then dress the wound. But we couldn't even start on that until we could see how deep it was. "Don't tell Ms. Stephanie I said that, she'd probably give me a brain duster."

Another laugh, but then Dove sobered. "I'd protect you."

"I know you would. What I'm trying to tell you is that while we can't undo things and maybe we can't eliminate it entirely, we can learn to not do the things that will upset you. I know you don't want your ass touched, specifically along your anus."

She tensed so swiftly, if I hadn't expected it, I might have been startled. As it was, it made me a little sick to push her.

"That right there," I told her calmly, keeping everything even. "That is why I want to discuss your triggers. Help me help you, Dove."

"I have talked about some of it," she admitted.

"Yeah?"

She nodded, but then chewed at her lower lip. A knock at the door interrupted before she could continue, and I kept my hands on her hips when I called, "What's up?"

The door swung in to admit Kellan and Dove's expression lightened at his arrival. Yeah, that might be exactly what we need. Backup for me, but also support for her.

"Am I interrupting?" He glanced from me to Dove and then back.

"Not at all," I told him. "We were going to have a talk about her triggers and her boundaries. You mind if Kel stays, Dove?"

She turned wide eyes on me for a moment, but it was Kellan's expression that registered first. No surprise, which meant he did know *some* of it. Good. That would help us both.

Blowing out a shaky breath, she said, "I don't mind. I think it might be easier to just tell it once than have to keep repeating it."

After he shut the door, Kel toed off his shoes and then walked around to take a seat on the other side of my bed. "Come here, Sparrow."

At the request, she gave me a light kiss and then scrambled over to crawl into his arms. I'd be jealous except some of the tension and fear leaked out of her as soon as he held her close.

"Would it help you if I started?" Kel asked, and Dove gave me a look. Was that alright with me?

"Whatever works," I assured her. "This isn't about us right now."

"No," Kellan agreed, then focused on her, too. "This is about *you*. What would help you?"

CHAPTER 35

KELLAN

didn't make the offer lightly, but I was serious. We all had different pieces of the puzzle. I wasn't sure how much the others knew versus what she'd told me except that she admitted she'd talked to Rome. He'd never reveal her secrets.

Frankly, *none* of us would. Sparrow would come first, and we would only dig deeper into that hole if we had to in order to help her. I didn't want this coming down to another Pine-tree situation.

Ever.

The ease with which she slid into my lap quieted some of the concern curling in my system. The fact she relaxed as soon as I wrapped my arms around her, and the tension leaked out of her, did more to settle my own temper.

Vaughn was a good call for this conversation. He was a calm guy *most* of the time. Where Jasper's temper rode a razor thin line and Liam's combative, in-your-face style got results, Vaughn was steady.

It was that steadiness that earned Sparrow's trust first—well, first after she lost faith in me. That was the past and I'd earned her trust again.

"I can start," she said slowly. "This is apparently a conversation I need to have with all of you."

"Dove," Vaughn said as he shifted to sit sideways and face her. "You don't have to do anything. Remember that. If you want to just set rules that you would prefer we follow, then that's what we do."

I agreed, to a point. She had told me that "he" had hurt her via ass play. While she had been circumspect about naming who the "he" was, I had a solid idea. It had to be either her uncle or her father.

Process of elimination leaned me in her uncle's direction. He was the one who set Liam up to meet him *elsewhere*. He'd been the one mentioned in all the "missing" stories. He'd been the one she left with to *protect* us.

Currently, he was also the only one we couldn't track where he was. The father was in Vegas at some "conference" as far as we could tell, but that sounded like a cover for gambling.

She turned those soft brown eyes on me. Every shadow of pain that had ever darkened those eyes was another mark in a column of retribution that needed to be taken on her behalf. A retribution we *would* deliver. She deserved freedom from that pain and from ever worrying about it again.

"I won't say you don't have to say anything," I told her, selecting my words carefully. "Vaughn is right though, first and foremost is that you know we will never do anything that hurts you. You told me some, and I can tell him if that makes it easier." I'd already offered to do this. At the same time, Sparrow's well of strength was depthless.

She made a face, but I resisted the urge to smile or laugh. Distraction. Deflection. These were the tools of a survivor. Jasper recognized them even before he understood what they were. I had to wonder if he even realized how much he'd seen.

Looking back at my time with her *before* the show and then after—the clues were there. We made excuses though. The partner. He was guilty, but not the only one who was guilty.

"I don't like ass play," she said, enunciating each word with care. Not once did she look away from me as she formed them. Pride unfurled in my gut. That took a lot of courage to say again. It had cost her the first time, but she squared her shoulders as she straightened.

At my nod, she glanced at Vaughn. Next to us, he'd gone still. I imagined that, like me, he was laser-focused on her. Every nuance of her expression, every waver in her intonations, and even the way her eyes flickered: I tracked all of it.

"Ass play," she continued. "As in penetration of any kind. Even—touching it with your fingers, it just throws me back to when…"

She pursed her lips and her eyes seemed to flatten a little as though she were seeing further away. The memories didn't get to have her right now. With care, I tightened my arms around her, enough to remind her that we were there, and almost at once she blinked then snapped her gaze to me.

I drew a circle against her hip with my thumb, and a smile flickered over her lips. There she was.

"When I was younger…for as long as I can remember…he has always wanted more with me. Touched me. Made me uncomfortable. Kissed." A flush stole over her face and she grimaced. "He—my uncle."

That slammed the last nail into the coffin where I wanted to bury the scalded remains of his body.

351

Vaughn clenched his hands. From the corner of my eye, I caught the whitened knuckles.

I'd heard this part. Didn't make it any easier to listen to, so I could barely imagine how difficult this was for her to verbalize. But one by one, the words spilled out.

From the first time he put his hands where they didn't belong to when he *punished* her using anal sex. Oh, the detail my brain absorbed to revisit a thousand fold on that walking corpse. As it was, I kept myself as steady as I could.

She didn't need my rage. Not right now.

Each time she glanced at me, decades of pain, loneliness, loss, and, fuck my life, *shame* burned in her eyes. She had *nothing* to be ashamed of. It wasn't until she let out a little cough that I allowed myself to cup her face. The tears spilling out of her eyes gutted me, but like any poison—we had to drain it all away.

"He wanted to hurt you," I said for her. "Even when he said otherwise, it was always pain."

How could it possibly be anything else? The truth would kill Milo.

The truth threatened to strangle anything civilized in me. We would have her pound in flesh extracted and then some.

She stole a look at Vaughn and he sighed softly. "Dove, he's the monster. Not you. You're perfect. You still shine no matter how much filth he tried to spread over you."

A hiccupping sob shook her and that was the cue to pull her in closer even as Vaughn moved. He braced a hand on my shoulder as he wrapped himself around us both. Between us, nothing would come anywhere near her.

In the midst of a sob came a laugh and then another hiccup. Shock and trauma. It went so much deeper than I could ever have imagined before.

We should have stolen her the first chance we got.

"Okay," Vaughn said, pausing to clear his throat as he

straightened. I caught his expression, the murderous rage glittering in his green eyes as he pulled back only enough to look at her.

His control was damn near perfect, the rage vanished behind rock steadiness.

"So, what do you need from us?"

I couldn't have phrased it better myself.

She swiped at the tears on her face, then glanced from Vaughn to me. I didn't need her to voice the question, but I also believed that she needed to say it herself. She needed to own this.

"You..." She swallowed and then tilted her head back to look at the ceiling. I gave her a beat, let her gather her thoughts and her breath. She could do this.

I had absolute faith in her.

"You said," she began again, her voice a little raw. "There were ways to make it pleasurable so we could take it away from him." Sucking her upper lip against her teeth, she shook her head once then looked at me before she glanced to Vaughn. "Kellan said that. When I told him some of it before."

"I did say that," I agreed. "There are ways to make it very pleasurable for you." The idea of ripping that nightmare to shreds was enough to turn my dick to solid steel, but my sparrow was a good girl. There was no way she could miss the erection, but she ignored it.

Because dicks did that and my dick could fucking wait.

"Your body is yours, Sparrow. No one here will ever dispute that. Ever. As for anyone else? Fuck them, they don't get a say." If some fuckhead even had a passing thought of doing so, I would take a nail gun to their dick to illustrate how much say they didn't get in the subject. If I bothered to let them live long enough to benefit from the lesson.

A smile flickered around her lips.

"That means," Vaughn said, picking up the thread. "You

don't have to do anything. That beautiful ass of yours feels good in my palms, but it's also just fine not ever being touched if you never want that."

She chuckled, but the wet laughter didn't add to the humor. "Wouldn't the piercing hurt?"

"Not if I can help it," he swore. "We would make sure you were ready for it and if you weren't, that's fine too. Kel's got a normal dick."

"Thanks," I said dryly.

"You know what I mean."

"I do, but still…" The teasing comments were perfect because some of the aching sadness in her expression fled.

"I like his dick," Sparrow championed me, and I had to swallow my own laughter as Vaughn appeared to consider that.

"Never examined his personally," he said instead. "Just on a scale of one to five, do you like it more than mine?"

"Vaughn." Scandalized, but very real laughter erupted from her and I mimed slugging his arm but mouthed a very quiet thank you over her head as she covered her face with her hands. "I'm not answering that."

He chuckled. "Cause I'd win, that's okay. We know."

I rolled my eyes but accepted the ribbing because it did more to help relax Sparrow than anything else. She was still chuckling when she wiped her eyes. The tears were humor and pain. I wanted to take away all that pain.

Every damn drop of it.

"Your body is yours," I repeated. "We can experiment. We can test what you like and what you don't. We can go as far as you want and stop the moment you say stop. No one will ever take that away from you again."

"Agreed."

We could have been more sober or serious if we'd sworn that oath in blood. She studied us for a long time.

"I believe you."

"Good." Then because it needed to be asked, I said, "Who else knows, Sparrow?"

She let out a long sigh. We waited her out, but she didn't drag the experience out. "Rome knows all of it. So does Freddie."

That startled me a little, it shouldn't have, but it did. Freddie—Freddie was a good choice. He would die before he betrayed her secrets.

"Jasper knows I have issues with it and so does Liam. I told Liam what the rules were, what you said." The last was directed at me. The rules that her body was hers and everything stopped when she said so. "They don't know the details, and I know I have to tell them..."

"Dove," Vaughn said firmly. "You don't have to do anything. Telling them will be about what you need. They will want to know how to help, but neither one would ever demand it of you."

They probably wouldn't slow down on their way to kill Bradley Sharpe either. But that was a discussion for another day.

"Doc knows some," I said. He would have to after the medical exams. Like Freddie, he'd go to his grave before he betrayed her.

"Mickey does and doesn't," she said. "I mean, he's seen some of the scarring." Then she wrinkled her nose and shuddered. "It's so invasive and after...Pinetree..."

Yeah. I needed to check with Freddie on that part. If anyone from Pinetree that was involved in her mistreatment survived the place burning down, they wouldn't survive us coming for them.

"But I don't..." She trailed off and we waited again. Her taking ownership and direction of how she healed herself was more important than anything I wanted. If she gave me that power, then I'd make sure she got everything she needed and wanted.

To give that kind of power, she had to take it first.

"I guess I don't know how to start this and I don't know how to confront it. Sometimes when I panic…I lose track of who is there or why. I fight. I hit. I flee…" She winced. "I belted Liam really hard once." Then she flicked a look at Vaughn.

"I remember," he murmured. "For all that he growls and grumbles, Dove, Liam would line the street with bodies for you."

"That's—graphically romantic," she said with another half-smile, half-grimace.

"If you want bodies, Dove, just say the word, and trust me, we will lay them all out for you."

Yes, we would.

"That still doesn't change the fact I don't know what I'll do and I don't know how to do this." Good girl. She pulled us back to the topic at hand.

"You don't have to know," I said. "It will take us time. We'll have to push you some. Test your limits. Then ease you back each time. The only thing I need to know—do you trust us to help you?"

"Yes." Zero hesitation. "But I don't want to hurt you."

"We can take a few bruises," I promised. "But trusting us means telling us to stop if it becomes too much. Telling us what isn't working—don't worry about hurting our feelings. Whatever you do, please don't force yourself to 'endure' because you think it's what we want."

"I agree with Kel," Vaughn said swiftly. "Neither of us wants you to suffer. *Ever*. If it takes a day, a week, a month, or a year…it takes as long as it takes."

"But, let's be clear here," I added. "You make the rules. You decide when. You decide how. If you need help on any of that, you decide that too."

"Do I have to tell the others we're doing this?" It wasn't an unreasonable question from her.

"Do you want to tell them?" Vaughn met her gaze directly.

"Not really," she said with a sigh. "But it's not fair to exclude them."

"This isn't about fair, Sparrow," I reminded her. "No one is keeping score."

"Probably a good idea because...I would be winning if we were."

There was a slow blink from her before mischief flooded her eyes and her lips tilted up into the curve of real humor.

"She's not wrong," Vaughn told me.

"Nope. And I don't have a problem with that."

I slid my hand up to her nape, massaging the tension cording the muscles. "What do you need, Sparrow?"

"All of you," she whispered.

"That part is easy," Vaughn said. "What else?"

Come on, sweet sparrow. Ask.

"Will you both help me? I want—I want to erase him."

Oh, so did I.

"Yes," I told her in the same breath as Vaughn. "We'll help you."

CHAPTER 36

EMERSYN

The next morning at breakfast, Kellan treated me to a lesson in making pancakes for the guys. The lesson required him standing right up against my back, until his groin nestled against my ass. There was no mistaking his erection or how he moved to keep rubbing it against me.

At first, I stiffened up. I didn't mean to, but the way his body framed mine startled me. Then he slid a hand around to rest against my stomach and pressed me firmly to him before guiding my hand with the spatula. Honestly, a cold sweat gathered at the back of my neck and it took me a full three pancakes to remember to breathe.

"Just say the word," he murmured against my ear. "Remember?"

It was almost hard to hear him past the sudden jackhammer of my pulse. The soft rub of his cheek to my hair helped. The slow massage of his hand against my stomach.

Then I relaxed my hand as he guided it through the flipping of pancakes.

By the time we made it to the second stack of pancakes, I was taking deeper breaths. I was a lot sweatier than I liked for breakfast, but when Kellan sat at the table and patted his knee, I slid onto his lap easily enough.

A couple of days later, Vaughn wandered into the studio when I was practicing. He studied me, then he studied the silks that had been rehung from the ceiling after they'd done their upgrades.

I still hadn't used them. Between physical therapy and practice, I wasn't sure I was up to them—yet.

The *yet* was important. I was building my strength. I had a goal. I *would* fly again.

I was mid-barre routine when Vaughn slid in, and I glanced over at him—especially when he locked the door. "Don't let me interrupt, Dove."

Despite my quizzical look, he didn't offer anything more, just leaned against the wall as I went through my routine. When I paused to take a break, he pushed away from the wall and pointed me back to the barre.

"Grab that for me, yes?"

Since it was right in the mirror, there was no way to miss him so I gripped the bar and watched him as he drifted toward me.

"Stretch your arms and step back."

Curiosity speared me but reality sank in its sharp talons as I stretched until I was bent in half.

"Eyes on me, Dove."

I flicked my gaze up to the mirror and met his gaze. He was dressed in jeans, a loose t-shirt and a hoodie. He looked for all the world like he'd just come back from work. But it was early, so maybe he was going to leave for work.

"Dove."

I sucked in a breath.

"Better." He rubbed a hand over my back. "You have to keep breathing, that's a rule."

I swallowed and then nodded.

"We can just call it here," he reminded me. The silkiness of his voice helped. The soothing croon and the low timbre. His voice had been the first thing I really noticed about him.

"No," I said softly. "I'm okay to keep going."

"Yeah?" He tilted his head. "Do we remember what we say if we need a break?"

"Stop," I murmured. "I do remember."

"Good, I don't need Kellan coming after me for pushing you too hard." It was a teasing comment, but the sobriety in those green eyes suggested it was also much more.

"I really do want the help," I admitted and wiggled my ass at him to emphasize it. "I half-expected sex the day I asked but…"

Vaughn chuckled. "Dove, one of the things I've learned about triggers over the years—they strike when we aren't expecting them. You were ready for it then. You were focused on us, but you were also already exhausted from telling us what happened. It wouldn't have been fair to anyone, especially you."

I hadn't thought of it that way. "I'm sorry…"

"Shh," he murmured, then hummed as he began to run his hand up and down my back. "Nothing to be sorry for, Dove. We wanted to talk, too. We wanted to figure out how we will make this work for you. He had some ideas. I had some ideas."

Heat scalded my face. "You guys talked about me?"

"We do that sometimes." A smile pulled at his sensuous mouth. "Does that bother you?"

"No?" Did it bother me? I turned it over in my mind, but then shook my head. "No, it doesn't. I guess I just didn't think about it that way but—is it weird that I'm glad you guys do talk?"

"Worried about misunderstandings?" If he was guessing, then he was definitely on the right track. Somehow, I didn't think it was speculation though.

"I never planned on all of you." It wasn't an explanation by any stretch. "From the first day I woke up here to the first time…to the first time I walked into the bathroom while you were showering. I never planned on this."

His smile gentled even more and he leaned over to press a kiss between my shoulder blades. "Dove, I know Jasper had issues with sharing in the beginning. Hawk's a tough guy and he's always struggled with the idea that what he cares about will leave him…"

I swore my stomach sank. "You don't have to tell me his secrets."

"Not telling you too much," he soothed again, rubbing his hand along my back and then down to my hips. It really did help to relax the tension that came in waves. "Just—I get it. I get that you've always been afraid to claim what you want."

That startled me and I jerked my gaze up to his.

"You don't hide a best friend for years, keep them a deep, dark secret, if you don't want to protect them. The more I learn about your family, the more I see why you didn't trust us—you couldn't. Not when you first got here."

I swallowed hard. He cupped his palm over my right asscheek and began to massage it. The movement firm and so very present. "I trust you now."

"And that," he whispered, "is everything."

He grinned at me and that was when I realized he was massaging both ass cheeks. A shudder and shiver collided in my center and I laughed. It was both strangely scary and liberating.

The next three days passed in similar fashion. They found

me wherever I was and made a point of squeezing my ass or massaging it. Sometimes they just held me close so they could rub against me, other times, I would just sit on their lap. For the most part, I could handle it.

The day Kellan slid into the shower behind me when I had soap in my eyes led to a bad moment. I just shut down and when I came out of it, he was sitting on the floor in the shower with me in his lap, rocking me until I recognized where I was again.

Two steps forward, a half-dozen back.

"I hate this," I said, not quite stomping out of the shower in Vaughn's room. We were still sleeping in here for the most part. Another couple of days and we could start carting the furniture up to the new bedrooms.

"It takes time, Sparrow," Kellan reminded me. He and Vaughn were so damn patient.

"I don't want it to take more time." I wanted to throw something. Or break it. Or just—do anything that would make this stop.

Instead of trying to soothe me with words of comfort or excuses, Kellan dried off and dressed. Then he waited for me.

"You're not going to try and make this better, are you?" I was dry for the most part but why bother with clothes. I just —sure I couldn't walk around naked even if I wanted it. Milo was here and that was just too weird.

"You don't want me to make this part feel better."

I stared at him. Was he for real right now? The calm certainty in his voice aggravated the hell out of me. How could he just stand there like everything was okay? I fisted my hands together and fought the urge to scream.

"Come on, Sparrow," he murmured. "Get dressed. We have things to do."

The temptation to throw myself down on the bed and just refuse was right there. Instead, I just sat down on the edge and hung my head. "Kellan… What if I never get over this?"

"Then you don't."

Not exactly the answer I wanted to hear. He pushed away from the wall and moved over to where I sat, then crouched down so I had no choice but to look at him.

"Sparrow, no one said this would be easy. You spent years suffering this abuse, building up walls and defense mechanisms. You found ways to hide from it in your mind and in your life. A few days of easy play with us is not going to push you over the edge that fast. We're going to make mistakes, you're going to get scared."

"I don't want to be scared." This time I did stamp my foot. "Great, now I sound like I'm five."

"No, you sound like a survivor who has fought so many battles you've lost count and you just want the war over."

Yeah. I kind of did.

He caught my hands in his and pressed them together. "But here's the thing. You aren't waging these fights alone anymore. We're here. We'll get there. I just need you to keep fighting. We can take a break for a while. Rest and let you catch your breath. Then, we'll dive back in tomorrow."

I made a face. "That sounds a lot like running away."

"You can run away if you want, no one here will complain. Cause we'll be running with you, covering your exit." He tilted his head. "Covering that sweet ass of yours one way or another."

A laugh escaped me, along with a tear that I tugged a hand free to wipe away. "I hate this."

"I know," he said. "That's why you asked for help. We'll get there."

Instead of just being grateful, I was complaining and I hated that even more. "I'm sorry."

"Don't need to be sorry, let's just get some clothes on that beautiful ass before I'm tempted to push you and you don't need to be pushed today."

When I would have argued that, he gave me a firm look and I kept the words to myself. No, I'd already had a moment, the exhaustion from that was in my bones.

The rest of the day we spent at the shooting range. I fired so many guns, I was sure my arms were going to fall off. But I could take apart and put three different kinds of handguns back together. I learned how to clean them, shoot them, and then keep shooting them even when I was tired.

That night, I fell asleep snugged between Vaughn on one side and Rome on the other, while I sprawled on Kellan. We'd been watching a movie. At some point, Jasper and Freddie came in and I woke up enough to smile at them before I went to sleep again.

Work on the renovation took point, though the guys were taking longer and longer trips away. When Jasper headed back out on a run, he took Vaughn with him. By the time they got back we would have the new sitting room done.

The ginormous sofa Liam had delivered stunned me. It was big enough for most of us to sprawl on it and be able to be comfortable. Freddie threw himself down in the middle of it and stared at the ceiling.

"I think Liam's got delusions of grandeur. This thing takes up way too much room."

Kellan chuckled as he tugged me to him. "It's so we can all curl up and share Sparrow when we watch movies or shows. The poker table and pool table will be down in the main living room. This is just for us."

I kind of liked how that sounded. A place we could lounge where it wouldn't rub it in Milo's face. Though there was a bite of regret at that idea too.

When Kellan dipped his head, I rose up on my tiptoes to kiss him and he slid his hands under the waistband of my loose pants and gripped my ass. It gave me a shock and I fisted his shirt.

For a moment, my heart stuttered and I blinked my eyes open to find his gaze on me. It was Kellan and I was safe. The only other person here was Freddie. That soothed more of my racing heart.

"Good?" he asked as he lifted his head and I grinned at him.

"Good."

He let go of my ass then nodded once before he delivered a light slap. I jumped and Kellan grinned when I laughed.

"Even better." He pressed another kiss to my forehead. "Milo's downstairs. Doc will be by later today. You two stay put, yeah?"

"Will do, Daddy K," Freddie said with a smart salute. "Come on, Boo-Boo. Movie time, you and me."

After Kellan left though, Freddie didn't turn on the television, he studied me.

"You okay, Boo-Boo?"

I dropped onto the sofa next to him. It was huge and soft, there was more than enough room for us to sprawl and starfish and we probably wouldn't touch each other. It was also designed more like a bed than a sofa, though it was definitely a sofa.

"I think so," I said slowly. "Should I not be?"

"Kel grabbed your ass." The blunt words served as a dash of ice water.

"Yeah, he did."

"Do I need to talk to him?" He was so serious that I scooted over to him.

"No, it's fine."

Doubt crept into his blue eyes and he raked a hand through his disheveled hair. "Are you sure?"

"Yes." I crossed my heart. "I promise, it's fine. I—" I

glanced at the closed door then back at Freddie. Rome knew, and while Liam and Jasper definitely suspected, I hadn't talked to them yet. And I still needed to talk to Mickey.

Maybe.

One hurdle at a time.

He held up his pinky finger and I hooked mine to his. "I told Vaughn and Kellan about my uncle."

All the air seemed to whoosh out of him.

"They're helping me."

"By grabbing your ass?" He definitely didn't look convinced.

"Yes." I summoned a smile because this really was okay. "Even when it's scary—actually because it's scary. They are helping me to face the nightmares that anyone touching my ass triggers in me."

I didn't have to explain it further. Freddie's eyes darkened and I squeezed his pinky.

"Stay here with me," I pleaded and he refocused on me.

"I don't want them to hurt you."

"They aren't hurting me. They push me because I asked them to. If I say stop, they stop. I don't want my uncle to control *anything* about me anymore." The words came out more vehement than I intended, but… Wait. No buts. "I don't want anything to do with him anymore. I don't know if I'll ever like anal sex, but I want the chance to discover what it can be without someone trying to hurt me."

Freddie grimaced.

"I don't know how it will all go, I just know I don't want to be afraid of you guys. I don't want to be afraid when I *know* you won't hurt me."

Still studying me, he rubbed his lower lip. "They stop when you tell them to stop?"

I nodded. "Sometimes, if I—if I have a moment, I don't even have to tell them. They know to do it and they take care of me. I won't lie, it hasn't been easy. I mean sometimes it is and then…something happens and I get triggered."

"But you're not giving up?"

"No." On this I was resolute. "I won't give up. Kel says even if it takes a month, a year—ten years. They're not giving up either. We take it as fast or as slow as I need to go, but I'm the one who decides."

He looked thoughtful. "Do you think…" Not finishing the question immediately, he studied me again. I wished I could read him at that moment, but there was so much darkness in his eyes. So many questions.

Some of those shadowy places could drag you in and suffocate you. But I kept ahold of his pinky. I was here and I wasn't going anywhere.

"Do you think it will really help?"

"I hope so." I wouldn't lie to him. "Kel and Vaughn have ideas. They're talking. Working together to try and help me. I think…I think if I told everyone, they would want to help too."

"Probably." He gave me a wry smile. "I know you're working on this, but do you think we can try the same thing for me? Just—you and me. I'm not sure I'd ever be comfortable with the guys…"

He didn't have to explain that. "Anything you need. We can go as slow or as fast as you want. I—I'm no expert. But I'll do whatever you need me to do."

The corners of his mouth quirked and he shifted his grip from interlocking our pinkies to just holding my hand.

"This works?" He lifted our joined hands and I nodded.

"Totally works."

"Okay then. Let's hold hands and watch something really bloody and violent."

Laughing, I leaned over and froze before I pressed a kiss

to his cheek. But Freddie didn't leave me out there, he closed that gap and I gave him the kiss.

"Blood and violence makes you happy?" Freddie said with mock surprise. "You are so the girl for me."

I laughed again, then we made ourselves comfortable while he looked for a movie for us to watch. Not once did he let go of my hand.

CHAPTER 37

JASPER

Doc arrived too fucking early, in my opinion. I'd barely had a cup of coffee. Considering Emersyn was already in her studio when he got there, I guess that was the reason he came so early. I'd gotten in too fucking late the night before, to do more than check on her before going to bed.

Since she was already curled up with Rome and Kel, I'd left her where she was. We needed a schedule. I scowled at the idea of having to sign up for time with her. Scratching the bristle that I'd begun to let grow back in, I caught Doc's questioning look.

"What?"

"It's a little early to be that annoyed."

"Eh," I said with a shrug, then grimaced. The stitches were out, but the area was still tender. I didn't want to be laid up any longer. There were things I could do—like drive—that meant I could alleviate some of the burdens on my brothers.

"Went to bed late, alarm went off too fucking early and I haven't had coffee."

"If you wanted to reschedule your therapy…" He raised his hands at my glare, but there wasn't anything about his manner that suggested he was really cowed. "Or you can keep scowling at the world. Get it out of your system now. Little Bit doesn't need to try and comfort you while she focuses on her own PT."

"Thanks," I muttered while rolling my eyes. "Otherwise, I would have just been the grouch who pissed all over her morning."

Lips twitching, Doc waited for me to finish my coffee before he moved to get his own. I needed to figure out the new machine they'd set up, but some days I just wanted normal black coffee and Doc seemed to be in the same mood.

"What?" I asked when he kept smirking. I thought Doc's dickish vibes were new when he came back, but now I was starting to wonder.

"Drink your coffee, Jas. Pick a fight with me later. You're going to need that extra energy for the lifting today."

Lifting?

"What are we lifting?" I had to follow him as he strode out of the kitchen, coffee in hand.

He didn't answer, pausing at the closed door to the studio and knocking. We'd soundproofed it, so she might not hear us.

"Hit the button," I told him.

After a beat, he pressed a button next to the door. It turned on a light just inside that she could catch in the mirror.

Depending on how loud the music was, she wouldn't hear a bell. A moment later, the door opened to a sweaty, flushed Emersyn who grinned at both of us.

"Jas, this was the best idea," she told me and my own smile grew. We'd only installed it a couple of days earlier.

Smug, I saluted her with my coffee.

"Also, good morning." She blew me a kiss and I made a show of catching it and tucking it away in my pocket.

"Time for physical therapy," Doc said dryly. "We're out in the warehouse today. The guys have set up some weights that we can use out there."

I frowned, then glanced down at her feet. Except for the little sock things she wore over the ball of her foot, they were bare. "You need shoes." While I wanted to say more clothes, since she was in a crop top that left her midriff bare and dance pants that looked spray painted on, I didn't.

First of all, she could wear whatever the fuck she wanted. Second, I'd just get rid of the rats or poke their eyes out. Though...

"You need to grab a hoodie or a sweatshirt," Doc said. Fuck yes, he could be the bad guy. "It's too cold out there and you're already warmed up. No getting a chill."

"I can do that. Give me five?"

He nodded and stepped back to let her out of the studio. She paused to brush my lips with a real kiss and to snake my coffee. I chuckled as she stole a sip, then grinned at me. "I'd offer to make you one of yours..."

"Nope," I told her. "This is great. Probably a good idea to wait on the other until after Mickey beats us up."

Doc snorted. "I'm not going to beat you up."

Pivoting, she backed away, a playful expression on her face. One that had been somewhat lacking over the last few days. Or maybe I'd just missed it. Either way, I was damn happy to see it.

"You say that *now*, and in a little while it will be—'push, come on, you can do one more. Look at that, it was easy.

Give us another.'" The perfect mimicry of Doc's encouragement made me snicker.

"Just for that, I'm adding pushups," Doc teased her, his disgruntled expression turning into a smile after she blew him a kiss and vanished up the stairs laughing. "She looks better."

The sobering comment gave me pause. "She's been looking better for days."

"She has," he agreed, heading back to the kitchen where he grabbed his bag. "But she's also been pushing herself, and some of the fatigue has been sneaking through the cracks."

"The renovations are taking longer than expected and we're running into a lot of dead ends." That frustrated all of us. The renovations were going well though. We were almost ready to start furnishing the bedrooms, but we'd had to wait for the rest of the plumbing items, including the new shower and bathtub we'd gotten her. Her bathroom would be larger than all of ours but then again, what space did we really need?

"She likes that part," he said, pushing the electronic release for the lock that let us into the anteroom, before we headed out into the warehouse itself.

Fuck the air out here held a biting chill to it. Cars had been shifted and moved so that a workout area could be set up. They'd pulled out the benches and free weights. The floor was base concrete, no mats of any kind. But we'd fix it inside when we were ready. In addition to the safe room, we were going to turn some of the other bedrooms into a free gym.

That just meant more reno and knocking out walls. It was probably the most comprehensive renovation we'd ever done to the clubhouse since we built it. Knocking back a long drink of the coffee, I scanned the interior of the warehouse.

The rats were not in evidence, though there should be some out on the street or nearby, keeping watch. The truck

I'd brought in the night before waited for offloading, but that would be later today.

We had a number of trucks out and three were due back by sundown tonight. The crews would come in and do all the offloading, inventory, then sorting for delivery.

"I know she likes it," I said, glancing back at the door before focusing on Doc where he went to work setting up the weights. Like me, he was dressed in loose clothing, sweats and a sweatshirt, though his read Army in bold letters across the front and looked worn as hell.

Mine was an old gray and black sweatshirt with Braxton Harbor in stylized lettering. I didn't even remember where I got this one. It was comfortable though, and I'd grabbed it more out of habit than anything.

"So what are you worried about?" I asked when he didn't comment about her liking the renovations. Clearly, *something* was bugging him.

He moved the flat weight bench over and then gripped the larger barbell. He'd only put two twenty-fives on it, so fifty pounds, which wasn't that much.

I waited him out this time as he tested it before he pointed me at the bench.

"I can do a hell of lot more than fifty." Fuck, Swan could probably do a hell of a lot more than fifty.

"Just because you can doesn't mean you are. This isn't about a strength contest, it's about building back muscle tone and lost flexibility. We also don't want anything tearing. So you're starting with fifty."

The order chafed. No, it wasn't the order so much as the finality in his tone and the implied *don't push me*. Just made me want to push him. Clamping my teeth closed, I swallowed the first comment that came to mind.

Doc was back. He was in. He'd been in for a while, I'd been watching. The urge to slug him had diminished, though it hadn't vanished entirely. Grinding my teeth together, I turned away to put the coffee down and to roll my head from side to side.

Temper fisted, I went to the bench and laid on it. Doc moved to spot me. Yeah, that just made me glare at him. "You didn't answer my question."

"I told you this is about restoring lost muscle tone—"

Gripping the bar, I snorted. "The question about Swan. What are you worried about?"

"Not a conversation we're going to have."

What the fuck?

I eyed him, but Doc just met my gaze.

"You want to explain that part," I said, not sure I wanted to issue an invitation that he could in part decline. However, I did want answers. If Doc saw something I didn't where Emersyn was concerned, then I wanted to know what it was.

"She's my patient," he said as if it explained everything. "Now, focus on what you're doing. The weight is light but we're going for reps more than resistance."

Adjusting my grip, I lifted the bar off and lowered it to my chest then pushed it up. Yes, it was light. Fifty pounds wasn't a strain.

"Give me fifteen, nice and steady," Doc ordered, but I only half-listened to that part as I turned over his statement in my head. "That's good. Take a breather…"

"I don't need a breather." So I kept going and he didn't comment. "She's your patient," I said at rep twenty. A light burn had begun to work its way from my arms to my shoulders. "So whatever it is you think would violate confidentiality."

Had something else happened that he hadn't told us about?

"Jasper," Doc said on a sigh, gripping the bar when I pushed it up and halting my reps. "You can interrogate me and tear apart this worry or you can focus on your healing and getting better. You can't do both."

Letting go so he could rack it, I rolled to a sitting position and ignored the immediate stitch in my side as I faced him. "Who says I can't do both? If something affects her then it affects me. I can't help her if I don't know what it is."

"You can't help her if you collapse either, and it ties her up in more knots worrying about you." The dry observation struck like a slap in the face. Arms folded, he glanced back at the door, and I did the same. She still wasn't out here.

"Talk to me," I said, then blew out a breath before I added, "Please."

That earned me a surprised look. Fine, fuck it, I deserved that.

"Doc, she's important to me."

His expression eased as he raked a hand over his head. "Kid, I know she's important to you."

He hadn't called me kid in a really long fucking time. I used to hate it back then, but it didn't bother me so much now. Usually, it was a title he reserved for Milo.

"She's important to all of us."

I accepted that truth for what it was.

"But I gave her my word, anything she says to me or talks to me about—I don't share. As her doctor, I wouldn't anyway. I'm also her friend, or trying to be again."

Grimacing, I put my hands on my hips and glared at the weights. "If it's bad..."

"It doesn't matter what it is. If you asked for my word on your condition or anything you told me, then I wouldn't share yours either. In fact, I haven't. Not you. Not Milo. Not Kel. None of you."

Fuck.

I wanted to swear, and at the same time I couldn't. "I fucking hate that I respect that."

He chuckled. "Well, hate it all you want, but get your ass back to work." He pointed me toward a step bench.

I stared at it then looked at him. "I can walk up and down stairs."

"Didn't ask. Get your ass over there. Or we can keep arguing about this when she gets here."

Whatever. He showed me what he wanted me to do. It seemed pretty fucking straightforward. Step up, hold, then step down, hold. Only, I needed to keep all my weight on one leg on the way up 'cause the hold was with the other leg in the air. Then the same on the step down.

As straightforward as it was, I started sweating by the fifth rep. My balance wasn't as rock solid as I'd like. Swan's arrival on the tenth step let me take Doc's order to break for a breather without complaint.

Goddamn stitch in my side was worse, too.

"Walk it out," he told me, then summoned Emersyn with a curl of his fingers.

"Are you okay?" she asked, her gaze fixed on me. I pasted on as cocky a grin as I could.

"Kicking ass and taking names. Just taking a break so Doc can focus on you."

A skeptical frown tightened her forehead and she switched her attention to Doc. Between leaving us and coming back, she'd pulled her hair out of a bun and put it in a ponytail. She'd also washed her face of the sweat. Or maybe she'd just cooled off.

Either way, dressed in one of Rome's paint-stained sweat-shirts, she made an adorable picture that smelled a lot like vanilla and citrus when I passed close to her. The scent was enough to settle some of my restlessness.

"He's fine, Little Bit. Focus on your workouts so he'll focus on his."

The echo of what he'd told me was right there and I shot

him a look as I continued my circuit. He met my gaze easily. He could have told her I pushed it and that I'd had a bit of weakness at the end. He could have said I'd overdone it with the barbell and wasn't listening.

Instead, he just focused on her.

As olive branches went, it wasn't a bad one. Once he got her working on the free weight, I moved back to the step.

"I'm still on this?"

Doc nodded with an easy smile. "Yep. Another set of ten, then walk to cool down."

Swan spared me a look, but Doc clucked his tongue to get her focused back on what she was doing. The barbell had been shifted from fifty to thirty pounds.

She seemed to be having as easy a time with it as I had with the fifties, but he wasn't building our strength.

It wasn't until I was on my third set of steps and my muscles were protesting with a burn but not giving out that it all registered.

After the barbell, he gave Swan a couple of lighter fives then had her doing walking lunges. None of this was *hard* or going to build intense muscle. But it was pushing us to maintain a certain level of output.

Son of a bitch.

He was working on our endurance.

Doc met my gaze when I paused mid-stride and raised his brows. Okay, Doc. I see you. I see what you're doing. I smirked.

"What's next?"

CHAPTER 38

EMERSYN

*I*t had been almost six weeks since the Vandals came for us. Forty-four days since Adam traded himself for me. According to Freddie, almost eighty days of sobriety for him. It was also one day since I had to say goodbye to Lainey again.

She'd left a wrapped present for Milo with me, along with another for me personally. That was when it hit me that we were in the midst of the holidays. She had to go home because Andrea would be going home. Adam was still missing, according to their family, and there would be repercussions.

Her goal was to avoid those as much as possible, but how could she? Really? We had no idea where he was. Who had him. Or when he would be back. It had to be a when. No ifs allowed. Liam had been circumspect on the possibilities, but it didn't seem like a secret he was keeping so much as an answer that continued to elude him.

A personal affront from the way he acted. It was also a subject he changed whenever I brought it up. While he didn't seem to want to discuss it, he couldn't quite hide his worries. I swore every time we seemed to get close, he retreated.

After the couple of days I'd spent with him, he'd been absent more than around. I didn't want to yell at him, but I had a feeling that keeping track of Liam would be a full-time job.

At least I didn't hate PT as much anymore. Vaughn did weights with me on alternating days. Jasper had joined my PT sessions, and he was getting stronger. Mickey? He always seemed patient and steady, and even when I wanted to push further, he would just hear me out and then redirect me back to the slow, but steady path.

The results were there. I was stronger. The pain in my arms seemed more like a phantom than anything else. I traced my thumb over one of the scars. Had they faded? They weren't red and angry anymore. They'd begun to whiten out. Eventually, Mickey had said, eventually I'd be ready to tattoo them because the scar tissue would be less.

Vaughn had even begun to draft some designs with Rome offering his own ideas. Freddie had joked that I needed a social meter on each arm—one for when I wanted company and the other for when I wanted people to fuck off.

A knock on my bedroom door dragged me out of my melancholy. "It's open."

We'd only had furniture in here for the last couple of days, so I was still getting used to the new space. I had to admit though, my favorite thing was the painting Rome had put on the ceiling. It was the night sky and he'd done something so that the stars actually twinkled.

I needed to remember to ask him what that was. Liam nudged the door open and I grinned.

"Hey!" I'd just taken a shower after coming back from the

shooting range. Kellan had taken my shooting practice seriously. Twice a week, no excuses. Although he didn't make me shoot for hours on end like we had that one day.

Bullet therapy, he'd told me, was good for some things, but not all of them.

This late in the day, I was just pulling on loose pants under an oversized t-shirt. But I had them in my hand so I dropped them on the bed as I went to greet Liam. He scooped me up into a hug and his lips found mine like we were two magnets snapping together.

Electricity skittered over my skin and I let out a groan as he lifted me up. Arms wrapped around him, I savored the very thorough invasion of his tongue as he darted in to play with mine. Humming and half-tempted to twist and drop him on the bed, I groaned when he gave my hip a gentle pinch.

"What?" I grumbled, lifting my head and his whole expression softened.

"I've missed you, too, Hellspawn. While I'd like to do nothing more than spread you out on this new bed and christen it with your screams as I eat you out until you can't see straight, we have a meeting to get to."

Heat rolled through me and I swore my cunt spasmed at the very delicious promise in his words. Then the rest of his sentence registered.

"What meeting?"

Amusement curved his sensuous lips and he shifted my weight to band an arm beneath my ass before he sat down on the bed with my knees landing on either side of his thighs.

"The meeting Kel is pulling together downstairs. Vandals business."

Vandals business. My heart clenched. "And it's okay for me to go?" I wanted to be there. More than that, I longed to just be one of them, but sometimes they didn't want to discuss everything in front of me.

He leaned his head back and squinted at me. "Of course it's okay for you to go." Between one blink and the next, his eyes narrowed. "Did someone tell you that you couldn't?"

"No, just…I know sometimes it's easier to discuss some stuff when I'm not there." I mean they did talk when I wasn't around and it wasn't like I knew how everything worked…

"Hellspawn." The snap of command in his voice pulled my gaze to his. "I came to get you because we're not starting until *all* of us are there. You're part of all of us."

Below the command was an air of quiet confidence particularly when he said "us."

"I'm glad you're back," I murmured, then cupped his cheek. A hint of yellow-green bruise decorated the corner of one eye. The bruises had been fewer and further in between, this one was almost healed. "With the Vandals and with me."

When I would have kissed him, he leaned his head back a fraction and eyed me. "You *are* one of us."

"I—"

"No arguing on this one, Hellspawn. In fact—you know what. Get those pants on because I can tell those panties are way too thin and I really don't want to have to break Milo's jaw for bitching if we didn't come down." Not even waiting for me to respond, he rose and set me on my feet.

When he snatched up my pants and knelt to help me put them on, I swore my face scalded again, but the impatience with which he shook the pants made me hurry up. As soon as I had them on, he frowned at my toes.

"Socks—one sec."

"Why do your feet look that bruised?" The growl in his voice should be downright illegal.

"Dancing," I told him as I dropped to sit on the bed, then

tugged on the fuzzy socks. "I've been upping my training. Dancing can be brutal on the feet."

"Hmmm."

Someone wasn't happy. Rising, I slapped a hand to his chest. "Deal with it, O'Connell," I told him, lifting my chin. "Performance can be pain, but it's a pain I crave." I punctuated the sentence with a kiss to his jaw before I headed out the door.

"Fuck," he swore behind me under his breath. "You did that on purpose."

"Nope," I told him, tossing a glance over my shoulder. "Just a happy byproduct." I sprinted once I got to the door to the hall though before he could catch me, and laughed all the way down the stairs.

I jumped the last two and slid on the new wood floors like I'd meant to do that. It also snared the attention of everyone present in the newly-finished "living room" with its stuffed sofas, recliners, a ninety-inch television, pool table *and* poker table and three standup arcade games.

When those arrived, I'd been a little startled but Rome just said, "Liam." It made me smile. Freddie had claimed Galaga for himself and currently had the top seven scores. No one else was even on the board.

I kind of loved that.

"Running away, Sparrow?" Kellan asked, flicking his gaze behind me and I grinned.

"Liam said you guys were waiting for me and I didn't want to hold you up."

He patted his knee and I climbed over to settle there while everyone else grabbed spots.

Milo stared at us pointedly and Kellan slid a hand onto my thigh while he met Milo's stare. When my brother said nothing, just shook his head and hid a smile, I almost fist pumped.

So much winning.

Liam strolled over to the chair next to Kellan's and dropped into it. "Setting my alarm. In seven minutes, she's moving over here."

"How long do you think this meeting is going to take?" Vaughn asked as he handed me, then Liam, a beer before he settled on the end of one of the sofas where he had a beer of his own. "And Freddie, pause that game…"

"I'm almost—"

"Freddie," Jas and Liam said in the exact same voice. I had to clap a hand over my mouth to keep from laughing, especially when the game made the whining sound of the character dying.

"Apparently," Freddie said, "I'm done."

He sauntered over to join us and paused next to me to press a kiss to the top of my head.

"I'm only joining you dicks 'cause Boo-Boo is here."

"Noted," Kellan said with no small amount of amusement. "Come on guys, get in here and let's do this." When Kellan nudged me back, I slid further onto his lap and draped my legs over the arm of the chair. "Better," he murmured, before pressing a kiss behind my ear.

Rome came down the stairs, hair damp. I hadn't seen him before I went up. He circled the room and claimed a beer from the table next to Jasper before trailing his fingers down my cheek. I caught his hand and squeezed it. He looked me over and I smiled at him. He nodded then moved to take a seat.

It wasn't until he shifted that I caught Milo watching me, almost thoughtfully. Mickey sat next to him on that sofa and when I glanced at him, he raised his beer in a quiet greeting.

I liked this. Everyone was here. It would only be more perfect if Lainey hadn't had to go home.

"Now that we're all here," Kellan said. "We've got a few

topics we need to discuss. We're starting with Liam… what have you gotten on Brixton so far?"

That yanked my attention to him, and I wasn't the only one. Over the last few weeks, I'd done my best to not dwell on Brixton, the shock collar, and forcing Rome to take that beating. But I hadn't forgotten him.

Him or Adam.

"Nothing," Liam said with a scowl. "I had a call with the king earlier this week. He knows even less, and he's not happy about that either. Pretty much every single Royal is being dragged into the hunt." That definitely didn't make him happy. "It's going to be a bloodbath, because this is a chance to curry favor with the king and some of these guys are just pawns who've never been given a shot before."

"What are the chances they're going to be gunning for you?" Milo asked and I stiffened. Before I could really react though, Kellan squeezed my leg gently. When I looked at him, I read the request to trust them right there in his eyes.

I nodded and he gave my leg another squeeze then rubbed it.

"They aren't even looking at me. Hell, half of them don't even know my name," Liam said with a snort. "Being a bishop does have its advantages. The fact is—Brixton and his people are good. They walked in, took Rome and Hellspawn, threw Rome in a ring and managed to control them until we showed up. After, they vanished without a trace."

"What about the people running those events?" I didn't think Brixton ran them, because we'd still had to follow some rules. We'd actually been on our way to one of the fights before they even got the location. That didn't suggest control—unless that was an act.

"Too many layers to fight through to find the guys who run the palace. While nothing is impossible, Hellspawn, they aren't likely to be the ones Brixton is fronting for. First of all, they are very well aware of my twin. Rome has been to plenty of matches with me and secondly—it would be too much exposure for them."

I wanted to ask how but he sounded certain so I left it alone. I had more questions about the king but he didn't bring him up again, so I would wait.

For now.

When Liam's alarm went off, Kellan just gave him a look and Liam flipped him off. Everyone laughed, even me. It helped to ease some of the tension talking about Brixton had aroused.

The discussion turned to trucks and shipments. More about our renovations. Costs came into it and Kellan said we were going to have to delay a couple of things until we were back in the black the following month.

"I could help," I said before thinking about it. "I mean, I do have money." I just had to get access to my accounts.

"You are helping," Kellan said firmly. "You're staying safe, you're learning to protect yourself, and you're helping us."

How was I helping them?

"Hellspawn, put a pin in that. Going for your money right now means we have to deal with your family. If that's what you want to do, sign us up—but you don't have to deal with them until you're ready."

My family. Right.

I frowned.

"Besides," Liam cruised right on. "I'll take care of underwriting any more changes. I mean—I was part of the reason the place got shot to hell."

The conversation shifted but I was still back on dealing with my family. I had accounts. I even had trusts. I was eighteen—no, I was nineteen. Those were accounts I could access…

"Sparrow," Kellan said softly when the hum of conversation in the room surged. My skin prickled and I caught Milo still studying me so I raised my brows, but he shook his head.

Tabling that, I glanced at Kellan. "Sorry, I was thinking."

"Nothing to be sorry for; you were thinking about stuff you do not need to deal with right now. We have more than enough to take care of what we need. I meant it when I said, you don't have to deal with any of them."

"I know. Liam said the same thing." I kept my voice low just like his.

"Now promise me that you're not going to do something that might alert them without talking to me first." Not to all of them, just him.

"I promise," I said. "I don't really want to talk to them." I kind of wanted to see my mom, but that was a niggling feeling in the back of my head that I kept pushing away. Some days I almost forgot about being related to any of them.

I liked that a lot better.

"It's going to be alright," Kellan said gently. "You know that, yeah?"

"I want to believe it," I said. But sometimes it was hard. He studied me for a moment and when he slid his hand up to my throat, I leaned into the contact, resting my forehead on his. The hum of conversation rising and falling around us mixed with masculine laughter helped even more.

It was going to be alright.

Maybe if I said that enough it would be true.

CHAPTER 39

DOC

The day after the meeting, I arrived late for Little Bit's physical therapy. Jasper was already out on a delivery, but he had her vouch for him doing his exercises. Honestly, at this point, Jasper was probably fine. I could discharge him fully, but...

I liked having his activities semi-limited. If it kept him out of fights until he was one hundred percent, that was better. Then again... as much as I looked at all of them like kids, they weren't.

Little Bit was out in the warehouse when I arrived. The gym wasn't quite finished, though it was close. There were rats at work out in the warehouse too. I eyed a grouping of them who were in heavy discussion near a large stack of pallets on the far side.

They must have gotten a delivery that wasn't ready to go out. As the exterior door rolled closed, I slid out of the truck and frowned because there was another rat about fifteen feet from where she sat on a weight bench, phone in hand.

Her expression was intent on the screen and mostly oblivious to her surroundings. It wasn't until Milo exited the door to the clubhouse and the rat who was standing there straightened immediately that I relaxed.

Milo raised a hand, then gestured toward his sister before he sent the rat toward the others.

They'd been waiting for me. I crossed to greet Milo with a quick handshake. "Everything good?"

"Yeah. Just ran into some issues. Two of the trucks broke down. Kel's on his way to work on them. He took Rome with him, that left me here with Ivy and I need to get these guys on deliveries."

"But you weren't leaving until I got here." Understood. "Where's Liam?"

"He's in meetings." He made a face. "I need to meet him later for more with Warrick. So it might be just you and Ivy for a while. Freddie's with Jasper on the road."

That was more than a few unexpected delays. "I'll stick around until at least two of you are back." I didn't have to check the gun in the holster at my lower back. The jacket hid it. I had a pair of knives in my boots too.

There was another gun in the truck.

"I'm leaving four rats on watch. They won't bother either of you."

"Don't worry about us, kid." I clapped his shoulder. I could more than handle the rats. "If push comes to shove, I'll take Ivy with me."

"Right," Milo said slowly, then glanced over at his sister. She wasn't looking at us, but I had a feeling she was aware of the conversation. For all that she still held that air of fragility, it disguised a core strength. She'd just gotten good at "pretending" she didn't see everything going on.

392

Made you wonder just how bad it had all been before. That wondering though, was not something I could afford to dwell on. It made me plot real murder. Not for the first time, I was all right with that. I wanted peace. I preferred peace.

I was not afraid of war.

"What's eating you?" I shifted my focus to him. The last few weeks—especially since getting Rome and Little Bit back and while his girl was here, Milo had begun to settle. While I wouldn't say the barbed-wire perimeter had been removed, a path had opened up.

"I'm worried about her," he admitted. "Worried about Liam, too. This…Brixton person, whoever he works for, and the fact that they have Reed…" His mouth flattened into a thin line. "This shit with her family." He cut a look at me. "What the hell did I miss, Mickey?"

"Kid," I said, keeping my tone firm but quiet. "You did everything for her. You did everything for these boys. Let me tell you right now, if we missed something, it was because a lot of effort was expended to make sure we missed it."

"Pinetree?" His eyes flattened and his nostrils flared. "They jacked her up on drugs. Electroshock therapy." Yeah, I'd read between the lines on a lot of that too. Where I hadn't already been over the lines like I had with her toxicology.

"She's not there. We're never letting that happen again."

We would for fucking sure *never* allow her to be abused again. Not the sexual abuse. Not the physical abuse. Not the mental and emotional abuse. Milo may not know the details, but he was close. Even if he hadn't allowed himself to verbalize it yet.

"You know—"

"Don't," I told him, slicing a hand through the air then shifting it to rest on his shoulder. Little Bit had noticed our conversation. She'd gone still and her attention wasn't on the phone in her hand anymore. "Don't focus on that part. We

393

fight the battles in front of us. We prep for the battles that are coming."

"And the ones we can't see?" He locked his gaze on mine. For a moment it was too goddamn easy to see the boy he'd been in the man in front of me. The boy who'd grown up too damn fast and made the kind of emotional and physical sacrifices his parents should have been there to protect him from.

"Well, I have your back. You have mine. We'll have hers. We'll have theirs. They will have ours." Then, because of late it had grown more and more true, "Don't underestimate her or that firecracker of yours. They have been in this fight, and I don't doubt for an instant they won't protect us."

I shifted my gaze and caught her glance. Worry filled her expression, and I did my best to give her a smile.

"And on that note, I'm going to go work with her on physical therapy before she decides we're keeping things from her."

Milo sighed then glanced back at her before he faced me. "I don't know that I'm ever going to be okay with her dating everyone or with her actively choosing this life."

Somehow, I wasn't sure if he understood how clear that was to everyone and not just me. "That's your prerogative. You want the world for her. But this is what she wants. Sometimes…we have to accept that those two things don't have to be the same. Her choices are the ones that matter."

A faint but real smirk touched his lips. "Be careful, old man, your feelings are showing."

"Get out of here before I remind you how not old I am and slug you." I gave him a friendly smile of my own and he chuckled before lifting a hand to wave to his sister.

She dropped any pretense of ignoring us as I headed toward her.

"Is he okay?" she asked by way of greeting when I got

there. As she stood, she looked so damn fierce despite the oversized clothes, sneakers that seemed almost too big for her feet and her hair pulled up into a ponytail while she sported a pair of fingerless lifting gloves.

They looked good on her and it made me feel better to see her wearing them. When I gave them to her at our last session, she'd been a little skeptical.

"He's fine, Little Bit. He's doing what brothers do, which is worry about their sisters."

"I'm fine," she declared, her chin lifted in defiance even as she folded her arms to assume a defensive posture.

"That doesn't mean he won't worry. Just like you worry about him."

Her nose wrinkled as she made a face. For all that she had a natural elegance and class, she was every bit the stubborn little shit her brother was. I should have seen it from the beginning.

Speaking of which… "Shall we get to work?"

She spared a look to where her brother had gone then back to me before she slid the phone into a pocket on her leg that I hadn't noticed. It was a tight fit and it held the phone in place.

"I'm ready," she told me. "Do you have to go right after?"

"No…something up?"

"I'd like to talk to you…if you have time."

I'd make time. "Done. Let's do this then."

As much as I'd rather just go ahead and push her to tell me now, I gave her room to breathe. The weight she'd put on during recovery, not only from her injuries but from the blows her confidence had taken, continued to be breathtaking. While I knew she was dancing, she hadn't taken back up with the silks.

Not when any of us had seen. That didn't mean she

hadn't. So that continued to be an area of concern. Again, not pushing. Not yet.

If I were to guess, it would be Jasper or Liam who goaded her when they tired of patience. I didn't want to force her hand. Not when I had to rebuild trust.

Then again, I wasn't doing her any favors if I let her get away with not achieving her goals.

One step at a time.

We didn't talk much as I walked her through her weights. She'd increased how much she lifted in short order. She'd also added reps. Then again, it took almost an hour before Milo and the crew of rats finished loading those pallets and crates on various trucks and headed out with them.

I wasn't a fan of Milo running only with rats for backup, but we couldn't leave Little Bit here by herself. As the sounds in the warehouse diminished, though, she relaxed.

We needed to do something about her discomfort around the rats. I got it. They wouldn't lift a finger in her direction other than to do as she told them. But did she know that?

"Be careful with overdoing it," I reminded her. "We want to strengthen you, not injure you again out of fatigue."

"I know," she murmured. "I'm only increasing my reps by ten and my weights by five. But I need to feel the burn."

Some of my skepticism must have shown, because she unzipped her hoodie and shrugged out of it. Despite the cold in here, she had been working, so I imagined she wanted to cool down. After she laced the hoodie around her waist, she glanced at me.

"I really do know," she assured me.

"I heard you, Little Bit. I'm allowed to be concerned. You've been making a hell of a lot of progress, so I don't have any complaints at all."

Her expression brightened. Oh, was that it? Fuck. I could kick myself.

"You're doing great," I continued. "Let's get to these next few, then we can grab a coffee after you hydrate."

A warmer smile stretched her lips. "I'd like that."

When she moved back to the weight bench to begin lifting, I followed to spot her. If she needed praise then I'd fucking shower her in it.

Rather than let her drive herself too hard, I called it after another thirty minutes. The fact she didn't argue to push a little more suggested more than anything else that either she was good with being done or really did want to talk to me.

"Do you want to shower?"

"Um…" She did a cautious sniff check. "I don't think I'm too terrible. I did shower after my workout this morning."

"Sweat never killed anyone, Little Bit. Let's get you some coffee." I'd say keep hydrating, but she'd been drinking out of a thermos of water since she started her workout. "Do you want to get it here or would you like to go for a ride?"

That caught her off-guard. She blinked slowly. "Actually —I kind of would like to go for a ride. Is it okay for us to go by ourselves?" She did a quick scan around her. "I just need to grab a bag."

"We'll be fine. I told Milo we might head out for a bit and if I had to go, I'd take you with me. We can alert the guys to you being with me so they aren't worried when they get back. And you take your phone…"

"Which has tracking on." The swiftness of her grin was another kick in the crotch. A kidnapping on the heels of what she went through at Pinetree had definitely left its mark.

Ten minutes later, she and her bag were in my truck. Kel had answered my message while she was inside. I told him we were going out for a ride and I'd have my head on a swivel. While he wasn't thrilled, he said to just keep him updated.

Liam's smart ass said he'd be heading in this direction in the next hour or so, he'd just follow her phone. Fine by me. Once we were out of the warehouse, she had her sneakered feet on the dashboard, and her hands stuffed in her pockets.

"Okay, Little Bit. Now you're worrying me." I hadn't intended to just kick off the conversation that way, but it was time. "Tell me what's going on."

She sighed. "I know I said I wanted to talk but now...now I'm not even sure where to start."

"Wherever you want," I suggested. "Tell me how you're doing—for real."

Rolling her head so she faced me, she said, "I'm okay. I think I'm better than okay. It's kind of scary to look too closely at it."

"Because you don't know if it's real or not?"

"I know it's real, but... I love—oh look at that." She cut herself off and sat forward abruptly. The decorations all over the street and in the different storefronts captivated her. "I keep forgetting that it's almost Christmas."

"Well, we can do something about that."

"We can?"

Oh, we were *definitely* doing something about the holidays for her. "We can," I said. "We will. Trust me?"

The last two words slipped out without me meaning to just drop that rock in the pond. Instead of withdrawing she stared at me intently. "I want to."

"I'd like it if you did again, too." Fuck it. "But I can also wait for when you're ready."

"Mickey..." She sucked in a deep breath and then let it out in a rush. "I know you learned a lot about me from your exams. You know...about the assaults."

My grip on the steering wheel tightened, but I kept everything neutral. That neutrality was a total facade, but it was one she needed. "Yes."

"You...you asked me why I didn't go inside when you took me to the hotel, but I couldn't tell you then."

"I remember."

"I need to tell you about how I grew up. About my family and..." She licked her lips. "About why things like Pinetree happened." The barest hint of a quaver in her voice had me peeling one hand off the steering wheel and I held it out to her.

After the briefest of hesitations she slid her hand into mine. Her fingers were like ice.

"You—may not like what you hear."

Oh, I already hated it. "I can handle it, Little Bit. Tell me what you need me to know."

She took another breath and then the words spilled out of her in a rush. The story registered but I had to keep a lid on every single reaction.

Her. Uncle.

Her. Fucking. Uncle.

"I can't tell Milo," she said in a voice so heavy I wanted to pull over and just pick her up so I could carry the burden. I hadn't bothered with stopping anywhere yet. No, I just kept driving.

"Little Bit, Milo loves you more than anything else on this planet. You can trust him. He will *never* blame you."

"That's not it," she admitted. "It's—he'll be so damn disappointed, Mickey. He's told me over and over how he wanted me to have this better life. That the family who adopted me... the world they took me to...that it would be everything he couldn't give me."

And they not only failed at every single promise they'd made him, they'd *hurt* her. It would break him if he thought she didn't trust him.

I needed to know everything about these people. I'd

399

thought her uncle was just a control freak. Some arrogant jackass who wanted to control her because of a class thing.

This was so far from that it wasn't funny.

Yes. Milo would be furious. But he would also go hunting for blood for her. All of us would. "You've told the others."

"Not everyone yet," she admitted, the fine tremble in her hand betrayed how hard this was for her. "But I'm working on it. But Kel and Vaughn are right. Everyone needs to know. We're all…together…" She shot me a questioning look and for the first time since I'd tried to shove her away, the door looked open again. "It's weird…it gets a little easier each time I tell it."

I'd promised to keep my head on a swivel, and I did. It was the only reason I noticed Liam as he drifted into the lane behind us. He lifted a hand as if to wave at me and I nodded before glancing at her.

"Does Liam know?"

"Not all of it, but—some."

"Okay," I said, then lifted her hand and pressed a kiss to the knuckles. "He's right behind us."

She swiped at the tears dampening her cheeks, and twisted to look back. But not once did she let go of my hand. When she waved, I kept a watch over her. His presence helped her.

They all did.

Good. She'd need that.

Me?

I'd need blood.

A. Lot. Of. Blood.

CHAPTER 40

EMERSYN

*T*elling Mickey had been a lot harder than I'd thought it would be. He listened to every single word, without comment, until I finished. When he held out his hand like a lifeline, I clasped onto it.

Each time I had to tell the story, it was like I used a scalpel to tear myself open, rip out my soul and spill all the dark viscera out to be examined. It—hurt. Yet, it hurt less each time.

Whether it improved because I was growing scar tissue where I tore myself open or because each time there was a little less darkness to spill—I really didn't know. I wasn't sure I wanted to know.

If I asked, I was fairly certain Kel would tell the others for me, but this... This was my secret. I'd lived with it for so long, that it had bound and gagged me even when I was thousands of miles away from them.

No more. I needed to cut away the bonds holding me prisoner. I didn't think I could ever wash away all of it, but maybe I could bleed it out of my system.

"You ready?" Milo stood in the open door to the sitting room where I'd just sat down to pull on Uggs. The shadows beneath his eyes had lightened some. And he'd gotten a haircut in the last few days, neatening it up. He was dressed in jeans and a polo shirt, that was like the first time I'd seen him semi-dressed up at all.

Like everyone else, he seemed to favor jeans and t-shirts. Not that it was bad, but the polo gave him a different look. "Won't you be cold?" It was a short-sleeved shirt. I'd opted for a pullover sweater, more because I wanted to stay warm than hide the scars.

Yes, the scars were tangible evidence of what happened, but I'd gotten used to them. Over the last few weeks, between the scar gel Mickey had me using and the rolling therapy, the jagged marks had faded. They weren't gone.

They'd *never* be gone. But I didn't flinch at the sight of them anymore.

Improvement, right?

"I'll be fine, Ivy," Milo said with a wry smile. "If we were going to be outside for any length of time, it'd be different."

He had a point. I glanced down at myself. I'd gone with the soft sweater and a pair of leggings. The Uggs would keep my feet warm. I had a jacket I could take, but I wouldn't be putting it on unless we were outside for a while.

"Are we bringing something with us?" I smoothed down the sweater as I stood and twisted to call, "Freddie! Milo and I are leaving. Vaughn's downstairs and I think Kellan and Rome will be back with dinner soon."

"Got it," he yelled back. "Bring us dessert especially if Ms. Stephanie made cheesecake!"

I grinned. "Cross my heart."

"Yeah, if she made cheesecake, there won't be much left," Milo said, pitching his voice a little louder.

"Man, Raptor," Freddie complained. "You suck. Boo-Boo has my back. Don't you, Boo-Boo?"

"Absolutely." I was still laughing when I shouldered my bag and joined Milo. It was more like a tote than a purse, but it also held my gun, along with a can of pepper spray and a brand new panic button. Kellan had added both to my stash of items.

The stapler sat in the corner of the new sitting room on its very own table that Freddie had set up. It was ridiculous and perfect. Above it, hanging on the wall was an axe. Jasper had been pretty pleased about that too, but Kellan had just rolled his eyes.

It was the little things about setting up in here that I enjoyed the most. The guys kept saying we were making it more like a home, but it was already the best home I'd ever had.

"Five bucks says there won't be dessert left over," he teased as he motioned me to precede him down the hall.

The changes to the place continued. Rome had begun a mural in the main hallway, and it was a stunning rendition of all the guys. Kel working on a car and Jasper standing to the side, bat across his shoulders as he waited for something. Vaughn working on a tattoo, but you couldn't see his client. Even Freddie was depicted, though he looked like he was napping on a sofa with an open book on his chest.

He hadn't added Milo, Mickey, himself, or Liam yet, but each day something new would appear. I loved it. Downstairs, Vaughn looked up from where he had a phone to his ear.

"She and Milo are leaving right now," he said, then

crooked a finger to me. I needed no real encouragement to drift over and brush a kiss to his lips. He shifted the phone to my ear with a wink.

"Hello?"

"Heard you had a date, Hellspawn." Liam's droll voice sent a shiver right through me.

"Well, I do believe I texted you this morning that I was going to dinner with Milo at Ms. Stephanie's. Probably going to be a couple of hours."

"Sneak some cheesecake out if she makes it."

I laughed. "Freddie just asked for the same thing. I'm assuming her cheesecake is amazing." Vaughn's eyes lit up and he nodded firmly.

"Ms. Stephanie makes great treats, but her chocolate mousse cheesecake was something special she kept in reserve for Milo—or at least the kind she made with the dark chocolate chips."

I swore my mouth watered.

"Okay, I will try to bring extra of the dessert home."

Vaughn mimed pumping his fist as Liam let out an elongated "yes!"

"I'll be there when you get back." The promise from Liam sent another shiver through me. Right, I needed to not get so turned on before dinner with my brother, a woman he considered family, and whatever family she invited to share the meal with us.

"I'll see you then," I said, before blowing a kiss. This was to both him and Vaughn. Vaughn winked as I handed him back the phone.

"Let's go," Milo said, laughing. "I actually plan to eat dessert, so I don't think any of these assholes are getting any."

"We'll see." If I only had one piece, I'd bring it back to share with them.

It wasn't until I was in the passenger seat and Milo was

pulling out of the warehouse that it occurred to me, we didn't have backup. "Aren't we supposed to always have a third person if I'm going out?"

"We'll be fine," Milo said. "Trackers are on the cars, on your phone, and you have the panic button." From anyone else, I'd have assumed he might be teasing. Not Milo, though, he was grimly serious. "Everyone knows where we're going, when we're supposed to be there, and that we will check in. I promise, Ivy, we have this covered. I won't let anything happen to you."

I wouldn't let anything happen to him either. "Got your back," I said, and he flashed me a quick grin.

"I know you do."

That—I didn't have words to explain the feeling surging through me at his response. Unsettling disquiet and even more wild euphoria threaded through my veins. It was like an adrenaline dump hitting my system the second I stepped out onto the stage. The moment between reality and performance, when everything gelled.

"Are you crying?" Milo asked, sharp concern in his voice. I lifted a hand jerkily to swipe at my cheeks.

"No, yes… maybe." I laughed at myself. Even forming words properly seemed to be escaping me.

"Thank you for clearing that up. What's wrong?" While the last two words might have been a question, they struck with the force of an order. But even the domineering command couldn't dislodge the tipsy sensation of belonging.

"Nothing is wrong," I said, making sure I got all trace of the dampness from my face. "Just—you didn't even blink when I said I had your back. You didn't growl at me that I didn't need to protect you and you didn't—" How could I describe a feeling that was both disbelief and elation? They weren't mutually exclusive, but they were also not identical reactions.

"I get it," he said after a moment. We were paused at a traffic light and he glanced over at me. "I do get it. You didn't even flinch when I said you were safe and I'd protect you. You just accepted my word and believed me."

"I absolutely believe you." At some point in the last few months, he really had become the brother I'd always wanted and never known I was missing. For all his fierce protests and stony glares at the guys, he made space for me with them and he made a place for me.

We still stumbled over parts of it, but I also just—

"I trust you," I said. "I—I know there's nothing you wouldn't do, and it's important for me that you know I will do everything in my power to keep you safe, too."

"Done," he said almost too easily. "But I'm pulling older brother privilege, I get to make sure you're safe first."

"That's not a thing." It didn't sound like a thing.

"It's totally a thing," Milo said firmly. "Ambiguous language favors the person who wrote the contract. I arrived first, I set the rules, ergo, I wrote the contract."

"Ergo?" I twisted sideways and studied him. "Are you going to lawspeak me into compliance?" It took some warming up to get to teasing, but that was also getting easier.

"Huh," he said after a moment, tapping the steering wheel. "I think the wording is coming back to me with all the contracts, and organization documentation I've been reading lately."

I made a face. "Should I say sorry?"

His laughter was deeper, a little richer, and filled with some genuine humor. "Not at all. I never thought I'd enjoy reading the fine print, but it's taking me back to my pre-law studies."

Oh. Shit. I grimaced. "Can you still study law?"

"Sure," he said with a shrug. "But would anyone hire a jailhouse attorney?" He paused a beat. "You know, never mind, they might. But there are rules of conduct, years of coursework and…let's just say that the patience I used to have has been severely tested."

"Maybe," I said, grinning at the holiday lights and all the decorations. We hadn't gone out much, but the guys were planning to do a tree soon. We had time. So many holidays spent on the road, I had forgotten what it was like to need to do the decorating.

Usually, the hotels and the venues had all the decorations I would see.

"I think you're incredibly patient and really smart. You could probably turn every ounce of your experiences into academic credits and finish your degrees if you wanted."

"Maybe," he said, echoing my earlier sentiment. "We'll see. Not as committed to it now as I was then."

"Would it help, now?" Before, he'd said that his whole goal had been to build up his resume and the Vandals' wealth to be a part of my world. Was that the only reason he'd studied law?

He didn't answer immediately; instead he seemed to be considering it. When he nudged up the Christmas music, I didn't chafe at the non-answer. He might not know and I was *very* familiar with that.

When we pulled into the driveway of Ms. Stephanie's, the *wild* display of holiday lights captured my focus. The entire front of her house was one huge scene right out of some movie. The lights danced and reflected different images. There was a Santa on her roof, reindeer in her yard, and even presents scattered across the lawn because of the sleigh "wrecked" in her tree.

"This is—"

"Over the top, but the absolute best," Milo said with a fresh wave of enthusiasm. "Mickey said you've been missing

Christmas, so this is a great way to enjoy it. I know she'll have her tree up."

I climbed out of the car in a hurry, bag in hand. Then I paused again to just soak all the madness in.

"Ivy?"

I glanced at him.

"Being a lawyer might help now. I'll keep thinking about it."

I grinned slowly. "Whatever you need."

"Right now," he said, rubbing his hands together. "I need to get you inside and out of the cold."

Laughing, I went with him up onto the porch. He knocked twice before opening the door. Holiday music spilled out on an array of twinkling lights and rich aromas of meat and something infinitely sweeter and definitely like chocolate.

My stomach rumbled as I followed Milo inside. He pulled off his shoes and set them to the side, then offered me an arm so I could take off my Uggs.

"Come on in," Ms. Stephanie called from the kitchen. She wore an apron over her festive top and jeans. "Mickey's already here and hard at work. We've got drinks and hors d'oeuvre and we can get all caught up."

"Mickey's here?" Surprise flickered through me as Milo's smile turned a little smug.

"Come on," he said. "Evening, Ms. Stephanie, we should definitely introduce Ivy to your brother."

In the kitchen, standing at the stove wearing a droll expression was *Mickey*. Fresh shock rippled through me. I jerked my gaze from Mickey to Ms. Stephanie to Milo. What the hell?

"Don't be a dick, kid," Mickey informed Milo before shooting me an apologetic look. "Ms. Stephanie is my sister,

Little Bit. Don't hold it against her. Trust me, she really is the angel she appears."

Ms. Stephanie swatted him then hustled over to us. She enfolded Milo into a hug that he returned easily and I frowned.

"How did I not know this?" Had I completely missed all the clues?

"Because these boys think they're funny," Ms. Stephanie said with more than a little reproach directed at Milo and Mickey. "Are you up for a hug or are we still hands off?"

After the earlier conversation with Milo, the lights, and finding Mickey here, I was a lot easier with some things than I would be normally. "I think we can try a hug."

"Yes!" Ms. Stephanie raised her hands in triumph before she swooped in and gave me a fierce hug. She smelled like sugar cookies and honey. "Fantastic. Also, you look much better than the last time I saw you."

She motioned us to the table and to where there were already cold veggies circling a bowl of dip and also some hummus with slender cuts of bread. "We're going to be a few, so help yourselves. I've got soda and water if you'd like, Emersyn. I'd offer wine but you're still too young for that."

Bemused, I slid into a seat and caught Mickey's eyes as he grimaced. Had we never talked about his sister? All the guys had to know. Yet...

I was so going to get them.

"I hope you like mocha chocolate cheesecake," Ms. Stephanie said and I swore my stomach growled. "I know it's Milo's favorite, but I did a special mousse for it because a little bird told me that you enjoyed dark chocolate and coffee."

I did. I really did.

"I'm not even going to ask who ratted me out," I said,

stealing a phrase from Freddie's book and that earned me a laugh from Milo as Mickey grinned. "I *love* cheesecake. Freddie and Liam asked me to bring back any extra if you didn't mind."

"I don't mind at all. I'll make sure we have slices for all of them." Ms. Stephanie looked pleased, but Milo rolled his eyes and I just grinned.

Score one for me.

CHAPTER 41

"They're on their way," I said to Liam. "How far out are you?"

"Around the corner," Liam answered. "Kel and Rome are already on their way back. Can't be more than ten minutes. Jas should be there."

"He is. Just not happy about having to sit this out." I rubbed my thumb against my lower lip. "Not thrilled that we're not telling Dove what we're doing."

"This is housekeeping," Liam said, and I had to admit his tone was exceptionally reasonable. He wasn't wrong, it was housekeeping. Housekeeping we needed taken care of sooner rather than later. "Hellspawn could handle it, but she doesn't *need* to handle it."

"Anyone ever tell you that you split hairs well?" I didn't mean it as a compliment, and his laughter didn't carry much humor.

"A lot of practice." The sigh was there. "Too much sometimes. See you in five."

He didn't wait for me to say anything, just hung up. Jasper descended the stairs with Freddie behind him.

"Everyone else is on their way," I told him.

Freddie flung himself down on the sofa and sprawled. "Well, I'm sure Daddy K already has a plan."

Jasper gave him a look. "You really need to stop calling him that. It's disturbing."

"Nah," Freddie said, grinning. "It's funny, especially when he makes that face."

The door to the warehouse opened. The soft hum of sound that echoed through the downstairs meant we'd always hear someone coming in, too. It was the little things. The secondary door disengaged with a series of rolling locks.

The scent of Chinese food filled the air and I climbed to my feet. "Kitchen."

"Aww…" Freddie mock-pouted. "I'm comfortable. Come on, Daddy K. Tell Vaughn I can stay out here and eat."

Kellan rolled his eyes, but his grin was more exasperated amusement than genuinely annoyed. Not that he had to respond to it, but Freddie had already rolled off the sofa.

We didn't bother with plates, just sorted out the cartons, grabbed utensils, and dug in. Good plan, because I was starving. Liam popped open a water rather than a beer. But none of us were drinking.

Not until the work was done.

"Where are we starting?" I asked because we had a limited time frame to do everything we wanted to do before Dove got back.

"Here," Kellan answered and I wasn't the only one who gave him a long look. "I've been thinking about this for the last few weeks. Truck heists. Details on Sparrow's movements. Details on ours. The fact someone knew the full layout of the clubhouse including where the studio was. They also had the right ammo to penetrate the walls."

Putting his food aside, he leaned forward and braced his arms on the table.

"Coincidence? Entirely possible. For example," he continued holding up a single finger. "We know her uncle hired people to watch us."

Watched us. Photographed us. Provided him with material to convince her she had to leave us to protect us. We'd dealt with *some* of those problems, but not all of them.

"That said, we know the 19Ds were involved in the heists. They were doing jobs, watching us, reporting on truck movements. Tracking some of the trucks."

Even as he ticked off facts I was already aware the back of my neck itched. The 19Ds were history, but they'd caused way too much trouble in the meanwhile.

"When Milo and Mickey shook down a runner a couple of weeks back, we got a name, Jason Chaser. From Weavil's description, it sounds like he might have been linked to Warrick's charity, but there's no one named Chaser there or on their books that we've been able to find. Liam's people turned up another…"

"Constantine," Liam supplied. "Don't know if it's a first name or a last name. Do know they have ties to the palace crew, but we're not getting the information from them directly. The king doesn't know who they are either. The questions I have are if they are tied to Brixton. So far, we've come up empty on every avenue to approach them."

He spared a look at his brother.

"Rome and Hellspawn have described their interactions with Brixton. He told them they were working for an employer, that everything he had Rome—me—doing was for his employer. But he never mentioned his employer by name."

Rome nodded once.

"The guard names were all singular and didn't tell us much either. Grunts are grunts. They can come from anywhere."

That included the one Dove killed. Pride fisted in my gut. It was tempered by the sour taste of reflux in wishing she hadn't been in that position in the first place.

"Everyone is on the same page. Any questions?" Kellan took lead again. Jasper just shook his head.

For some reason, I expected him to want more. Then again... like the rest of us, he just wanted this shit over and done.

"Jas?" Kellan said.

"Freddie and I have been vetting the rats, all of them. Since I've been laid up, it gave me a lot of time to watch them."

"And they pay fuck all of attention to me," Freddie volunteered with a frankly devious little smile. "Asshats expect me to be stoned ninety percent of the time. You'd be amazed by the shit they say when I'm around."

I shifted my gaze to him and I wasn't alone. It rippled around the room. The rats were going to get a hard lesson in manners. One they wouldn't forget.

"So, we used it to our advantage," Jasper picked up the thread. "Even if I'm wounded, they know better than to fuck off in front of me. It let us apply pressure in different places to see what they would do."

"Nice," Liam said slowly and I had to agree. That was fucking brilliant. Timing their observations let them compare notes. It also revealed those most likely to fuck up and separate them from the guys who just wanted to do their damn jobs.

"Thank you," Jasper said with a smirk. "I have my moments."

"You're about to have one right now," Liam retorted in the same tone.

"Children," Kellan said in a dry tone. "Don't make me separate you."

Rome slid a five onto the table. There was a moment, then Freddie slid another five out.

"Bros, you better be betting on me," Liam informed them. Rome answered with a middle finger.

Chuckling, I put my hand on the fives. "We'll table this bet for later, cause I'll put my money on Kel."

"Damn," Jasper said. "That's cold."

"Ice cold," Liam agreed. "We could take all of them."

"Yes, we could." The firmness of their resumed alliance entertained me. It probably shouldn't be so funny, but fuck it. How long had we all been pulling apart, drifting away from each other and the grounding that having each other's backs provided?

"Put a pin in that," Kellan informed them as he rose and began to clean up the trash from the food. "Rome... you know who we need?"

"Yep." He rose, boxing up his leftovers and tossing the empty cartons before heading out to the warehouse. Liam didn't follow. None of us did. Rome was the best one to send; his actions and reactions were unpredictable for anyone who didn't know him.

The rats tended to just do what he said because he didn't ask and he didn't waste time on "pleasantries."

I kind of hated that I would miss that part. The moment Rome left though, we all moved. Cleanup, then we would go out and clean up.

Fifteen minutes later, I followed Kellan into the office. Jasper and Liam were watching the main warehouse and Freddie was on the cameras. Rome waited inside with our guests. The fridge door was cracked open.

Rather than walk right in, Kellan paused at the desk. The office itself was in much better shape these days. New desk, chair, and set up. Filing cabinets and more added to the aesthetic. A faux wall hid the fridge door so we could slide it closed.

Dove had stumbled in there in the first place when she'd been trying to escape all those months back because she'd been looking for a place to hide.

"How much do you think?" Kellan asked me. The unspoken sentiment referred to how much violence did I think it would take.

I shrugged. "Depends on how much they're paying." Or more accurately, how much they were being paid. This wasn't a conversation we needed to have.

"Need something solid to lead with…" No, this conversation was all a show for our guests waiting in the fridge. They'd been called in there by Rome, now they stayed put and would hear us.

We were in no way trying to be quiet about it. Them listening was the point.

"Everybody lies," I said and caught a flash of amusement in his expression as he turned to face me. The humor vanished behind sobriety. "Solid or not, if we have questions—chances are they are lying about something. If they're lying about something…"

"They could be lying about everything. Getting jaded in your old age, Falcon."

With a careless shrug, I flipped him off with the hand I used to card through my hair. One gesture to hide another. Games like this were more Liam's forte than mine. I preferred the direct approach.

"I accept what I'm shown. Words only mean so much. Actions? They say a hell of a lot more." It was an old but solemn truth between us.

"You may have a point." Translation: he agreed. "How do you feel about getting us started?" Did I want point?

"Can I do what I want?"

He tapped a pen against his palm as though he needed time to consider. "Fine, but it had better work." Damn, the exasperation and impatience he put into that sentence almost made me think he *was* annoyed.

Not wasting time, I crossed to the fridge door and yanked it open. The interior had been cleaned, and then some. The walls had been hosed down in a hydrogen peroxide solution to remove the stains and then plied with several gallons of hot soapy water and bleach. It actually didn't smell too bad, just a bit musty. Good work on our part.

Inside, Rome leaned against the wall, arms folded. His neutral expression seemed almost bored. It wasn't his reactions I was interested in.

Not slowing as I entered, I decided to just go with the flow and seized Shaun, the rat closest to the door, by his shirt front. The fabric stretched, but since I had two handfuls of it, he didn't get far as I half-lifted him and dragged him toward a wall to slam him against it.

Eyes bugging out of his head, Shaun jerked a wild look to Rome—yeah, no help there buddy—then to Kellan—good luck with him—before finally returning to me.

"What the fuck? I didn't do anything." At first he clutched at my hands like he would try to peel them off. The scrape of his nails on my skin barely registered.

It took a flex to keep him off his feet and pinned against the wall. But I was ready for his feet to flail. Predictable as hell.

"C'mon, Falcon—words man. I haven't done anything!" His voice climbed as the panic set in. Staring at someone often unnerved them.

Staring at someone you hoisted a foot off the ground had

a way of shaking a lot of things loose. He tried to kick me, I twisted slightly and took the blow against my thigh, then slammed him against the wall a couple of times.

Fight or flight was a bitch. A teacher I had in high school told me once that my very size could trigger it in other people. I was big. Imposing. It had nothing to do with my personality and everything to do with primal genetic coding or some shit.

I didn't care, except it reminded me to be gentle with the ones who needed it and that I didn't always have to say a word to imply violence and get what I needed.

The minute the smell of urine stained the air, I knew we had Shaun.

"It was just some oxy," he said, as he began to babble. "Not a lot. I needed some, cause I got pain you know and then I needed more. Doc wouldn't give me a prescription so I picked some up and then a little more and you know how it is, if I wanted more I had to give them some info…"

I dropped him while he kept talking and turned my attention to the others in the room.

Critter. Ratchet. Bobby.

Bobby surprised me, but then Bobby was a follower. He didn't think for himself. A problem in any line of work, but especially ours. We didn't use Bobby for much beyond general grunt labor because he was too easy to persuade. He was a genuinely nice guy without an ounce of deception in him.

Critter, like Shaun, had been around a while. They'd both come in with JD. It surprised me that we had Shaun and not JD in here. Then Ratchet. He was sweating.

The only one of those three who were.

Behind me, Shaun continued to blubber as he gave Kellan a list of names. One was Jason Chaser. Well, look at that. Ding ding ding. We had a winner.

"Okay, I get all of that," Kellan said in a kind, understanding voice. "I understand running the drugs. I understand calling it deliveries cause you're not actually doing the selling, you're just the errand boy."

"Yeah, that's it. I swear. I wanna stop. I've tried, but they threatened to break my kneecaps. I owe them a lot, Kestrel. And you know with my back…"

"I understand," Kel continued, his tone soothing. It was a velvet-lined trap. "It's a real bitch when you've got an addiction and someone uses it against you. Why didn't you ask us for help?"

"'Cause—no drugs. That's the rule. We all know it. But this was a prescription. I didn't do it on purpose."

"No, of course not. And I'm really sorry about all that, Shaun. Truly. Telling us would have been hard, so I can get why that was a challenge." I kept an eye on Ratchet even as I managed to look bored and like I was just waiting for the word. "What I don't get is why you'd sell out Freddie and the rest of us?"

"What?" Shaun's voice climbed an octave. "I didn't—"

Ratchet made a break for it. He didn't even reach the door before Rome caught him and flung him back to me. I gripped his shoulder, real friendly like. "Hey Ratchet, whatcha doing?"

There was a flash of a knife. I threw Ratchet into Critter and there was a grunt of sound. Critter stared at his friend then up at me as they both began an almost slow-motion tumble.

After he jerked the knife out, Critter backed up. Bobby fled to a different corner and I pointed a finger at Critter. "Stop."

"Yeah—sorry guys, I can't do that."

Then he slit his own throat.

CHAPTER 42

JASPER

Critter killing himself *after* he gutted Ratchet was not an end any of us saw coming. Shaun melted down into a sobbing puddle of piss. It was bad enough, I genuinely felt for the guy. Bobby, though, was in full panic mode. The only reason Bobby had made the cut was he didn't think beyond the directions he got.

We tried to stabilize Ratchet, but he was bleeding out too fast. The interior of the fridge stank of blood, urine, and death. I still couldn't quite wrap my mind around the fact that Critter cut his own throat. His blade was sharp, but still. Liam currently had Bobby sitting out in the office, talking the guy down.

Ratchet bled out too damn fast to get anything out of him. Critter was dead after spraying artery blood all over Vaughn.

Fucker.

"This is a shit show," Freddie commented as we stared

at the gory mess in the fridge. Considering how much effort had gone into cleaning the damn thing, I was less than impressed. Particularly because we got fuck all out of them.

Except…

"Jas…"

…whatever Critter knew made him wary enough to commit suicide rather than divulge it. That—that was some serious level of commitment. It also said he'd *never* been our rat. Maybe I was jumping to a conclusion. But that kind of loyalty had to be earned, it wasn't bought. I'd die before I betrayed the Vandals, but they were my brothers. Would I willingly die for one of the rats?

That answer was a lot more nebulous. I'd definitely risk myself to protect the rats because they were ours.

"Jas…"

The problem, now, was we didn't know whether Critter was tied to the enemies we already knew about or one of the more nebulous figures we hadn't identified.

He had friends among the rats. Those friends would have to be questioned. The minute they learned of his death, however, the useful ones would probably rabbit.

Or would—

"Jas!" Freddie snapped his fingers right in front of my face and I glared at him.

"What?"

"They're on their way back."

I switched my attention to his phone where he held up a picture from Emersyn. It was a photo of dark chocolate cheesecake. It was a miracle any of it survived Milo to get back here to us.

Then again, Swan was a bit of a miracle, too.

"Let the guys know. We're going to have to deal with Shaun."

"What about Bobby?" Freddie glanced over to the open office door. "He's not a bad guy."

"No, he isn't. I think we're going to volunteer him to go to Ms. Thompkins for a while—or that would be what I would do if I were in charge." Not that I was in charge.

"That's a good idea," Kel said from behind me and I pivoted to see him rubbing the back of his neck. A weariness marked his eyes. That kind of tired I understood. It was the kind that came from carrying a burden you couldn't—or wouldn't—put down. "I'll call her."

"I can do it," I offered. "Vaughn good?"

"He's washing up." He shook his head. "That's got to be one of the most fucked up things I've ever seen."

I didn't dispute him. It was a strange enough thought to imagine and I only saw the aftermath. I hadn't been in the room. "Take a beat," I told him. "I'll get Bobby sorted out. We need to decide on Shaun. Then we're going to need to go through the other rats."

His sigh was almost palpable. "Thanks, Hawk."

"You got it. Milo is on his way back with Swan. Just a heads up. We all need to have it together when she gets here." Just the mere mention of her seemed to lighten Kel's load as his shoulders relaxed a fraction and his chin came up. "Hey, Freddie, feel like making coffee for everyone?"

It was a better job than sticking around out here. Especially if we had to make a hard call with Shaun. Freddie didn't need to worry about that.

"I'll figure it out." He didn't mince words arguing or trying to offer to do something else. This rattled him. A lot like it had rattled Kel. Fuck, it rattled me.

"He okay?" Kel asked, tracking Freddie on his way to the door to the clubhouse.

"No," I told him. "But he will be. Just give time to process. Right now, he's asking himself what we missed."

"You guys didn't miss shit," Kel told me, his eyes blazing. "You called it almost perfectly. Bobby bugs me but then the more I look at this, the more I don't think Bobby needs to be in this mess until we've dealt with anyone coming at us who'll exploit him."

Pulling out my phone, and a pack of smokes, I paused to light one before I said, "There is no such time as one when someone won't exploit an innocent to get what they want. We can sideline him because it will protect us, but are we doing that at the cost of what it will do to him? Or do we partner him up with someone we trust so that we can offer him the protection he needs while also shielding ourselves?"

Head canted, Kel gave me a long look. "That's way too fucking reasonable for you."

"Look, I know I was a little wild there to the end, but I did run shit for over three years with precious little knowledge of what the fuck was going on with Liam or why Milo took that deal. I do know how to look after our people."

Lips twitching briefly, Kellan nodded. "Yes, you do. You might be an asshole, but you're our asshole."

"You're welcome," I said, with a smirk then held up the phone. "I'll get Bobby sorted out. Go deal with the rest of that shit like the boss you are."

"Asshole."

Chuckling, I walked away from the mess and worked out what I wanted to tell Ronnie. Veronica Thompkins had known us all long enough that we didn't have to bullshit her. That said, she didn't need to have *all* the facts. Just the ones she needed to have.

Pushing the door open to the outside, I stepped out into the bracing cold. The warehouse was chilly, but the air out here had a real bite of frost in it. I checked the sky as I exhaled a stream of smoke and then flicked a look at the camera just over the door.

We had a dozen of them placed strategically. That camera was the one they could see. There were three more that gave this alley as much coverage as possible. I needed to give Liam shit for the peeping Tom tendency he'd developed.

He knew *way* too much about cameras.

The scuff of a shoe and the clearing of a throat had me pivoting to where JD slouched against the wall. Like me, he had a cigarette in hand. His wasn't lit.

"Sorry," he said, straightening. "I came out here to get my head together and—" He wore bewildered well. And I kind of hated myself for judging his reaction.

Unfortunately, it had to be done. I pocketed the phone, then tossed him a lighter. He caught it and stared at it a minute before it seemed to register what it was.

"Thanks."

I exhaled and just waited for him to light his cigarette. The flicker of flame illuminated his face, revealing shadows and worry. Rather than toss it back, he handed me the lighter.

"Is it true?" the question was a little ragged, so rather than assume, I shrugged.

"Depends on what you're asking."

"Shaun was running drugs?"

Oh. That little nugget. "He said he was." Not much more I could offer him. "He's your friend, right?"

"Yes, he's my fucking friend." Real anger blossomed in his voice. "He hurt his back last year."

I remembered. "Took a few weeks to recover." We'd also paid for some physical therapy. "Came back and said he was good to go."

JD paced, agitation in his jerky motions as he sucked on the cigarette like it had done him a personal injury. He exhaled the smoke and vapor of warm breath in the cold air.

"I—fuck me. I knew he'd been struggling a little, but he said it was fine. Just a pussy problem."

"So you didn't know he was still using?" I could try to keep it conversational, but I was too fucking irritated right now. JD whirled to face me. His spine went stiff, but he didn't fire an answer back.

Apparently, he could think on his feet even while he was furious. Good quality.

Didn't stop me from just tracking and measuring everything he said and did.

"I didn't know he was still using…I mean he took a lot of aspirin. Bitched about headaches. Like I said, pussy problem." He pursed his lips, sometimes realizing the bullshit in someone else's answers came too late. Then you were stuck with the bitch of an aftertaste.

"Pussy have a name?"

"Bella? Blair—Beth—fuck if I know, it's a B-name. I don't pay that much attention beyond whether they got tits, ass, and a cunt to fuck."

Not a shock.

"It's why we stuck with strippers. Well, why I stuck with them. They are usually just using me to get off the same way I'm using them. But he got hung up on one. Been chasing her for the last—" He leaned to the side and spat. "Son of a bitch. For the last few months, since right before you brought that girl in."

"Did you meet this stripper?"

JD gave me a blank look as he stretched his arms. "Maybe? I just told you—I mean, I saw her tits at the club, got a mole just to the side of her right nipple and there was another on her left hip just where it dips down, you know. But she also did that glitter dust that smells and tastes like honey. Fucking Shaun stank of it."

That just tickled something in the back of my mind. "Was she one of the girls you two were fucking in the clubhouse?"

JD stopped dead.

Yes, Kellan had mentioned it to me. I hadn't killed them because they'd gotten their warnings then hadn't done it again as far as I knew. We'd been watching them closer.

Not close enough.

"Fuck, I don't know, Hawk. She could have been." He actually looked pretty broken up about it. "I mean—she was just a stripper."

Uh huh.

"Remember everything about her. Every distinguishing mark. Then where you guys met her. You know where Shaun's place is?"

'Cause we needed to go and search it.

He nodded.

"I want everything, the address. When he met her. How many times. How often he mentioned her. Did he ever take off and have you cover for him to meet her."

She could be a girl he had a thing for.

Or she could have been the bait on the hook to reel him in.

He put out the cigarette, grinding it under his boot. "I'll do that now…"

"JD," I said, before he got to the door. "Anything else you want to tell me?"

"No, I keep my head down and do my fucking work."

"So did Shaun," I reminded him.

"I don't deal drugs," JD told me flatly. "I like beer. I like smokes. I like pussy. I occasionally like to shoot the shit with the guys. I got a good thing here, and I'm not looking to fuck it up."

"Good. Go make the list."

If he wanted more comfort than that, he was talking to

the wrong person. As it was, I had a few issues of my own to sort out—not limited to where to send Bobby and then to figure out what else we'd missed in the last year.

Our enemies had been sniffing around for a long time, but we'd never had one get in this close before.

We couldn't afford to let it happen again.

Ronnie answered on the fourth ring. "You do know it's late, and I'm open over here."

"I know, Ronnie," I said. "I'd apologize. But it's an emergency and we need a favor."

"What can I do, Sugar? It's not Freddie. He's not here." All at once her hard-nosed tone gave way to something much friendlier. Like I said, she was a badass in her own right, but she'd been a friend when we needed one and we'd looked after her when people tried to rough up her or her girls.

"We need you to look after someone for us…"

CHAPTER 43

FREDDIE

Two days after Critter's—whatever the fuck that was—happened, I got to watch the guys carry in a Christmas tree. Well, attempt to carry one in. Seriously, when was the last fucking time we had one? It actually took Liam and Vaughn both to haul it. The challenge though, was getting it around the corner of the antechamber and into the clubhouse proper.

"You guys did not think this through," I said, nodding to where they had the doors braced open and were trying to ease the tree around the corner. It was easily seven or eight feet tall. It would fit in the living/game room area *if* they could get it into the front room.

"Unless you have a solution, you can hold all comments until it's in." Vaughn said, though he swore a moment later. "We might need to cut it."

"We're not cutting it," Liam said from the far side of piney needles that practically filled the entranceway. "We can do this. Freddie."

"I didn't do it," I said as I climbed off the sofa. The thing was so comfortable. I'd actually slept down here the night before.

"Is Hellspawn in there or is she in her studio?"

"Neither, she went to take a bath. She just finished PT with Doc and was hurting."

Vaughn immediately twisted to look toward the stairs.

"She's not hurting like that," I assured him. "She was just sore. She wanted to soak in the new bath and we haven't added all the reinforcement in case of splashing, so she bathes alone."

I had no idea if we'd done that or not, but Boo-Boo had been pretty drained. So she could have some time to herself.

"That's comforting." The dry comment from Liam actually pulled a grin from Vaughn.

"I'll let you figure it out while I go check on her."

"Nope," Kellan announced as he descended the stairs. His hair was slicked back and damp from a shower. He'd spent the day inside an engine and he'd smelled like it. "How big is that thing?"

There was absolute silence and I had to bite my tongue. Too easy. So. Fucking. Easy.

"What the hell?" Jasper's voice came from the far side. This was going to get comical. "Did you forget where we lived?"

Correction. It was comical. "We can always cut through the drywall…" I was not serious. We'd just reinforced that wall, if we tried cutting through it, we were gonna need more than just a reciprocating saw.

"We're not cutting through the wall. Back it out. We can set that one up out there and get a practical one for in here." Kellan sounded half-aggrieved, and half-amused.

"It smells fantastic." Milo sounded impressed as he descended the steps. I didn't even realize he was here. When had he gotten home? His expression, though, wasn't impressed so much as hungry. "When the hell was the last time we had a real tree?"

"We haven't," I said. "They never put up real ones at the group home."

We were lucky if we got the plastic ones from the store. But there was always some kind of tree. We even got presents, usually as the direct result of being on someone's angel tree or charity project, but the exchange on a solid present was totally worth it.

"There was one," Jasper said from outside. "Before we met you, Freddie."

"Well clearly, it couldn't have been that impressive, I wasn't there."

"That's right," Milo said. "Ms. Tappington's place. She was—"

"Crazy," Kellan filled in. "But she could bake."

"Which is good 'cause she couldn't cook worth a damn," Jasper said and they laughed.

When I glanced at Vaughn, it was kind of a relief to see he was as mystified as me. Sometimes... sometimes I forgot they all had lives and memories from before. I didn't think too hard about those years, and I sure as shit wasn't going to start on it now.

"Incoming," Liam called, and I ducked to see Rome sliding in under the tree. He practically eeled right out from under the tree and Vaughn had to shift before he stepped on him.

"Plastic sheets and drop cloths," Rome announced before glancing at me. I gave him a thumbs up and jogged up the stairs.

"You sure?" Milo asked behind me and I didn't catch Rome's answer. The drop cloths for painting and the plastic sheeting were all in the secure room right now. We'd finished most of the new bedrooms; we just hadn't moved all the furniture.

I hauled the lot of it down. Kellan and Milo met me at the bottom of the stairs and helped. Ten minutes later, I had to admit that I was impressed. So did Milo and Kellan.

Rome wrapped the whole tree up in plastic then used the drop cloths to slide it against the walls. It worked to let them stand it up inside the antechamber—barely— before they tipped it and then got it in the main door.

Most of the pine needles we lost were also on the plastic; it held up way better than I thought.

"Keep an ear out," Kellan ordered. "Distract her before she comes down."

"Okay, but I want to help decorate the tree." Better to be safe than sorry, 'cause that would be cool, I headed up to the new sitting room with my book in hand.

She was in the bath, so while they cleaned up the mess and set up the tree, I tumbled onto the bigger sofa in here and flopped on my back to read.

Weird. Even with the crazy crap with Critter and Ratchet, not to mention Bobby and Shaun, I'd been doing okay. The guys weren't happy with the Shaun thing, but I talked to him some. There were programs he could do, and while I couldn't really do any kind of heavy lifting, at least I had some first-hand experience.

Doc got him into one here in the community, where we could still keep an eye on him. The problem was, drugs were like mother's milk sometimes, and getting high was the only way to shut the voices up.

I checked my hand for tremors as I lay there. It was steady. That made my heart race and my skin go clammy. Tilting my head back, I focused on the ceiling as I tried to count my breaths.

I couldn't seem to get the numbers to go in the right order. The more I fucked it up, the more the panic began to scrabble at my insides. Shaun had been getting high for months and no one noticed it. Not even me.

Probably because I was high.

That could have compromised us all. He swore he didn't give up any information on any of us, but I knew what I'd do for a fix.

Rolling to the side, I sat up and put my head down. What I'd do? Look at what I'd already *done*. Stolen. Traded. Nearly sold myself...but that was a line I couldn't cross so I'd just followed some chick home, got her off and robbed her blind.

I didn't even remember her name.

Didn't want to remember.

The interior metal walls echoed back at me...

"Freddie," a soft voice intruded on the bleakness and the screams. Nothing I did stopped the sound. "Freddie, stop—you're going to hurt yourself."

Hands gripped mine as I yanked at my hair and pain lit up my scalp. I jerked a hand free and then I had my knife and—holy shit. "Boo-Boo." The blade was right there, on her throat, all I had to do was press a little harder.

The trembling that hadn't been present earlier was right there. As tightly wrapped as my hand was on the hilt, the quakes hit. She had her head tilted back, her soft brown eyes focused on me. Then she covered my hand with hers.

"Hi," she whispered. "Do you see me now?"

Did I—"Fuck!" I didn't jerk away for fear of cutting her hand or her throat, but I did pull back and she let me go. "Boo-Boo."

"You said that already," she murmured and I flipped, flicked, then closed the knife before I put it away. Jesus. I almost cut her throat. I wanted to pitch the knife across the room, but it was already in my pocket.

Scrubbing my shaking hands over my face, I glanced down at Boo-Boo again and she was right there at the edge of the sofa, watching me. Her hair was damp and hung straight over her tank top that was too thin.

I could see her nipples through it. I did not need to look at her nipples. I didn't deserve to look at them.

"I could have hurt you," I muttered. The urge to run was right there, but if I moved too fast, I might scare her. Goddammit.

"Can I hold your hand again?" The question punctured through the roaring in my ears.

"What?"

"Hold my hand," she said, then lifted her pinky. "We can sit back to back if you need it. Then you don't have to worry about me seeing you. But you're not alone, Freddie."

"I could have hurt you…"

"You didn't."

"But I could have." Didn't she understand? I gripped her biceps and pulled her up until she was facing me. The moment my knuckles went white, I loosened the grip immediately. I shouldn't even be touching her. "Boo-Boo… I kill people when I'm startled."

"You kill people when they threaten you. I wasn't threatening you."

But—

"And you stopped. You were so lost and you didn't hear me," she continued, grasping my hands when I would have pulled away. "I didn't want to yell for the others—"

"You should have," I told her. "I don't want to hurt you."

"You didn't hurt me," she repeated. "And I'll damn well stay here for you if I think you need me."

Was she— "Dammit, Boo-Boo."

"I know, I drive everyone nuts," she told me with a small

smile and I fought the urge to flee. "Liam and Kellan have both threatened to spank me."

A weak laugh escaped me at that confession. Dropping my gaze to where her hands gripped mine, I sagged. I didn't mean to just sit down. Yet, even as my legs gave out, Boo-Boo wrapped herself around me in a hug.

This was too much damn touching, and at the same time, fuck it was nice. I returned her hug just as fiercely. It was like the night in the drug den when I'd taken out John and his friends. Well, not friends.

Boo-Boo had come in then, too. Some place she never needed to be. She'd come in and she'd stayed with me.

"I'm sorry," I whispered.

"Me too," she answered. "But I'm right here. All fine. I didn't think you would hurt me, and I was right."

Thank fuck she was right because I'd have gutted myself... "Boo-Boo," I said, pulling back abruptly because I needed her to believe me. "If you ever see me like that again, throw something at me from across the room. Don't touch me."

Her expression crumpled, torn between ferocity and compassion.

"I mean it," I told her. "I wasn't me right then... I was him. I was back there. I could hear the sounds." Hear *them*. I didn't want to explain it. I didn't have to. Understanding filled her eyes.

"I'm sorry—"

"Just—promise me? I would die if I ever hurt you." I would die, too. I'd make damn sure of it.

"You will not hurt yourself," she snapped back at me.

"Did I say that aloud?" Holy shit.

"No, but I saw your face. You will not ever hurt yourself. I promise to throw something at you from across the room, and you promise that you will never hurt yourself like that."

"It's not the—" Woah. Her eyes went flat, her mouth compressed, and the promise of true violence flickered in her eyes. Man, she looked like Raptor when she got pissed off.

It was kind of funny.

Probably not the time to tell her that.

"You first," I mustered, rather than give into the crazy sense of laughter starting to bubble inside of me.

"I promise to throw things. I already said that."

"Right. Okay. That's good."

"Freddie…"

"You're super sexy when you growl." Probably not the best thing to lead with. Then she swallowed hard and I winced. "Sorry, bad joke—not the super sexy part. Or the growl part. Pretty pussy has bite…"

She lost the battle against laughter and her ferocious glare dissolved into laughter as she rolled her eyes. "You're terrible."

"And you love me for it," I informed her.

"Maybe," she countered and I clutched at my chest.

"Wounded."

"You will be if you don't give me my promise."

Letting go of a long breath, I pressed my forehead to hers. "I promise, Boo-Boo. I won't hurt myself. I'm not really a fan of pain."

"Me neither."

"That's a lie," I said and at her blink, I shrugged. "You're the one who said dancing was pain and you needed that pain."

"Oh." She made a face. "Fine. I do need that pain. I don't like you being in pain."

"Same." Then she wrapped her arms around me and hugged me tight. "What's this?" Not that I was objecting. I didn't want to let her go anyway.

"Pushing your boundaries," she whispered.

That was alright then. "Maybe we can hug for a while?"

"Yes." No hesitation. I only loosened my grip a little to move back to sitting on the sofa. Boo-Boo followed. But her grip never slacked off. I rested my cheek against her damp hair and breathed in her sweet scent until my racing heart calmed down.

Then I just kept holding on.

CHAPTER 44

EMERSYN

The tree was *enormous*. I stared up at it, more than a little impressed at the near *nine foot* tree. That was the measurement according to Vaughn who based it on me sitting on his shoulders to put the tree topper in place.

"What do you think?" Liam asked as he slid his arms around me from behind and pulled me back against him. "Milo said that you were missing Christmas."

"Not missing it—exactly," I said. "I kept forgetting it was the holidays. I didn't go home for them very much. The last time I had a Christmas at home, I was eight."

And that had been a double-edged sword I really didn't want to think about. A sense of restlessness had been itching under my skin for the last few days. I couldn't even put my finger on *why*.

"Hmm." Liam hummed a little sound as he rested his head against mine. "You're going to have to write a letter to Santa."

"Really?" I half-twisted to look up at him. "Santa?"

"Hell yes, Santa. Right Kel?"

Kellan leaned against the edge of the pool table, arms folded. "I think so. You need to write a very serious letter, Sparrow. Santa will have to decide if you're naughty or nice."

Okay, now they were joking. I just rolled my eyes and laughed. "I don't need any presents."

"Presents are never needed, they're given because someone wants you to have them." Liam tilted my chin up and before I could argue against his point, he kissed me. It was a slow, sensuous massage of his lips on mine. It sent a shiver cascading through me and then another.

Because we were far from alone.

Somewhere behind me, Vaughn chuckled. "Your turn, Kel."

"Yep." Then a crack of a ball hitting another at the pool table while Liam sucked against my tongue. Rather than lift me though, he just cupped my face and when he pulled back, I nearly fell into him.

"I'm next," Jasper said.

"To play me or kiss Dove?" Vaughn asked with so much amusement, I half-giggled.

Heat suffused every inch of my body. Then Jasper said, "How about both?"

"How about we play for kisses?"

"How about you losers settle your own debts?" Liam challenged, his eyes glittering as he winked at me.

"You don't want to play for kisses?" I teased.

"Fuck no, I want to play to take you home with me."

"Oh damn, look at the time," Jasper said. "You have to go. You mentioned it earlier."

"Bite me, Hawk." Despite the grumpiness in his voice, he was grinning.

Ignoring their teasing, I focused on Liam. "You have to go?"

"Unfortunately." At my frown though, he dropped another kiss on my lips. "Stealing Rome…"

"You're going to fight."

The bruises around his eyes and on his cheekbone had mostly healed, though there'd been a fresh scrape or two.

"It's what I do, Hellspawn. Rome will watch my back."

I still didn't like it. "You're hunting for Brixton. You both should have someone watching your backs." Rather than respond, Liam glanced up and over my head for a moment.

"They'll be fine, Sparrow," Kellan said from just behind me. "They've been doing this for a while. Rome will watch his back."

Just because they'd been doing anything for a while… Liam had been the original target.

"'Yes," Rome said as he arrived. Wrapping my hair around his hand, he tilted my head back and kissed me. It wasn't a deep or lingering kiss, but more a brush of his lips over mine. The light touch seemed almost more intimate. "I'll watch him."

"Rome—he was the one they wanted." I shouldn't have to tell him that.

"I know." He gave me a very firm look. Yes, he did know.

"C'mon, Hellspawn, walk us to the front door then bring that sweet ass back inside." Liam tucked me under his arm. "She'll be right back guys."

"I'm timing it," Jasper said on the end of a laugh, but there was a watchfulness in those gray eyes. I liked how relaxed they were with each other, but they were all trying just a little too hard.

Or maybe I was just overthinking all of this. Rome closed the secondary door behind us and Liam pivoted so he faced me and Rome bumped up against my back.

"Hellspawn," Liam said firmly, cupping my face as Rome wrapped his arms around me. "I will be fine. I've been doing

441

this for years, first for fun, then because it helped build up my credentials with the king. It gets me closer to the throne. To the people threatening us."

"You fight in the fights for him so he can leverage others and dish out punishment to those who disobey him. That's giving *him* power, Liam. It's not your power."

"You're right," he said slowly. "And you're wrong. I know you don't like this especially after what happened…"

"Of course, I don't like it after what happened. They hurt Rome…"

He just stared at me and I sighed, because I was shouting and he didn't deserve me shouting at him.

"Don't be scared," Rome murmured. "I'll protect him."

That pulled a smile out of me.

"And I will protect him," Liam told me. "We will protect you."

"What do I do? Sit here and look pretty?" That bothered me way more than I realized. "You guys are all taking risks. I see it in the silent conversations you're having. I see it in how you come and go at all hours. Then you throw in my problems…"

Was I being so selfish in wanting to stay? I'd brought more trouble to their door. I had to help fix it.

"Your problems," Liam said in a soft voice, "are our problems."

"Then your problems are *my* problems." I glared when his eyes flattened. He finally gave an exasperated sigh as he glanced up at the ceiling.

"Hellspawn, we'll argue about this later. I promise. For now, don't worry about us. I promise we'll text when we're done. Does that help?"

Not totally but… "I'd like it if you let me know you guys get out safe."

"Done," Rome said in a firm voice. I tilted my head back to find him staring at Liam like he was going to punch him. That Liam met that stare with one almost as frustrated as when he'd been looking at me made me smile. "Good night, Starling."

He kissed the top of my head, then entered the code to open the door. I kissed the corner of Liam's mouth. "Be safe," I told him.

"Yes, ma'am," he said with a bit more sobriety than teasing, but the teasing was still there. "You behave."

"I'll think about it," I retaliated and he laughed. Then I kissed Rome and let him nudge me back inside. After the door was closed, I sighed.

"They'll be fine, Swan," Jasper promised as he hugged me to him. "They know what they're doing and if someone tries to take them—well, we'll just go and find them."

That definitely helped.

A few hours later and after Jasper had gone to bed—he had an early morning run and Freddie was going with him—I sat on the edge of my bed, brushing my hair. The restlessness from earlier in the evening was back.

The knock on the open door had me glancing up as Kellan leaned against the doorframe. "You okay?"

"I'm…" I didn't want to lie, but I didn't have the words for whatever this…unsettled feeling was. I wanted to get up and run or scream or just throw myself back on the bed and pitch a temper tantrum. "I don't know how I am."

"Wanna talk?" He offered and I pulled the brush through my hair like I needed to just get out every single tangle and this weird feeling would go away. Probably not, but I wasn't sure how the guys would feel if I went down and locked myself in the studio.

"No?" I said, testing the answer. "Yes?" Neither one sounded right.

"Well, now that we cleared that up." Kellan nodded to the bed. "Mind if I come in?"

"You're always welcome," I said and he smiled as he crossed over to the bed. "You don't have to get permission." I tilted my head back as he leaned down to press a kiss to my forehead.

"I will always ask because you always have a choice. Most of us will."

I considered that. "Rome doesn't have to."

"No, because you already told him he didn't. He will wait for you to tell him he has to again." Affection marked his words. "I suspect you will never mind him."

"I don't expect to mind any of you."

At that, Kellan chuckled, then he sat down on the bed and laid back, one arm below his head. "Hmm-hmm. Liam and Jasper?"

I had to think about that, and then I swatted him. "That's mean."

"But you had to consider it."

I did. "That just makes me mean, too."

"Sparrow, we're a handful. All of us. Sometimes we get along great. Other times we fight like junkyard dogs over the same bone."

I made a face at that comparison and glanced back at him. "Please say that I'm not the bone."

His slow smile was half-serious, half-teasing. Oh, I hoped it was half-teasing. "We would *never* call you a bone."

"No," Vaughn said from the doorway. "You're too much a prime rib to ever be a bone."

Kellan snorted another laugh and I made a face at Vaughn. "I don't know if *that* is better."

"Totally better," Vaughn told me. Not even the sweet croon of his voice could make calling me steak sound good.

"A thousand percent better. Though, I think you're more like the decadence of chocolate ice cream."

"Chocolate ice cream," I repeated, tilting my head. "Do we want to follow this food metaphor to its conclusion or should we just call it good?"

"I love chocolate ice cream," Vaughn said. "It's sexy, sweet, and melts on my tongue. Sound like something you'd like?"

Kellan released a genuinely pained sound. "Falcon..."

"Hush," I told him, gaze locked on Vaughn. "I like where this is going."

Nudging the door closed behind him, he drifted toward the bed. "The best thing about ice cream is you can share it with your best friends, because even when there's only enough for a spoonful each, it's still the best damn treat ever."

A thrill rippled through my abdomen then unfurled through my whole system. I gave a little shudder at the thought of a "spoonful each." I didn't realize I could be quite so greedy or hedonistic.

"Sound good to you?"

I had to lick my lips when Vaughn took the brush from what seemed like my suddenly nerveless fingers. "It definitely sounds like a lot of fun." I shivered, that sounded like *more* than fun.

"Good," Vaughn said as he curled his fingers beckoningly and I took his hand. He pulled me up and lifted me right into a kiss. The firm feel of his mouth on mine was enough to blot out all the noise in my head. More, it seemed to set fire to the restlessness invading my system.

I gripped his hair as he wasted no time delving his tongue against mine. The warm, masculine heat of him chased out even a hint of chill. Lowering us to the bed, he dueled with my tongue, then pulled on my lower lip. The heavy weight of him blanketed me as he kissed a path to my throat.

He made short work of my shirt, then my panties were off along with my sleep shorts. Fierce pressure locked around my nipple as he sucked it against his teeth. He caressed my other breast and then continued his sensual path to my abdomen.

"Hmm, love this ink," he murmured.

"Need to add some to it," Kellan said almost idly in response. I lifted my lashes to find him gazing down at me a moment before Vaughn nudged my legs apart then pressed his mouth right against my cunt.

I'd forgotten Kel was still there.

"That's it, Sparrow," he said, stroking his hand through my hair. "Let Vaughn eat you up. He wasn't kidding about loving cream."

Oh hell, that turned me inside out. Vaughn hummed as he teased around my clit. He wasn't wasting any time on building me up slowly. I hadn't even realized how on edge I was until he pushed me right into an orgasm.

Hand around my throat, Kellan kissed me and swallowed every single one of my cries. Vaughn deepened the carnal kiss against my cunt, thrusting his tongue against me like he couldn't get enough. The first orgasm just crashed into a second as Kellan squeezed my neck and Vaughn eased two fingers into me.

Riding a haze of pleasure, I couldn't decide who to focus on or how. Kellan's mouth dominated mine even as Vaughn shifted against me. The sudden abandonment of his mouth was a cold dash against my senses. Not for long though, because he pushed my thighs wider and then the heaviness of his cock was there. He pushed in, the relentless stretch, the perfect burn.

"Switch," Vaughn said in a heated breath. The word registered as I swam up from under the pleasure they were drowning me in. Kellan lifted his head and I could still taste him on my lips as he released me.

All at once Vaughn was there and I could taste myself, him, and Kel all at once. He rolled until I straddled him. Rocking my hips in time to his, I savored every place our skin touched.

He clamped his hands on my hips, the push and pull a cooperative effort. Warm hands moved over my back and lower to my ass. A gasp escaped my lips as I dragged my head up.

"I'm here, Sparrow," Kellan whispered as I turned my head and kissed him. Vaughn kept filling me, every thrust of his hips sending sparks dancing through my system. More. I just wanted more. "You can have more," Kel promised.

"You can have everything," Vaughn said between explosive breaths. "Come here." I bit Kel's lip as he kissed me once more before letting me go to Vaughn.

"I'm still here," Kellan told me and I wasn't sure why until something warm and wet dribbled against my ass. The shock sent a bolt through me and I forgot how to breathe as I clamped down every muscle.

Vaughn stilled beneath me but he rubbed my hips as he murmured against my lips. "You're safe, Dove. All safe. Who is touching you?"

"You," I said on a half-sob.

"Who else?"

Warm fingers trailed up and down the crack of my ass, the wet spread against my anus. "Kellan," I said, shaking. His name came out broken.

"Yes, Sparrow, it's me." He pressed his fingers against my anus, the pressure gentle. It was there and gone again. "Do you feel me?"

I had to breathe. It took effort, and when I opened my eyes, Vaughn wavered a little in front of me.

"Sweet Dove, can you tell us in words?"

"Yes." I could do that. I could absolutely do that.

"What are the rules?" Kellan asked me, his lips at my ear as he whispered and my gaze snagged on Vaughn's beautiful green eyes.

Rules? There were rules. Vaughn nibbled at my lower lip. "Talk to us, Dove. We need to hear you."

Why? I almost wanted to sob, why did I have to think? All I could feel was Vaughn's gorgeous cock impaling me. His piercing lit me up. His fingers were heavy and strong against my hips.

His kisses—his kisses were like the best drugs ever. I needed so much more. Kellan, oh sweet Kellan, was there. His breath teased the shell of my ear and his kisses were filled with bite, giving and taking.

The pressure against my anus increased as Kellan pushed his finger against the tense ring of muscle. Too much. So much...

All at once the pressure vanished to be replaced by a sharp, hot sting as a palm landed a slap against one of my ass cheeks. Air flooded my lungs as I gasped. The hot massage of Kellan's fingers against my stinging skin seemed to melt me.

"Fuck that's intense," Vaughn swore.

"Get ready to stop if she doesn't surface here with us..." Kel's tone allowed for no arguments. The crack of command had my cunt clenching even tighter around Vaughn's cock and I wished it was both of them.

"I'm here," I said, forcing the words out on a half-sob. I sucked in another breath. "I'm here. Oh fuck me, I'm here. I can feel you."

"Good girl," Kellan soothed, that steel in velvet invitation was there. "Who are you with?"

"Vaughn...Kellan...I'm with both of you."

"Very good, Dove," Vaughn encouraged as the finger pressed against my anus again, more warm liquid dribbled down my crack. The heat of it was almost too much and not enough. "Tell Kellan the rules so he'll let us come."

Oh, rules. "No pain for me." I licked my suddenly dry lips as I looked from Vaughn's pleasure-tense expression to Kellan's dark intensity. His eyes seemed to laser into mine and everything inside of me was open and bare. I didn't even care. "My body is mine."

"Yes, it is," Kellan encouraged as he pressed a finger even deeper and I rolled my hips. I had to. The pressure was so intense.

"If I want to give myself to you—" I could hardly shape the words, but I had to. "I can. If anything hurts or scares me —or if I just want you to stop—all I have to say is stop."

"Oh, so sweet for me," Kellan whispered before he kissed me. The slow, sensuous tease of his tongue mirrored his finger as he pressed the full digit into me and Vaughn pushed up at once.

"So perfect," Vaughn echoed, he shifted one hand to my breast and he began to caress, and tease and twist. Kellan added a second finger and the burn started all over again. The stretch was too much.

Too much, I started to thrash as I gasped for air. They stilled and no—no—I forced my eyes open. "More," I demanded as I looked right at Kellan.

"Yeah?"

"Yes—*more*! Now. Please, Kellan…it hurts."

They stopped.

"No, not hurts like that." I gripped his shirt as I pressed my free hand to Vaughn's chest. "I'm so full…I need more."

Kellan studied me a beat then he began to scissor his fingers, gliding in and out of my ass as Vaughn began to thrust and somewhere in there, my vision went white and I shook with the pleasure unfurling within me.

The burn. The motion of his fingers. The thick weight of

Vaughn's cock stretching me. The way they both moved me and I just shook apart.

I surfaced somewhere around wrecked to the soft hum of Vaughn's voice as he stroked my back. There was a warm cloth against my ass and I was sprawled over Vaughn entirely. Sticky with sweat and shivering, I opened my eyes to see Vaughn's smiling face.

"There she is," he whispered. "Look who's back with us, Kel."

Kellan leaned to the side so I could see him. That was good, I wasn't sure I could lift my head. His smile filled me with a fresh wave of absolute warmth. I was so damn glad to see him. To feel him and Vaughn both.

I was sore and aching. I could definitely feel my ass but it was nothing at all like before. That thought drifted in and right the fuck back out as I floated on a haze of pleasure. At some point, the ability to speak would return to me and I'd try to remember the words for thank you.

Yes. Thank you would be a good place to start.

CHAPTER 45

ROME

Starling moved a little slower today than she had the night before. We'd messaged after the fight, but it was too late to wake her up. Rather than stay the night, Liam had gone back to his place.

Vaughn and Kellan had slept with her, which meant they could chase away any bad dreams. I'd gone into my new bedroom and spent the night painting. It had been a while since I could just let go and work on a project.

Even then... the shadows on the wall didn't have the shape I wanted. I was still in there when Starling woke. She brought me coffee and food, but I wanted to paint. For a little while, she sat with me, stretching. But then she wanted to dance.

The barest hesitation marked her movements. A stiffness. Had she hurt herself? I was still thinking about that when my phone vibrated. The message from Liam was just a question mark.

How was Starling?

She had been smiling when she came in. She smiled when she left. The physical soreness wasn't bothering her. At least not her mood. I sent him a thumbs up.

Alone?

I sent back a *yes*.

When it rang, I answered. "What?"

"Morning to you too, Sunshine," Liam said. "Am I interrupting?"

"Do you care?" There were times Liam truly did care. Most of the time…

"No, not really. Unless you have Hellspawn with you in which case, give her the phone."

"No." It was a pointless question since he'd asked if I was alone. I studied the outline on the wall. The shading and colors weren't right. Whatever needed to go here wasn't clear. It was like I had the image but it was out of focus. The plan was to use her body to paint again, but I was still reaching for what I wanted to create.

"I love you too."

"I know." Still, the sentiment gave me pause. "What's wrong?"

"You alone?"

"You asked me that already."

"Yeah. I got a message from Adam."

I glanced away from the wall. "No."

"You don't even know what he said." Not that Liam was denying it.

"You want to meet him. Not a good plan."

My brother sighed. "Maybe not, but he's spent the last several weeks with Brixton. If he's calling me, it means he's got some measure of freedom. We need to know what he knows."

"He could have told you on the phone."

"You know it doesn't work like that, Rome."

I disagreed. "When?"

"Ezra will back me up."

"When?"

"You need to stay with Hellspawn and look after her."

I said nothing and waited.

"Goddammit Rome…" Despite the swearing, there was no heat. "Who's with Hellspawn?"

"Freddie is here."

"No, he's not. He's on the road with Jasper."

I'd forgotten. I frowned. Kellan and Vaughn had work today. Starling had said that. I look away from the wall.

"Milo is with Doc." Liam had already checked.

I didn't like this.

"You have to stay with her," my brother continued. "If she finds out, she'll want to go."

"I should tell her."

His sigh echoed over the phone line.

"She worries about you," I told him. "She keeps telling you. You need to hear her."

"I do hear her. I hear the pain in her voice when she talks about her past. I hear soft sounds of sobbing in all the things she doesn't say. I hear the freedom she has now. I hear *her*. I also heard the fear for you—"

"And you," I interrupted. "She won't like this."

"Well, I can take my lumps after."

"I don't like this." Not him going without me. Not telling her. I didn't like either option.

"Rome, been doing this for a while. I'm letting you know so you can follow if something comes up. I've got a tracker in my shoe. Testing it out for Hellspawn anyway. I'll send the info once I'm on my way and I'll send a message as soon as I'm free."

"If she asks me, I'll tell her." It wasn't a threat, I just didn't want to lie to her. "Don't make what I say a lie."

"Deal. Give her a kiss from me."

I thought about it. "No." He was laughing when I ended the call. I turned to look back at the walls again. I still didn't know what belonged on them. Her room, the sitting room, even the other guy's rooms and the hall. I could see the art that belonged there.

Why couldn't I see what I needed?

Leaving it for now, I went downstairs with the plate and cup she'd brought up to me. The kitchen was mostly clean, so I loaded them in the dishwasher.

A note on the fridge from Kel said he would be grabbing some supplies on the way home. I didn't need anything except for Starling, so I got water bottles and headed to her studio. She hadn't been in the sitting room or in the living room, so the studio was the next place I could think of.

I pressed the button and waited. The door opened to reveal her sweaty, flushed face and she grinned. Music spilled out around her.

"Hey."

"Water," I said as I held out a bottle to her. She should hydrate if she was going to be working this hard.

"Thank you, Rome," she said, pushing up to kiss me. I ducked my head for her. "Do you want to come in and watch?"

"Yes."

I wanted to be right where I could see her and she could see me. I had my phone in my pocket. When Liam contacted me, I wanted to know where both of them were.

After I opened the water bottle, I passed it to her before I followed her inside. The door closed, bottling us inside with the music. I could check the cameras on my phone if I wanted.

Liam had shown me how. But he hadn't put any cameras in the studio yet. He must not have talked to Starling. Or she told him no.

Now I wondered which it was.

The music changed and I shifted my attention to where she stood in front of the mirrors. She'd set her over-half-empty bottle down next to a towel and switched the tracks on the CD player.

Liam wanted to upgrade the sound system, but it was one of the few things that *hadn't* been damaged. I moved to sit in the corner and settled with my legs crossed.

It was out of the way but gave me a full view of her as she picked a new song. When she lifted her head and glanced at me in the mirror, I found a smile for her.

Starling summoned smiles in me. Just like she made looking in her eyes easy. I could look if I wanted, but I didn't have too. My brother and my starling. They never needed more than me.

As she began to move, I forgot about everything else. Starling dancing was the most perfect art. I could never create what she did. The fluidness of her movement, the way she shifted from strength to flexibility back to strength. Her leaps were a little higher and her dips a little lower and at no point did she seem like she was real.

Animated.

It was like watching animation come to life. I'd tried to paint that once, capturing the motion in stillness. Transforming stillness to motion. I could watch Starling all day and never master it as she had.

As she arched her back following a spin, I followed her gaze to the silks hanging above. They were untouched. I didn't think she'd reached for them since she came back from Pinetree.

No, I knew she hadn't. It was why Liam and I wanted to

give her a surprise for her birthday. A surprise Brixton had ruined. Liam and I needed to do it again. Her birthday had come and gone, but there was Christmas.

I would tell Liam when he checked in. For now, I watched her as she descended to the floor and then held there. The rise and fall of her chest betrayed how ragged her breathing was.

The music changed and she rolled over into a handstand and then over again until she was in the splits. This dance was far more athletic. She bounded from one side of the studio to the other. Her leaps took her very high as she did splits in the air.

Where she'd been lighter than a feather, now she moved like a predator. All strength and dominance as she covered the room. Every spin, lift, tap, and beat resonated with the song. Then she danced toward me, every movement like lightning striking as if she held it for just an extra second before she danced into the next.

It crescendoed with her sliding to her knees and coming to a stop directly in front of me and the music ended. The silence was almost startling. Even more, it brought her into sharp relief against the backdrop of her studio, and the sweat gliding over her skin seemed to just add to the texture.

Movement.

Grace.

Beauty.

"I want to paint you." It wasn't the first time the urge came to me.

"You have painted me."

"Yes, I want to paint you again."

"Right now?" Head tilted, she accepted my hand when I stood.

I pulled her to her feet, careful to watch her. The stiffness from earlier seemed gone. "No."

Not yet. There was something more I needed to capture the motion and the stillness in the same breath. I touched a finger to her cheek, then followed the sweat with my fingertip as it slid down to her throat and then along her chest to disappear into the dip of her top.

"Hurting?" That was always a concern.

"No," she said slowly. "Trying to out dance my demons I guess."

That made her look down, so I touched my finger to her chin to ask her to look up again. "What demons?"

"Kellan and Vaughn are helping me—push my limits. To take what hurts and what scared me—and help me not be afraid anymore."

I frowned.

"I asked them," she told me and there was no deception in her eyes. "It—was wonderful and at the same time...I was sore this morning and it just..." She looked away again.

"The pain reminded you."

A sigh escaped her.

"Can I help?" What could I do to take the pain away?

"You help me all the time." She pressed her hand to my chest and I covered her fingers with mine. I liked it when Starling touched me. I liked touching her. "You make me feel like I belong."

"You belong."

"So everyone keeps saying," she said. "I'm not fishing for you all to make me feel better about it. Sometimes—the voices in my head... Even when they whisper, their words can leave scars."

"Words can hurt." Then I pressed my lips to her hair before I whispered, "You need us to shout them down."

"I'm working on that part." A real laugh filled her expression with light. Her eyes softened and even though she was still flushed and sweaty, she seemed better. "I really am."

I glanced around the room for a moment. There was something I could do.

"Stay." When I pointed to where she stood, she gave me a half-smile, but she did as I asked. I crossed over to the mirrors and snagged her bottle of water. After I gave it to her, I went back to take off my shoes.

She waited for me while I went through the CDs.

"What are you looking for?"

"I don't know." I didn't. But I would know it when I found it. It was on the third CD. I traded that CD for the one in the player. I began to cycle through the choices until I found the bluesy piano tune I was looking for.

When I backed it up to the beginning, I glanced at her in the mirror.

"Will you dance with me?"

She finished the water then put the bottle down where I'd been sitting before she walked toward me. Hitting play, I pivoted to face her.

"This is from my first solo performance."

"Shadow dancing." I remembered. "You danced with your shadow."

I'd watched it over and over. The dance had changed as she got older, but the steps were as familiar to me as her heartbeat. I followed her as she began to move. When she retreated, I went forward. As she surged toward me, I backed away.

"You can dance alongside your shadow," she said as she raised a hand and I mirrored the motion. "But you never touch."

Our hands moved like we were mirroring each other. Her smile grew wider as we glided from step to step. "Shadows follow us," I reminded her. "We can pretend we don't see them, but they never leave us."

When she shifted to holding her hands behind her back

and we continued to glide, more like we were on ice skates than on feet. I matched her motion for motion.

"It's sad in a way."

"Only if you want it to be," I said.

"Shadows are darkness…"

"Shadows are where you block the light. They do not exist without you. They are not bad, Starling."

"Broken isn't bad," she murmured and I nodded. "Shadows are not bad."

"No. Liam is my shadow."

"He can be bad."

I considered that then smiled. "Yes."

"But he isn't."

She inclined her head, then winked. They were alike, my brother and my starling.

"No," I agreed. "He is not."

As the song came to an end, she drifted to her knees and I followed her down. My knees hit the wood with a thump. Hers did not.

"I love how you know my dances." She marveled at me.

"Do you want to do another?" I did not look at the silks. My starling needed a lift to fly, and I could do that.

"Yes," she said, pushing to her feet and holding a hand out to me. "I'll pick one this time?"

Anything she wanted.

CHAPTER 46

LIAM

It was barely lunch time when I pulled into the parking lot of the chain restaurant off the interstate. When was the last time I ate at one of these? I couldn't even remember. As stupid as it was, because the last place she needed to be was right here, I wished Hellspawn was here. Hellspawn and Rome both. Then I could entertain myself with them looking at the menu items full of puns.

But they weren't here. She had already had too much exposure to this side of my life. We could wait until after the holidays, maybe after the king had been dealt with, then her family. Or her family, then the king.

Either way, both needed to go. I gave myself a solid mental shake. I needed to get my fucking head back in the game. Even if I'd rather be buried in her body and fucking her until she screamed.

Then make her scream again.

My dick was totally on board with that. "Yeah, one taste and we're all in for her, huh?"

My dick didn't have to answer. We'd been all in for her since the day she gave me that salty fucking look in the kitchen and she'd been bleeding through her pants like it was no big deal.

Hellspawn.

Another mental shake and I checked my phone before securing the second one. The one I used to talk to the king. *That* wasn't going in with me. I locked it into the console and then headed inside.

The skies were steel gray and the wind cutting. I hunched my shoulders as I strode up the ramped walk to the doors. Holiday music filtered through the speakers, though it had a faintly tinny quality. Decorations covered the various flat surfaces around the register.

There weren't that many patrons, maybe less than a dozen. Four exits, including the one behind me. Two fire doors, one on either end of the restaurant, and then doors to the back.

There were always exits from the kitchens and the back storage, even if it just took you to the dumpsters. It was an exit. The various scents of coffee, grilled bacon, and more filled the air. My stomach grumbled. It definitely smelled like more.

A silver-haired waitress hustled away from the pass-through window expertly handling a tray that was about twice her size. "I'll be right with you, hon. Or you can just grab a table and sit anywhere."

She didn't wait for my response, so I finished my scan of the restaurant. I headed toward the side that was shaped like an L. Unsurprisingly, Adam waited for me in the back corner. It gave him a solid view of the restaurant while also keeping him out of direct view.

Nice.

I gave him a once over before I slid into the seat opposite him. Turning sideways, I planted my back against the wall where I could watch him and the restaurant.

"You look healthy," I said by way of greeting. Not only that, he looked like he wasn't wearing that shock collar they'd put on Hellspawn.

"Looks are always deceiving."

That sounded very much like a warning. I spared him a look, eyebrows inching up a fraction. "Something we're both well acquainted with."

"Some of us more than others," he said before he took a drink from his coffee.

"Coffee hon?" the silver-haired waitress asked as she bussed a freshly empty table near us. She stacked up the dishes with a kind of careless expertise. Then again, she'd probably done the same motion a hundred times.

"Yes please," I said. "Have you ordered?" The last I directed toward Adam.

He shook his head then shoved a menu at me. I flipped it open. I already knew what I wanted but since he wanted me to look at the menu, I did.

A single note waited for me with a phone number on it. Ten digits, so most likely a phone number. I memorized it and let it slide into my hand where I could crumple it.

After the waitress brought me coffee and refilled his, we gave her our order and she left us to chat.

"You know," Adam said slowly. "I've been meaning to ask you something."

"Not like you to hold back."

He snorted. "You'd be surprised."

"Ask," I said before I took a sip of the coffee. It was fresh but bitter as fuck. A little like me.

"You set us up at school," he said slowly.

"Did I?" I raised my brows. "I didn't approach you."

"No, you played it really well. Made yourself interesting and then waited to be recruited." He rubbed his chin as though he were truly pondering it. "How did you know it would work?"

"All I did was get a blowjob. You were the guys who walked in."

He snorted then shook his head. "Someday, you're going to have to tell me how you knew."

Maybe. I shrugged. "Some things were just fait accompli."

"Right." He took another drink. "How is she?"

"My girlfriend or yours?"

"You mean my fiancée," Adam countered with a hint of a smirk.

"So not your girlfriend." If he wanted to keep needling me, I could return the favor. Adam's eyes flattened as he stared at me. "My girlfriend is fine. Worried about you, but she's got a kind heart that's taken enough bruising."

A far too kind heart that she'd kept under lock and key, buried beneath the rubble of a life that had been far from kind to her.

"I wouldn't think of it." He paused as the waitress returned with our food.

"Can I get you gentlemen anything else?"

"We're fine," I said. "Thank you."

"Sure thing. I'll be around to top up the coffee in a few minutes."

I did another idle sweep of the place. The other customers looked like what they were. An older woman enjoying her crossword puzzle while she nibbled on half of a grapefruit and chatted with the waitress when she wasn't running around. A couple of truck drivers.

There was a pair of mothers with young kids at a table far away from the rest of us who were talking while their kids tossed food at each other. Messy, but fun. There were at least one or two students in the mix, though I'd bet the one guy was a law student.

"Can you talk?" I asked as I shifted to face him rather than sit sideways. I could see a good chunk of the restaurant behind me via the reflective glass on the wall behind Adam.

"Some," he said. "I've earned some leash. But they will know I spoke to you."

"Sometimes you have to trade a little to get a little." I understood how the game worked.

"In this case, it's more like they gave me a leash so I could talk to you."

Then Brixton or whomever wanted something from me. Still.

Interesting. "I'm listening." I took a bite of the sausage with some of the egg.

"They suspect you might be open to working with them in the future, considering the nature of your relationship with the Vandals and the king."

I didn't snort or offer anything derisive. Instead, I kept my expression as neutral as possible. "Okay."

"I countered that you might be slippery and cunning, but you were loyal. Currently the king has that loyalty."

No comment. I picked up a triangle of toast and took a bite of it. Eating offered me a chance to play coy and mask my reactions.

"I also suggested that courting you by taking you *and* your girlfriend probably wasn't their best plan."

Thank you, Adam. I didn't smile, but I appreciated the sentiment. He'd continued to shield Rome.

"No," I said before draining the last of the coffee in my mug. "It definitely wasn't. They shouldn't have laid a finger on her much less that collar."

"She's stubborn," he retorted, but the grimace wasn't

faked. "The collar was their way of eliciting cooperation. Again—not the best plan. Let's just say they are learning."

"Are they?"

Our waitress returned with what looked like a fresh pot of coffee and she filled our cups. "You gentlemen still doing well?"

"Just fine," Adam told her. "Can you go ahead and leave the check?" He motioned to me. "He's paying."

I didn't roll my eyes, but I did nod to her. "Thank you."

She chuckled, then set the coffee pot on another table while she pulled out the check, totaled it by hand, then set it facedown on the table.

"Just give me a shout if you need anything."

I ignored the check as I looked at Adam. "So, did their method elicit your cooperation and trust?"

"In a manner of speaking," Adam said with a shrug. "I need you to pass a message on to the king for me."

"You're supposed to be dead."

"Exactly, and now I'm not. The being dead thing wasn't working for me anymore, but it would be better coming from you. We both know he's going to be looking into whoever these people are. Ezra was already antsy; this isn't going to make things any easier, especially…" He shook his head. "Just find a way to tell him."

"Especially?" I prompted. "Especially because of what?"

"It doesn't matter. If she continues to linger with my fiancée, I'm trusting your people to look after her."

"Keep calling Hellspawn that," I suggested. "I can send you back broken and bruised."

Adam chuckled. Dick.

"As for your girlfriend, she's back with her sister as far as I know."

He let out a breath.

"Probably back after the holidays, but I haven't asked Hellspawn. Do you want me to give her a message?"

Adam's humor dried up and he glared at me. "No."

Fuck this was going to get messy. "So, what message do you want me to give the king?"

"Easy," Adam said as he finished the last of his food, then wiped his mouth with a napkin. "It's war."

Yeah, that was going to be warm and fuzzy.

We didn't have much time after that. Adam told me what he knew about Brixton and his people—which was surprisingly less than I expected. Except... "Whoever they are working for is canny. Secretive. They remind me of the king in the sense that they are unseen, but you *know* their fingerprints are everywhere."

"What are you going to be doing for them?" They'd wanted me to fight. But how much of that had been to get the king's attention?

"Pretty much what I've always done," he said easily. Look after his own interests, protect his people, and find a way to break the leash.

Message received. "Let me know if you want to talk again."

"Will do," Adam said as he slid out of the booth. "Give me fifteen before you leave. Don't try to follow."

"Wasn't planning on it. Don't be a stranger."

Adam bumped his fist lightly to my shoulder and then he headed out. The waitress bid him farewell and I half-listened as I tracked his progress across the restaurant.

We still didn't know enough about these people and he wasn't exactly a fount of knowledge. Then again, they probably hadn't told him much. It wouldn't surprise me if they'd been listening to the conversation the whole time.

That would explain the focus on *my fiancée* versus asking

directly about Lainey. The mention of Ezra fit, too. But he kept Rome shielded. We discussed only the items our opponents already knew about.

I gave him the full fifteen minutes and finished my second cup of coffee before I counted out the bills and left a good tip for the waitress.

Cash transactions were better.

The late morning crowd had already dispersed, but the lunch crowd had begun to drift in. I kept my head on a swivel as I left. Even if we were hell and gone from the city for the meeting, that didn't mean someone else hadn't been observing us.

On the ride home, I paused at a rest stop, then went over my car. I checked under it and all along the edges including the inside of the tire well.

I found the tracker tucked into the frame near the front passenger tire. Assholes. I dropped it on the ground just behind the tire, then finished the sweep. I'd have to drop this off with one of my garages to get it fully debugged.

Backing over the tracker gave me a small amount of pleasure. Once I was back on the road, I sent a message to Rome. I kept it simple, just on my way home.

His thumbs up made me grin. I was tempted to ask him about Hellspawn, but I figured I'd already pushed my luck with him today. When I said I had to meet Adam, I'd already been on my way. It was easily a three-hour drive back.

Plenty of time to *think*.

I'd just dropped off the car and traded it for another when the king sent me a message.

The clock is ticking. I won't be issuing this as an invitation again. Bring the girlfriend to meet me.

I stared at the message for a long moment. Meet him.

Fuck.

In person?

The message sat unread for a long time. Long enough, I started the second SUV my guys pulled out and headed across the city toward the warehouse. By the time I got there it would be evening. I needed to talk to Milo and I needed to just lay eyes on Hellspawn and Rome.

CHAPTER 47

EMERSYN

*H*eat blanketed me on all sides. The teasing brush of lips against my shoulder intruded on the lazy dream where I could burrow deeper into the warmth. The scent of a cedar cabin with heavy wooden log walls. The crackle of a fireplace as the flames licked over the wood. Winter crispness and a hint of musk tickled my nose.

Cool air brushed down my side and I shifted, wiggling until I could tuck myself into the body next to me. The body —soft huffs of laughter shook him and chased away the last wisps of sleep. That laughter wasn't Rome.

"Liam," I murmured, savoring how his name tasted on my lips. "You came back."

"Yes, Hellspawn," he answered me in a soft voice, laughter coloring each word. "You going to wake up for me or try to hide inside my skin again?"

I debated the answer, especially with so much hard, hot

muscle wrapping around me. I wiggled a little more and the weight of his erection was right there.

"Keep it up," Liam teased and I grinned as I blinked my eyes open. Rome and I had collapsed in my room the night before. The guys were running late or still downstairs working when we'd gone to sleep. But one by one they'd messaged that they were home.

All except for Liam.

Speaking of Rome... I forced my eyes open. A light from the bathroom stretched across the room and highlighted the beautiful chest with its black ink and intricate designs that filled in half of it beneath my cheek.

Not only was Liam here and in bed, he was nude, hard as a stone, and pressed up against every inch of me. Didn't hurt that I was sprawled across the top of him. "Hmm, how did I get here?"

I glanced over to the other side of the bed. The indention in the pillow was still there. The sheets weren't all that cool. The sound of water running in the bathroom answered my question.

Rome was still here.

"You get very wiggly when you sleep," Liam informed me. He gave me a gentle squeeze, then lifted me by the hips and settled me more firmly on him. That also let his dick nestle right between my thighs. "I also like this t-shirt with no panties thing you're rocking. It's very nice for me."

"It's very nice for me too." I nuzzled at his jaw. The morning stubble was abrasive, but also soothing in its own way. He'd showered before bed. I must have been truly out when he got here.

Then again, Rome and I had danced half the day, then played half the evening. I had been very worn out when I went to sleep. Rolling my hips, I rubbed against the length of Liam's dick while he glided a hand up to gather my hair. It had to be a wild mass because I hadn't braided it or anything when I'd gone to sleep.

With a tug, he angled me closer until our noses brushed. His face was half in shadow from the way the light hit the room, but there was so much heat in his blue-green eyes it was like staring out at a Caribbean sea from a white sandy beach.

"Good morning," I said softly.

"Morning, Hellspawn." He leaned up and captured my lips in a heated kiss that ignited the banked heat in my system. It was like a backdraft as oxygen fed the flames. My scalp lit up as he gave my hair a firm tug.

There was no room for breath as he devoured my mouth. The rasp of his stubble against my cheeks added another layer of pain and pleasure to the moment. Need boiled over and I slid a hand down between us so I could wrap it around his cock.

He hissed out a sound as he pushed against my palm, then nipped at my lower lip. "No playing today, Hellspawn."

"No?" Disappointment surged through me. None at all?

"No," he repeated, letting go of my hip to close his hand over mine on his dick. I lifted my head as I pushed my knees down on the bed. "I need you too much. Can you take me now or do I need to warm you up?"

Oh...could I take him? I lifted my eyes to meet his gaze and began to tease his head against my entrance. My cunt might not be all the way ready for him, but the rest of me was and I wanted to *feel* him.

We lined him up together and I swore he looked right into my soul as I adjusted the angle of my hips. "Yes," I breathed out and I slammed down on him as he thrust up and fuck. So full again. The thickness was enough to rock me.

And I was definitely ready for him, but I still felt the pressure and the sting.

"Fuck me, Hellspawn," Liam ordered as he tugged my hair as if to get my attention. "Fuck me hard."

I planted my hands on his chest. "How hard?"

"Like my life depends on it." The darkness sliding under his words opened an ache in my soul. Loneliness. Need. Fury. So many conflicting emotions. But there was no conflict in this. I dug my nails into his shoulders to brace myself.

He wanted hard. I'd give him hard.

I arched my back and lifted my hips, rising up until only the tip of him was inside, then slammed back down again. The bruising force vibrated through me and the angle pushed him deeper.

"Yes," Liam exhaled and it was all the encouragement I needed. I writhed, rocking against him as I controlled the pace. He matched me thrust for thrust. Pleasure and pain met somewhere in the middle of where we touched. Sweat dotted my neck and slid along my skin.

Every thrust seemed to nudge us closer to the edge. He kept one hand on my hair and the other on my hip. If I slowed, even a minute amount, he would yank me down until it was almost violent how we came together.

"I need more," Liam said in between biting kisses.

"Take it," I offered. He flipped us so I was on the bottom and dragged one of my legs up and over his arm. When he increased the pace, I forgot how to breathe. Every thrust knocked the air out of me, and then he surged down to meet my mouth in another furious kiss.

I dug my nails in, locking my free leg around him as if to remind him that I was here and he wasn't alone. My vision began to white out as he pushed me right up to the edge, then his thumb pressed right against my clit as he gave a shout. His orgasm hit first and oh, I savored not only the hot rush of his release but also the way his whole face seemed to tighten.

It was agony and ecstasy. I clung to that memory before my own orgasm rushed over me and I bucked up, fighting for every bit of skin on skin I could get. His hips stuttered a couple of times as he pressed his face into my throat.

The hot pants of his breathing were another reminder that he was still there. The sting of bristle against my neck. Warm kisses behind my ear. As I floated, I began to caress his back in slow circles. As much to soothe him as to soothe me.

When the bed dipped next to us, I dragged my eyes open. "Hi," I whispered as Rome glanced from me to his brother then back. "I think he missed me."

A slow smile spread across Rome's face. "I told him to wake you up. He wouldn't."

"Next time, you wake me up if he needs me."

Rome nodded.

"Shut up," Liam grumbled but it lacked any real force and was completely undone by how tightly he clung to me. The weight of him pressed into me everywhere. I would wear a Liam imprint today.

I liked that.

I wanted to wear him every day.

"I need to get another tattoo or three," I murmured.

Head tilted, Rome looked at my arm.

"Well, yes, those too—but I was thinking about adding to the birds I already have. You guys all have ivy on you some-where. I should have birds for all of you."

"Vaughn will do it," Rome said. "Do you want me to draw it or him?"

"Maybe both of you? I would love to wear your art." Oh, that feeling was just heady. His smile grew.

Liam didn't say anything, but he also didn't try to move away so I kept rubbing his back.

"Can I ask you guys a weird question?"

"You can ask us anything, Hellspawn," Liam mumbled. "But if it involves me killing something or someone, I might need a minute."

"I don't," Rome volunteered and a real laugh shook through me. Not because they were kidding or it was a joke. No, they were absolutely serious and it was…so very sweet.

"I wanted to ask about maybe getting a Vandals tattoo."

Liam lifted his head. It let me savor the relaxation that had replaced the tension in his expression.

"I know, technically I'm not, but all of you have them. I mean, I haven't seen everyone's so I'm assuming." But I had seen Liam's, hidden there in the ink on his arm. It was buried, but it was there. "I would love to be one or at least have one… or is that too much?"

All at once my confidence in asking that question fled as they glanced at each other. They did that soundless communication thing. Their faces didn't move, no nuance of expression gave away anything of what they discussed, but I swore they were.

"Get dressed, Hellspawn," Liam said before he pressed a hard kiss to my lips and then rolled off me.

"Um…"

"Yes."

"Should I not have asked?"

"It's fine that you asked," Liam said as he looked around and then came up with a pair of boxer briefs. "Get dressed."

"Shower," Rome offered. "Then dress."

But that was it, they weren't saying anything else. I could argue or I could get dressed. The achiness from the day before had been joined by this morning's soreness, and I could still feel Liam like he was buried inside of me.

Not a bad feeling at all. It echoed the feeling of Rome and Vaughn. Then there was Kellan. A delicious shiver went through me.

"Move it, Hellspawn." And there was my grumpy bastard. For *that* I took my time, moving slowly over to the dresser to get out clothes. When I took an agonizing amount of time to open a third drawer, Liam let out another growl.

The next thing I was over his shoulder and staring at his gorgeous ass as he strode into the bathroom with me. He set me down gently in the shower, pressed a soft, almost sweet kiss to my lips that almost gave my heart wings.

Then he turned on the ice cold water.

My shriek just made him grin.

Fifteen minutes and actual *hot water* later, I followed the twins downstairs. The smell of breakfast filled the hallway, chasing away the scents of paint, cleaners, and the hint of sawdust that seemed to have become permanent since we started fixing up the clubhouse.

The kitchen was packed, it wasn't as late as I thought. Kellan was at the stove, Vaughn was staring at my coffee maker, while Freddie—he was back—slept in one of the chairs, head back and feet up.

Jasper was back as well, he had his phone in hand when we walked in, and I slid right over to give him a hug. Milo lifted his chin from where he sat filling out paperwork.

Wrapping an arm around me, Jasper set his phone down and pulled me into his lap. "Oh, this is the best welcome home. You smell good enough to eat."

"Feed her first," Liam said. "Also, she wants a tattoo or three, don't you, Hellspawn?"

That snagged Vaughn's attention. "More? Where do you want more, Dove?"

"More birds," Rome said. "For the rest of us." Vaughn laughed at that.

"She has the ones that count." Jasper nuzzled a kiss behind my ear and I twisted a little to look at him. He had more than stubble.

"Oh, you're growing your beard back?"

"Someone said she missed it."

"I think I just threw up in my mouth," Milo muttered.

"Suck it up," I told him. "I haven't said a word to you about the hickeys you left on Lainey."

For a moment, a real smile touched his lips, and he chuckled. But he didn't comment again.

"And yes, I want one for each of you. Might not be enough room on my abdomen, but I thought maybe we could do some on my back too."

"We can do whatever you want," Vaughn said, grinning a little wider.

"That's not the only tattoo she wants," Liam said, before nudging Vaughn. "Move over. I'll make the coffee."

"Thank fuck," Kellan murmured and Vaughn rolled his eyes, but I just laughed. This—this was perfect.

"What other tattoo do you want?" Kellan asked.

"Remind me to kick Liam's ass later."

"I'll do it," Rome, Jasper, and Milo all volunteered in the same breath.

There was a beat of silence as Liam glanced around at all of us. "Fine by me, with three of you, you might stand a chance."

They were nuts, but the laughter felt good. It was Rome who gave me a little nod though as if in encouragement that had me blowing out a breath. "I was asking if I could get a Vandals tattoo."

The silence struck the room so hard that the coffee grinder seemed especially loud.

As soon as it stopped, I added, "I know I'm not one but—

you all have ivy tattoos. I wanted one for all of you, too. One that means—I don't know—us?"

Were we an us? Was I overthinking this? Maybe I just should have kept it to the birds. The guys didn't say anything, They all looked at each other, and then one by one, they all turned their gazes on Milo. Even Freddie sat up. Twisting in Jasper's lap, I looked at Milo.

His expression was hard to decipher. Impossible really. He studied me, and I had no idea what he looked for, but his face didn't change. No smile. No frown. Just—neutral.

"Bad idea?" I tested. "Good?"

"Do you really want to be a Vandal?" The softness of the question gave nothing away.

I swallowed. "I know I might not understand all of it, but it means fierce loyalty and protecting each other. I want that. I want—this is the family you built, Milo. A family for all of you. I want to be that family, too."

The absence of sound save for the faint sizzling in a pan was palpable.

"We haven't added a new Vandal in a long time." The admission made me sad.

"Does that mean I have to be a *rat* first?" I made a face, but the resounding "no," from all of them chased away the trepidation and left me laughing.

Milo shook his head. "I said we haven't added anyone in a long time, Ivy. You are one of us. You've *always* been one of us."

Oh.

That took a moment to sink in.

Oh.

Twisting abruptly, I glared at Liam. "You could have told me that upstairs without all the drama."

"Nope," he said with a slow grin. "I couldn't. You needed to hear it from him and he needed to tell you, Hellspawn."

"I'll punch him for you, Swan," Jasper offered.

"To answer the question directly, Sparrow," Kellan said as he set a plate of eggs, toast, and bacon in front of me. "Yes, you can get a Vandal tattoo. Vaughn will probably let you tattoo anything you want."

"Yes," Vaughn said with a wide grin. "I will."

Warmth rushed through me as Kellan pressed a kiss to the top of my head before he went back to making breakfast. Liam brought me coffee and Jasper rubbed his chin against my shoulder.

Disbelief and elation vied for supremacy in my system. This was all kind of perfect. Even if we didn't get these moments every day, I loved it when we did. I stole a look at Milo and found him watching me again. Only instead of scowling or frowning, he had a small smile in place.

I grinned and saluted him with my bacon and he chuckled.

Yep. This was a good feeling.

CHAPTER 48

EMERSYN

Breakfast turned into a tattoo debate that included the guys getting out paper and pencils—well, Vaughn and Rome. The conversation revolved around how big or how small the birds had to be. More than once, I had to show the tattoo. That just had Milo rolling his eyes.

"I don't care where we put it," I said. "I absolutely want a raptor for Milo. And before you say it, yes, I know hawks are also raptors, but I want whatever Milo sees as his bird."

"Put a pin in that one, Ivy and we'll work it out. Vaughn is gonna have to find a way to balance the birds and their egos wherever he ends up putting them on you."

That just made me laugh. By the time breakfast was over, we had a tentative plan on paper. It was definitely not the final one. Vaughn wanted more time with that and I appreciated it. Nothing was going on my skin until he was sure about it.

Between waking up to Liam, asking about being a Vandal

and a Vandal's tattoo, then breakfast? My day was already amazing.

"As much fun as we're having," Kellan said. "Business meeting."

Groans met the statement but one by one, we all got up. I was kind of excited, but was I—

"Sparrow, you're a Vandal. There's nothing we're meeting about that you can't hear if you want. No one is going to say a word if you want to do your own thing though."

At Kellan's half-scold, I shot him a smile. "Am I that obvious, or are you just getting really good at reading me?"

"I'll never tell," he said gently then crooked a finger. Jasper took the plate and cup from me so I could wrap my arms around Kellan. He kissed me lightly then nudged me ahead of him and out to the living room.

The noise in the kitchen climbed as the water came on, and then it was just me and Kel.

"I mean it," he said. "You can stay and listen. Anything you don't understand, we can explain. Or—you can go dance, go read, hell go back to bed if you want."

"I want to be a part of this."

"You are a part of us, Sparrow. The most precious part. I won't lie to you, some of what we're going to discuss is grim." He traced his fingers down my cheek, then tucked hair back away from my face and behind my ear. "As much as we try to keep things legit—we do get dirty."

"I've seen the things you do," I reminded him. "I've never seen you hurt anyone who wasn't trying to hurt you."

"I appreciate that," he told me, his eyes sober and direct. "But we've all done some pretty damn bad shit. Chances are, we're going to do worse before this is all over."

"The dark doesn't scare me." Maybe it should. "I grew up surrounded by *perfect* people with perfect looks, perfect dress, and perfect manners. Most of them were perfectly awful humans. Some are worse than that. I can take you a little dirty, Kellan. I can get dirty if I have to."

I already had.

A flash of the doctor's face from Pinetree flickered through my mind. The guy who burst in here with his gun pointed at Liam. Then the guard at the fight. I could get bloody for them if I had to.

"I hope you never have to again, Sparrow," Kellan whispered before he pulled me in for a hug. "But thank you for being willing."

It wasn't long before the guys trickled out from the kitchen. Liam brought me fresh coffee and stole me before I could sit with Kellan. "He got you for the last meeting," was Liam's reasoning.

"You got her this morning," Rome said. "Mine now."

That started a whole other debate that had me in stitches. Kellan let them argue for a few minutes, before he whistled and sliced through it. "How about we let her sit where she wants?"

"Right, she wants to be here," Liam said as he settled me with my back to his chest. "Closer to the table for her coffee."

"Yeah, *that* is why she wants to be there," Freddie said with a smirk. That threatened to start another round of arguments, but he shifted to pull out his phone abruptly. "Holy shit."

That got all of us. "What?"

"Bodhi's here," Freddie said and I blinked.

"Pinetree Bodhi?"

"Who the fuck is Bodhi?" Milo asked, but I was already climbing off Liam to go look at Freddie's phone.

"Bodhi helped us. He's great," I said.

"He's also crazy," Freddie agreed. "But he's great and yes, he's here. Right outside."

"That's good right?" I looked at Freddie. "Did you tell him where we were?"

He pursed his lips. "No. But I did call and leave him a message."

"When?"

"When you were missing, Swan," Jasper said and that got him a dark look from Liam and Kellan. "You can all just suck it up. We didn't know where she and Rome were, and Freddie thought this Bodhi guy might be able to help, so we left him a message."

"That doesn't say why he's *here*," Liam stated as he checked the gun. I hadn't even seen him put it on. It was tucked into a holster on his back.

"He's a friendly," Freddie said. "Maybe I mentioned Braxton Harbor?"

"He helped us before. I think we should see him…"

"Wait," Kellan said, holding up a hand. "Everyone cool it." By everyone, he meant Jasper, Liam, and Vaughn—oh and Milo. Milo looked *pissed*. "Freddie, how sure are you about this guy?"

"Fifty percent?" Freddie offered. "He's—a little bit of an acquired taste. But I liked him. He looked after Boo-Boo, too. Helped us get out. Saved my life once, too. Twice if you count getting us out before he burned the place down."

"I count that," I told Freddie.

"Me too."

"Yes," Rome said.

Kellan looked at me. "Sparrow? How sure are you about him?"

"He was nice to me?" I said slowly. "A lot of my memories of Bodhi are kind of hazy. He came up with some really creative ways to kill people. It was one of his favorite topics of discussion."

The looks they gave each other might almost be comical

except our guest was out there and waiting. Freddie's phone vibrated again. I was close enough to read the message this time.

Here to see you and pretty pussy girl. Brought a present.

A selfie accompanied the message, and I laughed at the fact he was flipping off the camera.

"Is it okay if we go out and see him?" I asked because the guys weren't moving yet.

"Check the cameras," Kellan said finally. "I want to know if he's alone or if anyone else is with him."

"Already on it," Liam stated as he checked his phone, swiping through different camera angles.

Freddie asked Bodhi to give us five minutes, and it took more like ten before the guys agreed to go out. They didn't want me going at all, but I was one of the people Bodhi came to see.

They relented only because Freddie said, "I'll stab him myself if he even looks at her cross-eyed. Lighten up guys. You're gonna suffocate me with all that protectiveness."

I had to get a coat *and* boots, and then they were happy enough to let me go out. Liam wanted me to stand behind him but I was a little done with the chest thumping.

I agreed to *wait* inside while Freddie let him into the warehouse. Vaughn shadowed Freddie with Jasper. At least it wasn't just me they were being a little *overkill* about. Then again, after Pinetree—I couldn't really complain about overkill.

"Pretty Pussy Girl!" Bodhi called as soon as he came inside. He wore a somewhat happy, if manic, expression. "Long time no see—I thought you lost her?" He glanced at Freddie. "No, wait—you lost her, then you guys found her. I would have come sooner but you said you found her, so you didn't need me for that."

Turning away from those three, Bodhi headed straight

toward me, and I swore Liam and Milo just *appeared* directly in front of me. Bodhi laughed.

"New friends, PPG?" The new nickname made me laugh, but it would probably go over well.

"Not new, and they're good people. They're family." I debated circling the guys but stayed put for now. Bodhi could be unpredictable and that was probably the thing they were reacting to, I hoped.

"Family doesn't always mean good, PPG." He quieted so I nudged Milo cause he seemed *more* likely to move than Liam right now. Liam was so stiff, he might as well have become a tree.

Bodhi seemed to be studying all of them. Currently, they ranged around him in a half-circle. There wasn't more than three feet between any two of them. Milo peeled his stare off Bodhi to glance down at me.

"He's my friend," I said quietly. "Maybe not a close friend, but a friend."

"Oh, I'm definitely your friend, PPG," Bodhi supplied. "I like you. I like him." He jerked his thumb toward Freddie. "I don't know these guys."

"They're our friends," Freddie volunteered. "Our family. Best kind of family."

"You think they're the best kind?" Bodhi asked me and I smiled.

"They are absolutely the best kind. I really like them."

"Okay. Good. If you need me to bust you out, just say the word. I'll come and get you."

It was a very sweet, if slightly twisted offer. "Thank you, but I'm good here. Did you really come all this way just to offer to get us out?"

Not that I knew how far he'd traveled. "No," Bodhi said. "Had a present for you so thought I'd bring that, then the more I thought about it, I decided I wanted to see you.

Freddie said you were fine, PPG, but you were missing before right?"

"Yes."

"Do any of them need killing?" Interest sharpened in his eyes.

"Actually—" I began but Milo groaned.

"Rule number one," Bodhi said. "The word *allegedly* is your friend."

I bit my lip.

"Rule number two, when someone asks, you always say 'allegedly' then *how* you would do it if you had the chance—you know if you felt that way. But you never just say it. So do any of them need killing?"

"No," I said slowly. "I suppose if one *had* the chance, then probably. Do you want to know how I would do it, you know if I did it—allegedly?"

Freddie laughed, but it was Jasper who stared at me like I'd sprouted a second head, cause I was grinning. Maybe it was a "you had to be there" moment.

"Absolutely," Bodhi told me. "But later. These grumps are giving me a headache, and I don't have any of the happy happy juju to shake them off. So...how about I give you your present, and we'll talk again next time?"

He took a step toward me and Liam stiffened further. I put a hand on Liam's arm, just enough to remind him I was there.

"Look, O'Connell, I can take the stick out of your ass and beat the shit out of you with it in front of PPG, or you can chill the fuck out and let me give her a present."

"You know him?" I swung my wide eyes up to Liam's face.

"Oh, I know him. Didn't go by Bodhi when I knew him."

"Bodhi is my mother's maiden name. I prefer it to Phillip. Phillip is a tool. Bodhi is much friendlier."

I mean...he wasn't *wrong*.

"Okay, I knew you were a Cavendish."

Bodhi leaned to the side and spit. "Like I said, PPG, family doesn't mean good."

No argument here.

"Guys, let's all just take a beat. What did you bring Boo-Boo?" Freddie asked.

"Information, best kind of present." Bodhi grinned at me.

Oh, it was my turn. "What kind of information?"

"I know where your mother is," he told me. "Place is about as bad as Pinetree, and since you didn't want to be there, I'm guessing she didn't volunteer to take a trip on the Mayflower."

The Mayflower? "Wait, what? Where is my mother?" My stomach sank. Was she alright? Uncle Bradley had said...

Even thinking about him made me want to vomit. Hot and cold blew through me as I tried to remember what he'd said about my mother. She was sick?

Had that *not* been a lie?

"Pilgrim Hills, it's a hospital for long-term patients of a delicate state," Bodhi answered. "Pinetree, but with more syllables."

She was in a hospital.

They locked *her* up in a hospital, too?

I swiveled to look at Milo, and his expression was fierce. "We have to go and get her," I said. "She doesn't belong there. She's not crazy."

She wasn't crazy. Right?

"How do you know she's there?" Freddie asked. "How do you even know she's Boo-Boo's mother?"

Bodhi shrugged. "When I get bored, I have someone commit me. Lady was named Sharpe. PPG is named Sharpe. Not hard to figure that out."

"Kellan..."

She had always loved me. She didn't always agree with

Daddy or with Uncle Bradley. More than once we'd stolen away together.

We had to get to her.

She wouldn't have ever agreed to Pinetree.

She hadn't, right?

"Hang on, Sparrow," he told me. "I heard him. Mr. Cavendish…;"

"Fuck no, just call me Bodhi."

"Fine, Bodhi. Can you give us some more information on how you found her? And where she is?"

Milo slid an arm around me and pulled me close. I let myself lean on him as the information tumbled around in my head like a dryer on spin. She was in a *hospital*. How long had she been there?

Were they doing to her what they did to me?

Had they done it before?

We had to get her, right?

Yes. We had to.

She was still my mom.

~

The Vandals will return in Merciless Spy

To keep up with Heather and all her series join her reader's group:
Https://www.facebook.com/groups/HeathersPack/

MERCILESS SPY

Preorder Now

The fierce twin.

The dark brother.

The wild one.

I don't give a damn about labels. I never have. Not when it comes to me. But stay the hell away from my brothers. All of them. I've sacrificed a lot for them, and I'm more than willing to give a lot more.

If my blood, sweat, tears, and life were needed, I'd give it all up. Every damn drop. For my brothers, there was nothing I wouldn't lose.

Until her.

Reckless, ferocious, and seemingly born to match me in temperament and spirit, Hellspawn is not the fragile flower they all think she is. I don't think she ever has been. She will not be left behind, she will not hide, and she will not take the crap that life has been throwing at her.

She's saved our lives, defended us, fought for us, and sacrificed herself for us. I have no questions about what she would do if they tried to leverage us against her. This is why I won't allow anyone to put her to that test. She has nothing to prove to us.

She's a Vandal.

My name is Liam O'Connell. Hellspawn is mine. Emersyn is ours. We aren't going to wait around for the next attack. No, we're taking the fight right to them.

MERCILESS SPY is a full-length mature dark, new adult romance with enemies-to-lovers/love-hate themes. The dark romance aspects of this tale continue. Please be aware some situations may be uncomfortable for readers. Trigger warnings can be found in the foreword should you require them. This is a why choose novel, meaning the main character has more than one love interest. This is book seven in the series.

AFTERWORD

Yes, that happened.

Yeah, I know.

You're welcome.

xoxo

Heather

Reader group: facebook.com/groups/heatherspack

Spoiler group: facebook.com/groups/teammadatheather

ABOUT HEATHER LONG

USA Today bestselling author, Heather Long, likes long walks in the park, science fiction, superheroes, Marines, and men who aren't douche bags. Her books are filled with heroes and heroines tangled in romance as hot as Texas summertime. From paranormal historical westerns to contemporary military romance, Heather might switch genres, but one thing is true in all of her stories—her characters drive the books. When she's not wrangling her menagerie of animals, she devotes her time to family and friends she considers family. She believes if you like your heroes so real you could lick the grit off their chest, and your heroines so likable, you're sure you've been friends with women just like them, you'll enjoy her worlds as much as she does.

Follow Heather & Sign up for her newsletter:
www.heatherlong.net
TikTok

ALSO BY HEATHER LONG

82nd Street Vandals

Savage Vandal

Vicious Rebel

Ruthless Traitor

Dirty Devil

Brutal Fighter

Dangerous Renegade

Always a Marine Series

Once Her Man, Always Her Man

Retreat Hell! She Just Got Here

Tell It to the Marine

Proud to Serve Her

Her Marine

No Regrets, No Surrender

The Marine Cowboy

The Two and the Proud

A Marine and a Gentleman

Combat Barbie

Whiskey Tango Foxtrot

What Part of Marine Don't You Understand?

A Marine Affair

Marine Ever After

Marine in the Wind

Marine with Benefits

A Marine of Plenty

A Candle for a Marine

Marine under the Mistletoe

Have Yourself a Marine Christmas

Lest Old Marines Be Forgot

Her Marine Bodyguard

Smoke & Marines

Bravo Team Wolf

When Danger Bites

Bitten Under Fire

Cardinal Sins

Kill Song

First Chorus

High Note

Chance Monroe

Earth Witches Aren't Easy

Plan Witch from Out of Town

Bad Witch Rising

Her Elite Assets

Featuring:

Pure Copper

Target: Tungsten

Asset: Arsenic

Fevered Hearts

Marshal of Hel Dorado

Brave are the Lonely

Micah & Mrs. Miller

A Fistful of Dreams

Raising Kane

Wanted: Fevered or Alive

Wild and Fevered

The Quick & The Fevered

A Man Called Wyatt

Going Royal

Some Like It Royal

Some Like It Scandalous

Some Like It Deadly

Some Like it Secret

Some Like it Easy

Her Marine Prince

Blocked

Heart of the Nebula

Queenmaker

Deal Breaker

Throne Taker

Lone Star Leathernecks

Semper Fi Cowboy

As You Were, Cowboy

Wolves of Willow Bend

Made in the USA
Middletown, DE
05 October 2022